A Pride of Dolphins

Other books by
Mark Hebden

The Eyewitness
The Errant Knights
Grave Journey
Mask of Violence
A Killer for the Chairman
The Dark Side of the Island

Mark Hebden

A
Pride
of
Dolphins

Harcourt Brace Jovanovich
New York and London

Library of Congress Cataloging in Publication Data

A pride of dolphins.
I. Title.
PZ3.H24218Pr3   [PR6058.A6886]   823'.9'14   74-26710
ISBN 0-15-174031-3

First American edition 1975

B C D E

AUTHOR'S NOTE

I am indebted for information to my friends in the Royal Navy who so willingly gave me their time, and to the captain and crew of H.M. Submarine *Artemis* for their painstaking willingness to explain things when I went to sea in her.

Part I

Chapter One

It wasn't the day for dying. It wasn't even the time or the place. And James Thomas Nanjizel, of Looe, in the Duchy of Cornwall, who was heavily involved in an affair with Daphne Eltney, the wife of a fellow petty officer in the Royal Navy, had no thoughts of death in his mind.

Mrs Eltney lived in Portsmouth, not far from the submarine headquarters, H.M.S. *Dolphin*, to which Petty Officer Nanjizel was attached. Her husband, George, was serving in the anti-submarine frigate *Persephone,* at that moment in time doing a tour of the Far East. Eltney had once served in submarines with Nanjizel, and they had been friends for years. Which was why Nanjizel was suffering from a guilty conscience.

Daphne Eltney was less troubled by thoughts of guilt. She was well known around the naval base for being more interested in men than was good for her, and she had had more than one affair while her husband was at sea. She was petite, with a good figure, a ready smile and large slanting eyes that, with her jetty hair and smoky lashes, had a deadly effect, and produced a devastating line in kittenish seduction.

Nanjizel had met her with men on several occasions and, though admiring her figure, if not her morals, had worried over and over again whether he should set down his suspicions on paper and send them to his friend in the Far East before George Eltney received the inevitable 'Dear John' letter. Before he had been able to make up his mind, the matter had been unexpectedly set to one side when Daphne had awakened to the fact that James Nanjizel was a good-looking man. The Spanish-black hair and cornflower-blue eyes of Cornwall had attracted her immediately, and Nanjizel had never had a chance. At her

9

devilish best one evening, and a little excited by a few gins-and-tonic, she had swept him off his feet.

It had worried him for some time afterwards, which was no help to his work, because he was already somewhat perturbed by a variety of odd incidents that had occurred in the last few days. Several times he had been approached in bars by men who had talked in oblique phrases. They had been difficult to understand, but gradually what they'd said had begun to jell. At first he had thought they were newspapermen nosing out some scandal for one of the Sunday sensationals. Then it had seemed that their interest was in his last ship, the nuclear submarine *Jellicoe*. At least, when they had talked of 'his ship,' he had assumed at once that they were not referring to the broken-down old wreck to which he had been attached for the last month or two to await his approaching discharge from the Navy. *Achates* had been built in 1945 for the Pacific and, severely damaged by an internal hydrogen explosion six months before, had been lying at Portsmouth while being systematically stripped of her weapons system and most of her electronic equipment before being sailed to a breakers' yard. When the pestering continued, with such regularity it was obvious the meetings weren't accidental, his suspicion that the three men were reporters changed to a belief that perhaps they were after some dockyard fiddle and that they were policemen. Only in the last forty-eight hours had they finally made it clear to him that they were neither policemen nor reporters; that they wanted him less for his knowledge than for his skill, and that they wanted him to use that skill for something that was not honest.

Nanjizel, a straightforward man, had wondered for a while whether to go to the police or to his commanding officer, but in the end, thinking that he might well make a fool of himself, he had said nothing. Within a week or two he would be free of the Navy and beyond their reach – for the matter, thank God, beyond the reach of Daphne Eltney, who, he was beginning to realise, was as dangerous as highly volatile gelignite.

The strangers had been not only persistent, but also threatening. When Nanjizel, who was no coward, had offered alternatively to black their eyes or go to the police, one of the men had said: 'I wouldn't do that. That would be very unwise indeed.'

When he hadn't seen them for the last two days, he had come to the conclusion that they had probably decided he was just a bad bet. In that, he was dead wrong. They were sitting in an old van stolen from behind a Southsea cinema which at that moment was not far from Daphne Eltney's house. Which was a tragedy for James Nanjizel and for George Eltney, too. Because, as it so happened, James Nanjizel was in bed with George Eltney's wife.

Although the district was old, Daphne Eltney's house was new, and spotlessly clean. She had a sharp native intelligence and good taste, and given other circumstances might have made an excellent job of her marriage. Nanjizel admitted to himself that he enjoyed being with her because she was a good cook and knew how to make a man feel wanted, and the thought made him writhe inside.

'It's all wrong,' he said.

Daphne smiled and reached for a cigarette. As she leaned across him to pick up his lighter, her soft white bosom touched the matted black hair on his chest. Her flesh was warm, and Nanjizel, stirred uncomfortably by the touch of her skin, drew a deep breath and moved restlessly.

'It's all wrong, Daph,' he said again. 'I feel a proper rat.'

She laughed and lay back on the pillows, her eyes bright from the gin she'd drunk. With her hair ruffled and the pink flush on her cheeks from their recent exertion, she was enough to stir a bishop. Nanjizel was no bishop; he gave up trying and reached for her.

She pushed him away. 'I'm smoking,' she pointed out. 'Want one?'

He nodded miserably, his mind occupied with his friend George Eltney, sweating out his stint in H.M.S. *Persephone*. 'What the hell would George say if he found out?'

11

Daphne chuckled. 'George won't find out from *me*,' she said. 'All the same.'

She gave a guilty wriggle, like a small child caught with its hand in the jam. 'A girl can't sit at home for months on end. Just doing nothing. Seeing nobody. Going nowhere.'

'You could have joined George at Singapore if you'd wanted.'

'I have to keep an eye on my mother.'

Nanjizel turned his head. He knew about her mother. She lived not far away at Fareham and, from what he'd been told, had been another like Daphne in her day. 'You know damn well it wasn't your mother, Daph,' he said.

She shrugged. 'I'm not like some of these other wives. I can't sit at home and twiddle my thumbs waiting for George to turn up.'

'I told you, you could have joined him.'

'In some lousy married quarters, surrounded by a hundred other Navy wives?'

'*That's* why you wouldn't go. You'd have had to behave yourself.'

'Well, why should I?'

Nanjizel stirred. 'But, *me*, Daph! Why did it have to be me?'

'You were as eager as I was. I couldn't hold you off.'

'Not when I first came here. George was my mate. I came to warn you that people had started talking.'

'And stayed to climb into bed with me.'

Nanjizel looked at his cigarette, frowning. 'I've wished many times that I hadn't,' he admitted.

She laughed and moved closer to him, fitting her small shoulder under his arm. It was hard to keep his fingers off her, and he cupped her breast with his hand. She moved contentedly. 'Is that why you kept coming back?' she asked. 'Because you wish you'd never seen me?'

There was no answer to that, of course, and Nanjizel could only fall back on the same dogged formula. 'George is my mate,' he muttered.

She giggled. 'He's my *husband*. And *I'm* not moaning.'

12

'Oh, Christ, Daph—!'

She gave a soft snort of disgust. 'You men give me the creeps. You're all the same. You have a good time with a girl and then moan about what rotten beasts you are. You think George is a snow-white angel?' She got out of the bed and stood beside it, stark naked, a small white figure with a mass of tumbled hair. 'Look at me. Jimmy Nanjizel,' she said.

He tried not to, but she just stood there, her small breasts thrust provocatively forward, the light falling on the smooth round surfaces of her stomach and thighs.

'Don't you like me?' she demanded.

'Yes,' he admitted. 'I do.'

'Well, then! Try to tell me you aren't glad it happened.'

He grimaced. 'Aw, hell, Daph. Stop prancing about and come back to bed.'

She looked over her shoulder at him. 'You want me to?'

'Of course I do.'

'Well, stop moaning then.'

'All right—' He gestured. 'I've had a lot on my mind lately.'

'Going home to Looe and leaving me here?'

'Yes,' he agreed. 'That. And those fellers who've been bothering me. You saw 'em. You were with me when they picked me up in the Lord Nelson.'

She sat on the end of the bed, smoking, fully aware of his eyes roving over her. 'What did they want?' she asked, unconcerned.

'They were trying to get me to work for 'em.'

'What as?'

'They were only interested in my service in submarines.'

'What good's that to them? What good is it to anybody once you leave the Navy?'

Nanjizel didn't answer. The three men who'd been pursuing him had finally made fairly plain what they wanted, and he still didn't believe it.

She gazed at him. 'I'll tell you what,' she said.

'What?'

13

'I'll take your mind off 'em, if you like.'

He looked at her, then grinned and stubbed out his cigarette. 'Smoking in bed,' he said. 'It'll never do. Especially in your mate's bed. And with your mate's wife.'

'That's better.' She giggled. 'Now you're talking.'

He pushed the bedclothes back. 'Come on.'

She took a final pull at her cigarette, carefully, knowing the wait would make him all the more eager, and let the smoke dribble slowly out through her mouth and nostrils.

The man in the driving seat of the van threw his cigarette away as he slid the old vehicle to a stop between a line of cars outside the St Vincent Arms and a station wagon belonging to the owner of a fruit-and-vegetable shop who could never find anywhere to park at night. Quickly, he pulled on the hand brake and closed the window. The interior of the van was stuffy, and the windows were so steamed up it was impossible to see inside. He sat still, watching the last of the passers-by, then, abruptly, he leaned over the back of his seat and unfastened the catch of a heavy briefcase in the rear. There was a neon light switching on and off outside the cinema at the road junction just ahead, and he waited for the moment of darkness to reach inside it. As the darkness came again, he handed something to his companion. It was a Luger fitted with a silencer.

The other man took the gun and, holding it low under the dashboard, checked that it was loaded before carefully stuffing it out of sight in an inside pocket. A second silenced weapon was passed to another man, who sat on a box in the rear. At the next moment of darkness, the driver produced a third silenced gun and stuffed it into his own inside pocket.

'Right?' he said.

'Right.'

The driver opened his door.

'How do we do it? '

'We ring the bell.'

'Suppose he nips out the back way?'

'There's an eight-foot wall. He has to come round the front. You wait alongside the house in case he does.'

'Suppose she won't open up?'

'She will. She's got neighbours.'

'What about him?'

'*He'll* lie low upstairs until he finds out who it is, won't he? If he thinks it's anybody he doesn't want to see, he'll try to slip out the bedroom window. It leads to the top of the downstairs bay, and it's easy to get down. But it won't help much. Because you'll be alongside the house, waiting.'

Daphne Eltney had been in James Nanjizel's arms for some time when the bell rang. Her eyes were closed and her lips parted. Her dark hair tumbled about the pillow as she moved her head slowly from side to side, but as the harsh noise of the bell woke echoes in the silent house, the ecstatic expression on her face died at once. She wriggled from under him, and Nanjizel sat bolt upright, as if he'd been shot.

'Who's that?' he said.

For a moment they sat there, frozen.

'It's all right,' she said, relaxing. 'It'll be nothing.'

Nanjizel wasn't so sure. Men in his position never are. 'People don't ring doorbells at half past twelve at night for nothing,' he said.

She pushed her hair back and reached for a cigarette, flushed and beautiful, though the worried Nanjizel was in no mood to notice.

'For a senior non-commissioned officer of Her Majesty's Forces,' she said, 'you aren't half nervous.'

'Where I am right now,' Nanjizel pointed out, 'I've every right to be nervous.'

She laughed. 'I'll go and see. You stay where you are. Nobody'll come up here.'

'Except George.'

'George is in Singapore.'

'He might have come home.'

'Oh stop worrying,' she said. 'You can always get out the

15

back window. It's dark. You can get from the top of the back bay to the dividing wall, and then you can slip down the drive, if it's George.'

Nanjizel looked at her accusingly. 'I bet it's been done before, hasn't it?'

She ignored the question and, putting a hand on his chest, pushed her small fingers into the matted black hair with evident pleasure.

'Stay where you are,' she said. 'Or weren't you enjoying yourself?'

Nanjizel considered. He had been enjoying himself very much indeed, and he decided to see it through.

The bell rang again.

'Who'll it be?' he asked.

Daphne shrugged. 'Perhaps the neighbours. Sometimes they bring a parcel round from George. Since I work during the day, the postman leaves parcels and things next door.'

Nanjizel wasn't entirely satisfied, but just then the bell rang again and he didn't argue any more as she snatched up a nylon robe and put it on.

'Fat lot of good that is,' he said, grinning. 'I can see right through it.'

He heard her going down the stairs, and heard the front-door bolts slipping back. There was a scuffling sound and a short squeal broken off short, then the thump of feet coming up the stairs at speed. Making a wild guess that it was George, home somehow before he was expected, he dived from the bed for his shirt and trousers, but as he did so the door slammed wide, bouncing against the wardrobe and back against the arm of the man who had flung it open.

At first, Nanjizel saw nothing but a face distorted and blurred by a nylon-stocking mask, but then his eyes fell, and he saw the pistol in the man's hand. His jaw dropped just as the trigger was pulled, once, twice, three times.

The first shot hit Nanjizel in the chest, and he was flung back against the bottom of the bed and toppled over, stark naked, to sprawl on the white sheets, his blood staining the

16

linen. The second hit him in the throat as he was staggering back, and the third in the face as he fell, neatly punching out his nose. Twice more the man with the gun fired into his body before turning and hurrying down the stairs. At the bottom, Daphne Eltney, the inadequate nylon housecoat wrenched aside in the struggle, was standing with one arm forced up behind her back and the other masked man's Luger at her white neck. Her green eyes were wide with terror.

'Okay?' the man who was holding her asked.

'Okay. Let's go.'

Daphne was swung round and given a tremendous shove. She fell to her knees and went slithering on a rumpled mat along the polished hall, crashing on the way into a walnut stand with a tiled top which held a Busy Lizzie plant. The whole thing went down with a crash, shattering the pot and scattering earth, and she crashed into the kitchen door with a wallop that threatened to break the thin plywood panel.

The front door slammed, and she heard an engine rev up. Crouching motionless, terrified by what had happened, she wondered if her husband had found out what she had been up to and had sent a friend round to sort her out. But realising that she had come to no harm, apart from a bruised wrist and shoulder, from crashing into the plant stand, she arrived at the conclusion that perhaps *she* hadn't been the object of the intruders' intentions at all. She got slowly to her feet and padded down the polished wooden blocks of the hall.

'Jimmy,' she called softly up the stairs. 'Are you all right?'

But there was no James Nanjizel hurtling down the stairs – neither in alarm nor promising vengeance – and her heart began to thump.

'Jimmy,' she called again.

There was no reply, and she stood at the bottom of the stairs staring upward.

'Jimmy!'

There was still no sound, and then, through her panic, she remembered hearing the bedroom door slam open and a crash. For a moment longer she remained motionless then, clutching

17

the nylon housecoat round her, her heart pounding, she began slowly to climb the stairs.

There was an acrid smell on the landing, such as she had smelled when the signal guns fired from Portsmouth as naval ships entered harbour, and somehow it seemed ominous. She pushed open the bedroom door and saw Nanjizel's body on the bed, his legs hanging over the end. He was naked and lying on his back, his shirt and trousers in his hand, and the whole of his chest and head seemed to be covered with blood. It seemed to be everywhere, and was soaking into the rumpled bed linen and the mattress. His hairy white body looked like a slaughtered animal's on a butcher's slab, and her stomach heaved.

'Jimmy,' she whispered, but there was no reply. Nanjizel's handsome eyes went on staring at the ceiling, one of them twisted out of true by the bullet that had smashed his nose. Then she saw to her horror that there was blood on the carpet and even on the wall.

'Oh, God,' she breathed. 'What'll George say?'

Chapter Two

'Mo's back!'

Venner looked up as Daisy's head appeared round his door.

'When?' he asked.

'Just now.'

'What was the weather like?'

'Rained, of course.'

Venner grinned and bent again over the filing cabinet where he was working.

The room was a small one looking over St James's but now the view was blurred a little by mist, and the lake was a flat leaden sheet below the towers and turrets of Westminster. It was a new block of offices, an old building gutted and reconstructed, and the occupants were mostly civil servants, though the small suite on the top floor bore no notice on the door, and not many people knew why it existed. Venner had once suggested that since they received so few callers, it would be a good idea to mark it 'Ladies'. Certainly the typists didn't know what went on and, for the most part, worked on drafts fed to them by other departments. Outwardly the group was an extension of a set-up originally started in Germany to hold a watching brief on the steady under-the-counter selling of NATO arms, not only to emergent countries, but also to the underworlds of Europe. But its instructions had always gone further than that.

Venner closed the drawer of the filing cabinet with a crash and sat down at the desk. After perusing the sheets of paper he had extracted, he slipped them into a folder and picked up *The Times* to wait. The front-page headlines were the usual miscellany of speculation and disaster. There was the kidnapping of an English boy in Paris, the usual strikes in the car industry, and trouble in West Africa where a newly arisen demagogue by the name of Chief Olmuhi was giving sleepless nights to half a dozen neighbouring countries and more than one great power. There were complaints by students about university authorities and by university authorities about students, a demonstration by agitator-stirred locals at Ewerton, the chemical and biological research centre on the edge of the Mendip Hills, and the usual summing up of non-existent clues in the latest murders. NO LEAD IN PORTSMOUTH SHOOTING, one headline said. Without developments, the case had dwindled in the last day or two from the dignified two-column heads that *The Times* reserved for sensation to a single-column, four-paragraph story well down the page.

Flicking the paper straight, he began to read. Immediately, the bell rang. He folded the paper carefully, taking his time about it because it suited his particular kind of pride to feel he couldn't be summoned like a slavey, then he picked the folder up from the desk, made sure he had a pen and a notebook in his pocket, and headed for the door at as leisurely a pace as he could manage.

Mostyn was sitting at his desk, also reading *The Times*. His expression had been serious and preoccupied, but as Venner appeared at the door, it changed subtly, the hard, alert eyes becoming vague and blank as he put on the special expression he wore to face the world.

'Mornin',' he said.

'Have a good holiday?' Venner asked.

Mostyn put the newspaper aside, folding it as carefully as Venner had, before placing it with a fussy neatness on his desk.

'No,' he said. 'Rained.'

'Hard luck.'

Mostyn shrugged. 'Always does.'

He rose from the chair, the whole lean six foot three of him, tall, slender, and graceful, the absolute antithesis of Venner, who was square and dark and built like a boxer. There didn't seem to be a line or a curve on Mostyn's face or body that had any strength in it anywhere, and his hair and eyes were pale to the point of anonymity. He walked to the window, limping slightly, took a flat gold watch from a fob pocket, glanced at it, and stood staring at the view. He seemed pre-occupied.

'Thought you went to Italy,' Venner said encouragingly.

Mostyn nodded. 'Did.'

'Wouldn't have expected rain in Italy at this time of the year.'

'If I took a trip to the middle of Death Valley, they'd have rain.'

Venner grinned. 'Go alone?' he asked.

Mostyn nodded again, but Venner guessed there'd been some bright little dolly bird somewhere, or some luscious Italian jet-setter intrigued by the title that lay somewhere behind Mostyn. There always was, because his background was enough to make any girl starry-eyed.

Venner looked at him curiously. He seemed in an odd mood, not at all as if he had just returned from holiday, and Venner tried to jerk him out of it.

'Where did you go?' he asked.

Mostyn took a yellow Gauloise Riz from a monogrammed gold case and lit it carefully with a languid hand. 'Where *didn't* I go?' he said. 'Venice. To look at pictures. "Martyrdom of St Stephen" repeated *ad nauseam*. Cold as charity, and St Mark's Square like a prison exercise yard. Florence. Ankle-deep in the Piazza della Signoria. Elba. Bouncing a foot high off the pavements in Portoferraio. Finally to Sestri Levante in desperation.'

'Get some sun there?'

Mostyn studied the view again. 'Yes,' he said. 'Two hours. Then it started to rain again. What's it been like here?'

'Heat wave.'

'Thought so.' When Mostyn chose his vacation, the rest of the staff put a red ring round the date and avoided it like a

21

plague. They could almost guarantee perfect weather in England while the Continent sloshed about in floods.

'Spent most of my time sitting in bars,' Mostyn went on. 'Ankle-deep in pistachio nuts, staring at the television.'

Venner almost laughed. He could never, not even by the wildest stretch of imagination, imagine Mostyn tamely sitting in a bar surrounded by steaming Italians crowding in out of the rain. More likely he was in bed with some dainty contessa in a pink-and-cream palace somewhere in the Tuscan hills.

Mostyn took a last glance towards St James's, brushed a fleck of ash from his lapel, and turned to Venner.

'What's happened while I've been away?' he asked.

Venner placed the folder on his desk. 'The Prime Minister went to Ireland,' he said.

'I bet that made old Lucas think.'

Venner grinned. 'Yes, it did a bit.'

Lucas, who occupied an office on the floor below, was the titular head of the department, but he knew nothing at all about its functions and merely provided the panic when an event of any moment occurred.

'Keep you busy?' Mostyn asked.

'Yes.'

'What else?'

'Those leakages from the Ministry of Defence, the secrets cast at Chatham, and the watch on Ewerton.'

'Ewerton?'

'Nerve-gas place. Bristol way. Microbiological Research and Chemical Defence Experimental. Chemical Defence covers chemical warfare and protective measures against it. Micro Research advises on biological warfare and how to combat it. They produce bacteria.'

Mostyn frowned and limped back to his desk. 'I thought that place was due to be closed down,' he said. 'They don't produce the gas there, do they?'

'No. One of the big combines does. It's only tested there. But, if you remember, they over-produced, and it was sent to Ewerton for storage. A few nuts started protests. There was a

22

statement in the House, and they promised to destroy the overstocks.'

'What *is* this damn gas, anyway?'

'Whatever it is,' Venner said, shrugging, 'it's classified. They call it X gas. They produce it to find the antidotes. In case the other side ever sees fit to use it.'

'What a murderous lot of morons we are. How're they going to get rid of it?'

'The Americans put theirs in an old Liberty ship – didn't they? – and sank it in one of the Pacific deeps.'

Mostyn was silent for a while, puffing at the Gauloise. 'Navy's in the news just at the moment, isn't it?' he went on conversationally. 'This petty officer shot dead in Portsmouth.'

'Old old story,' Venner said. 'Husband in Singapore. Wife doesn't like being alone in the house at night. Someone writes a letter.'

Mostyn didn't seem to think it was quite so simple. 'Doesn't usually end in a couple of gunmen blowing a feller in half,' he pointed out.

This was something that hadn't occurred to Venner. 'That's true,' he agreed.

Mostyn glanced at his newspaper. 'Well at least,' he said, 'it wasn't the husband. He's being flown home.'

'Might have had friends.'

'Who'll shoot his wife's lover? It's usually a black eye or a few missing teeth. Wife's, if the lover's bigger than the husband.'

He sat down at the desk and began turning over the papers in the folder.

'What about this youngster kidnapped in Paris?' he went on. 'Son of the Naval Attaché. They're wondering if someone's trying to put pressure on him to hand out secrets. Ex-submariner. This chap at Portsmouth was a submariner, too. Think he'd been supplying information?'

'It might be worth looking into.'

Mostyn screwed out the Gauloise in the ashtray by his elbow. 'Weren't *you* a submariner?'

Venner frowned. 'Once,' he said shortly. 'But there was a bloody stupid dockyard matey and a torpedo. It fell on me and that was the end of that.'

Mostyn rose and limped back to the window. 'With me it was a tank. Wonder what happened to Daisy? Washing machine fell on her, I suppose.' He was silent for a while. 'Why do men volunteer for submarines?' he asked thoughtfully.

'The extra dough, I suspect.'

'And something else, I reckon.'

'Responsibility at an early age, perhaps. They like to consider themselves the élite. Everybody likes to imagine he's somebody special. Even me.'

'You are,' Mostyn said flatly, without a trace of warmth. 'Wouldn't be here otherwise.' He sat down and looked at the newspaper as though what he'd been thinking had slipped from his mind. Then he tapped it slowly with his finger, changing the subject again. 'This feller Olmuhi's throwing his weight about a bit, isn't he?' He leaned over the paper and read. ' "I'll have the weapons. . . . Soon I'll have Africa." ' He frowned. 'Politicians don't talk like that unless there's something behind it. He's probably expecting something. Something in our line, shouldn't wonder. What's our old friend Henry Latisse up to these days?'

'Last we heard he was buying guns for Middle East guerrillas. Perhaps he's in Ireland.'

Mostyn suddenly seemed to have lost all interest. He pulled his newspaper forward and made himself comfortable. 'Look him up, will you?' he said.

Back in his own office, Venner took out a file, studied it, then picked up the telephone and asked for a number. After a moment or two the reply croaked in his ear.

'Ministry of Defence.'

He gave an extension number, and a female voice answered.

'Mr Aubrey, please,' he said.

The reply came back pat and at once. 'Mr Aubrey isn't available.'

'He'd better be,' Venner said sharply. 'This is James Venner.'

During the ensuing silence, he could imagine the operator busily conducting a hurried conversation with someone better informed than she was about priorities and departmental protocol. The voice came back again, but there was no apology.

'Mr Aubrey's on the line now.'

There was a click, and Aubrey's voice came, feline and placating. 'My dear Venner. Sorry about that. One has to protect oneself, you know.'

'What from?' Venner asked.

Aubrey ignored the question. 'What can we do for you?'

The voice on the telephone was smooth as cream – like Aubrey himself. Pale, fleshy, lacking everything that was hard or tough. It was said that Aubrey had reached his position less through hard work than by his skill at shooting down his opponents. In many ways he was much like Mostyn – languid, amiable, not given to getting excited – but there was always a core of hardness in Mostyn that lifted him clean out of Aubrey's class.

'I'm interested in Latisse,' Venner said.

There was silence, and he guessed that Aubrey was about to start fencing and was thinking out the moves. He endeavoured to put the case straight from the start.

'You know the chap,' he said briskly. 'Naturalized Englishman. Born in Yugoslavia but says he comes from France. He's been making London his base recently. Tall chap. Big nose. Cleft in his chin that's so deep it looks like a scar.'

'Got him,' Aubrey said gaily. 'Henry Latisse. Czechoslovakian, actually. Real name's Chudoba.'

'Have it your own way.'

'Involved in recruiting arms for the Congo, the Black Septembrists, and odds and ends in Uruguay and Brazil.'

'And probably Ireland.'

'And probably Ireland,' Aubrey agreed with a little laugh.

'Have you had wind of him lately?'

'I thought that was *your* job.'

25

'So it is. We get our information from the manufacturers, the men on the spot – and *you*.'

'Yes.' There was a long pause, and Venner could tell that Aubrey wasn't going to be very forthcoming. 'That's true, I suppose. But I'm afraid our good friend Mr Latisse seems to have gone into hiding.'

'Since when?'

'Since October last year.'

'He must be up to something then.'

'Oh?' Aubrey's voice was non-committal, and Venner frowned.

'Unless he's dead,' Venner said. 'Latisse is a born trouble-maker, and if he's lying low, he's either sick or working up to something.'

'Such as what?'

'There are enough trouble spots in the world to keep a man like Latisse busy,' Venner snapped. Aubrey's dodging was irritating him. Why the hell, he thought, couldn't he stop this stupid game of keeping everything to himself? What he had he seemed to think he should keep.

'Latisse moves in high society these days,' Aubrey said. 'He made money. He's not easy to keep in touch with.'

'We can try,' Venner rapped. 'Has he been seen lately with that dame he used to be seen with?'

'Dame?' Aubrey spoke the word as though it offended him, as though it were something that never passed across his immaculate desk.

'Woman,' Venner corrected himself.

'Ah! Which one? There was a countess he used to go about with in Paris and the South of France—'

'Aubrey,' Venner interrupted angrily, 'I'm not interested in the one he *used* to be seen with. I'm interested in the one he was seen with here – in London.'

There was a long pause before Aubrey's voice came again, heavy with offence. 'Can't think who you mean,' he said.

'Try,' Venner suggested. 'Hard!' He knew the woman's name but he was determined to get it out of the hated Aubrey.

'Stop dodging and get your mind on it. Your department came up against her over those Middle East Centurions. Latisse was after them, and she was going about with him then. Come on, man, for God's sake!' he snapped. 'I'm not getting off this telephone until you come out with it!' He smiled as he imagined Aubrey holding on to his temper. He had a tongue like a viper when he was roused.

'Holcombe,' Aubrey said after some time. 'Dorothea Holcombe.'

'That's the one,' Venner said cheerfully. '*The* Dorothea Holcombe. The one with the money.'

'You knew all the time!'

'Oh, yes,' Venner said, 'I knew. I just wanted to hear the name from your own sweet lips. I don't like departments falling down on these things, you know.'

'We're not falling down! She's of no interest to us. Or you either. She's not a criminal.'

'Sheer luck,' Venner said. 'With less money, she might have been.'

'I'll see she learns what you say,' Aubrey retorted. 'She'll enjoy sueing you.'

Venner ignored the threat. 'Do you know her? Personally?'

'I've met her.'

'Out of your league a bit, aren't you? She's First Division. *You* belong in the Reserves.'

There was a long silence. Venner could picture Aubrey staring down his nose at the telephone, his nostrils pinched and white and offended, his eyes angry, and he felt a small glow of satisfaction. It wasn't often anyone was able to score off Aubrey.

Chapter Three

Venner was just about to put the telephone down when Aubrey said sharply, 'By the way, we've been having complaints from Ewerton about the demonstrators.'

'*We?*'

'This department.'

'What sort of complaints?'

'That they keep trying to get inside the compound.'

'Try giving them a whiff of X gas,' Venner said. 'That ought to stop them.'

There was a shocked silence and Venner smiled. 'Are *you* running that show?' he asked.

'This department is.'

'Well, guarding places doesn't come within our brief. You ought to know that. We already have a man there keeping his eyes open.'

'Is one enough?' Aubrey asked, irritatedly.

'They haven't started breaking things yet, have they?'

'No. I suppose not.' Aubrey's voice was stiff. 'Perhaps you'll pass on to us anything you find out.'

'Yes,' Venner said. With the sort of willingness with which you pass on information about Latisse, he thought: when it suits.

He slammed the telephone down, deliberately refraining from thanks. If Aubrey could be rude, so could he. He sat staring at the instrument deep in thought for a moment then he reached for the internal telephone.

Daisy answered. Her real name was Philomena, but, because he pretended he could never remember it, Mostyn had christened her Daisy, and it had stuck. Everyone used it now,

28

even Daisy herself. She had once worked for Venner, and there had even been a short and highly explosive affair between them that had rocketed backwards and forwards between her flat and his. But it had ended abruptly, without tears or recriminations, and perhaps even with a greater respect for each other than had existed before. There had been no argument when she had promoted herself to be Mostyn's secretary, but Venner still called on her from time to time because she was the only individual in the department, apart from himself, Mostyn, and their agents, who knew what went on. She was spruce, attractive, intelligent, and good-humoured, and they often used her for discreet enquiries.

'Think you could be a dress shop?' he asked.

'Dress shop?' Daisy sounded surprised. 'What exactly do you mean by a dress shop? A boutique?'

'Okay. A boutique.'

'I've no head for accounts, and at twenty-seven I'm out of date.'

Venner grinned. 'I don't want you to set up in business. Just ring Dorothea Holcombe—'

'*The* Dorothea Holcombe?'

'The very same.'

'What are we interested in this time? Black power, anarchy, Communism? You name it, she's tried it.'

'She used to know our friend Henry Latisse.'

'We're after *him* again, are we?'

'We're always after him,' Venner said. 'But he's big now. Wealthy. Got into the habit of going around with Dorothea.'

'And why am I a dress shop?'

'She's a woman. She wears clothes – expensive clothes.'

'They're certainly not little somethings she runs up on Mum's sewing machine.'

'Right. Tell her you're putting on a fashion show and would she be interested.'

'Suppose she is?'

'Tell her you'll send her a ticket with date, place, et cetera. Then forget it. I just want to know if she's still around.'

29

Hanging up, he studied the file again. The telephone rang. It was Daisy.

'She's not,' she said.

'Not what?'

'Around. The number was answered by a woman called Richards. She says she bought Dorothea's flat last October and she doesn't know where she moved to.'

'Didn't she leave a forwarding address?'

'No. I asked. The Richards dame said she thought she'd bought a house in Surrey. She arranged to pick up her mail herself from the caretaker.'

Venner frowned. 'She's being bloody secretive, isn't she? I wonder why.'

'You could try the caretaker. He might know.'

'Never mind. I'll try somewhere else. I don't want her to know I'm asking.'

'Just one thing—'

'What's that?'

'If you're really keen on putting on a fashion show, you've got a customer. The Richards dame said *she'd* like a ticket.'

Venner sat tapping his pencil on the desk, then, on an impulse, he picked up the external telephone and asked for a Mayfair number.

It was answered by a maid.

'Miss Gore, please.'

The maid seemed to have been brought up in the same school as Aubrey's telephone girl. 'I don't think Miss Gore's available,' she said.

'Oh, Christ,' Venner murmured. 'Look,' he said to the telephone, 'please get Miss Gore to the telephone and please don't tell me she isn't available, because I think she is. This is James Venner.'

There was an abrupt silence. The maid sounded as offended as Aubrey's girl had been. After a while, he heard a clunk as the telephone was picked up.

'Susie here. Hello, love.'

'Susie—'

The voice at the other end interrupted him determinedly. 'I said "Hello, love." '

'Hello,' he said shortly.

'—love.'

'Yes. Hello, love.'

'You might at least *sound* interested, even if you're not.'

He relaxed at last and grinned. 'I am. Just busy, that's all.'

She seemed hurt. 'I don't believe you for a minute. I suppose you decided "Oh, well, it's a spare night, and there are no typists wanting bedding; I'll give Susie Gore a ring." '

'No, listen—'

'Eventually, you know, I shall stop lying down and letting you walk over me.'

'If I found *you* lying down, old love, walk over you is the last thing I'd do. Look—'

'I bet you don't mean it.'

'Susie!' He almost bawled down the telephone. 'Shut up for a minute.' In the silence, he drew a deep breath. 'I want some information,' he continued.

'Is that all? I thought you might want *me*.'

'Susie,' he said gently, 'just shut up for a minute and listen to me. Do you know Dorothea Holcombe?'

There was another silence before a small uninterested voice said, 'Yes.'

'Where does she live?'

'Can't imagine. Seems to have sunk without trace. Why?'

'I'm interested in her.'

'Then you've got a damn nerve asking *me* for her telephone number!'

'I'm not interested in her in that way.'

Sounding more willing, she asked, 'Is she in trouble? Because, if she is, my paper would like to know.'

'You keep your damn paper out of this! It's nothing like that. I want to know what she's up to. Where she goes. Who her boy friends are. You know these people. You move in the same circles.'

'I wouldn't be seen dead in her circles!' Susie's voice was indignant. 'I only write about these people. London's biggest evening pays me money to help produce a column of what it considers juicy snippets about the wealthy and unpleasant, that's all. It's my mother, God help her, who *knows* them.'

'Susie—' Venner was pleading – 'go and ask her for me.'

He had almost forgotten his request when Susie rang back. He snatched up the instrument. 'Yes?' he snapped.

'You should always state your number,' the voice at the other end said. 'And then your name. Clearly! James Dennison Venner. Dark. Handsome. Taciturn. And, cool, man, cool—'

'Susie, come off it. Have you spoken to Mum?'

'Yes. Dorothea's moved out of London. She's got a house in Surrey. Esher way. At Hinchley Wood, just off the A3.' He made a note of the address as she went on quietly. 'If you like, I can take you to where she's dining tonight. I can even show you her latest boy friend.'

'Who is it?'

'I wouldn't know as of this moment. But she's in town, and they'll be at Caligula's. The Ma came up with the information. It's her birthday and a table's ordered in her name.'

After a pause, her voice came again, terse and faintly aggrieved. 'You might say "How about joining me for a meal there?" '

Venner grinned. 'How about joining me for a meal there?'

'You took a bit of nudging.'

'I was going to have a beer and a sandwich and go to bed with a good book.'

'Why not go to bed with a good girl instead?'

'Good girls don't interest me.'

'She might manage to be a bad one for you.'

'I don't believe you, Susie,' Venner said, smiling. 'You've got more scruples than a priest. It's just talk.'

'Yes, it is,' Susie said quietly. 'I'm old-fashioned. I'm saving myself for marriage.'

She was out on the pavement almost as soon as the taxi

stopped by her door and she was wearing a dress that took Venner's breath away.

'How does it stay up?' he asked.

'Hope, mostly, and a chest full of breath.' She grinned at him, looking like a small schoolgirl caught in a misdemeanour, and his heart thumped awkwardly.

Susie Gore had been chasing him on and off ever since she'd met him early the previous year, but every time he felt like succumbing, he always came back to the same answer: he couldn't afford her.

Her mother had been a member of New York society when she married Boston-born Calvin Simpson Gore in London. The match hadn't lasted very long, and since then she had been married twice more, both times to Englishmen with titles. She was now more a member of the landed gentry than the landed gentry itself, while James Dennison Venner's wealth consisted solely of a few hundred in the bank, a small pension, and his salary. There were no investments, no inheritances, not even any wealthy aunts. You could hardly offer that to a girl whose family had a house – a house, mark you! – in Mayfair, another one in Sussex, which they called a week-end cottage but was big enough to put away half a dozen families in comfort, who stayed regularly in Switzerland and on the Riviera – *stayed*, not went on a package tour – and who had mixed all her life with the right people and was always surrounded by young men of good breeding from the right schools and universities, both British and American, all dressed in trendy gear with the latest trendy phrases on their lips to captivate her. Susie Gore was more Mostyn's speed, not James Dennison Venner's. It might all have been different but for that torpedo.

'You could at least look pleased to see me,' she said. Although Calvin Simpson Gore had been killed in an air crash some years before, Susie, despite her English accent, stubbornly retained her father's cheerful, pugnacious, unorthodox American spirit.

He realised his thoughts had taken over his expression. 'Sorry,' he said. 'Things on my mind.'

She gave him a shrewd look. 'That ship you never got?' she asked.

Venner turned. She had an extraordinary gift for knowing what he was thinking. 'A bit,' he agreed. 'But not entirely.'

She was looking out of the corners of her eyes at him, and he found himself wondering for the thousandth time how anyone as vital, noisy, and bursting with energy as she was could also at times manage to make him think of youthful birthday parties with little girls in frilly pink dresses lifting up their faces to be kissed.

'Is it going on all evening?' she asked.

'What?'

'Silences and a face like thunder. Because if it is, I'd just as soon you dropped me at a Wimpy bar for a hot dog and let me make my own way home.'

Caligula's was one of those restaurants which appear and disappear in capital cities like mushrooms – expensive, discreet, and over-staffed – and they had drinks at a price, Venner saw with alarm, that was enough to knock his eye out. When they ordered food, however, he noticed that Susie picked the cheapest item on the menu. He caught her eye on him, and she gave him a small apologetic smile.

'I'm wondering if I've let you in for a hell of an expense,' she said.

He waved a hand airily, as though it didn't matter that he'd have to go without drinks for the rest of the week, and she went on earnestly.

'I'd offer to go Dutch,' she said, 'but if I did, you'd get that stiff-upper-lip look on your face, as though you were three other people, all disapproving.'

She hadn't missed a trick. 'When I take a girl out for a meal,' he pointed out, 'I don't expect her to pay.'

'Pride? Poverty-stricken parents? Struggle to make ends meet?'

He shrugged. 'Principle of the thing.'

'Oh, God!' Susie sounded weary. 'Not that again!' She

34

looked at him angrily. 'Do you trot that out to all your other girl friends? You've had a few, I know. That girl from your office, for instance. She's been to your flat, hasn't she?'

There was an awkward pause while he wondered how she knew. 'That's been over a long time,' he said. 'And *you* could come, too, if you wished. Tonight, if you like. I have a hi-fi for the sweet music and could even provide soft lights.'

'No thank you,' she said. 'When I finally go into the big scene, it'll be on my honeymoon.'

There was another pause while she watched him, and he wasn't certain whether her expression was one of doubt or pity.

'What is it that bothers you so, Jimmy?' she asked. 'You always seem to be searching for something.'

He said nothing because he suspected she might be right. She looked up at him with the sort of look the chairman of a charitable organisation might have given to an obstreperous pauper. 'I know you better than you think I do, Jimmy,' she said quietly.

He doubted that she did, but she seemed to be looking for compliments and he rose to the occasion. 'I suppose you do,' he agreed.

She frowned and stared at her hands before her on the table. 'Then why in God's name,' she said sharply, 'don't you some-time get around to asking me to share your life?'

He deliberately ignored the question, and there was a long silence. He stared pointedly across the restaurant. There was a large table, prepared apparently for a party.

'Looks like Dorothea's having a night on the town,' he said, but she didn't even bother to look.

She suddenly seemed a little depressed, and when the food arrived they ate in silence. He was just beginning to wish he'd never come when a crowd of people appeared in the doorway. The men were in dinner jackets and most of the voices were loud.

'Sounds like Dorothea,' Susie said, without turning her head.

It was. She was a tall woman, with a mass of ash-blond

locks, who seemed to have been poured into her dress.

'Quite a head of hair,' Venner said.

'It's a wig,' Susie pointed out coldly.

Venner managed a glance over his shoulder. There were three other women with Dorothea, all of them young and attractive, and four males.

'Who're the men?' he asked.

'The fair one's Freddie Trimble. And the little one's Tom Watson, the National Hunt jockey. The one next to her's a Frenchman who's been around a bit lately, Jean-Pierre Something.'

'And the big one?'

'That's her brother. He's one of those.'

'He doesn't look it.'

'Some don't. He's supposed to be in love with Tom Watson.'

Venner studied the group; then he noticed Susie's eye on him.

'Who were you hoping to see?' she asked.

'Just a chap I was interested in. He went around with Dorothea for a bit. A rather unpleasant Middle European, but he made a lot of money and got into her league.'

Susie turned her head and glanced at the party at the other end of the restaurant. 'Must have chucked him,' she said.

'It happens,' Venner agreed.

There was a wistful look in her eye. 'With some people,' she said, 'it never even gets that far.'

36

Chapter Four

Latisse seemed to have disappeared. By the time Venner had tried every contact who might have had any information about him, and come up each time with a blank, he decided the disappearance was intentional.

'I wonder what the bastard's up to?' he said to Mostyn.

'Probably got an atom bomb from somewhere he's wanting to sell,' Mostyn suggested. He was dressed as though he was about to leave for the country: immaculate tweeds, white shirt, ochre tie. Faintly old-fashioned but bizarre in a way that somehow managed to appeal to the girls. He lit one of the strong Gauloises that made the place smell like the inside of a French taxi. 'Pity we lost him,' he said, making it sound as though it were Venner's fault.

'We'll probably find him again,' Venner pointed out. 'I saw Dorothea Holcombe the other night. With a bunch of admiring males. Any of 'em might know where he went.'

'Who were they?'

When Venner told him, he raised his eyebrows. 'I didn't know Tom Watson was one of those,' he said. 'Must be all those horses he has to deal with.'

He noticed a copy of *The Times* on Venner's desk. 'Read your paper this morning?' he asked.

Venner glanced at it. 'Not all of it.'

'Small ads.' Mostyn gestured. 'Bang in the middle.'

Venner flicked the newspaper open. His eye fell at once on what had interested Mostyn. 'Submarine expedition to Galapagos. Ex-crewmen required.' There was nothing else except a box number.

'I made enquiries,' Mostyn said. 'It was inserted through an agency in New York. Try Capp in Washington. Ask him if the big American papers carried it, too.' He paused. 'And while you're at it, see if anybody answered it. The Director of Officers' Appointments at the Admiralty might come up with a few likely names.'

Venner made a note on his pad. 'Right. I'll try Gosport, too. H.M.S. *Centurion,* the naval pay and records centre. In case there were any ratings. H.M.S. *Dolphin*'ll probably have a few ideas as well. It's not only the permanent submarine head-quarters and school, but Flag Officer, Submarines has his offices there, and everyone who joins submarines passes through it. Think it concerns us?'

Mostyn frowned. 'Just funny everybody should be interested in submariners,' he said.

'Everybody?' Venner lifted his eyebrows. 'One shot. One wanted.'

'One with his son kidnapped,' Mostyn reminded him. 'In Paris. Kid by the name of Snell. *He* hasn't turned up yet.'

Though Mostyn didn't know it, he was about to. Just at that moment a big black Citroën was moving rapidly through the Porte d'Italie, on its way from an apartment at Villejuif to another at Belleville, the man at the wheel carefully watching the people and the dogs that filled the road. In the rear seat another man sat alongside a small boy, who was lying back, out of sight from the street. He was a fair boy wearing an English school uniform. He'd been wearing it, to return to school in England, when he'd disappeared at Orly airport.

An undersized, sober-faced boy with large blue eyes, his face a mask of innocence, he'd been a good captive and had shown no sign of trying to escape. He'd co-operated well with his guards throughout his stay in the shabby apartment over-looking the Avenue de Vitry, and his guards had relaxed a little. They'd had instructions not to harm him and, since he was an engaging little chap, they'd even played chess with him and allowed him to watch the television, translating where necessary for him. He'd picked up quite a lot of French during his visits to his parents, but there were words that he stumbled over, and they'd endeavoured to be helpful, providing ice cream to keep him quiet and even allowing him a vermouth in the evening, which was something his parents, who knew him better than the guards, wouldn't have dreamed of doing.

His sobersides Englishness had amused his guards, and they'd cracked jokes with him, and even allowed him to examine the guns they carried. Had they only known it, they were being extremely foolish, because although Stephen Morton Snell might have been innocent-looking, a glance at his record at the preparatory school where he boarded in the south of England might have changed their minds considerably. It was enough to give his mother nightmares. His headmaster had long since discovered that Stephen Morton Snell was not only determined, but also extremely cunning.

He was being cunning now.

'I think I'm going to be sick,' he announced suddenly.

The man in the back seat sat up abruptly. The boy had eaten a colossal meal just before they'd left, and he was horrified at what might result. He jerked a hand at the driver. 'He says he's going to be sick,' he snapped.

The driver craned his head round to flick a scared glance over his shoulder. 'He doesn't look very sick,' he said.

But already the boy was growing red in the face and beginning to look distinctly ill at ease.

'He does now,' the man in the back said.

'We can't stop here,' the driver bleated. 'Open the window.'

The man in the rear seat rolled down the window and indicated it.

'You said I had to lie down,' the boy pointed out.

He was beginning to make heaving motions with his shoulders, and the man alongside him edged to the opposite side of the car.

'*Ça va*,' he said nervously. 'Sit up.'

The boy's eyes were wild now. The driver felt distinctly alarmed, because the boy had his hands on the back of the seat, and his mouth was uncomfortably close to his ear.

39

As the car hurried down the hill, neither man had his mind on anything but what might happen if Stephen Morton Snell *was* sick. They were both dressed in expensive suits, and neither fancied being too near him.

This was exactly why Stephen Morton Snell chose that moment to lean forward and sink his teeth into the driver's ear.

As the driver shrieked with pain, the car swerved violently, collided with a passing truck, slewed round, and came to a dead stop, flinging the driver against the wheel and the man in the back to the floor. Before either of them could recover, the boy, who had thought it all out carefully and had cushioned himself against the back of the driver's seat for the sudden stop, had opened the door and was running as fast as he could.

'Bright kid,' Venner said.

'Make a good criminal,' Susie agreed.

They were watching the television news in Venner's flat, lounging on the settee, with their feet on a pouffe. Coffee cups were on the floor.

'Ought to be popular at school when he gets back,' Susie went on.

'Hero of the Lower Fourth.'

As the weather forecast began, Venner switched off the set and reached for her. She moved towards him willingly enough and responded enthusiastically at first, but then she seemed to have second thoughts and, after fighting him off half-heartedly for a while, managed to push him away.

'What's wrong?' Venner asked.

'Wind-up.'

'With me?'

'Especially with you. A girl's plumbing is different from a man's, and she gets emotionally involved. It's trickier.'

He reached for her again but she pushed his hands away. 'It's time I was going,' she said.

'Why?'

'Because I have to work tomorrow.'

'It's pouring.'

'I can afford a taxi.'

'There's a spare bed.'

She kissed him, taking care to keep her distance. 'No, thanks. I know what it would lead to. You're not the only one with principles.' She jerked her skirt down and, getting to her feet, changed the subject adroitly. 'Ever find that chap you were after?' she asked. 'Dorothea's friend?'

Frustrated and faintly irritated, Venner didn't attempt to rise. 'No,' he said. 'He disappeared.'

'You know the story's going round that she's getting hitched to that Frenchman she was with – Jean-Pierre Thing.'

'He didn't look all that exciting to me.'

'He asked her to marry him. That makes any man exciting.'

Venner stood up abruptly. 'Fancy a last drink?' he asked quickly, and Susie's eyes became angry at once.

'Why do you always dodge the subject?' she demanded. 'You're as nervous as an elderly spinster who can't find the loo.'

Venner frowned. 'It wouldn't work, Susie.'

'It works okay when I come round here.'

'That's different.'

'It doesn't seem so different to me. You could even dispense with the ring and the piece of paper, so long as it was permanent.'

'No, Susie.'

'I think you're afraid I'll start throwing my money in your face. Or do you feel girls born with a silver spoon stuck down their gullet aren't so likely to be faithful?'

'I don't even think about it.'

'It doesn't stop you grabbing.'

'I nearly go down on my knees.'

She pouted. 'When I get married I'm going to be entire.'

'That's the word they use for horses.'

'It'll do for me.'

Venner studied her small angry face. There had been several times when they had come perilously close to sealing their affection for one another physically, but at the last moment some small mental objection had always made her draw back. He didn't blame her for it and he knew how she felt. Despite her cries of protest, she was a surprisingly moral person.

Her anger had faded, and she was looking at him with eyes that were suspiciously bright.

'You know, Jimmy,' she said, 'I think you're a damn fool.'

Venner said nothing, and she went on, beginning to lose her temper again. 'Just because I happen to be well-heeled.'

'It's not that.'

'What is it, then? Because you lost your promotion and felt you had to resign your commission in despair?'

He didn't reply.

'You're a bit old for that sort of histrionics,' she said. 'Do you think I mind that you never became an admiral?'

He almost wished he could have done. She'd have made a wonderful admiral's wife. She had the sort of poise that would have remained unshaken if the man next to her at a party had dropped dead drunk at her feet, the sort of confidence that would have enabled her to step over him and continue the conversation with her nearest neighbour without turning a hair.

She interrupted his musings angrily. 'I'd be quite happy with a plain Mister, you know,' she said. Then her expression became sad. 'I guess one of the happiest days I've ever spent – you, too, I suspect – was when we went down to Buckler's Hard that time and ate at that pub in Portsmouth.'

When he still didn't answer, she went on wistfully: 'The Admiral Jervis, wasn't it? That friend of yours, the Pole, put out the red carpet for us. We borrowed his boat, and I sat in the stern while you made with the sails. I thought you must be terribly important. You said, "If you ever want me in a hurry, go see Polaski."'

'That was a long time ago.'

'Gosh, haven't we aged?'

'I mean things have changed since then. I don't get to Portsmouth these days.'

42

'You're telling me you don't. But it *was* different. On the way back to London I fell asleep in the car with my head on your shoulder. I was romantic enough to feel that was happiness.'

Venner turned towards her. 'Susie—'

She swung away, her head down. 'Don't bother to apologise,' she said abruptly. 'See you.'

As the door slammed, Venner stood looking at it, feeling a heel, as he always did when she left him like this.

Faintly depressed, he lit a cigarette, but screwed it out almost immediately. Given different circumstances, he thought, they might have meant something to each other.

The following morning Colonel Capp's reply arrived. There *had* been an advertisement in *The New York Times*, but the request for the insert had come from the same agency which had put the advertisement in the London *Times*, and it had come to the agency via a Paris address – Rue Royale, 175, Meudon.

'Seem to be covering their tracks a bit, don't they?' Mostyn said. 'Not for fun, I'll bet.'

'At least in Paris we're nearer home,' Venner pointed out.

'Right.' Mostyn nodded. 'Let's contact Luciani. If we're nice to him, he might put a man to watch the place.'

During the afternoon, Mostyn hung about like a shadow, deep in thought and filling the room with smoke. Finally, he vanished, returning just before tea-time with a newspaper, which he threw on Venner's desk.

'Middle page,' he said. 'I marked it.'

The item was a paragraph, no more than ten lines, telling of the case of three naval ratings at Plymouth who'd been dismissed from the Navy after being picked up by the police with drugs in their possession.

'Engine Room Artificer Donald McAvoy,' Mostyn read aloud over his shoulder. 'Ordinary Seaman Alexander Williamson. Ordinary Seaman Derrick John Phillips.'

Venner glanced at the date at the top of the page, saw it was two months old, and lifted his eyes to Mostyn's.

'Thought I remembered some case of this sort.' Mostyn sounded almost apologetic. 'Do they get much of it?'

'Crops up from time to time,' Venner said. 'They always get rid of them. Bad influence. How did you find it?'

'Went along and saw the editor.'

Editor, Venner noticed. No less. Not the librarian or the chief reporter. What it was to have a title in the offing!

'Turned it up in no time,' Mostyn went on. 'How do they handle these things these days?'

'Minor offences are remitted to the authorities by the magistrates. If they're committed in R.N. ships and shore establishments, they're dealt with under the Naval Discipline Act.'

Mostyn limped slowly about the office, his hands in his pockets, deep in thought.

'Ordinary Seaman Williamson,' he said, 'is now back in Kirkcudbrightshire, with his father – an ex-petty officer, I might add – hanging over his shoulder threatening to break his neck if he steps out of line again. Local police enquired for me. Ordinary Seaman Phillips signed on for unemployment pay at Colchester, Essex, and is still waiting for a job.'

Venner looked up. 'And E.R.A. McAvoy?'

'Disappeared,' Mostyn said, smiling. 'Wife contacted the police. No sign of him.'

Venner said nothing, waiting. Mostyn would get around to it eventually.

'Shore-based lately,' Mostyn said. 'But not always. Know what branch of the service?'

'Submarines?'

'Got it in one.'

Mostyn prowled round the room a little more, flicking the ash from his cigarette to the floor. 'Know any places in Portsmouth where we could get a decent meal?' he asked.

'There's the Admiral Jervis,' Venner answered. 'If you saw the chap who runs it and put on the old act a bit, I'm sure he'd give you red-carpet treatment. What's on in Portsmouth? Someone pinch a battleship?'

'Not quite.' Mostyn waved the smoke away. 'It's that murder. Seems people had been having a go at this chap Nanjizel. It's thought he might have been involved in selling secret equipment.'

Chapter Five

Portsmouth was not at its best. The sky was grey, and there was a blustery wind blowing that brought spatterings of rain from the direction of the Isle of Wight. A big slum-clearance plan being carried out on the north side of the city had left whole streets looking as though they'd been devastated by bombs.

Into the bargain, at the back of the room at police headquarters stood the brooding figure of Petty Officer George Eltney, a vast man with thick shoulders and bitter eyes. His presence made his wife nervous, and she seemed to find it difficult to answer questions properly. Perhaps the traces of a black eye had something to do with it.

She sighed. 'He was always saying "What about George?" '

'I should bloody well think so,' Eltney observed. 'He was supposed to be a mate of mine.'

She rounded on him, her eyes flashing. 'You're no snow-white angel,' she said.

Eltney lifted his brooding gaze, and it occurred to Venner that he would probably black the other eye when they'd gone.

'*I* never went with women,' he said heavily.

'What about that one in Plymouth?'

'That was before we were married. I've never been with anybody but you since.'

Mostyn interrupted before another of the cat-and-dog scenes that had been going on all through the interview started. 'What about these men Nanjizel complained about?' he asked.

He was leaning against the wall, smoking, and looking as though he weren't even very interested. Venner stood by the window gazing out at the bleak view of the city. The detective-inspector who had set up the interview for them, a dry-mannered man named Prothero, sat with his hands in front of him, the fingers entwined, not moving, simply allowing his eyes to flick from one to the other as they spoke.

'They picked him up first in the Lord Nelson,' Mrs Eltney said. 'It's a pub.'

'When did he tell you this?'

'He didn't. I was with him.'

She stopped to glance at her husband and lifted one hand wearily to her black eye.

Prothero glanced at Mostyn. 'Would you prefer to conduct the interview alone?' he asked. 'I mean, without—' He nodded at the bulky figure of Eltney.

'Might be a good idea,' Mostyn answered.

Prothero looked at Eltney. 'If you'll just wait outside,' he suggested.

Eltney glowered. 'I'm entitled to hear what she has to say,' he observed. 'It happened in my house, and I want to know what she's been up to. All of it. Every damn bit of it.'

Prothero sighed and rose to his feet. 'These gentlemen aren't here to enquire into morals,' he pointed out. 'They're interested in something that might be much more important than that.'

When Eltney still seemed inclined to argue, Prothero put a hand on his arm. 'Don't make it difficult,' he said. 'I can make you, if I have to.'

Eltney glared at him, then at Mostyn and Venner. He finally directed a look of intense bitterness at his wife. Without a word he got to his feet, as slowly as he could, and turned to the door with a look that would have had him up on a charge of 'dumb insolence' in the service. The policeman in the passage outside, who was having a quick drag at a cigarette, tried to look innocent, but Prothero wasn't interested.

'Give Petty Officer Eltney a fag, Joe,' he said. He turned away and closed the door firmly behind him. 'Now say what you have to say, Mrs Eltney,' he suggested.

She glanced at the door. 'Will *he* find out?'

'We don't supply information.'

'Not even to him?'

'It's none of his business.'

She sighed again, and answered their questions automatically. There was little sign of the sparkling gaiety that had attracted James Nanjizel. She seemed to feel that life had suddenly become very real and very earnest, and she didn't appear to be looking forward to the future.

Venner felt sorry for her, and he wondered if it was simply because she was so small and helpless-looking, or because of the blatant feminity of her. But she wasn't the first wife who'd slipped off the straight and narrow because the demands of the service had kept her husband from her side. Eltney was no Adonis, but, as far as they could make out, she'd always behaved herself when he was within reach.

Mostyn, who had said nothing during this passage, offered Mrs Eltney a cigarette. Venner noticed it was an English cigarette, and wondered bitterly why *he* was never offered anything but Gauloises. Mostyn lit the cigarette for her and went back to lean on the wall again.

'You were telling us about the three men,' he encouraged.

She pushed her hair back and shrugged. 'It was one night in a pub,' she said. 'He told me how they'd picked him up before and got talking. After that, he said, they bumped into him again and again. He said they were after him.'

'What for?'

'He said they only seemed to be interested in him for his service in submarines.'

Venner glanced at Mostyn, but Mostyn was studying the end of his cigarette with a look of incredible vacuity on his face. 'Go on, Mrs Eltney,' he said.

'He couldn't make out what good that would be to them,' she went on. 'He said that whatever it was they were after didn't sound honest to him. He said he'd told 'em he was thinking of going to the police. I think he would have if they'd gone on. In spite of what they said.'

'What *did* they say?'

'That it would be dangerous if he did.'

It *had* been dangerous, anyway, Venner thought – fatal, in fact.

'He asked them why they were interested in *him* – there were plenty of other submariners – but they said *they* were all in the Navy. *He* was due to leave.'

Venner caught Mostyn's eye. This time there was a spark of interest.

'What did they look like?'

'Just men. One was tall and thin. One was broad. The other was fat.'

Prothero pressed her to enlarge on this, but all she could really offer was that they had had all the usual features, including arms and legs. Because of her interest in Petty Officer Nanjizel, she hadn't even looked at them much.

'Any idea who they are?' Mostyn asked Prothero.

The Detective-Inspector grimaced. 'Could be anybody,' he said. 'Villains follow patterns, but recruiting submariners isn't one we've come across before.'

He turned to Mrs Eltney, who was sitting with her hands in her lap, dejected, pathetic, and small. Even in her misery she seemed to exude sex.

'What about the men who burst into your house?' he said.

She looked up at him with wide eyes and suddenly began to weep. The sight of Jimmy Nanjizel's naked blood-stained body had never left her for a minute. She'd cowered at the bottom of the stairs for ten minutes after the shooting, wondering what to do, before she'd finally realised there was no way of avoiding her husband's wrath and the sneers of the neighbours. Her husband, flown home two days after the murder, had blacked her eye at once, and since then they'd hardly spoken. Even her mother had seemed to feel she'd been stupid to allow herself to be caught.

'I wish I'd gone to Singapore,' she said. 'I could have.'

'How's your French?' Mostyn asked as they headed back towards London.

Venner shrugged. 'Passable.'

'Better ring Luciani when we get back. Arrange for us to visit him. I'd like a word with that boy.' Mostyn fell silent, obviously deep in thought. 'What sort of men would you say submariners are as a whole?' he finally asked.

Venner considered. 'A lot end up on the admirals' list,' he said. 'A submarine posting's a step towards an early command. And now, with nuclear power, they're no longer merely submersibles; they're genuine submarine vessels. That's why the best men want to serve in them.'

Mostyn nodded, concentrating on his driving. 'Interestin', all this chasing after submariners, isn't it? Would you say Nanjizel was a good submariner?'

'He'd done his stint in nuclears.'

'He wasn't in one when he was murdered.'

'He was thirty-eight. That's old by submarine standards. It's normal enough for a man at the end of his stretch to serve out his time training new intakes or doing odd jobs about the base. No one's going to promote a man due for his discharge.'

Commissioner Luciani was a Corsican, swarthy, vigorous, vital. His hands were strong and covered with black hair, and his mind was as keen as a razor. He spoke perfect English with an American accent.

'We have been watching 175, Rue Royale,' he announced. 'It appears to be occupied by a man named Pierre-Jean Viollet. He's an oceanographer.'

'Qualified?'

'And genuine. The advertisement appeared also in *Le Monde*, as well as in *Nordsee-Zeitung* in Bremerhaven and the *Hamburger Morgenpost*. I took the precaution of finding out.'

'And Viollet?'

'He has some idea of building a self-powered bathyscaphe. He produced a few plans.' Luciani gave a vast Gallic shrug. 'I think he's a crank.'

'Or a front.' Mostyn, who had been staring at the glowing end of his cigarette, brushed ash from his suit and raised his eyes. 'Think we could find out if there've been any replies to these ads?' he asked.

'I think we can.' Luciani nodded and made a note on a pad. 'I'll contact Naples and Taranto, as well, for you.'

'I'd be obliged.' Mostyn smiled. 'What about the boy who was kidnapped?' he asked.

'Stephen Morton Snell?' Luciani grinned. 'He ought to go far. He is – what do you say? – a most resilient individual.'

Stephen Morton Snell was indeed resilient, and certainly didn't seem to warrant the fluttering concern his mother manifested. He appeared, eating an apple and with a roll of comics under his arm. Mostyn introduced himself, saying merely that they were the police.

The boy sat in a chair in his father's study with his legs dangling, finishing the apple and looking a little bored by the whole business. He had been interviewed by newspapermen and TV reporters so many times it was old hat to him now.

'I just said I was going to be sick,' he pointed out. 'That's all.'

'That was very clever, dear,' his mother said.

The boy smiled. 'Everybody does it,' he said. 'Going home from school in the train. We ask each other how our measles are. Or our mumps. All the women with kids disappear like a flash, and we get the compartment to ourselves. Pretending to be sick's another one. You should have seen their faces when I said that. While they were still wondering how to keep clear, I bit his ear. It was easy, really.'

Venner decided that Stephen Morton Snell was going to be able to carry off his new-found fame when he went back to school without being spoiled by it.

His father seemed less confident. 'I didn't think they'd touch my son,' he said.

'They?' Mostyn looked up. 'Who, Commander Snell? You didn't think *who* would touch your son?'

Snell gestured. 'I'd been approached by three men. Englishmen, I think. Perhaps Americans. I found it hard to tell what

51

they wanted from me. It didn't appear to be money. They seemed to want an experienced submarine commander.'

'You are one?'

'This is my first shore job.'

'Nuclear?' Venner asked.

'Both.'

'Did they say *why* they wanted a submarine commander?' Mostyn asked.

Snell shook his head. 'They didn't mention that at all. It was all very puzzling. Even now I'm not sure if it was connected with my son's disappearance.'

The telephone rang. Snell answered it and held it out to Mostyn. It was Luciani.

'We have just picked up the men who kidnapped Stephen Morton Snell,' he said in a flat uninterested voice.

'You have?' Mostyn said cheerfully. 'Have they said anything?'

'No. Nor are they likely to. They are dead. They were pulled out of the Seine near St Cloud. Someone had the wits to notice that one of them had a severely bitten ear. They had both been shot. I thought you might like to know.'

'Any clues to their identity?'

'None whatsoever. Or to why they'd been shot. But I can guess. Because they might talk or because Stephen Morton Snell might identify them. Someone seems to be very afraid of being involved.'

Chapter Six

It didn't take much imagination to guess that something was in the wind, but just what it was defied both Venner and Mostyn. Enquiries across northern Europe revealed that Viollet's advertisement had appeared in newspapers in Holland, Belgium, Norway, and several other countries. Beyond that, they were unable to advance at all until certain events in London on Midsummer Day set the enquiry moving once more.

That year, midsummer fell on a bright day with a blue sky full of puff-balls of cloud. The English weather had pulled out all the stops for the occasion. London had an air of festivity about it as the sun fell on the pale-ochre fronts of the buildings at the bottom of the Mall and round Buckingham Palace. Even the traffic seemed to flow more freely.

At ten-forty-five in the morning, a large blue vehicle like a Security Corps van cruised along Baker Street, its four occupants wearing dark police-like uniforms and black crash helmets. At ten-forty-nine the van stopped in a vacant space outside a row of offices and shops, and the men inside began to watch the clock on the dashboard. At almost the same time, not far away a grey Jaguar also pulled into a vacant space. In both cases, the spaces had been occupied by insignificant private cars, which had been there for some time and conveniently evacuated their parking spots together. It was significant that in both cases the drivers of the disappearing cars glanced at the drivers of the new arrivals and nodded.

There was nothing unusual about either the blue van or the Jaguar, but a keen-eyed observer might have noticed that the van was parked outside a bank and the Jaguar outside a small but fashionable jeweller's which catered to affluent customers from the West End, and that the street was wide and had a free flow of traffic. Every man in the two vehicles was wearing headgear of some sort, but what wasn't obvious to people outside was that underneath the headgear, out of sight, they were also wearing nylon stockings.

John William Bird, the man alongside the driver of the Jaguar, studied the clock. Everything was going well, he decided. It had all been worked out carefully for them in the shabby house in Willesden that he called his headquarters. Overlaid with smoke grime, it was no beauty spot, but it was in a district where the neighbours were never much interested in who occupied the house next door. With the great prison of Wormwood Scrubs not far away, people weren't inclined to be fussy, and it made a good hideaway.

He had been a little surprised at being asked to do this job, as a matter of fact, because he wasn't a clever man and hadn't managed to stay out of prison for long at a time. But he had big ideas, and it gave him a great deal of pleasure that someone of apparent moment had called on *him*.

As they waited, he fished out a small cigar and stuck it between his teeth. There was something of the Walter Mitty about Bird, and a cigar between his teeth made him feel important, a big wheel instead of the small cog he really was. He liked to dress smartly, and he had a girl who worked for one of the pin-ball saloons that operated round Piccadilly. She liked smart clothes, too, and smart wisecracks, and Bird spent a lot of his time reading books like *Matt Helm* in the hope of picking up a few that would make her laugh. She had a flat in Islington which she shared with another girl, who was always willing to move out when Bird moved in.

Bird's eyes gleamed as he glanced again at the clock. 'Minute to go,' he said. 'You guys ready?'

Grunts from the rear seat told him that everyone was prepared, and his eyes narrowed behind the wrap-around dark glasses he liked to affect. They not only hid his identity – a useful asset in his profession – but also gave him a mystique, an air, a big-time look.

He took off the glasses, carefully folded the earpieces, and placed them in his pocket. Then he patted his inside breast pocket for the hand gun he carried there. It was a Smith & Wesson five-shot .38, and it had cost him seventy-five pounds in a pub in Covent Garden; it was his prize possession.

'How about the cannon, Alf?'

The thick-set youngster in the rear seat reached down to the hold-all at his feet. A gleam of metal showed below the un-zipped top where a sawed-off shotgun nestled under a bundle of rags.

'Okay. Loaded.'

'Tug?'

The other man in the rear seat slapped his pocket.

'Right.' Bird nodded. 'You know what to do.'

'I got it, Birdy.'

'Right. Just coming up to eleven. Are the others in place?'

The man with the shotgun glanced out the window. 'Right outside the bank,' he said.

The clock down the road chimed eleven, and the driver started up the engine. As though at a signal, they saw the puff of blue exhaust smoke as the van's engine started, too.

'That's it,' Bird said. 'Us first. Them three minutes after.' After glancing at a policeman standing further down the road, at a point approximately equidistant between the two vehicles, he swung the door open. 'Right,' he said. 'Let's go.'

The three armed men climbed quickly from the car and crossed the pavement, just as the men from the van up ahead cautiously opened their door. Once inside the entrance to the jeweller's, they reached up and pulled the nylons over their faces, so that they immediately became unrecognisable.

It was unfortunate for John William Bird, however, and even more so for the man called Tug, that in the jeweller's shop quite the wrong man should have been buying his wife a ring for a twenty-fifth wedding anniversary. He was an ex-major of paratroopers named Snow, who had won two MC's

55

as a young soldier in Korea and, though severely wounded, had added a third some years later in Malaysia just before he'd left the Army. An expert in unarmed combat, he was the last man in the world to be afraid of weapons handled clumsily by men who were obviously inexpert. He made sure his wife was safely out of the line of fire before calmly hooking the handle of the heavy walking stick he had to use because of his shredded right leg round the elbow of the man holding the sawed-off shotgun, the thick-set youngster called Alf. Snow's jerk swung the gunman round and caused him to pull the trigger, and Tug, holding a German Luger, caught the blast full in the back of the head. The tightly grouped pellets tore into his flesh in the area just below and behind the left ear and, travelling upwards, ripped their way without obstruction through muscle and sinew to shatter the brain. He was dead when he hit the floor.

Startled and shocked, Alf tried to give the contents of the second barrel to Snow, but, despite his game leg, Snow was too fast for him, and the handle of the heavy ash-plant came with violent force across his nose and sent him staggering away. The blast from the second barrel brought half the ceiling down.

Seeing the whole plan fall apart in front of his eyes, Bird fired at Snow as he dived for Tug's Luger. The shot missed and brought plaster from the wall. As Snow's fingers closed on the Luger, Bird decided it was time they left. It didn't take him more than a fraction of a second to realise they couldn't do a thing for Tug, who was sprawled on the floor with a head that looked as though it had been through a mincing machine. He grabbed the nearest tray of rings and, kicking the half-blinded Alf to life, bolted out of the shop. Half-falling, half-staggering, they dropped into the waiting Jaguar.

'What about Tug?' the driver shrieked.

Bird was panting and wild-eyed. 'Never mind, Tug,' he said. 'He's had it! Get going!'

The car accelerated and took off, flinging Alf, sobbing, on

to the rear seat. The constable half-way down the long street started to run. Just as he disappeared inside the shop, the van outside the bank began to pull away, too, and one of the clerks hurtled out to the pavement screaming for help.

'The dead man,' *The Times* report stated, 'has been identified as Desmond Stewart Bowden. He served in the Army for three years, ending his time in Aden. After leaving the Army, he had had a variety of jobs. He was the youngest of five brothers, three of whom are in the Forces.'

'The point being,' Venner said, 'that one of them is in the Navy—'

'And?' Mostyn asked.

'And at the moment not on the payroll.'

Mostyn's eyebrows rose – which was as much as he normally allowed to show when he was surprised – and Venner went on. 'Two months missing,' he said.

'Deserter?'

'Right. And a submariner, too. Or ex-submariner, to be exact. He's a telegraphist.' Venner placed his newspaper on Mostyn's desk, the report on the robbery uppermost. Alongside the report was a photograph of a man, bare-headed and casually dressed, which was captioned 'Desmond Stewart Bowden.'

Mostyn studied it. 'Flowered shirt,' he pointed out. 'Taken on holiday.'

'As a matter of fact,' Venner said, 'it wasn't.' He gestured at the picture. Behind the man's head were towering masts, heavy yards, and a spider-web of rigging.

'I recognised the ship,' he said. 'It's *Victory*. Nelson's flagship. She's set in concrete in a dry dock in the naval dockyard at Portsmouth. No one who's sailed in or out of there would ever fail to recognise those masts.'

'And the shirt?'

'Serviceman's mufti. It was *Victory* that started me thinking, and I enquired of the police. They found the picture in Bowden's wallet, and because the face fitted the one on the body, they issued it. There was another, too, though, and in that one he was wearing a roll-collar white jersey.'

'So?'

'Submariners wear white jerseys,' Venner pointed out. 'So I made enquiries. The Navy had no Desmond Stewart Bowden on their lists. Naturally – because Desmond Stewart Bowden was in the Army. But they did have a Dennis Sidney Bowden.'

Mostyn stared at the picture of the man in the newspaper. 'Then why was Desmond Stewart Bowden wearing a naval jersey and why is he standing in front of *Victory* in this picture?'

'A little understandable confusion,' Venner said smugly. 'It seems that Desmond Stewart and Dennis Sidney were identical twins. The pictures they found on the body weren't of Desmond, but of his twin brother, Dennis, the one in the Navy. Someone obviously took the flowered-shirt picture as he went off duty from his ship. They're allowed to wear what they like these days, and sometimes in summer they look like refugees from a Bermuda beach. I pinned him down at Naval Records.'

'Go on.'

'He'd served in nuclears but he'd been found unsuitable and was finishing his time in general service. He disappeared two months ago while on leave after returning from a stint at Gibraltar.'

He studied Mostyn's face, expecting praise.

Mostyn's expression didn't change. 'Interestin',' he said. 'How about having a chat with this chap Bird?'

John William Bird still looked a little shocked that the thing had gone wrong, that Tug was dead, and, above all, that he was now in custody and unlikely to enjoy his girl friend's charms for a long time to come.

Major Snow had done more damage to Alf's face than he had thought. Not only was his nose shattered, but the heavy walking stick had also broken his cheekbone. So it hadn't surprised Bird much when he heard that Alf had been picked up. He'd decided it might be wiser to go to the country for a few days. The police had stopped him near Guildford on his way west. 'Going somewhere, Birdy boy?' they'd said.

'Name of John William Bird,' the detective who now ushered him in announced to Mostyn. 'Calls himself a director. Can't think what of.'

'I got a garage,' Bird said angrily.

'A shed, a vise, and a can of petrol,' the policeman said. 'Small-time crook. That's all.'

'Thanks,' Bird said. 'For nothing.'

'Don't mention it.' The detective gestured. 'The job was arranged, and they were told what to do. Even the Jag was pinched for 'em. They didn't draw a share. They were simply paid to do the job.'

'Who paid 'em?' Mostyn asked.

The policeman glanced at Bird, who shrugged. He was well aware of the code. The one thing you never did was give information, and he didn't really know, anyway. 'Tug Bowden did all the fixing,' he said, 'and he's not here now, is he? His brother was behind it somewhere.'

'Dennis Sidney Bowden?'

'I think that's his name.'

'What happened to the jewellery?' Venner asked.

'It was hidden in his girl friend's flat,' the detective said. 'He hadn't had chance to get rid of it.' He glanced at Bird. 'We've got all we can out of him. There won't be any more. He's a small-timer. He was set up to draw us off the other lot. They knew he wasn't much good for anything else, and it's been done before.'

'Same gang?'

The policeman nodded. 'Same method. Some pathetic nit like this one draws the fire while the real snatch goes on somewhere else. It happened in Willesden. A hundred and fifty thousand quid pinched there. At Heathrow. Diamonds that time. At Leicester and Manchester and Coventry. Same method exactly, every time.'

Back in the office, Mostyn was thoughtful. 'Same method,' he repeated. 'Same gang. Know how much they got away with?'

'Forty-seven thousand, I'm told, give or take a little – and a tray of rings.'

'Not this lot,' Mostyn said, frowning. 'The other occasions. The ones that detective mentioned: Willesden. Heathrow. Leicester. Manchester. Coventry. Works out around three hundred thousand quid.'

'Good haul.'

'Wonder if it was to pay wages.'

'Wages?'

'Big criminal enterprises these days,' Mostyn pointed out, 'are planned like big business. They pick the experts. But they have to guarantee payment even before they pick up the loot. Wonder if that's what it's all about?'

'What have you in mind?'

'Submarines. With our friend Bowden, the link exists.'

'And?'

'If they're recruiting experts for something – as they seem to be – they'll have to pay them until they're ready to use them, won't they? They tried to get Snell, a submarine commander of some experience. They tried Nanjizel. They might already have got McAvoy. They might already have got Dennis Sidney Bowden.' Mostyn stared at his finger tips. 'Wonder if it'd be possible to find out if anyone approached Bowden or McAvoy before they disappeared. As they did Nanjizel and Snell.'

'I'll put it into orbit.'

Mostyn continued to stare at his fingers. 'Wonder what it's all about,' he said. 'Have there been any attempts to sabotage any of the new nuclears?'

'I thought of that,' Venner said. 'The answer's "No".'

'What have we got these days?'

'More than you think. Four Polaris, eight nuclear fleet submarines, twenty-five diesel conventional – mostly "P" and "O" class – with *Sovereign*, a fleet nuclear, just launched, and ready for service as soon as she's completed.'

Mostyn nodded, making notes on a pad, and Venner went on.

'Polaris and fleet subs are at Faslane, near Helensburgh, Scotland. Fleet and conventional are at Devonport, conventional only at Portsmouth.'

'And building?'

'Four fleet subs, to bring the total up to twelve.'

Mostyn rubbed his nose. 'Been any trouble at the yards?' he asked.

'Not a thing. A little fuss at Greenock, but not connected with us and nothing to hold up the building. Nobody was worried.'

'No attempts to collar the plans?' Mostyn looked up at Venner. 'That's what they're supposed to do, isn't it?'

'It used to be. Perhaps times have changed.'

Mostyn sat for a long time studying his fingers. They were long and tapering, and Venner had heard he was a good pianist who used his skill to seduce the girls he took to his flat. Soft lights and sweet music. Oh, Colonel Mostyn, how clever you are!

Mostyn's pale eyes were curiously empty. But Venner knew that the brain behind them was whirring like a time bomb. He had a built-in early-warning system.

'I think you'd better go over this whole business,' he said slowly. 'It's beginning to have rather an unpleasant smell.'

Chapter Seven

Commander Axson, Venner's naval contact at the Ministry of Defence, was a breezy, honest man who seemed baffled by the vagueness of the enquiries Venner was making.

'You know as well as I do,' he said, 'that they don't get many deserters in submarines. Something keeps them there. High pay, pride, I don't know what. Perhaps it's just that the selection's tough.'

'There must be an occasional maverick slips through,' Venner insisted.

Axson nodded agreement. 'Oddly enough,' he admitted, 'we had two in the last five months. Francis Frederick Bonser. Leading hand, seaman branch. From *Confounder*, in the Clyde. History of family trouble. And Jeremy Luck, another leading seaman, also seaman branch. Disappeared from *Orion* at Devonport. Orphanage background. Recently in hospital with V.D. but discharged recovered.'

'Any history of them having been approached at all? Like that case in Portsmouth. Nanjizel. Three men had been badgering him for some time.'

'What about?'

'I wish we knew.'

Axson studied Venner, more questions trembling on his lips, but he resisted the temptation and glanced instead at his sheet of paper. 'Nothing here,' he said. 'But I could enquire.'

'Do that, please.' A new thought occurred to Venner. 'Who knows about these desertions? Apart from you and me.'

Axson smiled. 'The whole bloody Navy, I reckon.'

'Nobody else?'

'Not normally.'

'Do you have their files?'

Axson went to a cabinet and opened a drawer. 'You'd better have a look in here,' he said. 'You'll know as well as I do roughly how many men are discharged in the course of a year due to sickness, injury, or time-expired. We keep their records for pension rights and things like that. Details are entered if they're unusual. Or if there's anything special.'

'Such as what?'

'Injury. *Any* injury. In case they later claim it was caused during service. Bad record—'

Venner's eyebrows rose, and Axson explained.

'Security officers are always on the look-out for heavy drinking, sexual perversion, marital problems, extreme political views, maintenance of a standard of living higher than normal. There've been a few slip-ups, because nobody likes ferreting out his shipmates' aberrations. We keep the records for another reason, too.' Axson grinned. 'Surprisingly enough, some of these men who're discharged as unsuitable come back. They feel lost in Civvie Street. It's not hard to spot 'em, though, even if they change their names, and when they turn up we remember not to accept them. They're less trouble outside.'

'Officers *and* men?'

'The files are in the cellar.'

'Are they available to *anybody*?'

'Anybody in this building.'

'Isn't that dangerous?'

'Why should it be?' Axson looked surprised. 'This is the Ministry of Defence. With integration of services, there are always queries.'

'Do civilian personnel have access to them?'

Axson shrugged. 'There are a hell of a lot of non-service personnel in this building,' he said. 'About two thousand, I reckon.'

'Could they get a look at the files?'

'Not without permission of the Keeper. Nobody sees them without good reason, and certainly not without two signatures.

That applies to everyone – except departmental heads, of course.'

In the corridor as he left, Venner almost fell over Aubrey, who looked at him coldly, his pale skin curiously fishlike, his eyes full of distaste.

'Hello,' Venner said with exaggerated cheerfulness. 'Glad I saw you. You might like to know we're not interested in Latisse any more.' Since Aubrey had a habit of lunching with Wither, the Keeper of the Records, who was a known gossip, it seemed wise to keep their enquiries quiet. It also pleased him to torment Aubrey, and the reaction he received was all he could have hoped for.

'*You're not?*' he said.

Venner beamed. 'No. He appeared to be interested in United Nations weapons imported into Cyprus, and the Greeks were worried they'd find their way into the wrong hands in any conflict between the administration and its opponents. It seems they were wrong.'

When he returned to the office, Mostyn was sitting with his feet on his desk. He looked half-asleep, but Venner noticed sheets of paper in front of him covered with hieroglyphics scrawled by the expensive gold ball-point that lay across them.

'Been making a few enquiries,' Mostyn said, speaking in short clipped sentences, as though he found talking exhausting. 'No special interest in *any* of our submarines – *anywhere*. Not even a dirty little demonstration. So I wondered if it were a foreign one they were after, and I sent a warning to Capp. After all, this *might* be international. Things often are these days, and the U.S. has nuclears at Holy Loch and at Rota in Spain, to say nothing of one or two building. Capp couldn't be specific.'

He paused. 'Then I wondered about the French. *They* like their share of nuclear glory, too, and they're building a class of nuclear ballistic submarines at the moment. The first – *Redoubtable*, *Terrible*, and *Tonnant* – have already been completed. At Cherbourg. I warned Luciani we thought something was in the wind.'

As he finished, he sagged in his chair. The long speech seemed to have worn him out. 'What did *you* find out?' he asked.

'The names of two more deserters,' Venner answered. 'One from *Orion* at Devonport. Name of Luck. One from *Confounder* in the Clyde. Name of Bonser. '

Mostyn's eyes opened. 'What branch?' he asked.

'Seaman. I made further enquiries. On his last ship, Bonser's job was on the foreplanes. Luck's, oddly enough, was on the afterplanes.'

Mostyn's expression seemed to indicate it was all a lot of Choctaw to him, and Venner explained.

'Submerged,' he said, 'there are certain essential posts which have to be manned. There's the captain, the navigating officer, the first officer watching the trim, the engineer officer, the telegraphist, and the radar and asdic operators. In addition, there's a man at the helm, one on the blowing panel, one on the foreplanes, one on the afterplanes. If these two deserters have been swept into the same net as the others who disappeared, then our friends are half-way to a control-room watch.'

'That *is* interestin',' Mostyn said. 'Good at finding 'em, too, aren't they?'

'Not so difficult as you'd think,' Venner said. 'They've got a cabinet full of likely names at the Ministry of Defence. Very useful if you're looking for specialists who might decide to opt out.'

Mostyn made a note on his pad. 'Surely to God,' he said slowly, 'they're not thinking of *pinching* a submarine, are they?'

There was a long silence in the office, during which the muted sounds of the traffic outside and the bellow of a siren from the river came up to them through the window. Mostyn's question had stopped them both dead. The idea was so fantastic it didn't bear thinking about; yet there was something ominously repetitive about the defections in a branch of the service that didn't normally suffer much from them.

Venner found Mostyn's eyes on him. 'It's a thought,' he admitted.

Mostyn nodded. 'It is,' he agreed. 'Under the circumstances, it might be a good idea to tighten security all round. Even a few words in the right ears at the N.A.T.O. embassies. Who do you know?'

'I have a contact at Grosvenor Square. Lieutenant Commander Turk.'

'Well, he's a start. See him on your way home.'

When Venner arrived at the office the following morning, he was early and in an uncertain mood. Lieutenant Commander Turk, at the United States Embassy, had not responded to his warning with much enthusiasm.

'Hell, man,' he had said, 'we have trouble enough of our own without this. The U.S. Navy's a mess right now. You've read the goddam papers. You name it, we've got it. Deserters are nothing new.'

'Deserters from nuclear submarines are,' Venner had pointed out.

'Yeah. That's true.' Turk had run his fingers through his hair. 'But we've nothing to go on. It's pure conjecture.'

'It's worth watching.'

Turk had moved restlessly in his chair. 'Is this official or unofficial?' he had asked.

'Call it officially unofficial.'

'Oh, Christ!' Turk had looked bewildered. 'One of your goddam people got the wind up?'

'You might say we're covering our rear.'

'Okay!' Turk had waved a disinterested hand. 'I'm a great one for watching out for kicks in the ass. Let's have the facts.'

For a change, the day had been hot, but the evening had become thundery and muggy. Venner had arrived at his flat tired and frustrated, like Turk, from the way they seemed to be

66

groping around in a fog for something that didn't appear to exist.

He'd pushed open the door to find the telephone was ringing. It was Susie, fishing for him to ask her round, but he'd not taken the bait and they'd quarrelled. It was only later, when some of the harsh things she'd said about him had ceased to hurt, that he'd decided her anger had been caused by his own lack of feeling, and he'd promptly rung her back to put things right.

By that time, however, it was too late. She'd gone out. He'd tried several times during the evening, even up to midnight, to reach her, but the telephone had not been answered. He had been left with a feeling of inadequacy and bloody-mindedness, and he had only managed to run her to earth before leaving for work that morning.

'I feel like a rat,' he said.

'Rats do, I guess,' she said without much sympathy.

'Susie, I'm sorry.' He was prepared to go the whole way. 'I don't make things easy.'

'I'd say,' she rejoined briskly, 'that you made them pretty damn hard. A brush-off isn't easy to take.'

'I'm not brushing you off.'

'What *are* you doing then?'

'Oh, hell—' It was hard to explain, bound up as it was with money and vanished hopes.

As usual she seemed to know what he was thinking. '*I've* got the cash,' she said. 'And *you* could get a new ambition.'

Her shrewdness startled him, as always, because it didn't seem to go with the innocent little-girl face, or even with the charity chairman's expression that appeared occasionally. He managed to ignore the jibe.

'Susie,' he said, 'let's stop quarrelling. Let's have a meal together tonight. Not Caligula's. It'll be more like a Wimpy bar, given the state of my finances. And don't offer to pay or I shall be angry again.'

'Okay.' Her voice became gentle, still faintly hostile but more pliable. 'A Wimpy bar. With wine?'

'If you like. A vino bistro.'

'Sounds wonderful.'

She blew him a kiss down the telephone, completely won over, and it helped a little to feel he'd put things right with her, even if it was only a temporary measure that merely altered the mood between them and never the circumstances – the money and the lost ambition.

On his desk was a report from the Foreign and Commonwealth Office on Chief Olmuhi. 'Ibrahime Olmuhi,' he read. 'Thirty-eight years old. Married. Two wives. Youngest son of senior chief of Makro tribe by third wife. Army sergeant under French. Officer after independence. Promoted self general on acquiring power . . .'

It continued with a run-down of his ambitions and ended with a résumé of his character that made Venner sit up. 'Signs of deep-seated psychological disturbances which drive him to do strange things and keep him in a state of tension. Rigidity of personality, feelings of persecution by the West, perfectionist anxiety and obsessive sense of self-righteousness, suggesting a paranoid personality . . .'

'Oh, charming,' Venner murmured out loud. 'Bloody charming! No wonder half Africa's scared stiff of him.'

There was also a report from Luciani. There had been advertisements for submariners in the Naples and Taranto papers, but the replies had been collected long since and no one had any idea who by. Venner threw it into Mostyn's tray and picked up the police report on the men who'd tried to recruit Nanjizel. As he'd expected, nothing had emerged from their enquiries on this. The thought that they were getting nowhere didn't help his temper; nor did Lucas, who seemed to have got wind of their suspicions and called from the floor below just as the office began to spring to life, demanding to know what was going on. Venner put him off with a whole lot of technical data he knew he wouldn't understand – blinding with science, it was called – and was just sourly wondering why work which appeared to be sensible and essential had to be hidden under a smoke-screen of civil-service activities

68

when Axson rang up with his replies to Venner's enquiries about Bonser and Luck.

'It seems Bonser *did* have approaches made to him,' he said.

Venner sat up at once, reaching for a notebook and pencil. 'What sort of approaches?'

'We don't know.' Axson sounded worried, as though *he*'d decided it was important, too. 'His wife was pretty thoroughly questioned, and it seems he was visited more than once. He told her he'd been offered a job, and when she asked *what* job, he said a shore job for when he got out of the Navy. Since he had another two years to do before he was time-expired, she thought it a bit odd, to say the least. She thinks now it probably had something to do with his deserting.'

'I'm damn sure it did,' Venner said. 'What about Luck?'

'Nothing much there. Luck was the sort of chap who liked his own company, but the night before he vanished, he was seen in a pub in Glasgow talking to a couple of civilians. A tall thin one and a short thick-set one. He never went back to his ship. Do you want more than that?'

'Is there more?'

'Shouldn't think so. I got that lot from the regulating branch. There was another man in *Confounder* due for discharge who says he was approached, too. Name of Evans – Engineer Mechanic Evans. The report came through his commanding officer, who unearthed it during his enquiries when Bonser disappeared. Nothing came of it though. Evans changed his mind about his discharge and signed on for another nine years, and they left him alone.'

'Perhaps he was lucky,' Mostyn suggested. 'If they'd said any more to him, they might have decided to knock *him* off, too, like Nanjizel. I think we ought to go and see him. I'll get Daisy to fix it.'

'Now?'

Mostyn raised his eyebrows. 'No reason why we shouldn't, is there?' he asked.

69

'People have private lives,' Venner tried.

'Not in this department.'

Venner thought of Susie. 'I suppose I could make a telephone call,' he said.

Mostyn didn't seem too keen. 'So long as it's quick,' he said.

It took Venner all of five minutes to find a room without anyone in it where he could telephone his apologies and behave contritely. Daisy seemed to be entertaining the entire floor in his office, so he went to hers. Immediately people poured in. In the end, he claimed his own office back and rang Susie's newspaper. Everybody there seemed to be stricken with congenital idiocy. Twice he was put through to the wrong extension, and when he finally reached her department he was told she'd just gone out.

'Couldn't have been more than two minutes ago. Hang on. I'll try the front office.'

But, of course, the front office was as slow as everybody else that morning.

'She's just gone.'

'Where to?'

'God knows. Some enquiry of her own. She's picked up some sniff of scandal in high places and asked permission to ask around.'

'Haven't you any bloody idea *where* she is?' Venner snapped in a fury.

The voice replied in kind. 'No,' it said. 'We bloody haven't,' and slammed the receiver down.

Venner glared at the instrument and called the number again. This time, a different voice answered. There was nothing to do but leave a message. He was just wondering if it was worth ringing up a florist and sending a few flowers to make the apology more abject when Mostyn returned.

'Ready?' he asked.

Knowing it would take at least five minutes just to find the name of a florist, Venner looked round for Daisy to do it for

70

him, but by this time her office was bafflingly empty. He would have to let it slide.

'Yes,' he said, defeated. 'I'm ready.'

He fished in his locker for the overnight bag he always kept at the office for emergencies like this. Mostyn was waiting by the door, looking impatient, and they descended in the lift in silence.

They made the mid-morning plane to Abbotsinch by the skin of their teeth, and Mostyn sat back, bland and indifferent, blinking at the sunshine.

'Have a date?' he asked.

'Yes,' Venner said.

'Pity.'

Venner gave him a dirty look. 'Don't *you* ever have dates?' he asked.

'Never any I can't break.'

Venner frowned, wondering which of the office secretaries Mostyn was currently sleeping with. What he had said was quite true. He was a bachelor and still young enough not to experience much difficulty. Most of the girls in the office blushed when he spoke to them – even Daisy, who was old enough to know better. It must be the money everybody said he had, Venner decided bitterly.

Engineer Mechanic Evans was a placid man with a thick line of black eyebrow that ran straight across his forehead. It gave him an evil look that didn't seem in keeping with his character, because his last four years in the service had been blameless and there wasn't a mark on his record for that period.

There was a cold wind blowing down the loch from the north, gusting between hills that were tawny and blue. The water was steel-grey, and there was no light in the sky to highlight the curves of the great vessel, with its tall fin. It looked sleek and menacing, a vast complex of intricate machinery and electronic equipment that represented one of the deadliest weapons in the world.

The Officer of the Day, his nose blue with the cold, met

them on the casing. 'Commander Queripel's waiting for you,' he said.

They negotiated ropes and wires to the hatch in the fin, the clean-lined version of what used to be called the conning tower, and climbed down inside the vessel to the warmth and the purr of machinery.

The captain, Commander Queripel, was a surprisingly young man, who wore his hair longer than he ought, and his uniform, though it looked neat at a distance, was old and frayed from long wear. 'You can use my cabin,' he offered. 'Smoke if you wish.' He picked up the intercom microphone. 'Captain here,' he said. 'Engineer Mechanic Evans to my cabin.' He turned as he put the microphone down. 'What's Evans been up to?' he asked.

Mostyn shrugged. 'Nothing at all.'

'Good.' Queripel seemed pleased. 'I wouldn't want him bothered. He's done well, and I want him to keep on that way. He got in with the wrong lot at first, but he pulled his socks up and now he's signed on for another nine.'

Mostyn looked blank and innocent, as though the enquiry were really Venner's and he'd only come along for the ride. 'Nothing to worry about,' he said. 'He's done nothing wrong. You're welcome to sit in and listen, though we don't promise to explain what it's all about.'

Queripel smiled and rose to his feet. 'I'll take your word for it,' he said. He glanced at Venner. 'I'm sure I know you, don't I?'

'I was in *Odysseus*,' Venner said shortly. 'She was alongside when you came to *Dolphin* in *Oriflamme*. You were a first lieutenant then. So was I.'

'Where are you now?'

'In my office,' Mostyn said quickly, and Venner caught Queripel's pitying look, the arrogant, superior look of a man who'd made it for a man who hadn't. He seemed to be expecting an explanation, but Venner didn't bother to tell him about the torpedo.

'Always thought they said the Navy was known for its tact,'

72

Mostyn observed when Queripel had gone.

'Not me,' Venner said. 'I don't say it.'

'Got any friends, Venner?'

'Not many.'

'Thought not. That's why I picked you for my team.'

Venner's head jerked up indignantly just as a knock came on the door. It was Engineer Mechanic Evans. Mostyn looked at Venner as though for a lead on protocol.

'Better sit down, Evans,' Venner said. 'The Captain said we could use his cabin.'

'I'll stand, sir.'

Venner offered a cigarette, but Evans refused, and stood waiting in a relaxed attitude that spoke of self-confidence.

'We'd like to know a bit about you, Evans,' Venner said. 'Nothing to worry about, though. We've been investigating a few men who've gone absent, and we find there have been a surprising number of cases where they'd been approached by strangers and offered money. I believe you were, too.'

Evans seemed startled that they should know. 'Maybe it was my record,' he said. 'I had one. Then I sort of saw I wasn't getting anywhere and stopped overnight.'

Venner nodded. 'Did you ever talk much about this record of yours, Evans?' he asked.

'No.' Evans gave a bashful grin. 'I used to when I was younger. Like kids boast how much beer they can drink and how many girls they've been with. Mostly blow.'

'Anybody know about it?'

Evans shook his head. 'Only my ma. She wasn't very keen on it.'

'Father?' Mostyn asked.

'Killed in *Amethyst* after the war. Up the Yangtze.'

'No civilians?'

'Can't see how they could.'

'Oh, they could,' Venner said. 'You weren't the first man they found out about.'

Evans's eyebrows rose, and Venner went on. 'These men who approached you? What were they like?'

Evans frowned. 'I never really got a good look at 'em. Kept to the shadows. One was tall and thin and one was stocky. There was a fat one, too.'

'Nanjizel's recruiting sergeants,' Mostyn said. 'How did they go about it, Evans?'

'Met 'em in a pub. They seemed friendly enough. Bought me a couple of drinks. I didn't see why they shouldn't. People often do. Sometimes it's women. Sometimes it's men, after – well, you know what *they're* after. Sometimes it's politics. Sometimes it's nut cases.' He frowned again. 'I don't think these three were nut cases.'

'What was it they were after?'

'I never really found out. It seemed to me they wanted me to do a trip for 'em. In a submarine.'

'Which submarine?'

'We didn't get around to that. The next time they tried, I told 'em I was staying in.'

'Did they mention any names?'

'None I remember.'

'Ships' names?'

Evans struggled with his memory. 'No,' he said. 'I tried to get out of them what they were after, but they'd clammed up by then.'

'More than they did with Nanjizel,' Mostyn said when Evans had gone.

'Think we ought to warn him?' Venner asked.

Mostyn rose and reached for his stick. 'Leave it to you,' he said. 'Have a word with the Captain. On the quiet. Tell him about Nanjizel. Get *him* to have a word.'

He looked at his watch. 'Just time to check security,' he said, 'then we can pick up the plane south. It's Saturday to-morrow, and it'll be more difficult. Besides, I've got a dinner date and I don't want to miss it.' Smiling at Venner, he headed for the door. 'Suit you?' he asked. 'You had a date, didn't you?'

'I did,' Venner said. 'I shouldn't think I have any more, though.'

74

Chapter Eight

To all intents and purposes, the big black car beside the road on Portsdown Hill, overlooking Portsmouth harbour, belonged to a group of people taking the summer sunshine. There were other cars, too, their occupants sitting with the doors open and the windows down, watching the afternoon sun glint on the waters of the Solent between the south coast of England and the Isle of Wight. On the road below, the early-summer traffic hurried along the shoreline towards Southampton and the continental ferries in glinting bunches of colour.

It was possible to pick out, beyond the channel, the houses of Ryde, on the north coast of the island. A frigate was heading east past a group of small sailing craft near the entrance to the great sheet of water that formed Chichester harbour, and off the Nab a bigger vessel, which looked like a helicopter cruiser, swung at anchor. Further out, a tanker was moving slowly towards the naval docks with her cargo of fuel oil, and the ferry to the Isle of Wight trudged across the gold glinting Solent like a small beetle on a pond.

There were three men in the black car, and an observer might have decided that they were businessmen taking a breath of fresh air during their lunch break or relaxing in the sunshine after a business meal. One of them, a small man with a hard face, spoke with an American accent. Another was an older man, much older, with a scarred leathery face and a beard. The third, dark and cleft-chinned, looked like a senior executive briefing his colleagues, which, in a way, was just what he was. On his knee was a notebook with a neatly written list of items, and in his hand was a radio-and-television trade magazine with which he stabbed the air to punctuate his remarks.

'Have we the house?' he was asking.

'All set up.' The American spoke quickly, as though used to action and quick decisions. 'We're moving them there right away.'

'Isolated?'

'You couldn't get it more isolated. On top of a hill, in its own grounds, surrounded by woods. Near Selborne. It's been occupied by a sculptor, and it's been empty for some time. Nobody goes near it.'

'Is there somewhere we can set up the equipment?'

'The studio. It's in an old stable. The guy carved big statues, so there's plenty of room.'

'Good.' The man with the cleft chin looked at his notebook. 'We shall need a transmitter-receiver. Big enough to do what we want.'

'Big enough to stop the others from doing what they want, too,' the man with the beard said.

'That, too.'

'We have one.' The American made a gesture of derision, as though what they suggested was easy. 'It was taken from the R.A.F. two months ago. It was U.S.—'

'U.S.?'

' "Unserviceable," in their lingo. Damaged in transit from a base in Scotland. It was at the back of a shed, where it wouldn't be in the way.' The American grinned. '*And* where it was easy to get it out without being seen. As far as I know, they still haven't missed it.'

'Does it work?'

'It does now. We rebuilt it.'

'Will it do what we want?'

'I guess so. If we use it much, someone will be picking us up and wanting to know who we are. But we *have* tried it.'

'Where are we setting it up?'

'I haven't decided. There are always houses for rent along this coast, but we haven't found one off by itself.'

'What about a lorry?'

'I'm getting one.'

'The boats?'

'I've got 'em. One's an ex-naval tender. Privately owned, but she still looks the part.'

The man with the cleft chin looked again at his notebook, frowning. 'Uniforms,' he said. 'They're going to be a problem.'

'No sweat,' the American said. 'They don't wear uniforms, anyway. Working parties wear blue pants and blue shirts, with their trade and rank badges. And caps. Officers wear reefers and white sweaters.'

The man with the cleft chin managed a smile. It looked chilly. 'That seems to be all for the moment, then,' he said. 'We still have a lot to do, and we can't delay much longer. We're still one short.'

'It'll work out.'

'Right.' The man with the cleft chin tapped the magazine in his hand. 'One last thing. This.'

The American grinned. 'On its way tomorrow.'

Just off the A325 in Hampshire, near Great Mew, the area is heavily wooded, and, with no moon and a layer of cirrus obscuring the stars, the trees were pitch black but curiously alive with the creaks and movements of branches in the breeze and the occasional shuffle of a small animal in the shadows. As Police Constables Kevin Bawes and Brian Vench sat in their car knocking back a cup of coffee from a vacuum flask, they had more than once noticed bright eyes caught in the glow of the side lights.

'Always enjoy this place,' Bawes said, his voice full of enthusiasm. 'I like being out at night.'

'Perhaps your dad was a poacher,' Vench replied from behind the wheel.

Bawes smiled. 'P'ra'ps he was. He knew his way about, that's a fact. I was born in the country.'

'London, me,' Vench said. 'That's the sort of place I like. Always something happening. Even at midnight. None of this unnatural stuff like trees. Besides, when it's dark I like sitting in front of the telly, not on the edge of a wood watching rabbits off for a bit of tail.' He shifted restlessly in his seat. 'Now *that's* a good occupation for a dark night.'

As he finished speaking, a pair of lights came into the rear-view mirror, and he looked up. 'Bit late for the pub,' he observed, interested immediately. 'Might need to blow in the old breath bag.'

It wasn't a late carouser, however, but a large van, coming from the north. As it passed, they saw there was another behind it. Both were big and both unmarked.

There was nothing especially odd in two unmarked vans and it was perhaps only somebody with a big house, or an office, moving from London to the west. Bawes and Vench had once stopped a suspicious vehicle and found it stuffed full of files belonging to a London firm moving to a less expensive area.

'All the same,' Vench said aloud, reaching for the starter key. Bawes didn't argue, but pushed the coffee away as Vench put the car in gear and pulled out to the road.

They caught up with the vans two miles further along, just as they were turning west towards Winchester. It was no part of their job to stop anyone who was behaving himself but they made a mental note of the vans' numbers and their direction. It didn't mean much, but the top brass never clobbered a policeman for being extra careful.

'How about checking 'em?' Bawes said.

'Let's pass 'em and wait at the top of Hailey Hill,' Vench suggested. 'They'll be going slow there, and they won't be able to nip past.'

They did so and waited, with Bawes in the road waving his torch. They were pleased to see the vans pull up and stop one behind the other.

'Nah then, what's all this?' The voice had a Cockney accent. 'Think we've got the Bank of England aboard?'

Bawes was relieved to hear the cheerfulness in the voice. Midnight was not a time when most people welcomed being stopped.

78

'Just a check,' he said. 'What are you carrying?'

A thick-set, dark man with a cigarette drooping from his mouth thrust a bunch of manifests at him.

'Bit late to be on the road, isn't it?' Bawes asked.

'Not with the stuff we're carrying, mate. Sunday's always moving day for the people we work for.'

Bawes glanced at the manifests. They indicated that the vans had come from the Yvonne Arnaud Theatre at Guildford and were heading for Poole.

'Want to take a look?' the driver asked.

There seemed nothing wrong with the manifests, but an extra check always looked good on a report, and with a co-operative driver it was never a bad idea.

'No trouble,' the driver said. 'Nip up on the cab roof and shine your torch through the window.'

Bawes did as he was invited. 'What is it?' he asked.

'Theatrical flats. You know, them things they stick around the stage to make it look like some rich bloke's castle, or something like that.'

'What's this then?' Bawes was staring at pipes and dials. 'The plumbing?'

'It's a job lot,' the driver said. 'It's been bought by a firm of theatrical agents for disposal abroad. Bit of Shakespeare. Bit of Variety. I wouldn't know. I'm a telly man meself.'

'Other one the same?'

'Exactly.'

Bawes climbed down. 'Okay,' he said.

The driver lit a fresh cigarette and offered Bawes one.

Bawes shook his head. 'Why this time of night?' he asked.

'Take everything down Sunday after the Saturday performance. Next lot up for the Monday-night show. They probably wanted the place clear for when the new stuff arrives to-morrow.'

Bawes waved him on. 'Look out for the turn on to the bridge at Barsley,' he warned. 'It's tight. You'll need to take it easy.'

'Thanks, mate.'

The driver let in the clutch, and the van moved forward. The other moved off after it, the driver waving to Bawes as he passed.

Bawes slipped back into his seat in the car. 'Theatrical stuff,' he said. 'Everything in order.'

Vench shrugged. 'Put it down in the report. Bawes and Vench on their toes. Suspicious of everything.'

Bawes grinned and fished for his notebook. 'Might have been a battleship,' he said.

In fact, it very nearly was.

Chapter Nine

Mostyn held up his hand and ticked off the names on his fingers. 'McAvoy, engine room artificer. Bowden, telegraphist. Bonser, seaman. Luck, same. Four of 'em. Could it be that they've been recruited simply because one of 'em might know where to place a bomb?'

Venner listened without much interest. When they had returned from Scotland, Mostyn had gone off happily to his date, but Venner's telephone call to Susie Gore had remained unanswered, and nothing he'd done had enabled him to find out where she was. He'd been willing to apologise and explain with the right degree of humility and contriteness, but there had seemed to be a conspiracy of silence to keep him from finding her.

'We saw the security arrangements in the Clyde,' Mostyn continued, unaware of Venner's mood. 'We saw no reason to fault them, but it'll be a good idea, all the same, to demand extra precautions. At *all* establishments with submarines attached. Let's make it personal, as we did in Scotland. Carries more weight. I'll attend to Devonport.'

He smiled. 'I can spend the week-end up the Helford River. Might even take Daisy and do a bit of work between times. You cover Portsmouth. You could take that little dolly of yours and enjoy the Solent. Arrange to see the Admiral. And take a look at that ship of Nanjizel's – *Achates*.'

'Nobody's going to sabotage a ship that's heading for the breakers,' Venner pointed out.

Mostyn refused to be put off. 'Just look,' he said. 'Something might occur to you, especially since you were a submariner yourself.' He paused. 'Then go and see Mrs Eltney again. Go through every conversation she ever had with that chap Nanjizel. Every one. He might have told her something she's forgotten. People do talk in bed, you know.'

It was clear he spoke from experience.

Before he left London, Venner tried again to get in touch with Susie. He asked for her number and was put through to her office. She answered the telephone personally this time.

'Susie!' he said, aware of his heart lifting. 'This is James Venner.'

'Drop dead,' she said briskly, and hung up.

He sat with the instrument in his hand, staring at it. Then he slammed it angrily back to its stand and went to catch the Portsmouth train. The day was bright, but he had no eye for the weather and still less for the scenery as he brooded his way past Guildford and Haslemere to the drabber streets of Portsmouth.

Admiral Haythornthwaite, the Commander-in-Chief, Naval Home Command, like so much top brass, was intelligent and knew the value of good relations with others. He was handsome and confident, his face unlined and youthful, and he was polite, helpful, and friendly, but he clearly saw no future in sub-ordinating the Navy's arrangements to the demands of a small and unknown organisation which virtually wanted to close his bases to normal traffic. 'There'd be precious little work done here if we indulged in that sort of thing,' he said cheerfully.

'We had to in wartime, sir,' Venner pointed out.

'Bit different then. If we went in for anything like that, the whole damn thing would come to a grim grinding halt. We'd need a directive from the Minister.'

The Admiral remained friendly, however, and even took the trouble to arrange personally for Venner to be driven to the King's Stairs Landing for a boat to *Dolphin*, where *Achates* lay.

There was a lieutenant-commander waiting to meet Venner when the car arrived. He was a shrewd young man by the name of Cathcart, with a trace of accent that suggested he'd come up from the ranks and a decoration over his breast pocket that suggested he might well have deserved to.

'You police?' he asked.

'Not exactly,' Venner said.

Cathcart didn't ask any further questions, but Venner knew of the average naval officer's left-handed respect for the civil authorities. Like the civil servants they regarded with dislike but called 'our lords and masters,' the police were outsiders, and they did not enjoy having them involved in Navy matters.

As Venner followed him to where the tender was waiting, the salutes he acknowledged were evocative and unsettling, like the crying of the circling gulls and the soft putt-putt of the tender's engine.

They climbed ashore at the other side of a stretch of oily water dotted here and there with lean grey shapes and groups of smaller boats. *Achates* was lying further along the quay, her black paintwork, broken here and there by spots of rust, showing the attrition of long service. With her casing covered with ropes, crates, and pieces of machinery, she had a shabby, forlorn look. There were carboys on the quay alongside her and a couple of lorries waiting by a party of men struggling to lift what appeared to be a large piece of electronic equipment.

After a quick exchange of words and more salutes, Venner followed Cathcart on board. The control room had a bare look, and there were empty bulkheads, from which equipment had been removed. In the messes a livid scar of black ran across the white paint where the flames had ripped through.

'She'd had her time anyway,' Cathcart said.

'What happened?'

'Battery explosion. Somebody's bloody carelessness.' Cathcart spoke angrily, as though he felt for the submarine as he might have felt for a crippled horse. 'Three men were killed. Everything's still U.S.' He shrugged. 'Still,' he said, 'it probably reduced the number of cockroaches.' He indicated the scarred bulkhead door between the control room and the tiny ward-room. 'No longer watertight,' he said. 'It was damaged by the blast.'

For the most part, the messes were empty and unfurnished, though an attempt had been made to repair some of the damage with new paint, and temporary bunks had been installed.

'For the trip to the breakers,' Cathcart explained.

Dockyard workers' tool-boxes were stacked by the bulkheads, and temporary power cables hung in uneven loops. The deck was scuffed and littered with scraps of paper, strands of oily rope, and cigarette ends. There were loose ends of wire every-where, and holes in the bulkhead where pipes had been ripped out. It smelled of dirt and stale air.

'Wouldn't like to be aboard if she had to dive,' Cathcart remarked. When Venner said nothing, he went on cheerfully. 'Under the regulations laid down for safety, she can't, of course. Not with the holes in the bulkheads there. But you'll know that as well as I do.'

'What about all this equipment they're taking out?'

'Salvageable stuff. Nothing new. Nothing secret. All old hat. Like the ship herself.'

'Engines?'

'Normal and conventional. Solid injection diesels. Built by Vickers. Batteries by Chloride Electrical. They've been re-placed, but I can't think why. She'll be going on the surface to the breakers.'

They moved through the length of the ship. *Achates*, with so much of her equipment removed, was echoing and devoid of life. Standing in the fore-ends, one hand on the empty torpedo racks, Venner caught the familiar smell of fuel oil. The compartment was chaotic, more dead wires and ropes hanging motionless over the remains of pin-up girls. A group of narrow-gauge wired pipes ending in valve connections clamped to the deck-head caught his eye.

'What are they?' he asked.

Cathcart gestured at a small brass connection almost lost

among the maze of pipes and wires by the escape hatch. 'Evacuator valves,' he said.

'To evacuate what?'

Cathcart looked at him. 'Gas,' he said. Though he hadn't intended it, he spoke in a way that made Venner feel ancient and out-of-date. 'They were classified until recently. All boats are fitted with them.'

Venner studied the valve. 'What gas?' he asked.

'This stuff the government's getting rid of.'

'Do *submarines* carry it?'

Cathcart laughed. 'Good God, no,' he said. 'But if the other side's ready to use it, we have to be, too. I suppose now they're getting rid of the stuff, evacuator valves are useless, and they'll eventually be removed like all the other rubbish they stick on ships for fun and then take off again the next time the moon's full.'

Warfare had moved a long way even in the short time since Venner had been involved with it. He frowned and looked about him. He didn't know what he was looking for, or even if there was anything to find; he was conscious only of familiar smells and shapes, how easy it was to bark the shins, and how the damp lay over the dead ship like a miasma from the inside of a tomb.

'Nothing but radar and asdic left in her,' Cathcart said. 'She's going to Devonport under her own power, and they'll need them in case of fog. Everything that's left – engines, batteries, the lot – will be removed at Devonport, and she'll go to the breakers under tow.'

They moved through the scarred and blackened messes again to the after-ends. The scene of desolation didn't seem so bad there. Though the torpedo racks were empty, the great engines and electric motors were still in place, a petty officer working over them, and the bulkheads were unmarked by the removal of wires and pipes.

'Only part that's left untouched.' Cathcart made a gesture of finality. 'Well, that's the lot, unless there's something special you want.'

85

'No.' Venner shook his head. 'There's nothing special.'

After lunching in Cathcart's mess, a taxi summoned by an elderly petty officer took Venner to Mrs Eltney's home. Mrs Eltney herself opened the door for him.

'Oh,' she said. 'It's you.'

'May I come in, Mrs Eltney?'

She moved back and allowed him to step into the tiny hall. Like Mrs Eltney herself, it was spotlessly clean.

She opened a door. 'You'd better sit down. Like a cup of tea?'

She sat down opposite him, and he caught a glimpse of well-shaped thighs as she crossed one leg over the other in what seemed to be a particularly provocative manner. He wondered if it was deliberate. She had good legs, and he guessed that Nanjizel wouldn't be the last man to run his hand along them.

'You on your own, Mrs Eltney?' he asked.

She nodded glumly. 'He's gone,' she said. 'I don't suppose he'll ever be back.'

'I'm sorry to hear that.'

She shrugged. 'I'm not fussy,' she said, and he felt sure it wouldn't take her long to find another man. She'd obviously written off Petty Officer Eltney.

She was looking at Venner now as though it had suddenly occurred to her, too, that, with her husband written off and Nanjizel dead, she was a free agent again. She smiled at him. 'What did you come for?' she asked.

'To see you, Mrs Eltney.'

Her eyes brightened perceptibly, and Venner knew exactly what she was thinking. For a moment, he thought it, too. His affair with Susie seemed to be well and truly over at last, after a year or more of cat-and-dog bickering, and he was as free as Mrs Eltney was. He fished in his pocket and pulled out his cigarettes. She accepted one and made the lighting of it an intimate affair in a way he hadn't noticed when Mostyn had offered her one at the earlier meeting. Her hand was on his as he held the lighter, and her big green eyes were on his face.

86

She was expert at such small gestures, and he had to pull himself up sharp. For God's sake, he thought, no wonder Nanjizel succumbed; he hadn't had a chance.

Aloud, he said, 'We're still worried about Petty Officer Nanjizel, Mrs Eltney.'

'Oh!' Her eyes clouded, and to his surprise he realised she'd actually been wondering if he'd come back to see *her*.

'We're still trying to make out what it was all about?'

She studied him, the same look on her face that Cathcart had had. The question was the same, too. 'You police?' she asked.

'No.'

'You came with the police.'

'That's true. But I'm not a policeman.'

She said nothing and puffed at her cigarette for a while, eyeing him speculatively, as though she were wondering if he'd be likely to succumb to her tricks.

It wouldn't have been hard, he thought, in the mood that was on him after Susie's cold rejection. He decided he'd better get down to business. 'We've just been to Scotland,' he said. 'Talking to a sailor up there who'd been approached in the same way as Nanjizel. It sounded like the same men.'

'Did they shoot him?'

'No.'

Her eyes flickered. 'They did Jimmy Nanjizel.'

'That's why I'm interested in him,' Venner explained. 'We believe they told him something.' Feeling that he'd have to explain a little more or she'd think he was mad, he said, 'There's something on. We don't know what it is, but it seems to involve the Navy. They seem to be trying to make contact with Navy men. Submariners, to be exact. It could be secrets or it could be an attempt at sabotage.'

'The new ones? The nuclears?'

'That's what we think.'

'They're not here.'

He reflected that naval secrecy was all rather pointless when every Navy wife with her wits about her knew what was going on. 'No,' he agreed. 'But if it *were* sabotage, that wouldn't really matter. They were perhaps merely recruiting experts who could help.'

'Jimmy Nanjizel was a good man,' she said. 'He'd have married me eventually, I bet. I'd have got a divorce, and then it would've been all right. Especially with him due for his discharge.'

He tried to push her on quickly before she became sentimental. 'Did he talk much to you, Mrs Eltney?'

'Call me Daphne,' she suggested. 'Seems silly all this "Mrs" and – what's your name?'

'Venner.'

'You must have a first name.'

'James.'

'Do they call *you* Jimmy, too?'

Oh, Christ, he thought. This damn woman! She was arch and clever and a sight too attractive for his peace of mind.

'Some people do. Mrs Eltney – Daphne – did Petty Officer Nanjizel talk to you?'

'Yes,' she said, stubbing out her cigarette. 'More than that lump George did. All *he* ever did was watch the telly.'

'What did he talk about?'

'Me and him. What were we going to do about it – about us, I mean. He was worried sick.'

'Did he talk a lot?'

'Sometimes.' Her eyes lifted as she spoke, and he knew that she meant they'd talked in bed. Mostyn had been right. He wasn't surprised. She radiated sex, and it troubled him that he wasn't proof against it.

'Did he ever talk about these men who kept meeting him?' he asked. 'We think they were the ones who came here.'

She gave him a stricken look. The memory of Nanjizel's naked butchered body still troubled her. He leaned forward, and to his horror, he realised he had almost taken her hand. He sat up again quickly.

'Mrs Eltney,' he said, 'I've got to try to find out exactly what it was they said to him. Were they blackmailing him? It's the way it usually works.'

'I don't think so.' She shrugged. 'Any case, he was just working off his time. He couldn't give them any secrets. He was only stripping some old sub they've got. Taking out all the stuff that wouldn't be wanted, and making sure the motors would work in case they had to use them in an emergency.'

They talked for a long time, and Venner accepted her offer of a cup of tea. He didn't enjoy it, but it seemed to please her and he decided that she was probably one of those women who need a man around, to do things for, the sort who would always be lost as a service wife because half her married life would be spent without her husband.

They went over every conversation she could recollect. In the end, she fished out a bottle with a little gin in it. 'I feel like a drink,' she said. 'Could you do with one?'

A drink was what he wanted more than anything else, and he nodded. 'I really could,' he said.

When he left, she escorted him to the door.

'I'd like to come again, Daphne,' he said.

Her face lit up. She hadn't been expecting it, he knew. 'When?'

He had the whole week-end before him. 'Tomorrow?' he suggested.

'That's all right.'

'In the meantime, I'd like you to try to remember everything Petty Officer Nanjizel ever said. Something might occur to you, and it might be just the one thing I'm looking for.'

She nodded, her eyes bright. 'I'll be ready.'

She'd be wearing her best dress this time, he knew, and probably be tarted up to the eyes. And ten to one there'd be a new bottle of gin. He knew perfectly well what was in her mind, because, try as he might to push it out, it was in *his* mind, too.

89

Chapter Ten

'X gas,' the Prime Minister said, 'is not good after ten years, and we on this side of the house can be relied on to make sure that it will be properly taken care of in safety until that time has passed. I can give my honourable friends opposite the assurance that there will be no risk. They will, however, have to accept the fact that I cannot tell them where the gas is or how we propose to dispose of it. Clearly, such an announcement could be dangerous.'

The House of Commons had been crowded, not to hear the Prime Minister's observations on X gas, but because a row was brewing again over Ireland. The subject of the gas had been injected by the Member for Ewerton and Strowe, who was anxious to have it seen by his constituents that he was protecting their interests, and the Prime Minister's comment, waspish and sharp, had put him firmly in his place.

Venner tossed the paper aside. He could just imagine Aubrey enjoying the secrecy. 'Minister, we really ought to keep this information top secret. Of course, Minister, far too tricky to have this stuff lying about. Yes, Minister. No, Minister. Three bags full, Minister.' He loved to make a mystery of everything, loved to give himself a top-security rating that was three times as high as everyone else's.

Venner had had another passage of arms with him only that morning, a brush over a delayed file on Ewerton that he suspected Aubrey had been sitting on merely to show he had authority. It was childish in the extreme, and Venner knew he'd been childish to respond.

'I'll have you remember,' Aubrey had told him coldly, 'that your rating here is only a junior one and I'm a departmental head.'

Mostyn appeared. He looked as though he'd enjoyed his week-end. Daisy, too, was wearing the smug expression of a cat that had been at the cream. Neither of them seemed to be suffering from the remorse that was troubling Venner, who had arrived back ridden by guilt. Daphne Eltney had been enchanting and expert but, though the affair had seemed like vengeance on Susie for her rejection of him, he was finding it hard to live with.

'Aubrey's been in, complaining,' Mostyn announced.

'Thought he might,' Venner said.

'Shrill as an elderly spinster caught with a man in her room. Don't push him too far. We need his good will, and he's a sad chap really. Let him enjoy his bit of limelight.' Mostyn indicated the paper on Venner's desk. 'After all, *we*'re not concerned with the disposal of his blasted gas. That, at least, is one of the things that's decently guarded. Olmuhi worries me a damn sight more than that. He's saying now that he'll have weapons before long that'll give him the whole of Africa if he wants it.'

'He'll soon have to either put up or shut up,' Venner remarked. 'There are enough people waiting in the queue out there to get rid of him if he doesn't.'

'Think Latisse's selling him a nuclear submarine?' Mostyn asked.

The idea was a startling one. 'Wouldn't be much good,' Venner said. 'A struggle for Africa wouldn't be naval.'

'A missile fired from the sea to land on some inland city would be,' Mostyn pointed out. 'And if it came from a submarine, stopping it getting into position would be, too.' He tossed the paper aside. 'I suppose he's talking through his hat again. He seems to do a lot of it. But it was an idea, and he could afford it. He nationalised the Pelémelé Gold Mines last year, and they were very profitable when the French had them.'

Venner was silent and he went on quickly. 'Luciani was on the telephone,' he said. 'He has some names of men who might have been approached. He thinks one – electrical mechanic by the name of Arteguy – might well have been recruited. He also found out from Taranto that there've been enquiries in that region.'

'Kiel would be a good place, too,' Venner said thoughtfully. 'You must be able to scrape ex-U-boat men off the bars in dozens there.'

'That's what Luciani thought. He even discovered one or two the police knew of who've disappeared.' Mostyn lit one of his Gauloises, his expression bored. 'How about you? Find anything in Portsmouth?'

'Only a new bit of apparatus I didn't know about.'

'Was that all?'

Venner nodded, avoiding Mostyn's eyes, aware that he was being watched with interest, as though Mostyn suspected his time hadn't *all* been taken up with questions.

'Was there nothing else?' he asked. 'Not even from Mrs Eltney?'

'No.' Venner wished to God he could shake off his feeling of guilt. He'd done nothing that dozens of smart young executives didn't do regularly, and it was easy to blame it on Susie's intransigence. But these days, if what you did couldn't satisfy your conscience, it was fashionable, he supposed, to feel guilt-stricken. People were. Even nations. It must have something to do with over-civilisation.

'Didn't the damn man ever say *anything* to her that would give us a lead?' Mostyn asked.

'She didn't seem to discuss much with him except bed.'

'Didn't he talk about his work?'

'Do you? In bed?'

Mostyn stared back at him but refrained from comment. 'Didn't he mention any ships?'

'Sure he did. The ones he'd been in. *Jellicoe*'s the only one that would interest us.'

Mostyn scowled. 'Hadn't the damn man *any* special skills or knowledge?' he asked.

'Only so far as Mrs Eltney was concerned.'

92

'Smart little dolly, that,' Mostyn said.

Venner nodded, his face expressionless, guessing that Mostyn was hoping to trap him into a reaction.

'Not surprised men fell for her.'

'Not my type,' Venner said.

Mostyn kept his eyes on Venner's face, and Venner could tell he was making guesses.

'What the hell were they after?' Mostyn asked.

'Only his skill as a submariner, it seems.'

Frowning, Mostyn looked at a list he'd made. 'How many people are there in a submarine's crew?' he asked.

'Conventional or nuclear?'

'I suppose it's got to be nuclear.'

'A hundred.'

'As many as that?'

'They're big ships.'

'How many in a conventional?'

'Sixty, sixty-five.'

Mostyn rubbed his nose. 'If they were thinking of *pinching* one – not using it, just pinching it for its secrets, say – how many would they need? These men you told me about who handle the essential jobs.'

'Conventional or nuclear?'

'Let's have both.'

'Are they diving?'

'Can't imagine 'em getting away without, can you?'

Venner began to count on his fingers. 'In a nuke, one officer and about eight men aft to run the propulsion plant and distillers, instead of the normal three for a conventional. Forward they're much the same – an officer holding a commanding officer's ticket, a seaman coxswain for the control-room helm, and an E.R.A. for the hydroplanes. A man for the foreplanes, a man on the blowing panel, a sonar operator, a seaman in the fore-ends, and a communications rating. Something like that.'

Mostyn looked at his list again. 'Wonder if they've got 'em yet?'

As it happened, soon afterwards proof appeared that they hadn't.

At Parsonsteignton, down in Devon, Police Constable Trevor Routledge was driving slowly in a small blue-and-white police van along the edge of Dartmoor. Somewhere up above him in the darkness the great prison of Princetown stood, hidden by the slopes and the grey damp mist of the moor. Not that P.C. Routledge was concerned with the prison. It didn't affect him much. Occasionally, there was a panic when someone escaped. Then everybody in the area was called on to help, and there was a week of intensive searches, which meant going without meals and sleep, but it usually calmed down as the escapers were found to have left the district or were picked up again. Normally, his work comprised the mundane duties of watching empty holiday homes, traffic enquiries, and the handling of such things as offences against the orders for foot-and-mouth disease or foul pest. It was a pretty dull life.

Routledge was deeply immersed in his thoughts when he noticed that the sea fret which an unexpected drop in temperature had brought up the Dart was growing a little thicker. He was obliged to slow down; then, just as abruptly, the mist cleared, and he was able to accelerate once more. Almost immediately, however, he ran into another bank of mist, white and milky in the dark, and thick enough to be dangerous.

His thoughts drifted to his fiancée, Mona. Mona's parents, who farmed three hundred acres near Buckfastleigh, were both bingo enthusiasts and liked to drive to town once or twice a week to meet other people. This left Mona alone – or with P.C. Routledge – in an empty house with the certain knowledge that they wouldn't be back before ten o'clock, and with a long gravel drive and an iron gate a hundred yards from the house that clattered when it was opened. Since Routledge was a policeman, Mona's parents trusted him implicitly. This gave Routledge and Mona a lot of leeway, and they always waved the older people off from the gateway warmly, and securely fastened it after them. They often joked about Routledge being

94

good at judo and felt few qualms of guilt, because they were planning to marry the following spring, anyway.

Routledge realised he was letting his thoughts run away with him, and he coughed loudly as he forced himself to concentrate. At almost the same moment, he hit another patch of fog and, as he decelerated, he noticed a blur of colour in the ditch at the other side of the road. Seeing at once that it was a car, he slammed on the brakes. Leaving the engine running and the headlights on, and with the flasher on the roof going, in case anybody else came down the misty lane in a hurry, he walked back to where he'd seen the car and switched on his torch. He was shocked by the amount of blood he saw. It seemed to be all over the road and on the grass verge. There was enough for a massacre, and he wondered what in Christ's name had been happening.

Then he saw the brown hump half in the ditch and a long branch-like leg sticking in the air. Someone had hit a cow in the mist. The animal was dead, its entrails spilled across the grass and still steaming in the chilly air, but it had obviously thrashed around a little first and had scattered its life-blood everywhere.

'Jesus,' he breathed.

The car, a bronze-yellow Morris 1300 GT, was on its side, its right wheels in the ditch. Its front was badly bent, the wheels askew, and there was brown hair and blood on the paintwork. At first Routledge thought there was nobody in it, but then he spotted the circle of broken glass and flashed his torch inside. There was a body in there, he could see now, and here, too, there was enough blood to make him feel ill.

The incident seemed big enough for someone with more authority than he had, and he reached for the switch of his radio.

By the time the Inspector and the ambulance and two more men arrived, P.C. Routledge had recovered sufficiently from his shock to have made a few investigations. He had found several more cows grazing placidly in the ditch further down the road and the hole in the hedge where they'd escaped. It was neglected, and there was only a loose strand of rusted barbed wire to hold anything back. Somebody was certainly going to be booked for letting them escape – especially with a man dead.

The corpse inside the car was that of a small man with reddish hair. It was hard to see his face, but he was so obviously dead that Routledge made no attempt to move him. Only after several minutes of staring at him did he notice that the hole in the window was at the passenger's side, though the dead man was huddled on the driver's side.

Looking closer, Routledge figured that, from his position, the dead man hadn't been in the driver's seat at the time of the accident; in which case, he reasoned, someone else must have been. He peered about him. There were no other bodies. But he saw that the rear door on the passengers' side had not been fastened properly, and he found several bloody hand prints on the yellow paint. The driver must have somehow managed to scramble from under the dead man, over the front seat, and out through the rear door. There had been no alternative, because the doors on the driver's side were jammed against the ground. And if he climbed out, Routledge had thought, where is he now? Why hasn't he raised the alarm?

After the Inspector had made a cursory examination, Routledge put forward his theory. Apparently, the Inspector hadn't noticed anything odd. He looked closer and nodded agreement.

'Brighter than you look, Routledge,' he said. 'I think you're right.' He straightened up and looked around. The police car further down the lane was flashing its blue light through the mist, while Routledge's little van was flashing in the opposite direction. 'Just one thing,' he said. 'Where's he got to?'

'Wandered off, sir? Shock, perhaps.'

'Perhaps. Who *is* this feller in the car, by the way? Got any identification?'

'No, sir. Not yet. When I noticed he wasn't the driver, I

started looking for whoever was with him. Thought he might be injured somewhere.'

The Inspector craned his head to one side. 'See if he's got a wallet,' he said.

Routledge glanced resentfully at him. Give me the dirty jobs, he thought bitterly. He opened the car door and leaned inside, moving his hand gingerly through what clothing he could reach. Eventually he found a wallet in the dead man's left hip pocket. He handed it to the Inspector, who opened it and took out a driving licence.

'Trevanion, Edward Gerald, 176 Pearson Street, Portsmouth. Bit out of his way here, wasn't he?'

Routledge knew what he was thinking. When dead men appeared in Devon from the other side of the country, they were either holiday-makers, businessmen, or up to no good. And, judging by his clothes, the dead man fitted into neither of the first two categories.

'Got the car number?'

'Yes, sir.'

'Call Ashburton and get 'em to check with Portsmouth. Ask about the car and find out who he is.'

By the time the radio in the Inspector's car squawked its reply, Routledge was involved in measuring the marks on the road. The affair had passed out of his hands.

'Trevanion, Edward Gerald,' the radio announced. 'Known as Trigger Trevanion. Portsmouth say he's known to them – well known.'

The Inspector's guess had been a good one.

'Merchant seaman,' the radio continued. 'Though he no longer goes to sea. Believed to be involved in rackets and drugs. Record of assault and fraud, to say nothing of a string of driving offences as long as your arm.'

'Not a good type,' the Inspector said.

There was a ghost of a chuckle over the radio. 'Definitely not a good type.'

'And the car?'

'Hired. From Ajax Car Hire, Plymouth.'

'Smart car for a hire firm, isn't it?'

'Belongs to the owner's son. Because they hadn't anything available, he allowed it to go out. Since he also has an Alfa, I don't suppose he missed it much.'

The Inspector replaced the microphone and went back to the smashed car. Routledge was standing near it with one of the other constables.

'Car's all right,' he said. 'Hired. But our friend has a record as long as your arm. Wonder who his pal was and why he buggered off.'

It was Venner who first connected the incident near Parson-steignton with their own investigations.

The newspaper report was garbled because the police weren't saying more than they had to, but it suggested a mystery, and it was only because the driver was missing that he read it again. It was then he noticed that the dead man was a merchant seaman who seemed to have stopped going to sea and that he came from Portsmouth. He took the newspaper to Mostyn.

'Seen this?' he asked.

Mostyn looked up from his own paper. 'Just reading it,' he said.

'Portsmouth, you'll notice.'

'I will indeed.'

'Think it's worth investigating?'

'Might well be. I think we'll drive down. Got any dates for tonight?'

Venner looked at him bitterly. 'You must be joking,' he said.

The journey was a dull one, with the car radio going the whole way so that Mostyn wouldn't miss a single item on the news. After he'd listened to Chief Olmuhi's threats for the umpteenth time, Venner was moved to protest.

'Do you have to listen *all* the time?' he asked.

Mostyn shrugged. 'Sort of monitoring service,' he said.

By the time they'd reached Ashburton, the affair of the

dead cow and the missing motorist had passed into the hands of the C.I.D. They were as puzzled as Routledge had been.

The Detective-Inspector from Plymouth wasn't sure how to regard the case, any more than he was sure how to regard Mostyn. He was a Devon man, with a way of speaking – as slow and stolid as a farmer's – that went with his solid Devon name, Yelland.

'We've done our homework,' he said in his heavy, trudging way. 'We've found out that this Trevanion chap's been hanging around Torquay for the last two weeks. He rented a house with another chap, who must have been the driver of the car. Just the two of them, with a woman to look after them.'

'*Cherchez la femme,*' Mostyn said quietly.

Yelland knew his quotes as well as Mostyn. 'We did,' he said. 'We found her, too.'

Mostyn blinked, but recovered quickly. 'Clever of you,' he said. 'How?'

'Not very difficult. The chap at the car-hire firm kept his eyes open. It's a habit they have because sometimes the cars don't come back. They were able to describe them all. We've got their descriptions for you, if you want them. Also, a taxi driver drove a man with blood on his clothes to the station, and it seems he took a train to London.'

'Any chance of picking him up?'

Yelland shrugged. 'We're trying. We've seen the woman. She was also from London. With a record. Of course she didn't know a damn thing. They never do. But Records knows her. She gave a false name, naturally, but we identified her as Bridget Rawlings, well known as the lady friend of a gentleman by the name of Puffer Stephenson.'

Mostyn looked interested. 'I take it you know this Puffer Stephenson.'

Yelland shook his head. '*We* don't,' he said. 'But London does. He operates mostly on their midden. The woman Rawlings claims she's never heard of him, but they searched the flat she rents at Camden Town, and there was a photograph of Puffer as large as life on the mantelpiece. He must be the missing driver.'

Mostyn rubbed his nose thoughtfully. 'Do we assume that our friend Puffer is a dangerous criminal?' he asked.

'Depends on what you mean by dangerous,' Yelland said. 'He's not violent. Our little friend Trevanion was. He'd try anything. Puffer was best known as a springer.'

Mostyn raised his eyebrows, and Yelland explained.

'Used for getting people out of prison,' he said. 'You've heard of the springing of the spy George Blake, and Biggs, the train robber.'

Mostyn nodded.

'These chaps have their methods, and it's the day of the specialist, you know. They get well paid, too. Puffer was expensive.'

'And he was springing someone from Dartmoor?'

'That's what I think.'

'Who?'

'There you have me.'

'Think you could fix it for us to check?' Mostyn asked.

Yelland looked puzzled. 'What are you hoping to find?'

Mostyn smiled. 'Naval captain or two,' he said, and Venner saw by Yelland's look that he recognised this misquotation, too. 'But nothing worth a damn.'

The interior of the old prison was depressing. At the end of a passage painted pale green that looked more like part of an office block and was a great deal pleasanter than many, they were shown into the Deputy Governor's office.

The official he summoned led them away and began to produce folders full of typed sheets and photographs, which he passed across his desk.

'How long will it take to go through this lot?' Mostyn asked.

'Depends how fast you can read. What are you looking for?'

'Don't know,' Mostyn admitted. 'Ex-sailors. Ex-Navy men.'

'Ex-submariners,' Venner said bluntly.

The clerk leaned forward. 'We've got cross-references on them all,' he said. 'We keep pretty close records on them for the prisoners' aid societies and the people who try to place them in jobs when they get out. Let's look. '

It was simpler than they'd expected. Within ten minutes, the clerk was laying a file on the table.

'Galbraith, Lewis Duncan,' he said. 'Ex-officer, R.N. He's down here as an engineer.'

Venner looked at Mostyn. 'I've got him,' he said. 'He was a wartime lower-deck promotion, and he was trapped for two days in that sinking in the Thames estuary about 1950. It sent him round the bend a bit. He must be sixtyish, if he's a day, though. Our friends don't seem blessed with a lot of luck, do they? With Snell and that bank raid, this makes the third time things have come unstuck.'

'Local police moved too fast again,' Mostyn said. 'They've probably pulled it off five or six times, though,' he reminded. 'Perhaps more, if you include one or two we don't know about. And *that's* not a bad average.' He turned the sheets in front of him slowly. 'Could this chap Galbraith take a submarine to sea?'

'He'd be short on experience.'

'*You* could.'

'I've not been away from the game as long as he has. And I heard he went for the bottle, so he must be a pretty poor specimen now.'

'Could he handle the clock-work in a nuke?'

'Not a chance. But he *was* a bit unusual. He was a real up-and-comer, with a lot of experience and a gong from the war for bringing home a motor launch when the deck officers had all been killed. After the accident in the Thames, he was transferred to surface ships and, because of some problem he had with claustrophobia, he got himself a navigation course in the hope of transferring to the deck branch. It was more of a therapeutical thing than anything else, I heard, but the Navy was sympathetic because of his record. He turned out to be pretty good, as it happened, but it didn't work, and he

101

was quietly asked to leave. Then he got involved with the police and he seems to have sunk so low now he's dropped right out of the bottom.'

'Could a submarine engineer handle a submarine?' Mostyn asked, rubbing his nose.

'I bet Galbraith could. Think I should have a word with him?'

Mostyn shook his head. 'Might get to our friends and put 'em on their guard. Has he had any visitors?' he asked the clerk.

'A man and a woman.' The clerk was watching them curiously. 'They gave their names as Mr and Mrs Arthur Trevose. There's an address here in Torquay. Shall we query it?'

Yelland peered at the file. 'Don't bother,' he said. 'It's the one where Bridget Rawlings was living with Puffer and Trigger Trevanion.'

Venner and Mostyn exchanged glances. 'Might be a good idea to go and see Prothero in Portsmouth again,' Mostyn observed thoughtfully. 'I'll drop you off on the way back.'

Venner scowled. 'I thought you might,' he said.

Chapter Eleven

Mostyn seemed rattled when Venner returned. It was as though he felt they had their fingers on the solution to the mystery.

'If it's important enough to pay an expert like Puffer Stephenson to get an old lag like Galbraith out of Princetown,' he said, 'then they must be still in business. What about Prothero? Did *he* have anything on Galbraith?'

Venner didn't answer at once. Mostyn had dropped him in Salisbury, en route back to London, to make his own way to Portsmouth. Three days later, having had to buy a new shirt to keep himself going, he had picked up a train home. His mind was still dwelling restlessly on Daphne Eltney.

'Prothero knew him, all right,' he said. 'He had some curious friends.'

Mostyn beat the desk top softly with the flat of his hand. 'If only our friend Nanjizel had lingered in hospital and murmured a few words before dying, like they do in films.' He looked up at Venner. 'See Mrs Eltney while you were in Portsmouth?'

'Yes.'

She'd been delighted to see him. She'd opened the door immediately, and no questions had been asked. There hadn't been much interrogation on his part either; there hadn't been time. But there'd been a new bottle of gin.

'She remember anything?'

'No. We arrived at exactly the same point we did last time.'

'Thought you might.'

Mostyn was looking keenly at Venner, and Venner suspected he could read his mind. Even his comment seemed pointed. He stared at his fingers for a while.

The question he threw out next was unexpected. 'What was *your* line in submarines?'

'All of 'em,' Venner said. 'You start as fourth hand in charge of torpedoes, and progress through the other departments. As you move up, you handle communications, navigation, and so on. Eventually you end up as first lieutenant, by which time you can handle anything and you get your time in deputising for the captain until you get your "perisher" – your commanding officer's qualifying course – and your own boat.'

Mostyn digested this information. When he spoke again, his thoughts had taken another turn. 'Is it possible,' he asked, 'for a bunch of ex-submariners – all strangers, all different ages, probably all different types, nationalities, languages, and generations – to man a submarine?'

'They'd need to work up,' Venner said. 'Only one man can see when they're submerged, and even *he* has to rely on the man at the helm for his course and the man on the gauges for his depth. Besides, won't some of 'em be out of practise? Like Galbraith?'

'More than likely. Where could they do this working up?'

'They'd need an electronic simulator. A nuke's a big ship.'

'I take it,' Mostyn said after a pause, 'that the Navy's got these simulators.'

Venner nodded. 'They do attack training in them. At *Dolphin.*'

'Could a non-Navy crew – *our* crew, if you like, this hypothetical all-language mongrel crew we keep envisaging that's been recruited to sabotage or steal our nuke – could they get to use R.N. facilities?'

Venner shook his head. 'Not a chance! Nor anybody else either, except under treaty arrangements. The Navy doesn't like other people using their ships.' He grinned. 'Come to that, they're not even very keen on other people using their sea.'

'Where could they do it then? Abroad?'

'Egypt? Somewhere like that?' Venner said, after some thought. '*They* might be prepared to allow it. But they've got

104

no nukes, and they wouldn't touch it with a barge pole if it looked illegal.'

Mostyn frowned. 'There used to be a feller some time ago who went around selling battleships,' he said. 'To South America, the Far East, those places. He was one of *our* customers, as a matter of fact. Generation before Latisse. Ex-U-boat man called Hans-Gottfried Tutschek. He was damn good, too, I believe. *He* was involved in one or two shady deals. He might have found something for them.'

Venner waited, and Mostyn gestured. 'Check him,' he said. 'Tough old bird. Got his face carved up in his last brush with the frigates when he was captured at the end of the war. He's in the files. You never know; he might even have an old submarine for hire.'

It didn't take long for Venner to turn up information on Hans-Gottfried Tutschek. Customs and Excise said that he had indeed been seen around again, and they suspected he might be in the country. He'd been involved in arms smuggling with fast launches from Tangier and Morocco, and had even been seen in Rhodesia and North Vietnam. A trip to Kiel turned up a policeman named Pinow, whom Mostyn knew, who produced a picture of a salty-looking old pirate with a black beard marked with curious white streaks, and a scar on the left side of his face that twisted his mouth and drew down the corner of his eye.

'One of Doenitz's aces,' Pinow said. 'He speaks excellent English, and probably has several false passports.'

Since this didn't get Venner very far, he took the opportunity to go again to Portsmouth – this time to enquire about Tutschek. The man hadn't been seen there, despite his easily recognisable appearance – as Venner had expected, and he knew he had taken the step really as an excuse to see Daphne Eltney.

'Hello,' she said gaily when she opened the door to him. 'You on business *again*?'

He no longer felt guilty, because he hadn't heard a word

from Susie, and when he had tried to ring her before he left – in the faint hope, he realised, that if she'd answered and welcomed him, he might not have gone – he had got no response. Nevertheless, he wasn't pleased with himself, and he wondered if fornication had seemed easier in the days when guilt had not been considered an essential part of the human make-up.

By the time he returned to London, his head ached with thinking, he'd smoked so many cigarettes his mouth felt charred, and the amount of tea he'd drunk would have given an ulcer to an elephant.

He wrote a note for Mostyn and left it on his desk. 'Enquiries re Tutschek interesting,' it said. 'Not much demand for hired submarines.' He knew Mostyn would simply screw it up and throw it away, but it gave him some pleasure to be sarcastic.

He had a gin at a pub on the way home and, because he was tired, he merely warmed up one of the packets of frozen food that he kept in reserve in the freezing compartment of the refrigerator. Good for television suppers, the print said. Good for lonely bachelors, too. There was beef, gravy, peas, mashed potatoes, and Yorkshire pudding. They all tasted exactly the same and exactly like plastic.

Depressed, sick of work and bored with his own company, he felt a desperate need for Susie. It was odd the way it worked. When she was chasing him, he didn't seem to need her. When she was out of reach, he seemed to need her more than anything else in the world. On an impulse, he called her number. She was out, so he poured himself another gin and rang her office. She occasionally went there in the evening, and he was prepared to take a taxi up to Fleet Street. She wasn't available, however.

'Why not?' he demanded. The voice at the other end of the line sounded like the same one he'd offended last time, and it was giving nothing away.

'She's out, working,' it said:

'Isn't she ever *in*, working?'

106

'People doing leg-work spend more time out than in.'

'When will she be in?'

'Couldn't tell you.'

'Could I meet her wherever she is?'

'Shouldn't think so.'

'Why not?'

'She's out at Pinewood or somewhere.'

'Doing what?'

'Trying to make some unknown TV producer sound like a fugitive from Hollywood. It's a follow-up on an item in this week's *Radio Times*.'

'When will she be free?'

The man at the other end sounded bored suddenly. 'Look, I'm sorry,' he said, 'but I have other things to do besides look after Susie's love affairs.'

'I'm not a Susie's love affair,' Venner snapped. 'And if you'd got one ounce—'

'Sorry, chum. Have to ring off.' The voice sounded malicious. 'You can find out all about it from the *Radio Times* if you're interested.'

As he hung up, Venner knew he'd once more been too quick to fly off the handle. Savagely, he snatched up the new *Radio Times*, which the daily help had laid for him beside the television, and hurriedly began to turn the sheets. He tore several in his haste and fury before he found the article. He hadn't been expecting anything in particular, but his heart thumped and he sat up quickly as he found himself confronted by a colour montage of Lancaster bombers and guns – *and submarines*!

Moving nearer to the light, he began to read. The article dealt with a new series of television plays, due to start the following week.

'These plays are concerned with drama,' the story said. 'Not drawing-room drama, but the behaviour of people under enormous stress, and they include a famous German play of the thirties concerning miners trapped below ground. Others have been written specially for television from novels or from

107

memoirs. Every effort has been made to get the details exact, particularly for those dramas concerning the last war. "So many people of viewing age served in the Forces," Producer Willie Moffatt said, "it would be ridiculous to offer them the mock-up of the inside of a Lancaster bomber that wasn't right. The switchboard would sink under the protests." The sets have been made with the assistance of experts, and photographs of them are hard to distinguish from photographs of the real thing. One of the dramas is about a Lancaster crew on the Dresden raid, another is on the defence of Tobruk, while a third is based on "Thunderer," the autobiography of Commander Hector McEwan, submarine ace and holder of three D.S.O.'s. . . .'

Venner knocked over his gin as he reached for the telephone.

Chapter Twelve

'I'd be happy to have Leonard Cheshire or even Bomber Harris look over this one.' The property master was a talkative little man named Haddon, who wore a yellow shirt and a red silk scarf. 'I was a flight engineer during the war, and it makes my blood run cold again just to sit inside it with the studio lights out.'

Venner hunched behind the controls of a Lancaster bomber, looking at the maze of quadrupled dials on the simulated instrument panel in front of him. One side of the cabin was missing so that the cameras could get in, and movement was impeded by the crowded presence of lights and microphones, whose cables hung down in festoons. The whole thing, he thought, would produce a cramped, claustrophobic feeling in the viewers, especially with a dark night sky simulated beyond.

'Every bit of the action takes place in here,' Haddon went on. 'The play's about the relationships among the crew, how they gradually get on each other's nerves as they get to the end of their tour. And we've got the lot. Everything they saw you'll see. Fires on the ground. Machines in flight. Old film, of course, with a blue filter. There'll be searchlights outside, and the pyrotechnics people have fixed in some neat little gadgets that'll punch holes where we want them. It'll end up with an explosion in the nose and a hell of a gale from a wind machine blowing through. It'll be so rugged the actors'll have to go into training.' He gestured. 'In fact, they've *been* training in the North Kensington Community Centre, with chairs and bits of old furniture, for some time. So they won't look like crashing amateurs. The people in this series are supposed to be experts, and they've got to look it. No long hair or with-it whiskers. We're putting it on tape at the week-end. You're welcome to come and watch.'

Venner shook his head. He'd listened to Haddon's chatter for a quarter of an hour now without complaint. 'It's not really the flying episode I'm interested in,' he said. 'I'm interested in *Thunderer*.'

'Oh!' Haddon seemed faintly disappointed. 'That's already been done.'

'Done?'

'Yes. The set's been dismantled. That episode was one of the first to go out. It's one of the best, and we like a good one to start the series and a good one to finish it.' Haddon laughed. 'That way, any rubbish that turns up in the middle gets forgotten. It's taken from that chapter in the book when they were after the *Scharnhorst*. Perhaps you haven't read the book, though.'

'I've not only read the book,' Venner said, 'I also did my training on *Thunderer*. I was even on the same base as McEwan for a while.'

Haddon turned towards him, his eyes bright. 'Are *you* submarines?'

'I was.'

'You'll be interested in that episode then. The Navy gave us every assistance, and we could afford to make it good because there was only one set. To get the feeling of tension. To suggest the characters' dependence on each other when they're pushed too hard. Perhaps you'd like to see the pictures. We've got some good stills.'

The photographs he produced were so like the real thing, Venner wouldn't have known them as anything else, except for a subtle something in the faces of the crew.

'This was one of our best sets,' Haddon said. 'It was put together with a submarine engineer standing right alongside us every bit of the time. Even the dials worked when the wheels and levers were moved. The periscopes gave us a bit of trouble, because they have to go up and down, and you can't fake that. We got around it by building the whole thing on a ten-

110

foot platform, so they could disappear into the floor. It looks good on the screen. Like to see some of it? There are some clips that'll be going out as trailers.'

Sitting in a small cinema with three rows of seats, Venner watched the screen light up and a few numbers flicker. Then he was seeing the control room of H.M.S. *Thunderer* as she waited outside Alten Fjord for her tangle with the defences round *Scharnhorst*. He barely noticed the dialogue, which, apart from one small error that he picked up instinctively and without really hearing it, sounded true enough to life. His eyes were roving over the maze of pipes, dials, levers, and moving gauges, to the helmsman, the foreplane and afterplane operators, the stoker petty officer at the blowing panel, the first lieutenant, and McEwan (they'd even picked an actor who looked like McEwan) standing with his hands on the clips of the attack periscope with the rating opposite, his hands clamped on McEwan's, reading out the courses as McEwan peered into the eyepiece.

He was lost in nostalgia when the sound disappeared and the screen went white again.

Haddon looked at him enthusiastically. 'Good enough for an ex-submariner?'

'I think it's splendid.'

'Moffatt will be pleased. I'll tell him.'

'As a matter of fact,' Venner said, and he coughed apologetically, 'when we get down to basics, I'm not very interested in what Mr Moffatt's done. I'm interested in what *you*'ve done and what happened to it?'

Haddon's jaw dropped. 'What *happened* to it?'

'Yes. Where is it now? What happens to these sets when they're dismantled?'

Haddon shrugged. 'Parts of them get used for other plays. Doors, windows, that sort of thing, can always be used again.'

'There can't be that many submarine epics on TV.'

'No. That's right. But *this* one was sold.'

Venner's heart thumped. 'Who to?'

111

'I can find out. Sometimes foreign companies buy them as they are, if they've got something planned. The price is set against costs. The powers-that-be like that, and so do we, because it gives us extra funds to play with. I heard Independent Television was planning a documentary on the loss of the *Thetis*.'

Venner hardly heard him for excitement as he went on. 'This chap came with the authority of some company that makes films for TV. He sounded foreign and he brought an ex-U-boat man with him. Chap with a scar and a beard with white streaks in it. He said he'd seen a note in a trade mag a few days before. It was taken away a fortnight ago. Just as it stood. I'll find out where it went.'

As he replaced the telephone, Haddon lifted startled eyes to Venner's face. 'They don't know anything about it,' he said.

Venner was aware of a sinking feeling in his stomach. 'I didn't think they would,' he admitted.

'They say that they've got no submarine documentaries planned at all.' Haddon looked baffled. 'I can make further enquiries, if you like.'

'I don't think it'll be necessary.'

'It must have gone somewhere.'

'I'm sure it did,' Venner said. 'But I doubt if you'll ever see it again on TV.'

Mostyn's eyes hardened as Venner made his report. 'Well, that's that,' he said. 'Latisse's got his simulator.'

'He's also got his captain,' Venner pointed out. 'Haddon identified Pinow's picture of Tutschek. Passport Control suspects he got into the country on a document belonging to an American named Wendell.'

Mostyn's fingers beat a soft tattoo on the desk. He was already late for his plane to Paris for another talk with Luciani, and he was irritated at the delay. 'Would this studio mock-up be enough for them to go through the motions of training a crew?' he asked.

'For a group of men who'd been through it all once already, yes. It works.'

'But *Thunderer* was old! Older than *Achates*.' Mostyn scowled, reached across his desk, and, snatching up a list, began to read from it. 'The United States, Britain, France, West Germany, Russia, Italy, Spain, China, Israel, India, Egypt, Pakistan, Australia, Sweden, Holland, Japan, Turkey, Argentina, Brazil, Canada, Chile, Greece, Indonesia, Portugal, Peru, Norway, Yugoslavia, Denmark.' He tossed the list down. 'Every country with a frontier on the sea. The major powers have nukes, and the rest couldn't use one if they were given one. So where do we look?' Venner could see he was growing angry at their continued failure. 'Let's bring it down to basics. If there's nothing different in the controls between nukes and conventionals, then the people we have to consider most important are the engineers. Right?'

'Right.'

'And there are more nuclear engineers in the States than anywhere else in the world. Right?'

'Right again.'

'Okay.' Mostyn stood up and reached for his bag. 'Go and see Capp,' he said. 'See what he has to say.'

113

Chapter Thirteen

Second Officer Margaret Pratt, of the Women's Royal Naval Service, gave a wide friendly smile to the man standing opposite her.

'Leading Seaman Arthur Rowan Lemon,' she said. She held out a bunch of documents and a travel warrant. 'Discharged. There you are, Lemon, all correct.'

The sailor at the other side of the desk smiled back. He was a sharp-featured man with the sort of smile Second Officer Pratt would normally have distrusted from a mile away. 'Thanks, ma'am,' he said. He took the papers and glanced at the railway warrant, then he fished out his wallet to stuff the documents away. 'Better make sure they're safe. Wouldn't want to be picked up absent without leave.'

As he pushed the papers out of sight, Second Officer Pratt noticed the wallet was full of money. 'Everything straightforward at the Pay Office?' she asked.

'Yes, ma'am.'

'You look as though you've got enough to carry you over till you get a job.'

'Yes, ma'am. Shan't have to hurry. Me and the missis are going to have a bit of a holiday before I look for one.'

Second Officer Pratt smiled again. She was a pretty girl, and her smile was a dazzling one. She stood up and held out her hand. 'Good luck, Lemon.'

Lemon took the proffered hand. 'Thanks, ma'am.'

'Better be off now. Or you'll miss the train.'

Lemon grinned and stepped back. 'Yes, ma'am.' He threw her a salute. 'Last time, ma'am.'

As he disappeared, Second Officer Pratt sat looking at the door.

The Chief Yeoman at the other side of the room grinned.

'He's a right lad, that Lemon,' he said. 'Slick as they come. But I suppose he did his job, and at least he kept the place cheerful.'

Second Officer Pratt nodded, then she frowned, thinking of the contents of Lemon's wallet. 'For a man who's been so often in trouble,' she said, 'he seems to have done rather well out of the Navy.'

On an impulse she picked up the telephone. 'Pay Office,' she said. As the line crackled, she picked up a pencil and pulled a note pad nearer to her hand. 'Second Officer Pratt here,' she said. 'Leading Seaman Arthur Rowan Lemon, discharged to-day. Just as a matter of interest, what did he draw in pay? Yes, I'll hang on.' She sat tapping the pencil until the voice at the other end of the line came again. 'How much?' She frowned. 'Is that *all*?'

'That's all.'

'Had he any savings?'

'You must be joking. Lemon was noted for pouring his pay down his throat.'

'Been fiddling the Pay Office, has he?' the Chief Yeoman asked, as she hung up.

'No.' Second Officer Pratt was frowning deeply now. 'But he had a jolly sight more in his wallet than *they* gave him.' She shrugged. 'Oh, well,' she said. 'He's gone now.'

She began to work again, but the thought of Leading Seaman Lemon continued to trouble her. It troubled her most of the morning, though she wasn't certain why. He could, of course, she told herself, have drawn out savings from the Post Office bank or some account the Navy was not aware of. He might have been running a few fiddles on the side. He might even have had a lady friend who kept him well heeled in return for his services. Second Officer Pratt had been in the Wrens long enough to know what went on.

Once again she shrugged Leading Seaman Lemon out of her

mind, but insidiously he slipped back. Somehow there seemed to be something fishy about all that money he'd had in his wallet. Leading seamen didn't normally leave the Navy with wallets bulging with ten-pound notes, especially leading seamen with indifferent records and a penchant for drink.

She sighed and picked up the telephone again. 'Dockyard Police,' she said.

Venner's face was grim when he left for his office. He'd just returned from Washington, and it had been a rough trip. Daisy had telephoned ahead, and Capp had laid everything on – the car at the airport, the hotel room, and the food – but it had been exhausting nevertheless. The time changes had torn pieces out of him, and the long hours of sitting in the same position had played hell with his injured back.

Drinks had appeared and information had been exchanged about submarines, ship movements, secret equipment, and men. But, while it seemed that there were many ex-Navy engineers with nuclear experience in the States, it had been impossible to check on all those who'd been discharged or had retired. A few had put their knowledge into the hands of government installations or the business world, a few had found work in power stations, a few had simply retired. Three had been killed or had died, and two of them had simply disappeared. They could easily have been recruited by the men who'd murdered Nanjizel, or, as Capp had pointed out, they could simply be living quietly on a pension in Spain or Mexico.

'Anyway,' Capp had said, looking puzzled, 'what's in it for 'em? Who's behind it? Where's the payola coming from and where's it headed? Nobody would steal a submarine, for God's sake! They're too big, and it would start a goddam war.'

Venner had left Heathrow at three in the morning and hadn't slept a wink on the flight west. Yet when the plane had taken off for London, he was so tired he found it impossible to sleep. Back at Heathrow, his eyes gritty, and hardly able to straighten his back, he felt he'd been without sleep for days.

Daisy was out when he arrived at the office. Without her restraining presence, the filing clerk looked up and made a face at the junior typist. 'Sweetheart's in a bad temper again,' she said. 'Expect his beloved's chucked him.'

'How do you know?'

'That's his sex-frustration face. Different face altogether for office problems.'

Her guess was a good one. As soon as he'd reached his flat, jaded and in need of comfort, Venner had tried again to reach Susie. But once again he had had no luck, and it had seemed obvious at last that she had no wish to be called by him. His resulting low spirits had made it difficult for him to sleep despite his extreme weariness. As he now threw his briefcase down on his desk, he felt as though he hadn't a friend in the world.

The telephone rang as his door slammed, and the filing clerk answered it. 'Just a moment,' she said. 'He's just come in.'

As she put the call through to Venner's office, the junior typist smiled. 'Girl friend?' she asked.

'Not this time. Police.'

Venner's face had brightened a little as he picked up the telephone.

'We've found the vans that carried your film set away,' the voice at the other end of the line said.

'You did?'

'Yes. Empty. They'd been abandoned near Guildford. We found 'em in an old warehouse. They were seen to drive in, and two more drove out.'

'Have you found the second lot?'

'Yes. You can't hide a furniture van all that easily. One was found in Bristol and one in Swinton.'

'What the hell were they up to?' Venner asked.

'Putting us off their trail, I suspect. They'd been dumped.'

'Were they heading for Plymouth or somewhere?' Venner's mind immediately leapt to Devonport and nuclear submarines.

'Nobody saw 'em there.' The policeman's voice was flat and

117

discouraging. 'They'd been stolen, of course. In North Wales.'

'Good God!' It was planned like a military operation. 'Go on. Anything else?'

'We're concentrating our search in Hampshire. Some bright young copper there noticed two plain vans pass through Great Mew on the A325 at midnight on Sunday, the third, and had the sense to check. They told him they were carrying theatrical flats, and their manifests were in order. He thinks now – now that he knows what's missing – that it was your film set. They were heading south at that point, on the Portsmouth road.'

'Portsmouth!'

'We think the vans were unloaded somewhere in the area where they were seen and were taken away later to be dumped.' There was a silence for a moment then the voice came again, tinged with bewilderment. 'Why in God's name would anyone want to pinch a film set?'

Venner put the telephone down and glared at it, his face a picture of frustration. Almost immediately it rang again.

'Office of Flag Officer, Submarines, Portsmouth,' the filing clerk said.

It was Lieutenant-Commander Cathcart, and Venner's face tightened as he listened.

'*Another one?*' he said.

'Another one,' Cathcart agreed. 'I haven't the foggiest what you're up to, but when you were down here some of it seemed to concern naval deserters. It was just a guess.'

'It was a good guess. There can't be any mistake, I suppose?'

'No, there can't. He was discharged at Devonport last Wednesday and given a railway warrant to his home at Winchester.'

'What was he?' Venner demanded.

'Leading telegraphist. When he didn't turn up, his wife got in touch with his commanding officer. The report came here, as they always do, and I remembered what you'd told us about keeping an eye on our doubtful characters. He's not strictly one of ours, of course, except insofar as we're submarine headquarters, but I thought you might be interested.'

'By God I am! I don't suppose you've been in touch with the wife, have you?'

As Venner had already guessed, Cathcart was an intelligent young man. 'Yes,' he said. 'I have. Regulating branch went to see her, naturally. And since my home's near Winchester, I thought I'd go along for the ride. She couldn't tell us a damn thing.'

'Had he been approached at all?' Venner asked. 'Like Nanjizel.'

'I remembered that, too.' Cathcart sounded smug. 'I asked her. She said not to her knowledge. Of course, if she lives in Winchester and he's stationed in Devonport, she wouldn't be *likely* to know, would she?'

'Right.'

'There's just one other thing.'

'I'm all ears.'

'I heard an interesting story in the mess last night. We have a chap here who's resigning his commission. Name of Mere. Lieutenant Mere. First Officer of *Alliance*. A conventional. He'd been approached with the offer of a job, and, since it's not normal for firms to approach people with offers of jobs before they're out of uniform, it set me wondering. I got him on one side.'

'That was quick thinking. Who made the offer?'

'He doesn't know. No names were given. It was done by telephone to the mess. Nothing came of it because he doesn't need a job. Daddy wants him to go into the family business.' Cathcart sounded faintly contemptuous, as though no one could possibly prefer business to the Navy. 'He thanked them and told them no.'

Venner drew a deep breath. 'What was the job?'

'He couldn't tell. They didn't get beyond the preliminaries, of course, but he said they seemed to be interested chiefly in his skill as a navigator. He's still trying to work it out. Like to talk to him?'

'Yes, I would.'

'I'll fix it. Now—' Cathcart became impressively business-like '—coming back to Leading Seaman Lemon: there's someone at Devonport who knows him. A Second Officer Pratt. She had one or two things to say you might be interested in. We could get her over here and you could see 'em both at the same time.'

Venner thought of Daphne Eltney and drew a deep breath. 'Do that,' he said.

Mostyn was nose-down in a file when Venner appeared two days later.

'They're still recruiting,' Venner said at once, and went on to describe Second Officer Pratt's suspicions. 'She was interested enough to enquire a little further,' he ended, 'and it seems the Dockyard Police saw Lemon leave the docks and climb into a large black car which was waiting nearby. There was no doubt. They knew Lemon well.'

'Why?' Mostyn said. 'As if I didn't know.'

'He's a drinker. He's done time in the glasshouse. His C.O. gives him good ratings for his work but not for his character. He was transferred out of nukes to conventionals and finally to a shore job. He was a telegraphist.'

There was a pause while Mostyn thought over the implications.

'That wasn't the only one,' Venner continued. 'There was an officer. An expert in navigation. Nothing came of it because he wasn't interested, but it sounded like our friends again.'

'Two radio operators,' Mostyn mused. 'Two seamen, two engineers – with Arteguy, Luciani's Frenchman. All these, apart from those we know nothing about who might have been recruited abroad.' He put his fingers together in a steeple and stared at the ceiling. 'Be nice if we could throw 'em someone we could rely on to report back to us. A navigation expert, for instance. They're obviously still looking for one, and they're probably growing anxious by now.'

Venner said nothing, and he went on slowly. 'It's my bet that they weren't after Galbraith for his ability as an engineer.

120

They were after him because he was a navigator. When that didn't come off, they tried Mere.'

'There must be dozens of navigation experts available.'

'Not who know submarines. You told me that in addition to the captain they'd need someone in the control room to handle the trim and other things. Galbraith could. Mere could.'

The idea seemed intriguing. 'Okay,' Venner said. 'Where do we find one?'

'There's one I know.'

'Who?'

'You.'

Venner stared at Mostyn indignantly. 'You have to be joking,' he said.

Mostyn's eyes were cool and he wasn't smiling. 'Not so's you'd notice,' he said.

Despite himself, Venner was interested. He'd lived too long with the affair by this time not to be. 'How do I get in touch with them?' he asked. 'We don't even know where they operate from.'

'Don't think we need to,' Mostyn said. 'They'd get in touch with you.'

'Why the hell should they?'

'Almost certain to if you were kicked out.'

'*Kicked out?*' Venner's jaw dropped.

'Especially with trumpets.'

'What the hell have you got in mind?' Venner demanded.

'Suppose' – Mostyn spoke slowly – 'suppose James Dennison Venner suddenly appeared in a London pub rather the worse for drink. Suppose the police had to take him in for creating a disturbance. Suppose he was charged with being drunk and disorderly, and it came out in court he'd just been slung out of his job for fiddling—'

'Fiddling what?'

'Funds, documents. With the typists, if you prefer. What does it matter? That's a detail.'

'Suppose nobody noticed?' Venner said coldly.

Mostyn was unperturbed. 'They would,' he said. He paused. 'Perhaps it had better be typists,' he went on. 'Or some other deviation like sodomy, rape, or murder.'

'Thanks,' Venner said.

Mostyn smiled. 'You're welcome,' he said. 'That ought to stir up enough fuss for someone to notice.'

'And then?'

'James Dennison Venner's experience as a submarine officer would come out in court, and he would, of course, have to give an address to the police. A seedy hotel in London, with a bar on the corner. We know a few. Suppose he hung around there for a while and waited, having the odd noggin—'

'On expenses, I hope.'

'We could run to one or two. But not many. You can hardly charge expenses for something you enjoy.' Mostyn spread his hands. 'That ought to be enough to start things moving, don't you think?'

Venner looked at him bitterly. 'You can bet your life there'd be plenty of slimy bastards around this place who'd run straight to the files to see if there were any previous convictions.'

'We might even find out who.'

'I can tell you one now.'

'Who?'

'Aubrey. He'd be the first down there. He's got a thing about me. He thinks I'm watching him, I suspect. Sometimes I wish I were. I'd like to catch the bastard at *something*.'

Mostyn smiled. 'Perhaps I'd better get your file up here,' he said. 'After all, if someone's going to look, he'd better find something.'

Venner's face turned red. 'Such as what, for God's sake?'

'Things to make people say "I told you so." '

'And if I get run over the next day, there they remain – in my file.'

'Wouldn't matter then, would it?'

'I have a few people who have a little regard for me still.'

'Okay.' Mostyn waved a languid hand. 'I'll arrange to take

them out if you're killed. I'll be the only one who'll know how they got there.'

'Then, for Christ's sake, don't *you* get run over.'

Mostyn smiled again. 'How does it appeal?'

'I think it stinks.'

'Good,' Mostyn said. 'We'll start on it at once.'

Part II

Chapter One

The Olde Light Horseman was not a pub on a tourist track.
Those tourists who went from London to Oxford and
Stratford, then back again to do a final round of the high
spots before heading for Paris or Düsseldorf or New York,
confined their activities in the capital city to Trafalgar Square,
Piccadilly, and the Monument. The Olde Light Horseman was
tucked away in a back street, not far from the City, yet certainly not of it. It was a dark, old-fashioned place – not the
sort of dark, old-fashioned place that attracted City businessmen for a quiet beer and sandwich, nor even the sort of dark,
old-fashioned place that appealed to the young in their search
for Victoriana. It was just dark and old-fashioned.

Its clientele during the day came from among the clerks
and typists in nearby offices, none of them with much money
to spend, and therefore not warranting any major face-lighting
of the premises, and its clientele at night consisted almost
entirely of caretakers and cleaners, who merited even less a
smart up-to-date background for their drinking.

It was furnished with scarred plastic-topped tables and thick-
legged wooden stools, and round the walls ran red plastic-
upholstered benches marked by thousands of cigarette burns.
The barman was indifferent, and sloppy puddles on the counter
were left unwiped and there was a strong smell of stale beer.
The drabness came from the absence of sunlight, caused by
the office block opposite, which effectively shut out the
day.

Venner's stomach turned over at the sight of it. But now he
stood at the counter, imagining Aubrey, his smooth face
flushed with triumph, relating his story round the departments

('That fellow Venner. Not a bit surprised—'), could just imagine him, in the midst of his preparation of evasive answers for the Home Secretary, nipping down to the file room for a quick chat with Wither, the Keeper, and a brief exchange of scandal.

There had been a blazing row in Mostyn's office – well rehearsed the night before in Venner's flat – in which Daisy and the telephone girl and one of the typists had been involved, and Venner had marched out, flushed and hang-dog, leaving behind him a cold-eyed and silent Mostyn, and Daisy in tears at his departure.

As far as he could see, now that he thought clearly about it, he had risked everything, including his career, for one of Mostyn's bright ideas. If anything happened to Mostyn now – even if he were superseded, he realised with a shock – there was an even chance that he'd never be accepted back. It required only a change at the top, at ministerial level, for God's sake – and Ministers did get reshuffled, right up at the top, so far up, in fact, as to be almost out of sight – and the usual crumbling of the pyramid would begin. Appointees would disappear and *their* appointees would not long remain. If anything like that happened to Mostyn – and it could, he thought with horror – it would mean the end of James Dennison Venner.

He had tried to get hold of Susie Gore the day after his sacking. He wasn't sure why, because there wasn't much he could have told her. But she'd been in the south of France.

'Doing what, for God's sake?' Venner had demanded.

'Working,' the same cold voice as before had answered. 'We do, sometimes.'

'When will she be back?'

'God knows. If she's got any sense, never. *I* wouldn't if I had the sort of money she's got.'

Somehow, Venner felt, he needed her around more than ever now, because it had been surprising how little reaction there'd been in the office. Apart from Daisy, nobody appeared to have noticed his departure. It was as though the place had closed

128

over the spot he'd occupied, like water in a pond closing over a flung stone, with nothing more than a disappearing ripple. And there had not been one single offer of help.

As he ordered another whisky, the girl behind the counter studied him closely.

'You've had just about enough, I'd have thought,' she said.

'Let me be the judge of that.' Deliberately, at a gulp, he emptied the glass she had filled and pushed it back across the counter. 'See what I mean,' he said. 'Fill it up.'

He saw her glance at the barman, who caught the look, straightened up, and approached. He leaned solidly on the counter opposite Venner. 'Now, sir—' he began.

Venner pushed the glass at him. 'Fill it up,' he said.

The barman didn't move. 'Don't you think you ought to go home and sleep it off, chum?'

'No, I don't. And don't call me "chum".'

As he'd expected, the barman reacted strongly. 'Listen, brother,' he said, 'this is my livelihood, and I've every right to advise you to go home if I think you should.'

'I can do without your bloody advice,' Venner said.

'Maybe you can,' the barman agreed. 'But I still don't have to serve you.'

Venner moved quickly. He grabbed the barman's tie and jerked him across the counter. A glass whirled away and shattered on the floor. He heard a woman scream. The barman's fist flew wildly, and Venner shoved as hard as he could, so that the barman staggered back. Bottles and glasses went flying, and the barman was round the counter in a flash.

Venner could see the girl reaching for the telephone, so he pawed at the barman, deliberately missed him and just as deliberately went blundering past into a table. The table went over with a crash and the screaming of girls, and the barman lunged at him again. Reaching for a rolling beer bottle, Venner flung it and, as he had intended, it went through the window.

Almost immediately, it seemed, the door was full of blue serge as a policeman appeared. For God's sake, Venner thought, when you wanted them, they were nowhere to be seen, and when you didn't they came at once. He had hoped to make much more fuss than this.

He swept a soda-water syphon from the counter and saw people ducking and leaping for safety as the policeman jumped at him. Venner knew how to handle himself, and the policeman, who was only a youngster, reeled back, spitting out a tooth. But he was game enough, and, coming again at Venner, he was able to grab his hand and wrench it behind his back. Venner kicked out, and the policeman swore but got one foot round Venner's leg. A chair back broke off as they crashed to the floor. A man stamped quite deliberately on Venner's hand as the policeman heaved at his other arm, and a woman with glasses and a tight, loveless mouth threw her gin in his face. The spirit burned his eyes and made him gasp.

'Right, you bastard,' the policeman panted. He put a knee in the middle of Venner's back and dragged his hand up until Venner thought his shoulder was dislocated. 'Get a patrol car round here,' he said to the barman, who was kicking broken glass aside. 'But fast.'

The magistrate was a small, fat man with rimless spectacles and a mean mouth, and Venner thought he'd probably be sent to prison for a week. But the magistrate was just mean, and lacked courage. After enjoying himself with threats and a lecture, he merely fined Venner and sent him away.

'And don't come back,' the Sergeant said as he handed him his receipt. 'Because next time it'll be twice as nasty.'

Returning to the dingy hotel in Bayswater he'd chosen Venner lay back on the bed and stared at the drab ceiling. There was a crack in it, and the white paint was flaking off. Christ, he thought, what have I let myself in for?

He stayed there for the rest of the afternoon. As soon as the pubs were open again, he rose, placed a half-full bottle of whisky prominently alongside the bed, and went out to buy a newspaper. The story was on the front page: EX-SUBMARINER BLAMES SACKING FOR DRUNKENNESS – all that Mostyn could have wished. He took it into the nearest bar and stood at the counter reading it.

It was all there. Mostyn had obviously done his homework well. The court had been full of unexciting cases, and the reporters had not been much interested until Venner had said his piece in his defence. Then they'd sat up at once. Clearly, one of them had dug a little deeper, and there was an evasive quote from Authority which hinted that Venner's departure had been due to rather more than mere inefficiency.

He seemed not only to have dug his own grave, but also to have jumped into it and pulled the earth in on top of him. It was a wonderful scheme, but, he thought bitterly, it wasn't Mostyn who was likely to be affected if anything went wrong.

To keep the picture going, he asked for the telephone and rang up the one man he knew would refuse him help. Running true to form, the man hedged and said he was just on the point of going to the Continent.

'It's just that I'm a bit short of cash,' Venner explained. 'Twenty quid would do.'

There was a shrill artificial laugh. 'I wish I'd *got* twenty quid. I'm as hard up as you are.'

'Well, I'll come round, on the off-chance,' Venner said maliciously, and put the telephone down. There'd be quite a stirring-up, he knew, with his victim calling all their mutual acquaintances to warn them before disappearing down some private rat-hole of his own until he felt he was safe. Venner hoped he'd caused chaos and confusion, and it gave him a measure of satisfaction because he hated and was embarrassed by the image of himself he was having to present.

He had reached the stage of screaming boredom and was aching with self-sympathy when the landlady called him to the telephone. He was drinking his coffee after a late breakfast in the basement dining room when she appeared alongside him.

'I think it's you they want,' she said. 'James Venner.' It had apparently just dawned on her that he was the man who had featured so prominently in the newspapers, and she was

131

probably wondering if he were likely to run amok again. 'It's upstairs. In the hall.'

The hood over the telephone seemed to have caught all the smells that came up from the kitchen below, and was full of boiled cabbage and frying.

'James Venner?' a crisp, alert voice asked.

'Yes.' He made his voice as blunt and rude as possible.

'This is a friend.'

'Who?'

'Never mind who. Just let's say that we're interested in people like you. We saw the story in the paper.'

'I'm not interested in prisoners' aid societies.'

'Perhaps not. But you might be interested in a job.'

'Yes.' Venner was alert at once. 'I might. But it depends on the job. I'm not trained to do much.'

'I think you're trained to do what we want you to do.'

'What's that? Personnel officer at some pissy-arsed little factory. Because I'm not interested, if it is.'

The voice came back smoothly. 'I'd have thought that a man in your position—'

'What position's that?'

'You could find things difficult.'

'You bet your life I could. Nobody wants someone like me.'

'We might.'

Venner's heart was thumping now. 'Okay,' he said. 'Spit it out. What is it?'

'Not on the telephone. We don't do business on the telephone. Suppose we meet somewhere.'

'You name it.'

'Do you know the Old Theatre Club off Villiers Lane, Soho?'

'I can find it.'

'Be there this evening. Seven o'clock. Just ask for a drink. They won't ask questions.'

As Venner went out into the street, he noticed a newspaper seller on the corner whose face seemed familiar, and it dawned

132

on him that he was one of Mostyn's men watching the hotel. Walking slowly in the direction of Notting Hill, he went into the Underground and took a train to Victoria. Emerging there, he found a row of telephones. They were all occupied, by youngsters apparently arranging dates for the evening, and he had to wait a quarter of an hour before he could find a free one. He rang Mostyn's office.

Daisy answered. Pinching his nose so that she wouldn't know who it was, he asked for Mostyn.

Mostyn came on the line after a long wait, and Venner snapped at him. 'You might take the bloody trouble to be on the ball.'

'Ah,' Mostyn said cheerfully, 'our old friend!'

'Where've you been?'

'Conference. Top level. Aubrey's been complaining about my tightening up on the files. Suspect he's been trying to have a look at yours. He certainly doesn't like you, does he?'

'If that bastard gets anything on me, I'll never forgive you.'

'Don't worry. We look after our own. And he's too tied up with keeping his Minister supplied with the right answers to be bothered about you. What's happened?'

'Bingo,' Venner said. 'We've had a bite.'

'Interestin'.'

'Not so interesting as you'd think,' Venner retorted bitterly. 'I don't like this damn job.'

'Had second thoughts about it?'

'Yes.'

'Thought you might.'

'Quite apart from the bloody place where I'm having to live, I don't like the set-up at all. What guarantee do I have that that police charge'll be struck off?'

'I'll attend to it when the time comes. What happened?'

'Mysterious callers offering me a job.'

'What sort of job?'

'I'll tell you tonight. I have to meet them. In the Old Theatre Club, off Villiers Lane, Soho.'

'Might be a good idea if we had someone there to get a

look at 'em. If it's our friends the recruiting sergeants, the police might be interested in where they go. I'll fix it.'

'There's a lot you've got to fix,' Venner said darkly. 'I'll call tonight after I've heard.'

The assessment of the Old Theatre Club as a place where questions wouldn't be asked appeared to be correct. No one asked Venner about his membership, but the place was dark enough to make it almost impossible to recognise anyone anyway.

He went straight to the bar and ordered a whisky. He had had two others before he left the Bayswater hotel, so that, though he was neatly dressed and shaved, his breath stank of booze.

He carefully chose a seat under the only light and sat back to wait, lighting one cigarette after another, as though he were nervous. Almost immediately, a man in a purple suit and chiffon scarf tried to pick him up. Judging by his lisp, he wasn't the man he was waiting for, and Venner pushed him away. After a while he became aware of someone standing behind him. He heard drinks ordered and a conversation about sailing. Then, unexpectedly, one of the voices addressed him.

'James Venner?'

He was about to turn round, when a hand dropped on his shoulder. 'No. Stay just as you are.'

Venner stiffened. The conversation about sailing continued then the voice said, 'Thought you'd turn up. They usually do.'

'They?'

'You're not the only one.'

'Oh!' Venner fished a little. 'There are others, are there? How many?'

'Seven or eight.'

'What's the job?'

'It isn't due to start yet, but if you accept, you're on salary immediately.'

Venner waited for the voice to continue, but, instead, he heard only snatches of conversation about boats. He could see men behind him and noted that there were three of them in the group, all dressed in sober business suits, their faces in shadow. He tried again.

'Must be an important job,' he said.

The conversation stopped. 'It depends on how desperate you are for work,' the voice behind him said.

'I'm desperate, all right. What is it?'

'Don't rush. The best-paid jobs aren't always respectable.'

'I thought you'd already guessed,' Venner said. 'I'm *not* respectable.'

There was a low laugh. 'So we gathered. It's been going on for some time, hasn't it?'

Venner caught his breath. So someone *was* examining the files. There was nothing in his past, otherwise, to give any hint that what Mostyn had arranged had happened before. As his mind worked, the conversation behind him went on, arid, dull, the small talk of young businessmen trying to show off. He waited, and after a while there was a pause.

'Well?' the voice said.

'Okay.' Venner nodded without turning. 'I don't pick and choose. I tried the whole of last week, but nobody's playing, and I'm buggered if I'm going to sign on at an employment exchange.'

'Might come to that,' the man behind him said.

'Not on your life. What have you got to offer?'

'Interesting work.'

'Permanent?'

'Alas. But you'll be paid well.'

'I'm not robbing any banks.'

'We're not paying you for a strong right arm. We're paying you for special skills that you possess.'

'The only special skill I've got is what I acquired in the Navy. Navigation.'

'That's what we're thinking of.'

As a group of young men in brightly coloured suits pushed up to the bar, the conversation behind him started again, noisy and boastful. Venner's eyes flickered about, trying to find a mirror that would reflect, but the bottles beyond the counter broke up the picture too much, and, in the shadows, he was unable to see any recognisable faces. The young men in bright suits moved away with their drinks, and the conversation stopped again.

'What do you want me to do?' Venner asked. 'Run guns to Ireland?'

'Not really. You have other skills beyond navigation.'

'Only submarines. You can't be after that?'

'Suppose we were?'

Venner was thinking fast. 'Only one way that kind of skill can be used,' he said. 'That's in submarines.'

'So?' The voice behind him was still cool.

Again the conversation was interrupted for several seconds with talk of boats. Venner shoved his spoke in through a chink in the chatter, as though he was growing impatient. 'What are you up to?' he demanded.

The voice behind him came back quietly. 'Never mind what we're up to. We just have to know whether James Venner's sufficiently on the rocks to accept a job.'

'James Venner's very much sufficiently on the rocks to accept a job. *Any* job.'

'Even a job he might once have balked at?'

Venner drew a deep breath. 'For Christ's sake,' he said in a low voice. 'I don't know who you are or what you want, but if the bloody job's dishonest, then for Christ's sake say so, and let's get it over with. I'm in no position to argue.'

There was a long silence, and he sensed that the three men behind him were eyeing each other, trying to make up their minds.

'The job might well be called dishonest,' the voice said at last.

'Right! We know now where we are, don't we? What does it entail?'

'Exactly what we've told you. Navigation and control.'

'Of a submarine?' Venner asked. 'Because if it is, you have to be pinching the bastard. There are no submarines outside the Royal Navy or any other established navies. Where are you getting it?'

'We'll come to that when the time's right. The pay's one thousand pounds. For roughly one week's work.'

'What week?'

'It's not that simple. You'll have to leave London and lie low for a while, until we're ready. You'll be given money, which you'll be expected to make last until you're called on. There'll be a thousand pounds clear at the end of it.'

Venner nodded. 'I can't afford to argue,' he said. 'What do I do?'

'For the moment, nothing.' There was a pause, and he heard the rustle of banknotes. 'Don't turn round,' the voice said. 'There are five tenners going into your pocket.' He felt a tug at his jacket. 'That'll keep you going until we tell you what to do. For the time being, just go back to your hotel, stay sober and keep your mouth shut. Good night.'

Venner turned round as the figures moved away, but all he could see were three dark-suited men leaving by the door. As they disappeared, another man, who'd been sitting in a corner, finished his drink and left. Mostyn's tail, Venner decided. It seemed to be time to pass on the good news.

Guessing he'd be followed, he left the club cautiously. There was no one in sight, but that didn't mean no one was watching. He walked to the end of Villiers Lane and caught a bus. No one got on with him. He dropped off it again near Marble Arch and walked across Hyde Park. Still guessing he might be followed, he stopped and lit a cigarette. Over his shoulder he saw a man fifty yards behind with a girl, and he wondered if they were watching him. Inevitably, the men from the club would not be doing the tailing. If they were as clever as they sounded, they'd be giving Mostyn's shadow the time of his life as he tried to keep up with them.

At the other side of the park, he crossed Knightsbridge, dived into the maze of smaller streets round Montpelier Square, and headed into Chelsea. Picking up a taxi, he took it

137

along the King's Road and left it near Carlyle Square, then, finding a public house, he went in and ordered a drink. Since nobody followed him in, he assumed he'd managed to shake off any pursuers.

He stayed there for half an hour, then left hurriedly by the back door and headed for West Kensington Underground. He rang Mostyn's home number from a call box. As the receiver was lifted off, he heard music and a girl's voice in the background which he could have sworn was Daisy's.

'Mostyn,' a bland voice said in his ear as the music died and the girl's voice stopped.

'Who the hell have you got there?' Venner asked.

'A friend. What happened?'

'We're in business,' Venner said. 'And I'd like to cut your throat, I think.'

'Never mind the histrionics. What's on?'

'It's submarines, all right, and I think the balloon, whatever it is, is due to go up soon, because they seemed in a hurry. They didn't beat about the bush, as they did with Nanjizel and Evans and Snell, but came straight out with it. From what they said, they've already recruited seven or eight others.'

'What you said they'd need for a skeleton crew. Which ship is it?'

'I don't know yet. They don't appear to have one now, but they're getting one. It's a week's job some time in the near future.'

'A week, eh?' Mostyn was silent for a moment. 'Just long enough to take it out of the country and fly back. Anything else? Did they say when or where? Any indication?'

'None. What about the recruiting sergeants? Were they followed?'

'Yes. But we lost 'em. Did you get a look at them?'

'I'd have needed a miner's lamp on my forehead to recognise my own mother in that place.'

'Anything else?'

'They're offering a thousand quid, plus living expenses until they want me.'

138

'Well paid.' Mostyn's comment came flatly.

'It'll help towards the fine I had to pay. It was a stiff one.'

'Shouldn't think you'll be able to keep it, of course,' Mostyn said calmly. 'Be needed as evidence.'

'Like the fine.'

'You'll get that back.'

'In about ten years' time, when the wheels of the Civil Service have ground through the evidence.'

'That all?' Mostyn asked coldly.

'Not quite. Somebody's seen the files. They knew all about me.'

There was a pause. Just as Venner was about to put the instrument down, Mostyn said, 'Just one thing.'

'What's that?'

'That little dolly bird of yours rang me last night.'

'Did she ask where I was?'

'Yes.'

'What did you tell her?'

'That I hadn't the faintest idea,' Mostyn said smugly.

Chapter Two

Despite Mostyn, Susie Gore found Venner more quickly than he'd expected.

Venner was still angry about the casual way Mostyn had brushed off her enquiry, because, of all the people he'd ever known, she seemed to be the only one who was sufficiently concerned to wonder what had happened to him.

His case had aroused immediate interest in Whitehall and, with thoughts of another Kim Philby, the expected question had appeared on the list in the House. They were a bit late, Venner thought. Things had already started moving. The enemy – whoever they were – had recruited him with half the fuss they'd expected.

Two more days went past. No one tried to contact him, and he suspected they were checking up on him. No one wrote or telephoned. Once, he passed Aubrey in the Strand, and Aubrey's eyes narrowed with dislike. Venner turned deliberately, as though to cross the road to speak to him, but Aubrey seemed to be stricken blind and hurried away towards Covent Garden. Venner smiled maliciously, suspecting he'd been going to lunch at the intellectual club he frequented and hoping he'd made him late.

He was growing tired of the dreary hotel, tired of standing at bars where he wouldn't expect to meet anyone he knew, tired of reading the newspapers and lying on his bed staring at the crack in the ceiling. He was itching to ring Susie to let her know he was alive. Then he decided it was too late for that. It might have been possible before he'd got himself involved in Mostyn's half-baked plot, but now he was supposed to be an outcast and not the sort of man who sought the company of girls like Susie Gore.

Reluctantly, he put the idea out of his mind, hoping he'd be able to put things right later, when everything had been sorted out. If later weren't too late. If she hadn't given him up as a bad job. If she hadn't got herself married by then to one of those long-haired, chiffon-scarved young men of the right birth and breeding, with wide trousers and high-heeled boots, who were always hanging round her.

He had decided he *had* seen the last of her when, three days after his visit to the Theatre Club, he heard her voice in the hall, high-pitched, well bred, and haughty.

'He's not inviting a young woman into his room,' she was saying firmly to the landlady. 'She's *bursting* in. Now please get out of the way.'

He took a quick swallow of whisky to make his breath smell and lay back on the bed pretending to be asleep.

As the door opened, Susie was still arguing with the landlady. 'This is private,' she was saying. 'I'm trying to help him. I've not come to spend the day in his bed.'

The door slammed shut on the mutterings outside, and there was an ominous silence. For a long time he went on feigning sleep, but at last he turned over and opened one eye. She was standing by the bed looking down at him, haughty New England, yet clearly worried. When she was an old woman, he thought, she'd look at cripples and the sick and ailing in the same way, while she administered what she would inevitably come to regard as her own private branch of the Red Cross, pushing her workers about just as she'd pushed the landlady about and chivvying her cripples in the same way she chivvied him. He felt sorry for her sick and ailing, but also pleased to see her, so pleased he felt weak.

He pretended to be irritated. 'What do you want?'

'You, of course,' she said. 'I've only just got back. I got your address from the paper. You stink like a brewery.'

'I've drunk enough to float a brewery.'

She studied him. 'What's come over you? You were never

141

one for a lot of booze. I think that clever swine Mostyn's been up to something.'

She was brighter than she looked, he thought. She didn't miss a trick.

'Go away,' he said.

'Not likely.'

'What the hell do you want?'

'I've told you. You.'

'I don't want *you*.'

'I didn't want you either,' she retorted. 'Not after you stood me up last time. But I finally came to the conclusion I was wrong. Come on, you're going round to my place to sober up.'

'Go away, for Christ's sake!'

She ignored him. 'Don't argue,' she said. 'You need someone to look after you.'

'Leave me alone!' He'd look fine, he thought, taking refuge in Susie's home while his friends with the submarine tried to contact him here.

'You smell of stale cabbage and whisky. Yuck.' She reached for him, and he flung his arm out drunkenly, sending her staggering back so that she almost fell. He'd used more force than he'd intended, and he wanted to get up and apologise, to help her. Oh, blast bloody Mostyn, his mind screamed. Just when he was desperate enough to welcome her, he was having to make a show of rejecting her.

She had straightened up again. Her brow was smooth and her temper calm. He knew she was making a tremendous effort on his behalf. 'Have you eaten?' she asked slowly, patiently.

'Not much.'

'Then come to my place, have a decent bath and a meal and a drink. If you still feel the same afterwards, you can come back.'

He couldn't resist it; it made sense, the sort of thing a lonely man might do. 'Why are you doing this?' he demanded.

'Nobody else seems to be doing it,' she said, reaching into the battered wardrobe and producing his jacket. 'Do they?'

'Oh, Christ, Susie,' he begged, 'leave me alone!'

'If you insist on punching me in the nose and kicking my feet from under me,' she said firmly, in her best Red Cross chairman manner, 'then I'll go. But apart from that, or biting and scratching, I'm staying here till you've got your coat on and decided to come with me.'

There wasn't much choice.

She didn't talk much in the taxi. As she led him in silence up the steps to the front door of the big house in Mayfair, he realised he was looking forward to a bath and a good meal. Eating in caffs wasn't his idea of fun, and he seemed to have done a lot of it in the last few days.

'Mum know about this?' he asked.

She didn't look at him as she replied. 'No.' She let them in, and immediately went to the decanter. 'Drink be all right?' she asked, and to his surprise he saw that her eyes were full of concern.

'I'll go fix the bath,' she said, handing him the glass.

Half an hour later, he emerged, wearing a clean shirt and clean socks. 'Whose is the shirt?' he asked.

'He's a boy friend of the Ma's. He stays here from time to time. It doesn't look too exotic.' She stared at him unhappily. 'What's it all about, James?'

He refused to meet her eyes. 'Nothing to do with you.'

'That's where you're wrong,' she said.

'Well, then, you'll have read the papers. That bastard with the nasal voice in your office will have been pleased to show them to you.'

'Yes, as a matter of fact, he was. But I didn't believe a word of it. It's a put-up job.'

Oh, dear sweet Susie; darling, honest, decent, high-principled stiff-necked, gallant Susie; dear Red Cross chairman Susie! Out of all the people he'd known, only Susie was prepared to regard him as a reasonable risk. He could have kissed her, and very nearly did.

She cooked steaks, and there was lettuce, tomatoes, and peppers.

'Low calory content,' she said. 'I expect it's what the Ma intended for lunch. I know she's having someone round.'

She sloshed red wine into a glass and handed it to him. It was the sort he couldn't afford even for a treat.

'Mum's?' he asked.

'No, mine. I never touch hers.'

'Your principles are too high,' he said.

'Principles are never too high,' she said, and he thought guiltily of Daphne Eltney. 'Knock it back. You look as though you haven't eaten decent food for weeks. Who engineered all this? Mostyn?'

He could have hugged her for her faith in him, but it was no good. He couldn't afford to indulge in self-pity. 'No.'

'Who then?'

'Me.'

She looked at him, her eyes glittering and blue as ice. 'Somebody's lying, James,' she said. 'Either you or some other guy.'

He managed a jagged laugh. 'What's bred in the bone,' he said. 'My old man was a compulsive gambler.'

She snorted. 'Come off it! There was never anybody quite so stuffy as you.'

Her summation of his character startled him. Stuffy! It was a new view of himself.

'I'm not against all this,' she said, rather to his surprise. 'You've needed something like this to jolt you out of your introspection and kick a few boards loose. All that brooding over the ship you didn't get. Anybody with any sense would have faced up to it long since and thought of something else. What you need is a good woman to stir you up occasionally.'

'Like you, for instance?'

'I could do better than some of those stupid chicks I've seen you with from time to time. Have another drink?'

'What are you trying to do? Resurrect me or get me drunk?'

'How drunk were you?' she said.

'When?'

'When you were thrown out of that pub.'

'Pretty drunk.'

She didn't seem to believe him. 'Are you short of money?' she asked.

'Why?'

'I've got plenty.'

'I've got money.'

'You don't live in places like the one where I found you if you've got money.'

He shrugged. 'Beggars can't be choosers.'

'How much could you use?'

'None.'

'No need to get stuffy again.'

'I don't want your damned money!' he snapped.

'Okay, okay. No offence intended. If the idea of going back to that appalling hotel's too much for you, though, I guess you could stay here the night. I could find you a bed.'

Venner began to feel edgy. She was offering him the kind of help, the kind of faith in him, that was making the whole project ridiculous. No man in his senses would have refused her help, but he knew he had to.

'I don't want one,' he said. 'I'll shove off in a moment, and then just leave me alone.'

While they were talking, still sitting at the kitchen table, they heard the front door slam.

'The Ma,' Susie said. 'This should be interesting.'

'I'll leave by the back door.'

'Don't talk silly! It's nothing to do with her.'

'It's her house.'

Susie sniffed. 'As a matter of fact, it isn't,' she said. 'My father trusted her so little, he left it to me. It's mine.'

'God, we are wealthy, aren't we?'

'Don't be so goddam unpleasant!'

The door opened, and Susie's mother appeared. She was tall and blonde and beautiful, and looked a little like Susie except that the honesty was missing from her eyes. She looked coldly at Venner.

'You know James, Mother,' Susie said without emotion.

'Indeed I do. I hope *you* know him, too.'

'If you mean, have I read the papers,' Susie said, 'yes, I have. It doesn't make a damn bit of difference. I don't believe a word of it.'

God, Venner thought, what a girl to have batting for you!

'I have friends coming.'

'They needn't come in here.'

'I think, in fact, I'll ring the police and have him thrown out.'

Susie rose to her full height, and it was not inconsiderable; like so many Americans, she had long legs. She advanced on her mother and took her arm, jerking her round firmly and leading her out the door. Venner could hear them arguing in the hall.

'If you say one more word,' Susie was saying, 'I'll have *you* thrown out.'

'You wouldn't dare!'

'Try me and see.'

Venner rose. It seemed to be the point when he should leave. But he had to do something to stop Susie from following him. Now that she had her teeth into the saving of him, she'd never let go until she'd got him established in a decent apartment and with a responsible job among people with the correct philanthropic instincts.

Her handbag was on the window-seat where she'd dropped it when they'd entered. He crossed to it. The argument in the hall had grown more subdued, and he guessed that Susie was winning. The handbag was open, and her wallet lay at the top. He picked it up and flipped it open. It contained at least thirty pounds. He stuffed the money into his pocket. Nobody liked being kicked in the teeth when they were holding out a helping hand. Nor would Susie.

He sighed as he closed the door behind him. It was so bloody sad that it had to be Susie, he thought.

Chapter Three

Susie's money was burning a hole in Venner's pocket as he headed for Bayswater. He guessed that by this time she was beginning to have second thoughts about him. If her mother had found out about the money, too, she was probably even fighting a rear-guard action.

When he reached the hotel, the landlady, exuding an aura of frying, told him someone had been asking for him on the telephone and would ring again. He went to his room, hoping to God that Susie wouldn't turn up before the message came through. Exactly an hour later, the telephone rang, and there was a sharp rattle on the door.

'Telephone!'

As Venner had expected, it was the same voice that had spoken from behind his shoulder in the Theatre Club.

'Venner?'

'Yes.'

'Where have you been?'

'I have to buy cigarettes and have a drink.'

'We told you not to drink.'

'No, you didn't. You said stay sober.'

There was a pause. 'Okay, fair enough. Now listen. You're to go to Portsmouth—'

'When?'

'Immediately. Take the first train down there and get a room in a hotel. The smaller the better, but make sure it has a telephone and that you can eat there. We might want you in a hurry.'

'Do I use my own name?'

'No. You're William Vaughan, of Chatham. When you've

found somewhere, leave a message with poste restante at the general post office. For George Gardiner. And don't bother to enquire who he is, because it's a false name. Give your address and telephone number, and be there in case we ring. Don't leave except to buy cigarettes. We don't want you out if we need you, because we won't want to wait. Understood?'

Venner returned to his room and packed his belongings at once. He paid his bill, took the Underground to Victoria Station, and by afternoon was in Portsmouth. With the summer, it was full of holiday-makers from nearby Southsea.

He took a taxi to the Admiral Jervis, where he found a place at the bar and asked for Polaski. The Pole came from the kitchen, big and amiable and cheerful, but his smile vanished at once when he saw Venner. Venner thought he was going to cut him dead.

'This is a funny place for you to be just now,' he said.

Venner nodded. 'In a way. I'm after a job. But I need somewhere to stay for a while. Know any cheap hotels away from the docks?'

The Pole's face was expressionless, giving Venner an uneasy feeling he was wondering how he could get rid of him. He spoke to the barman and hurried back towards the kitchen.

The barman pushed another drink across the counter. 'Mr Polaski's compliments,' he said, and from the way he looked at him, Venner suspected he'd recognised him from the picture in the paper.

When Polaski returned, he had a slip of paper in his hand. 'There's an address here,' he said. 'It's not much of a place. It's out towards North End. The district's gone to hell and they're pulling down a lot of property. But I'm told it's reasonably clean and that you can eat cheaply.'

'Thanks, Polly.'

Polaski looked at him as though trying to work out how he could have sunk so low. 'The name's the Royal George,' he said. 'Everything around this damn place's named after an admiral or one of his ships.'

The Royal George, as Polaski had suggested, was a run-down place that overlooked a vast desert of demolished and half-demolished houses. The landlady seemed borne down by worries and very glad to see Venner.

The shabby and cheerless room was cleaner than he'd expected and, flinging his bag on the bed, he handed over a five-pound note on account. Outside again, he bought cigarettes and, with a pocketful of change, walked to the nearest telephone box.

The wind, coming at a half-gale from the sea, was tearing down the mean street like an express train, whipping up the dust and the fish-and-chip papers and the discarded football-pool coupons. The place looked dreary and Venner felt frozen.

The telephone clicked as he pushed his coins in and Mostyn answered cheerfully. 'Mostyn here.'

'And aren't you lucky to be warm and comfortable,' Venner said.

'Venner?' Mostyn's voice became wary at once. 'Where are you?'

'You'll never guess. Portsmouth. I was told to report down here. Royal George Hotel.' He gave the address. 'I've been told to wait there for instructions.'

'Could we put one of our men in there? As a waiter or something?'

'Don't be funny! The sort of places you've landed me in don't go in for waiters.'

'Why Portsmouth?' Mostyn asked after a pause. 'There are no nukes there, are there?'

'Not to my knowledge. I'd better go now. I've got to leave a telephone number and address for a chap called George Gardiner at the main post office. I'll do it tomorrow morning.'

'I'll have a man watching. And we'll have someone keep an eye on that hotel and have the phone tapped somehow. Is there any way we can contact you without telephoning?'

'There's a tobacconist down the road. Name of Kitchin. I changed a note there to ring you. He's an old man, and I

149

seem to smell Navy all over him. Try him. I'll leave messages there. I bet he'd do it for a quid or two and enjoy feeling he was involved again.'

It was only as Venner headed back towards the Royal George that he saw he was close to where Daphne Eltney lived. He stopped dead. Despite the insistence that he remain in the hotel at all times, he was free right now – completing the arrangements his instructions had called for. He started walking again, and gradually his pace quickened. Daphne Eltney wasn't a woman to ask questions, and he felt he had no need to suffer any feeling of guilt. When you were down in the gutter, it didn't matter much what you did.

He thought of Susie, but he brushed her from his mind. Susie was finished. Too much had happened. He didn't belong in the same league when it came to honesty and decency.

Mrs Eltney answered his knock so quickly that he wondered if she'd been expecting someone. She was wearing a housecoat and her big green eyes glowed. But the eager expression died quickly and changed to a harder one, lacking warmth and impulsiveness.

'Hello,' she said.

'Can I come in?'

She glanced along the street before opening the door wide, pulling him inside, and slamming the door behind him. There was a fire burning in the sitting room, but she didn't ask him to sit down. Smelling of soap and with no make-up, she still looked warm and vibrantly alive, and the sight of her made his heart thump. She was studying him speculatively, wary and puzzled.

'How are things?' he asked.

'Better than they were.' She looked up at him with none of the usual archness in her expression. 'Was that you in the papers?'

'Yes.'

'Are you one of that lot who were pestering Jimmy Nanjizel?'

'No. At the moment, I'm nothing.'

'Why are you here then?' She was so wary that he knew he'd made a mistake in coming.

'I'm in Portsmouth now,' he said, not entirely giving up hope. 'At least for a time.'

'What for?'

'Looking for a job.'

'I hope you get one. What did you want to talk about?'

'I didn't want to talk about anything,' he said.

'Oh!' She stared at her feet, unhelpful to the point of embarrassment. 'I had enough trouble over Jimmy Nanjizel. I don't want any more over you.'

His reception had been quite different from what Venner had expected. When he'd left her last time, at five-thirty in the morning, to catch a train to London, her eyes had been heavy with sleep. Now they were cold and unfriendly. He could see she wasn't prepared to melt. His idea seemed to have come to nothing.

'Under the circumstances,' he said, 'perhaps I'd better go.'

He heard the door slam behind him. He was left with nothing at all. Mostyn had a lot to answer for.

Chapter Four

Venner wakened slowly. His mouth was sour; his eyes felt gummy. His first view through the window was of a broken-backed roof across the road where a demolition contractor was hauling down a warehouse.

He moved sluggishly, bored and weary. The Nanjizel affair seemed to have occupied half his life, and these wretched surroundings all his old age. The sky was heavy, and the tap over the hand basin dripped monotonously. A bulldozer opposite roared as the scoop dropped and pushed bricks and earth and broken window-sills into a heap. Just beyond, two or three of the demolition men had built a huge fire from old floorboards and sooty timbers. Venner could hear it crackling and see the pale-blue smoke rising past his window.

Yawning, he ran his hand over his face. The sky had a red evening wash spreading across it, and grey and violet clouds were massing to bring darkness earlier than normal. He didn't find waiting easy.

He'd left his address at the poste restante as he'd been told, and, on his way back, he'd bought a bottle of whisky, for show, and placed it where it could be seen. But the day had dragged, and he had drunk more of it than he'd intended. The character was getting hold of him. If this went on, it would be too late to break out.

He looked about him again, his spirit weighed down by the drab surroundings. There was even a crack in the ceiling identical to the one in the Bayswater hotel. As he came to full wakefulness, hating himself and hating Mostyn and dreading the prospect of the evening, there was a tap on the door.

He sat up as it opened. At first he thought it was Latisse's people, who might have changed their plans for getting in touch with him. But it was Susie Gore.

His feet banged down on the floor. 'What the hell are *you* doing here?' he demanded angrily.

She was wearing her Red Cross chairman's face again. 'Looking for you,' she said, quite unperturbed.

'God damn it, can't you leave me alone?'

She began to take off her coat. 'What did you do with my thirty quid?' she asked.

Venner moved uncomfortably, avoiding her eyes. 'Spent it,' he said.

'What on?'

'Booze.'

'All of it?'

'Yes.'

'You must have shifted a bit. Anything left?'

'No. Why are you following me around?'

'I guess I felt I ought to.'

'Why, for God's sake?'

She looked angry. 'Don't you think you *need* following around?'

He almost groaned. She was clearly not intending to give up – no matter how much he insulted her. Then another thought occurred to him. 'Susie,' he said, 'did anybody follow you here?'

'Shouldn't think so. Oddly enough, I thought of that.'

'Why, for God's sake?'

'I thought perhaps Mostyn might be keeping an eye on you or something. So I came in through the back door. It was easy enough. If they'd stopped me, I was going to say I'd come to read the gas meter.'

He almost laughed out loud. Anybody less like a meter reader than Susie simply didn't exist.

'Why did you come here?' she asked.

'Oh, for God's sake, Susie!' His anger wasn't simulated now, because he was suddenly afraid for her. 'Because I wanted to.'

'You know—' she sat on the end of the bed '—something

153

queer's going on. If the Ma started all at once to show sweetness and light, if she threw off her boy friends and started behaving with intelligence and kindness, I wouldn't hang out flags. I'd suspect something bent was in the air. People don't all of a sudden jump out of their characters. Least of all you. That makes sense, doesn't it?'

It did, when he thought of it. But then, Susie knew him. Latisse's men didn't and, with the aid of those hints Mostyn had slipped into his file, which had undoubtedly been seen by someone who'd reported on him, they'd assumed that there had always been some latent dishonesty in him which, under the stress of trouble, had burst through to the surface.

Susie was still talking, though he hadn't been listening to her.

'I've thought often you might lie to me,' she was saying. 'About other girls. Things like that. But you were never lousy enough for *this*. It's so phony it stinks.'

'I took your thirty quid,' Venner muttered.

'Even that didn't make sense, because you'd just said you were all right for money. If you'd been desperate, you'd have accepted my offer of cash, not pinched it. Stealing's too tricky if you can borrow it.'

'Full of homespun philosophy, aren't we?' Venner said. 'How did you find me?'

'I went to Polaski. You always used to say, If you want me, go and see Polaski. He told me he gave you this address. It wasn't difficult.'

'Why did you guess Portsmouth?'

'Like to like. I thought you might come back here if London didn't want you.'

She'd guessed right every time but for all the wrong reasons.

'Still drinking?' she asked, looking at him with worry in her eyes.

'Like a fish.'

'What about eating?'

'Now and then.'

'You look terrible.'

154

I'm supposed to, he felt like saying.

She was silent for a while, then she leaned over and kissed him gently on the cheek. He felt like weeping.

'Why can't you leave me alone?' he said wretchedly.

'You must be dim,' she said quietly. 'Haven't you guessed yet? I love you. It's as simple as that.'

It took his breath away. He'd always thought it was just natural inbred bossiness, the poor little rich girl demanding something she wanted, the sort of thing that made successful Red Cross chairmen and presidents of flower-arrangement societies. But the straightforward unemotional way she said it told him how wrong he'd been. She wasn't asking anything of him – only permission to go on loving him, giving, not taking. The thought hadn't really occurred to him before, and now, in a flash of common sense, he knew he was in love with her, too. He'd always thought of her as someone to eat with, drink with, talk to, go to parties with, go to bed with – though she'd always been far too moral to allow him *that* pleasure – but, curiously, never anyone to spend the rest of his life with.

'Would you like me to stay?' she asked.

'Here?'

'It's warm enough and dry enough.'

'The night?'

'That's what I meant.'

'What's come over you?'

'Change of heart. Sympathy. Call it what you like.'

He managed a twisted smile. 'It's something I've thought of more than once,' he admitted. 'If you remember, you were rather against it.'

'My fault,' she said. 'Perhaps that had something to do with this.'

'It's a nice thought, but—' he shook his head —'love should be gracious, Susie.'

'The way I feel right now, it wouldn't matter one damn bit.'

He heard the telephone ring, and somehow he knew it would be for him. Sure enough, there was a tap on the door a moment later.

'Telephone, Mr Vaughan!'

She turned as he rose to his feet. 'Are *you* Mr Vaughan?'

'Yes.'

'Why?'

'Bit of incognito.'

'Not something somebody dreamed up for some reason?'

She seemed to be getting dangerously close. He shook his head.

'Don't go away,' he said. 'I'll be back.'

The voice was the same one as before.

'Venner?'

'Yes. Are we off?'

'Not at the moment. Just checking you're about. Don't go away. We'll be ringing with more information just before midnight.'

'Is that all?'

'That's all.'

Susie was stretched on the bed when he returned to his room.

'Who was it?' she asked.

'Someone who's offering me a job.'

'What sort of job?'

'A job I can do.'

'Aren't you going to tell me?'

'Not now. If it comes off, I'll be able to look you up, and perhaps then things'll be all right.'

'It's not a job at all, is it?'

'Of course it's a job. They're going to ring again about midnight.'

'You don't get jobs by mysterious telephone calls at midnight.'

'*I* do.'

'What are they paying you?'

'Quite a lot.'

She looked sad and disappointed. 'Informative, aren't you? Is it honest?'

'Yes.'

156

She sighed, but showed no sign of moving, and Venner shifted restlessly.

'What about you?' he asked. 'Where are you staying?'

'In one of those sea-front hotels at Southsea. It's quite comfortable. It's full of middle-aged spinsters in twin sets and pearls. They like comfort.'

'I'm sorry I can't see you home.'

'I'm not going yet.'

There was a long silence.

'I've come to the conclusion,' Susie said at last, 'that you and I have been wasting time.'

'I think perhaps we have. It'll be all right, though, in the end.'

'I didn't mean that.'

She had risen and was standing with her back to him, her hands at her sides, and he took a step forward and put his arms round her. She lifted his hands to her breasts and stood with her fingers over his. They stood like that for a long time. Then he felt her draw a deep shuddering breath before she moved in the circle of his arms and turned to face him, surprisingly still.

Suddenly her arms went round him and she was crying softly and he was kissing her tears away.

'It's all right, James,' she said. 'Really, it's all right. I'll try to understand, though I don't believe a single goddam word you've said. Just don't let's waste any more time.'

Her head down, she unbuttoned his shirt and slipped her hands inside, her fingers cold on his skin. 'It's all right,' she said again. 'Gore the whore. Susie the Floosie.'

'Susie, don't talk silly!'

'It's not silly. Really it's not. Right now, it seems the sanest, most natural thing that's ever happened to me.'

Chapter Five

It troubled Venner that he had been unable to see Susie back to her hotel, or even to find a taxi for her. She had been quiet and subdued when she left, but her eyes were shining and he thought that maybe she felt she'd won some personal battle. He knew *he* felt better; all his depression seemed to have fallen away.

He sat thinking about her while waiting for the call. As time passed and nothing happened, he fell asleep on the bed, yet when the telephone rang at eleven-fifty-five, he reached it before the bell sounded twice.

'Venner?' The voice was calm and sure.

'Yes.'

'Are you ready?'

'No.'

'You'd better be. You have five minutes.'

'Five minutes, for God's sake? I need to pack and pay the bill. And everyone's gone to bed!'

'Leave the money with your belongings in your room. With a note saying you'll pick them up later. You won't need anything but what you stand up in. We have all you'll need in the way of warm clothes.'

'Where do I go?'

'You don't. You'll be picked up. Be outside in five minutes. And don't hang about where you can be seen too much. We don't want the police around. Just be there.'

'Can't you tell me what it's all about?'

'You'll learn soon enough.'

They were sure of him, Venner decided as the telephone clicked. Damn sure. No threats. No wheedling. Just orders. He stood wondering what to do. There was no time to call Mostyn. He would have to assume that the telephone had been tapped, and that Mostyn would find out what had happened.

Leaving money and a hurried note on his suitcase, he reached for his jacket, wishing he could let Susie know how he felt about what she had done. He couldn't bear the thought that if he disappeared she'd feel he'd simply used her and walked out of her life. She deserved better than that.

When he stepped out of the hotel, it was raining. Most of the shop lights in the distance were out. There were few people about, and only an occasional car sped past, heading towards the residential areas of the city. He lit a cigarette, but he'd drawn hardly more than a couple of puffs when he heard a car slowing down behind him and knew he'd been seen.

A door opened as he turned.

'James Venner?'

'Yes.'

'Get in.'

He tossed away the cigarette and climbed in beside the driver. Only then did he realise there was another man, in the back, low down on the seat, his face in the shadows, his eyes hidden by dark glasses.

'Where are we going?' he asked.

'Don't let that worry you,' the man in the rear seat said. 'You'll be back in this country before anyone notices you've left.'

Daisy was enjoying her affair with Mostyn. As Venner had often suspected, it had been going on for some time now, but while she would have been pleased to bruit it about, Mostyn was inclined to keep it quiet, like so much else in his life. It didn't worry her much, however. Being with him meant living well, eating well – sometimes sleeping well – and his money and background made him a catch in anybody's language. More-over, behind her brisk efficiency, Daisy was a loving young woman who needed a man in her life.

She glanced round his flat. It lay in a highly desirable area,

159

and was furnished in style, and its size made her own place seem as overcrowded as a rat's nest. Only Mostyn's tendency to lapse into silence when his thoughts took hold of him, and his habit of vanishing behind his own face into a strange area of anonymity, ever bothered her. He was silent and thoughtful now, and, oddly enough, she suspected it was because of Venner. Ever since Venner had left the office he'd seemed to be waiting for the telephone to ring.

'Shall I make some coffee?' she asked quietly.

'Yes. We'll have a brandy and listen to Beethoven's *Emperor*. It's powerful music.'

'Powerful for what?'

'For what we'll be doing.'

When she returned from the kitchen, he still appeared to be brooding.

'Funny about James Venner,' she said. The words came out spontaneously, because Mostyn's silence had set her thinking about Venner, too.

Mostyn seemed startled. 'Funny?' he said. 'Why?'

'Going off like that.'

'Nothing funny about it. Half expected it. Been watching him for a bit.'

'Oh!' Daisy felt deflated. 'I didn't know that.' She decided she must be a bad judge of men, because she'd never suspected anything of the sort, and she'd known Venner for three years.

'I always got on well with him,' she said defensively.

'Bit difficult at times,' Mostyn insisted.

'Only with people he didn't like. Aubrey, for instance. He couldn't stand *him*.'

'Don't blame him. That's one of the few things I *don't* blame him for.'

'I don't like Aubrey either,' Daisy went on, still on Venner's side. 'He's the only man in the block who never made a pass at me.'

'Is that why you don't like him?'

Daisy shuddered. 'I wouldn't have him touch me with a barge pole. But since everybody else has tried to at one time or other, it always makes it seem there's something fishy about him.'

They had long finished coffee when the telephone by the end of the long settee rang. Daisy tried to wriggle out of the way among the cushions as Mostyn reached over her to answer it.

'Haggard, Portsmouth.' The voice that spoke was like a shadow. Which, in fact, was exactly what it was. Haggard was one of the men who'd tapped the telephone to the Royal George.

Mostyn's face was only an inch or so from Daisy's, and he saw she was staring at him with interest. 'Go on,' he said. 'It's all right.'

There was a pause, and they heard the man at the other end of the line draw a deep breath. 'Venner's gone,' he said. 'Midnight. Exactly.'

The surprised look that came into Daisy's eyes told Mostyn that she could hear every word.

'Where to?' he asked.

'We don't know.'

Mostyn sat up abruptly. Daisy slipped from under his arm and, swinging her legs to the floor, sat on the edge of the settee, jerking her dress down.

'Wasn't he followed?' Mostyn snapped.

'There was no time.'

'Dammit, why not?'

'They gave him only five minutes. By the time we got a message to the people watching down the road, it was too late. A black car – looked like a Ford – was seen. It went north. We didn't have time to pick it up. The whole thing was carefully arranged so they *couldn't* be followed. They said they'd have all he wanted in the way of warm clothes.'

Mostyn's mind ticked over. Warm clothes meant sea. And sea meant ships. And ships meant submarines.

Daisy's hands were busy with her hair when he replaced the telephone on its stand. She turned towards him. 'He said "Venner's gone".' Her expression was suspicious. 'I could hear what he said.'

161

Mostyn's face was blank. 'Yes,' he agreed. 'That's what he said.'

'That call came from Portsmouth. I heard him say so. Who was it?'

'Chap called Haggard. Follows people for me from time to time.'

'Tail?'

Mostyn gazed at her. 'What do you know about that?'

Daisy stared back at him, unblinking. 'What a question,' she said. She lit a cigarette and stuffed the lighter back in her handbag. 'Is Venner still working for you?'

'Yes.'

'And that scene in the office? It was all a put-up job?'

'Yes.'

Her eyes widened. 'God, you are a swine,' she said in a tone that was more awe than dislike.

Mostyn shrugged. 'Only way there was.'

'Are you going to Portsmouth?'

'Eventually, I suspect.'

Daisy made a face, but Mostyn seemed to be in his shutters-up mood and she didn't ask any more questions. She straightened up. 'Shall I make some more coffee?' she asked.

Mostyn shook his head. 'Better make it a couple of double whiskies,' he said.

As the car roared between the dark avenues of trees, Venner tried to remember the sign-posts in the hope of pinpointing his position. The route didn't seem to go with submarines at all.

They had headed out of Portsmouth and up the hill into rural Hampshire. He'd seen the Winchester sign several times, but now he realised they were heading towards Petersfield. After seeing Liss and Sheet and Farnham marked, he guessed they were somewhere behind Portsmouth, in the wooded country round Selborne.

While he was trying to work it out, the car turned off on to an unmarked road between trees, and turned again where the trees were thicker. He guessed they'd entered a private estate

162

or land belonging to a farm. Then they were pulling up in front of a large house, which was entirely in darkness, lonely and high against the sky.

As he climbed out, the driver touched his arm. He was carrying a torch. 'This way,' he said.

There were more buildings at the back of the house, and the driver stopped in front of one of them. There was no sign of life, but he tapped with the torch at a door. After a while they heard movement and bolts being drawn. The door opened into darkness.

'In here!'

As the door closed behind them, the light was switched on by an automatic device attached to the jamb. Venner saw that he was in what appeared to be a converted stable. Standing by the entrance was a man, fair-haired, hard-faced, and foreign-looking, whose accent sounded American.

'My name's Meyer,' he said. 'This way.'

He pushed open another door, and Venner found himself in an empty room with a corridor at the end leading to what looked like a shower and lavatory. There were a dozen Army beds by the walls, covered with mattresses and blankets. Clothes were scattered about the beds, and underneath some of them were suitcases. One or two of these looked like Navy issue, he noticed. The room smelled of cigarette smoke.

Nothing was said beyond what was necessary, so Venner followed Meyer without speaking. He was led down the corridor to a big door. Beyond it he could hear men's voices.

As Meyer opened the door, he saw men rising to their feet. Some were dressed in old blue serge trousers and jerseys that he again recognised as Navy issue.

Meyer stopped in the centre of the room, watched curiously by the men opposite. 'Venner,' he said, jerking his hand. 'He's the last.'

The men nodded their heads.

Meyer took him round them, making introductions.

'McAvoy,' he said, and a burly black-haired man stood up.

163

He looked wild-eyed, as though he'd been on drugs, but Navy was stamped all over him.

'Bowden ... Bonser ... Luck ... Lemon ...' They were all there, all the missing men, as well as a few they hadn't known about. 'Ryan. . . Madura – he's Dutch but he speaks English ... Arteguy, French ... Ekke, German – same applies.' The last was a man old enough to be Venner's father, and he guessed he'd been recruited from among ex-U-boat men in Kiel.

They all looked as though life had dealt harshly with them. Bowden's was a lowering face, McAvoy's a weary one. Luck seemed almost too young to be there. Bonser was small and looked ill, and Ryan limped heavily as he walked. Madura was an enormous man, at least six feet four, with the shoulders of an ox and a puzzled look in his blue eyes. Since they looked relieved, Venner figured that some of them had been waiting a long time. Only Lemon, a sharp-featured man with a saucy grin looked undaunted, as though he'd undertaken the adventure purely for devilment.

Meyer was looking at his watch. 'We can have a look round now,' he said. 'That's what they told me.'

He headed towards a pair of large doors at the end of the room. Taking a key from his pocket, he unlocked a padlock that was securing them. Just beyond, there was a partition with crude wooden steps leading to a door set ten feet high in it. On hooks near the steps were naval caps and blue shirts with badges. Among them was a reefer jacket with a naval lieutenant's rings.

'You'll be wearing these,' Meyer said. He had climbed the steps now and was pushing a key into the door of the partition.

'Right,' he said. 'Better come up.'

He thrust open the door, and they climbed after him.

McAvoy was first through the door. He stopped immediately. 'Christ almighty,' he said.

Behind him, Venner also stopped. The room beyond looked like a studio. There were big windows, but they had been covered with blankets, to keep the light in or sightseers out. There were daubs of paint on the walls, as though artists had

164

tried their brushes on them. But it was the middle of the floor that intrigued Venner. In it was a huge construction containing a mass of pipes, wheels, dials, levers, and levels, with, in the centre, two great polished tubes equipped with handles.

'Does it all work?' he asked.

'As much as we need,' Meyer said. 'It's exact in every detail.'

It was, too. It was the mock-up of the control room of Hector McEwan's *Thunderer*, which Haddon, the property man, had been so proud of.

Chapter Six

Down the long slope of the Somerset hills the lorries came, heading towards Salisbury. There were two of them, both articulated. Under tarpaulins they carried long dark-green torpedo-shaped containers bedded down on cushions of sacking and foam rubber and lashed in place with what seemed an extraordinary amount of rope and chain. They had no markings whatsoever on them.

A hundred yards in front was a police car, its blue light flashing, its siren filling the countryside with its rising and falling cadence. Behind it, just in front of the first lorry, was a Land-Rover containing a man wearing an Army officer's cap and a major's crowns, and three other men in uniform. Following the first of the two articulated vehicles was a lorry full of more men in uniform. Then came the second articulated vehicle, another load of uniformed men behind it, and, finally, another police car, bringing up the rear.

They had been on the road since the night before, and the reason they had made such little progress was their slow speed. They were moving as though they were carrying dynamite and a box full of detonators. They had headed south during darkness, moving quietly, halting miles outside villages to eat their rations. Just as dawn was breaking, they had passed near the end of Cheddar Gorge, following side roads as far as possible, the route worked out carefully for every inch of the way. At every major road junction, the convoy slowed down while the police car ahead checked the turn-off and halted traffic. The rear police car moved to the front to take the lead; the halted car joined on at the rear as the convoy continued. It was like a battle operation.

'I'll be glad when this is over,' the man wearing the major's crowns said.

Nobody answered him. The driver was concentrating on keeping his distance, as were the drivers of the big articulated vehicles.

At Preddy, a small village near Shepton Mallet, the cautious progress was noted by the proprietor of the Raglan Arms, the village inn, who was standing outside discussing the purchase of a new car with the owner of the local garage. The village constable was standing at the cross-roads as the convoy rolled sedately by.

'Wonder what they're moving this time,' the garage proprietor said.

'Atom bombs,' the landlord of the Raglan said.

The garage proprietor grinned and opened the door of the new De Luxe Ford he was demonstrating. 'Shake us if they were,' he said.

As the convoy passed on, the constable climbed into his white van and headed past the Raglan.

'Atom or hydrogen?' the landlord shouted to him.

'Christ knows,' the constable said. 'They dug me out of bed at five o'clock this morning to tell me they were coming.'

'Who did?'

The constable looked puzzled. 'I *thought* it was Traffic at Shepton Mallet,' he said. 'But now that you mention it, I didn't recognise the voice. And I ought to. Perhaps I should check back. You never know what the bastards are going to get up to these days, do you?'

About the time the convoy was drawing away from the out-skirts of Preddy, Mostyn was waiting for the Minister of Defence in the Strangers' Gallery of the House of Commons. He had seen the Personal Private Secretary and announced his request, only to be told that the Minister was on his feet in the Chamber.

The House was showing its usual mixture of virulence, backbiting, vote-grabbing, self-interest, and parish-pump spitefulness, and Mostyn was already bored when an attendant touched his arm.

'The Minister's available now, sir,' he said.

The Minister greeted Mostyn in his office with a puzzled expression. He listened quietly to what Mostyn had to say, but he took a great deal of convincing.

'It would have to be a matter of grave national urgency,' he said, 'before we could bring into force the sort of security *you're* demanding, Colonel.'

'I think the sabotage, or worse, of a nuclear submarine *would* be a matter of grave national urgency, Minister,' Mostyn said calmly. 'Don't you?'

The Minister passed a hand through his thinning hair. 'But do we have anything more than conjecture?' he asked.

'They've recruited one of my men,' Mostyn said. 'A man who was deliberately put up for them. He reports there are others. *That's* not conjecture, Minister. And if it involves what we think it *might* involve, it's worth a little inconvenience.'

The Minister pushed a small pile of papers about the desk. 'I can make sure that all bases are warned,' he said. 'We can also insist on even tighter measures than exist already and that there must be no slackness. But we can't bring ship movements to a halt. Would that suffice?'

'Coming from you,' Mostyn conceded unwillingly, 'it would at least indicate that the matter should be regarded as one of great gravity.'

'Very well.' The Minister made a note on a pad. 'It will be done. But I'm not very happy about the suggestion that we inform foreign governments. Surely their security's their own affair.'

'As far as N.A.T.O. countries are concerned, it's *ours*, too,' Mostyn pointed out.

'Can't it be done unofficially?'

'It's already been done unofficially.'

'I'd prefer it to remain that way. If it were done officially and we were found to be wrong, it would do us no good at all.'

168

The Minister pushed the last few piles of paper straight and rose to his feet to indicate the interview was over.

Back in his office, Mostyn brooded on ministerial caution, and reflected with some satisfaction that he had at least got his instructions down in writing, signed, sealed, and delivered. So at least his own rear was guarded, and if anything went wrong, and panic started in Lucas's office, he'd be able to shut him up. Yet somehow the whole thing remained incomplete. The leads he'd expected hadn't materialised. The man who'd picked up Venner's poste restante letter in Portsmouth had been followed all the way to London, only to be lost in a traffic snarl near Victoria. A police call had been put out, but he'd vanished. Mostyn had been left with no idea of his destination. As for Venner, he seemed to have disappeared off the face of the earth.

Daisy appeared. She'd been entertaining thoughts of a quiet August bank holiday, but, with the suddenly increased activity in Mostyn's office, she had a growing suspicion that something was going to go wrong. 'I've got someone in my office about James Venner,' she said.

'Who?'

'That girl of his.'

'Did you tell her Venner doesn't live here any more?'

'Yes. She said she knew damn well he didn't.'

'What's she want?'

'You, I suspect.'

'Tell her to go away.'

'I have, but she won't. In fact, she's so hopping mad, I think if I try anything, she'll clobber me with a typewriter.'

Mostyn looked alarmed. 'Perhaps I'll slip down to Lucas's office,' he said. 'Can you think of an excuse?'

'No, she can't, and if she could, it wouldn't wash.' The voice came from behind Daisy, who was brushed peremptorily aside.

Mostyn rose to his feet. His face didn't slip. Since there was no point in trying to dodge now, he simply pretended he hadn't been contemplating it. He waved Daisy out of the room and concentrated on pulling up a chair. Offering Susie a cigarette, he lit one for himself, took several puffs on it to give himself time to think, and sat down at the other side of the desk. He could see she was raring to talk and blazingly angry. 'Now,' he said.

'What's James Venner up to?' Susie demanded.

'Can't think,' Mostyn said. 'Doesn't work here any more.'

'I bet he does.'

Mostyn blinked. 'I'm not sure I understand what you mean.'

'I saw James Venner,' Susie said. 'In Portsmouth. In some awful cabbage-smelling, mouse-infested run-down hotel where he was staying.'

'How did you know he was there?'

'I guessed.'

Mostyn was startled, but he fought back. 'What's this to do with me?' he hedged. 'Venner's left this department.'

'I don't believe you,' Susie said.

Like Venner, Mostyn was struck by her inspired guesses.

'You must have seen the papers,' he said.

'I don't believe *them*, either,' Susie said. 'I believe he's doing something for you. I know James Venner, and I think this whole stupid business is a put-up job.'

Mostyn made a mental note to pick someone next time a little more dishonest than Venner apparently was. It seemed to be the moment to make a clean breast of things. He rose, crossed to the door, and turned the key in the lock.

'What are you going to do now?' Susie said. 'Rape me?'

The bland, bored look vanished from Mostyn's face. 'It so happens,' he admitted, 'that your guess is uncomfortably near to the truth, and I'm going to have to ask you to keep it to yourself.'

'I might.' She was making no promises. 'One of these days James Venner's going to be mine as well as yours. I decided that ages ago. I want to know what he's up to.'

''Fraid I can't tell you,' Mostyn said. 'This department isn't quite what it seems, y'see.'

'You've got to come up with a better one than that.'

Mostyn smiled. 'So happens,' he said, 'that it's the truth.'

'And all that nonsense about him in the papers was just a load of codswallop?'

'Exactly.'

'Who else knows about it?'

'Just me.'

'Then if anything were to happen to you, I guess it's a good job *I* know, too, now, isn't it?'

Mostyn shrugged. She had a point, he supposed. 'He'd no right to tell you, of course,' he said.

'He didn't.'

'And he'd no right to see you.'

'He had no option. He didn't know I was there, and I broke in. And why not? He needs me. He had a rough passage a few years ago and saw all his future go phut. He's probably hoping now that when what he's doing's all over, there'll be a bit of a life for him. I'm hoping so, anyway. With me.' She frowned. 'What *is* he doing?'

Mostyn shrugged again. 'Afraid I can't enlighten you on that point,' he said. 'Not just yet.'

She accepted the explanation without comment. 'And is all this why I could never get hold of him when I wanted him?'

'I expect so.'

'That's nice to know, anyway. Why he shot off to Portsmouth? And to Scotland?'

'Yes.'

'I thought he was chasing a woman. Is this department secret, or something?'

'In a way.'

It startled her. 'And is James an agent?'

'Not really. But we make rather specialised investigations for the government – for several governments, in fact. You will, of course, not use this in your newspaper.'

'I'm not with the newspaper any more.'

'Oh? What happened?'

'James Venner happened. He needs me more than the great British sporting public do. Is he in any danger?'

'We have police – even troops – at our disposal if we need them.' Though, Mostyn admitted to himself, if would be a whole lot easier if they knew *where* they'd be needed, and how and when.

Susie seemed reassured at last. 'All right,' she said. 'I'll keep quiet. But you've got to promise to hand him back the moment he turns up again.'

'Of course.'

'Because if you don't, and something happens to him, I'll raise holy war. I still have the ear of one of the most powerful editors in Fleet Street, and the Gores of Boston never did allow themselves to be pushed around. You'll remember that the War of Independence started there.'

It seemed to Daisy that Susie Gore's visit had unsettled Mostyn more than a little, and she knew he was feeling faintly guilty about Venner. He was still looking thoughtful when he picked her up for a meal that night.

Mostyn belonged to an organisation that gave him entry to a variety of country clubs. He firmly believed that the British upper class was the finest instrument for ruling ever invented and, as a member of that august body himself, regarded it as his prerogative to live up to the demands expected of him. The club he chose at Esher was new, swinging, and made very sure that moneyed men like Mostyn *would* have access. It was situated in fifty acres of wooded grounds ('Useful for a little necking,' Daisy had said as they'd driven through), and fell over itself to be discreet. The dining room was lit with red lamps that made it look like the back room of a foreign brothel. The customers were more than a little mixed, including the usual middle-aged men with girls who obviously weren't their wives. Despite the low lights, a lot of them discreetly wore dark glasses.

The place was intriguing, Daisy thought, and normally – especially by the time she had drunk two gins and a large glass of Traminer – she would have considered the occasion successful. This meal could hardly be called elated, however.

Mostyn was still brooding, and she decided they were behaving with as much circumspection as an old married couple.

'Venner?' she asked.

Mostyn looked up and nodded.

'Worried?'

'Bit.'

'About Venner?'

He nodded again.

From her privileged position, she thought, not for the first time, that there was more to Mostyn than met most people's eye. 'Because he's disappeared?' she asked.

The blank look on Mostyn's face vanished abruptly; the old indifferent, callous look returned, sharp, calculating, fireproof. 'Shouldn't worry your head about that,' he advised. 'You were set on this world to decorate it, not worry about it.'

Daisy smiled. He was good at flattery, and he was making an effort now.

But knowing she wasn't put off, he leaned forward to stop her from asking the questions that were clearly troubling her. 'Have some more wine,' he suggested.

'I shall be drunk.'

'All the better. You're always more enthusiastic when you're tipsy.'

'James Venner used to say you were a bastard,' she said, smiling. 'I think he was right.'

'In our ready-wrapped bite-sized cellophane-packaged world, there isn't much room for anything else.'

The bill, Daisy noticed when they'd finished, was enough to knock a normal man flat on his back. Mostyn didn't bat an eyelid. He tossed two ten-pound notes on the plate and waved it away.

The head waiter beamed and produced a ledger. 'We'd be grateful if you'd sign the visitors' book, sir,' he said. 'For the lady. The police have suddenly become rather strict about it.'

Without turning his head, Mostyn held up his hand for a

pen, filled in Daisy's name, and signed his own name in the members' column. The book was just disappearing when he pulled it back.

'That's fine, sir,' the head waiter said.

'I know,' Mostyn said coldly. 'I wasn't looking at *that*.'

At the top of the page, separated from his own by several days and several other names, was one he knew.

As they left, he sank into a thoughtful mood again, and Daisy sighed.

He was in the same thoughtful mood the following day when he rang his stockbroker.

'I'm interested in Dorothea Holcombe,' he said.

'Oh? Why?'

'Came across a couple of names I knew last night at a club out Esher way. Her brother's was one of them.'

There was a soft chuckle at the other end of the line. 'Whose was the other? Tom Watson's?'

'How did you know?'

'It gets around. What do you want to know about Dorothea?'

'She recently gave up a big flat in Mayfair. Know any reason why?'

'Plenty. In fact, I don't see how the Holcombes are still on their feet. Their money was in West African Tin, and Olmuhi knocked the bottom out of them. But I also heard she'd bought a big house at Hinchley Wood, which seems to suggest there's nothing wrong with her finances, after all.'

If *she* paid for it, Mostyn thought. 'How much did it cost?' he asked. The price made him whistle.

He immediately made a second telephone call. 'I want Dorothea Holcombe watched,' he said. 'I suddenly have reason to think Latisse might turn up on her doorstep.'

About the time Mostyn was replacing the telephone, the two articulated lorries, with their anonymous-looking cylinders, were coming down the hill towards Fareham, just outside Portsmouth. Since they filled the road, traffic was building up

174

behind them. But the police were taking no chances, and no one was allowed to pass.

'Torpedoes,' the driver of a Ford Escort following close behind the convoy observed knowledgeably. 'You can see the shape under the tarpaulin. They'll be going to *Dolphin*.'

His companion raised his head. 'Bit big for torpedoes,' he pointed out.

'New type. Self-steering, homing, magnetic super-de-lux.' The driver grinned. 'Perhaps that's *why* they're so big.'

They followed the two lorries slowly towards the town, the driver continuing to speculate on the identity of the long tubes.

'Army's with 'em,' he said.

'The Army doesn't escort torpedoes,' his companion said. '*Or* the police. I bet they're missiles.'

'There aren't any of *those* subs at *Dolphin*.' The little townships bordering Portsmouth were all whispering galleries of naval gossip, and the inhabitants knew their fighting ships – their functions, their classes, their ages – as well as did the editor of *Jane's*.

The man in the passenger seat was unconvinced. 'One of 'em might have arrived during the night,' he said.

At the roundabout where the route from the north crossed the Brighton-Southampton road, the convoy began to turn.

'There you are,' the driver of the Ford Escort said, pointing at the sign marked GOSPORT. 'They're going to *Dolphin*.'

As the Ford continued on towards the town centre, the convoy curled away and began to head through narrow streets towards the country again. The man with the major's crowns glanced at his map.

'I hope they were warned we were coming,' he said. 'We don't want to be kept hanging about.'

At the submarine base, the convoy came to a halt. There were a lot of policemen on duty, one of whom stepped forward to examine papers and passes. They appeared to satisfy him, and he waved the convoy through.

One by one the vehicles moved beyond the gates – the Land-Rover, the lorry-loads of uniformed men, the white cars with flashing lights and foot-high POLICE signs on their sides, and the huge articulated lorries with their silent ominous loads. Inside, they stopped in a line, surrounded by warehouses, coiled ropes, wires, white-stencilled warnings, and all the other signs of naval occupation.

The man at the wheel of the Land-Rover heaved at the brake and switched off the engine. Then he turned, grinning, to the man with the major's crowns.

'Made it,' he said softly.

Chapter Seven

A cool wind was blowing up the channel, rippling the surface of the dark water and sending little showering cascades of spray against the sea-wall. Even deep inside the harbour, the water, scummy with oil and the refuse that had swept in on the tide, was slopping noisily against the steps.

The men standing on the dockside looked cold, their bare hands and exposed faces pinched with the night-time chill of the unseasonable weather. Aside from them, the place was bleak and deserted, the yellow metallic lighting mercilessly picking out the harsh angles of the sheds and walls. In the shadow of a warehouse, the two articulated lorries were drawn up, with the other convoy vehicles parked further back in the shadows. The men, nervous and bored, were standing in a huddle, smoking. They were all in need of a properly prepared meal and sleep.

The man in the major's uniform was standing alone, his hands in his pockets, his head down inside his collar. Behind him, a man wearing a sergeant's stripes ground out a cigarette under his foot.

'It's taking a damn long time,' he said.

His eyes were on the dark shape of a submarine further along the wall, below the huge dockyard crane. Painted black, it was low, sleek, and menacing. There were no identifying numbers or names on her. Men stood about her casing, shivering in the wind. An officer leaned with his elbows hooked over the bridge coaming, his face shadowed by the peak of his cap. Alongside him, a younger man watched as the crane moved forward.

The area had been sealed off. There were no dockyard

workers about, and even the crane was being driven by a naval petty officer.

There was a whirring sound and a shout from the dockside. The officer on the bridge called down to the men waiting on the casing. 'All right,' he said. 'Stand by!'

The men near the torpedo hatch had rigged up rails and stanchions, which ran along about two feet above the casing like a tram-line and disappeared into the fore-ends of the submarine. One of the men waved his arm, and, with a warning hail from above, the jib of the crane swung over the side. Slowly, one of the big cylinders was swung out from the lorry and lowered. Two of the men on the casing grabbed the nose, and tail lines were thrown down. Then the two-ton twenty-foot steel cylinder, swaying a little in the wind, sank again, like a descending lift.

Twenty or so pairs of anxious eyes followed it. Three feet above the casing, it was steadied, the men making sure that the brass rollers on either side of the lifting band encircling the cylinder engaged the rails. Caught by the wind, the submarine pulled away a little at the last moment, and the rails punched up against the cylinder with an ominous clang. The officer on the bridge frowned, his eyes narrowed, but he refrained from saying anything. The men below him had been carefully chosen; they knew what they were doing.

There were a few more anxious moments before the rollers were finally slotted on to the rails. The nose line was dropped through the fore hatch, where, below, a man caught it and ran it through a snatch block on the forward bulkhead between the fore-ends and the tube space. The cylinder was drawn towards the hatch as the crane driver eased away.

The man on the bridge gave a sigh of relief as the tail of the cylinder vanished through the circular hatchway. They had been at the job a long time now, moving the big cylinders with care and precision, and everybody's nerves were on edge a little.

178

'I'm damned if I like this job,' he said to the youngster alongside him. 'There's too much could go wrong.'

While they'd been working, in London, Mostyn's telephone was ringing. He snatched at it.

'Packer,' a voice said. 'I'm in Portsmouth. Dorothea's down here. She's booked in at the Vernon's Head Hotel.'

The vultures were gathering, Mostyn thought as he replaced the telephone on its cradle. But why Portsmouth, for God's sake? With no nuclear submarines stationed there, it didn't make sense.

As he considered it, the idea of gun-running by submarine suddenly began to grow intriguing. Terrorists in Northern Ireland and elsewhere weren't without their supporters abroad, and there were those who found it useful to keep Ulster a running sore in Britain's side. Mostyn knew his history and remembered that this was an accepted form of foreign policy. Napoleon had found Ireland a fruitful source of annoyance to England, and so had the Germans in two world wars. Was someone doing the same thing now?

He reached for the telephone again and began to give orders. Ten minutes later he was still at it.

'Every one,' he was saying. 'Even the ones in dry dock, the ones on the stocks, and the ones in the fitters' hands. Even the ones that are going to the breakers. We've no authority to interfere with the functioning of the Navy – but *all* orders must be checked with the office of the Admiral.'

The telephone crackled.

'I know it's a lot of work.' Mostyn's voice was bland but deadly. '*And* a lot of men.' He frowned and drew a deep breath as the protests followed one another over the line. 'Then,' he said sharply, 'if you're as short of men as that, you'd better get on to the Minister. They could always introduce conscription.'

179

Chapter Eight

Mostyn remained anxious, but it wasn't until the following afternoon that the next snippet of information came his way. It came from Packer once more.

'Latisse,' he said. 'He's turned up at last.'

'Where?' Mostyn asked. 'The docks?'

'No. The Vernon's Head. Where Dorothea's staying. He saw her. They did a lot of telephoning together.'

'Get a man on the switchboard,' Mostyn snapped. 'We need to know what they're saying.'

As he put the telephone down, Daisy entered with a bundle of files.

'Get your coat, Daisy,' Mostyn said.

'Where are we going?'

'Portsmouth.'

She looked surprised. 'For dinner?'

'Dinner, tea, supper. Bed even. Tomorrow as well, and perhaps the day after and a week after that.'

'It'll be hell on the roads with the bank holiday,' she said.

An hour later they were heading towards Guildford down the A3 in Mostyn's Lancia. It was good bank-holiday weather – rain – and Daisy had been right! The roads *were* hell.

She was half-asleep while Mostyn drove, his mind busy. He had an uneasy feeling that somewhere they'd lost control of the affair and the men involved in it. They seemed, in fact, he thought bitterly, to be waiting with bated breath only for Packer's next announcement.

The car radio was playing pop music, and, when the news came on, he was miles away and missed the first few words.

Then his hand shot out and turned up the volume. A lorry roared past in the opposite direction, drowning the words for a moment. He felt a flicker of fear that he'd missed an important announcement.

But it was just the same dreary repetition of Chief Olmuhi's threats from West Africa, the same old sabre-rattling and the same old draughts of anxiety whistling down the time-worn paths of an ancient continent to set dictators and would-be dictators in the emergent countries looking to the foundations of their thrones.

When a string of lorries howled past on the wet road, he gave the volume the full treatment.

'... Bewilderment is expressed in Ghana because Chief Olmuhi's army is known to be under strength and to possess little in the way of armour ... Yet his threats have become so strident in recent days no one is taking any chances. The United Nations is to send a representative. ...'

'He's talking through his hat,' Daisy said.

'He's talking loudly, all the same,' Mostyn pointed out.

The last hatches had just been secured when a big Humber drove up alongside the submarine. The civilian who climbed out spoke to a burly man in the uniform of a naval captain who was waiting by the gangway with the ship's commanding officer. Captain Beaufort was a large, square man with a wide, humorous mouth and the calm temperament that was always an asset to a submariner. But now, as the civilian went on talking, he began to look distinctly impatient.

'Who's behind all this?' he demanded.

'Admiralty and Ministry of Defence.' The civilian produced an impressive sheaf of papers, which Beaufort read carefully, his frown deepening.

'I've not heard anything,' he said.

'The Admiral has,' the civilian said. 'I'm sorry. It's nothing to do with me. I didn't make the decision. But I have to inspect the orders. So there can be no mistake. Those are our explicit instructions, and I have the authority to carry them out. I have to make sure nothing leaves the harbour without genuine orders.'

'Of course they're genuine,' Beaufort snapped. 'I authorised them myself.'

'I'm sorry.'

Beaufort jerked a hand at the officer alongside him. 'Do they have to be *his* orders?' he demanded. 'They're supposed to be sealed.' When the civilian shrugged, he went on angrily. 'They were drafted on instructions I received from the Admiral.'

'And *his* orders?'

Beaufort looked startled and then irritated. 'Good God,' he said. 'How far back do we have to go?'

The civilian gestured wearily. 'I didn't make the decision,' he said again.

Beaufort sighed. 'Ship movements,' he explained patiently, 'are controlled by C.-in-C., Fleet at Northwood, who arranges fleet programmes. He takes his orders from the Admiralty Board, who are responsible to the Ministry of Defence. Ministry of Defence is instructed by the government. My instructions came from the Admiral. You can see them, if you wish.'

The civilian nodded. 'Very well. Yours would do.'

The captain of the submarine was waiting quietly, and Beaufort gestured. 'I'll be back,' he said to him.

The Wren officer in the outer office of the Captain's suite was remarkably pretty. Beaufort had never seen any reason why he shouldn't surround himself with attractive girls. Most attractive girls, he'd found, were usually efficient, too. The inefficient ones as often as not were equally inefficient at being attractive.

'I want the Admiral's signal,' he told her.

Two minutes later the file was placed in front of the civilian, who perused the Captain's orders carefully.

'There's no indication of destination,' he said.

'No.' Beaufort's face was expressionless.

'I must know.'

182

'Then you'll have to ask the Admiral. You say he's been informed.'

'Can't *you* give me an idea?'

'Not without instructions to do so. I've shown you the orders and I can vouch for them.' Beaufort turned to the Wren. 'Better put Mr Liversedge through to the Admiral,' he said.

'Will he be there, sir?'

'He will *tonight*. The Admiral can tell him himself then. I suppose *he'll* know why he's here.'

The information turned out to be correct, but the Navy was reserving the right to mind its own business.

'You've seen the newspapers,' the Admiral said. 'You've seen the signal I sent to Captain Beaufort. That will have to do, I'm afraid. Now I'd be glad if your department would release the ship.'

Liversedge sighed. 'Under the circumstances,' he said, 'I can see no reason why not. My instructions were to check, not to interfere. We were concerned only that all orders were genuine. I'm quite satisfied that they are. Thank you.'

As he put the telephone down, he turned to the Captain. 'There appears to be no reason for any further delay,' he said.

Packer met Mostyn as he stopped the big Lancia outside the Vernon's Head Hotel.

'They're still in there,' he said. 'In Dorothea's room.'

Mostyn glanced up at the front of the building. 'What about the switchboard?'

'We put a man on. What telephoning they're doing seems to concern a holiday in Paris.'

'Could be more than a holiday,' Mostyn said. 'It could be that they're preparing to bolt. Pick 'em up if they try it.'

'What do we make the charge?'

'Drunk and disorderly, if you like. I don't give a damn. Just grab 'em. What else? Any ship movements?'

'Liversedge has them. An anti-sub frigate, *Launceston*, bound for the Far East. *Holdfast*, a type 15 converted for anti-sub work, due for Iceland, and *Gladiator* undergoing engine trials.

Launceston and *Holdfast* are lying off Selsey Bill, checking radio, and *Gladiator*'s south of the Isle of Wight. Their orders are quite straightforward. Another frigate, *Warrior*, is due to move out after refitting, for Greenock. *Paladin* bound for Bermuda. Submarine *Archer* due for work-up exercises.'

'Is she watched and checked?'

'As if she were made of gold.'

'That the lot?'

'Apart from *Achates*, to the breakers. She's been due for some time.'

Mostyn was frowning thoughtfully. Then he came to life and turned to Daisy, who was standing nearby, head tucked in the collar of her coat, hands deep in the pockets. Her nose was pink.

'Get in the car, Daisy,' he said.

'Where are we going?'

'We're going to see Daphne Eltney again.'

Chapter Nine

They had set off just before dark, and nobody was saying much because they were all concerned with their own thoughts.

The lorry was painted navy blue and had R.N. plates. Venner sat in front with the driver, wearing a naval cap and the reefer jacket with the two gold rings of a naval lieutenant. The other men, huddled in the back under the canvas cover, all wore working rig, badged according to their rank, and the appropriate white-topped caps of seamen or petty officers. To all intents and purposes, they were a naval party going about their lawful business, their jerseys and oilskins with them.

The vehicle had appeared near the stables three days before, a perfectly normal dark-green ex-Army vehicle, with the chalk-marks of the makers still on its side. How it had been removed from the manufacturers, where it had been returned under contract for disposal, no one was saying. Within twenty-four hours, it had been stripped of its cover and sprayed the dark blue of the Royal Navy. Stencils and R.N. plates had appeared, and now it was a naval lorry.

The operation, whatever it was, Venner thought, had all the hall-marks of being well-planned. The group had been in Haddon's mock-up of *Thunderer*, getting used to their duties, when the ex-U-boat man Tutschek had appeared and explained what they were to do. The following morning they had started work in earnest.

The German was a hearty old pirate, who might have been likeable but for his record. He was a leathery-faced man, with a black beard, streaked with white, a patch over one eye, and a terrible scar that ran down his cheek in a tangle of purple-and-white marks.

'We will now learn how to work a submarine,' he had said cheerfully in the perfect English of a man who had done business all over the world. 'I know we all know, but *I* know best of all, because I was an expert. I have decorations to prove it.' He touched his face. 'Including this. So! By the time we are finished, we shall *all* be experts.'

There had been no difficulties beyond making the foreigners familiar with the English words of command, which Tutschek had at his finger tips. Several times he had turned the operation over to Venner.

'We will now see if *you* are an expert, too, Herr Venner,' he had said.

He had been well satisfied with Venner's knowledge, but had offered no explanations when Venner had probed. 'Navigation, Herr Venner' was all he would say. 'That is what you will be chiefly responsible for. Navigation and trim, because I cannot do everything.'

The other men had responded well. They knew their jobs and they didn't require much teaching. Only Madura, the big Dutchman, seemed to be having second thoughts.

'It is because of my vife,' he had explained gloomily. 'It is because she goes avay vith another man.'

Venner glanced out the window now and saw a sign to Chichester. He had noticed Winchester and Portsmouth signs earlier, and finally the villages through the South Downs. They were obviously making for the coast, but he was puzzled because it was clearly not towards Portsmouth they were heading, but further east. Then he saw the spire of Chichester Cathedral against the sky. They were heading along the by-pass south of the city. A big sign loomed up, THE WITTERINGS, and they turned right, to the coast. Dark houses and trees fled past while a slight drizzle of rain spattered on the windows. The driver, who was someone Venner had never seen before, didn't speak. When Venner had tried to pump him, he'd been told quite firmly that it was none of his business.

They came to a junction by a garage where the road curved right. Venner recognised it. He had driven to the coast past this point more than once with Susie on warm Sundays, and he knew now where they were heading. Soon afterwards, the lorry curved right again. They were heading for Itchenor, a small, fashionable sailing centre in the sweep of water that formed Chichester harbour, handy for Cowes, the Solent, and the Isle of Wight sailing grounds. Just short of the village, the lorry turned into a lane which swept in an arc to the shore, and finally ran into the yard of a large house.

'Vhere are ve?' Inevitably, it was the Dutchman.

'Seaside, mate,' Lemon answered in a jaunty way. 'It's bank holiday. We always go to the seaside at bank holiday in this country.'

'Vhy do ve come here?'

'Make sand castles. Or don't you make sand castles in that mud-heap you call a country?'

Two men appeared from the shadows, one of whom stationed himself at the back of the lorry to see that no one got out. No one tried to. They had all been well briefed. After a while a third man came and told them to climb out. They were led past the house and down a garden path to an uneven wooden jetty. There was a big clinker-built boat lying at the end, its engine running quietly.

'Get aboard!'

They climbed into the boat, crowding towards the stern. A man was standing at the wheel. Alongside him was another man, bearded, in oilskins. His face was in darkness, but Venner recognised him at once as Tutschek.

'Nobody will do anything until he is told to do it,' he said over his shoulder. 'Then you will act at once and without argument.'

'I do not like this,' Madura said stolidly.

No one took any notice of him and as the helmsman moved the throttles, the boat started forward. A few moments later, Venner saw the lights of the lorry vanish among the trees. Then a slash of spray hit him in the face, and he decided that wherever they were going it was likely to be a wet journey. Almost at once, however, the engine note died. They

187

were moving up astern of a big grey-painted vessel. He recognised it as an ex-naval M.F.V., and guessed it had been chosen because it might still be mistaken for a naval tender.

As the two boats bumped, Tutschek turned. 'Get aboard!' he said.

There were several men in oilskins on the M.F.V. already and when everyone had climbed to the deck, one of them pushed open a cabin door. 'Get below!' he ordered.

They went below, and the door was closed behind them. Through the porthole, Venner could see one of the men on deck changing all the life-belts on the side of the cabin round. One side bore the name *Leeway*. The other side was blank, naval fashion.

Tutschek, who had taken off his oilskins, was wearing a uniform with four gold rings on the sleeve. Even as Venner watched, he put on a cap with the scrambled eggs of a naval captain. The other men were wearing naval caps, too, now. While Venner was wondering what was going on, he heard the boat's big engines start and saw that a white ensign was fluttering from the stern.

The lights ashore moved as the big boat surged forward. An hour later, with the deck lifting and spray slashing against the portholes, they were beyond the bar and butting into the rising black waves a mile offshore. There had been little conversation beyond a few speculations as to what they were about to do. The men were inclined to be silent.

'God,' Lemon said. 'I couldn't half do a drink.'

'What the hell are the bastards up to?' McAvoy asked.

Lemon grinned. All naval parties had to have a funny man, and clearly Lemon was the funny man of this one. 'We're going to steal *Victory*,' he said.

Bonser jeered. 'Go on! We're submariners. Since when was *Victory* a submersible?'

'Didn't you know?' Lemon chuckled. 'That's how Nelson won the Battle of Trafalgar. I can tell you, he had the French puzzled.'

The conversation was the usual hearty chit-chat, light-hearted and blasphemous.

The M.F.V.'s movements altered from a steady butting rise and fall to a lurching roll as they heard the engines change their note.

'Hello!' Lemon shoved his face against the porthole. 'We've stopped.'

The engine noise had died away now, and the boat was wallowing in the dark water, the waves slapping at the chine with a monotonous sound. The cabin had a damp, misty look about it. A tin placed as an ashtray on the deck rolled backwards and forwards with a maddening clanking noise, while an oilskin hanging on the bulkhead swung in stiff jerky arcs. Lemon's cigarette smoke moved in a curiously erratic fashion to the roll of the boat.

There was silence. Then a voice came from the wheelhouse. 'There she is!'

'So!' The voice was Tutschek's. 'Call the shore.'

After a moment's silence, Venner heard the first voice obviously speaking into a microphone. 'We see her. We see her. We are in position. You can call her up now. I repeat. You can call her up now.'

The submarine had just passed the Langstone Bar Light off Hayling Island, the waves breaking against her saddle tanks as her bow dipped in the choppy sea, which lashed the fin with spray. In addition to the C.-in-C. and the Flag Officer, Submarines, her departure had been watched by Beaufort, the Admiral's chief of staff, the Admiral Superintendent of the Dockyard, and senior officials. The ninety-degree turn from Haslar Creek into the main channel round 'Promotion Point' had been accomplished in the last of the daylight with a flair which had not been slapdash.

As she had swung, the last rays of the sun catching her fin, a man watching with binoculars from an attic in Old Portsmouth had turned and picked up the microphone of a walkie-talkie.

189

'She's leaving now,' he had said.

The submarine had continued her turn round the point towards Stokes Bay, on the other side of the spit of land, where an M.F.V. waited with a heavy-browed lifting vessel. As she drew alongside them, the men on her bridge went below, and air began to bubble to the surface around her, turning the sea to boiling foam as she began to submerge. The officers on the bridge of the lifting vessel saw her slowly sink lower in the water and finally disappear.

'They're welcome to it,' one of them said.

They stood watching, their glasses in their hands, for any sign of trouble. Twenty minutes later, the water began to heave again as the submarine surfaced. Swinging, she turned her bow eastward. The man who had appeared on her bridge waved to the lifting vessel.

As she moved away, her exhaust smoke streaming behind her in the spray from her wake, a man on a cabin crusier just heading into Portsmouth near Gilkicker Point pressed the switch of an old Army radio. 'She dived,' he reported. 'She's up again now and moving east.'

Unaware that they had been watched, the men on the bridge of the submarine kept their eyes ahead in the growing darkness. Their duties lay with their own vessel, not with cabin cruisers that might be watching them. Because the vessel was in the hands of an expert, no one ashore was worried as she moved south-eastwards, leaving Ryde pier and the submarine escape tower at Gosport behind. The lights of Southsea fun fair lit the sky as the dark vessel moved on quietly, the crew settling down now to their jobs, hardly aware of the motion of the deck in the choppy water of the Solent.

The radio receiver started banging out a signal. The sub-lieutenant watching the antics of a couple of white mice in a cage stuffed incongruously against the bulkhead near the navigating table in the control room looked up.

Leading Telegraphist White, in the W/T office behind the ship's receiver, began to write automatically, as he stuck his head out and called to the Captain. 'Sir! Signal!'

190

It was in clear and it read: 'Job Chapter Seven. Verses nine and ten. Good luck.'

The sub-lieutenant turned a few pages of the battered Bible he already held in his hand. 'Felt sure they'd come up with one of those, under the circumstances.' He grinned. ' "*As* the cloud is consumed and vanisheth away: so he that goeth down to the grave shall come up no *more*. He shall return no more to his house, neither shall his place know him any more." '

'Apt,' the Captain said.

'Makes you wonder where they find them.'

The Bible had just been put away in the wardroom when the set started sounding again. This time it belted out unexpectedly loudly, with all the imperious blast of a powerful shore station not more than a few miles away. White had to turn down the volume control.

He noticed at once that the operator was different from the man who had sent the good-luck message. Any man used to Morse could recognise another man's 'handwriting' from the way he hit the key. The signal they'd received as they'd reached the Langstone Bar Light had been sent with all of Nobby Clark's usual élan. White knew Clark well and knew he had a gift for Morse and liked to show off. This man was not in the same class. He was correct, a little slower, and without any of Clark's flair; it was almost, the radioman decided, as though he were a bit rusty. Probably some petty officer who'd taken over for some reason and was out of practice. This seemed more than likely with all the high-rating prefixes that were coming through and the secrecy that had attended their departure.

The procedure and prefixes finished with, the message started, coming out in a way to blast his eardrums. When he realised it was coming through in clear again, he put his head out of his cabin and called the sub-lieutenant.

'Another signal, sir! Addressed to the Captain. Coming through in clear.'

The Captain was in the control room within half a minute, and the sub-lieutenant handed over the flimsy at once. The

Captain looked at it, frowning. The message was from the C.-in-C., Fleet, and appeared to have originated at the Admiralty. It was marked 'Most Urgent'.

ORDERS CANCELLED, he read. CHANGE IN DESTINATION. RENDEZVOUS MFV BULWARK ENTRANCE CHICHESTER HARBOUR. A position followed. The message continued: NEW ORDERS BY HAND. ONLY COMMANDING OFFICER TO BE PRESENT ON CASING.

He stared at the message, then glanced at the chart. 'Almost too damn late,' he said. 'We're dead on position already. Stop engines. Stand by.' He picked up the intercom telephone. 'Captain to bridge: Keep a sharp look-out for an M.F.V.! I'm coming up.'

There was silence aboard the M.F.V. as they all eyed each other, their bodies moving to the lurch and slide of the vessel with the lop of the waves. Then a harsh voice, which seemed to come from a loud-speaker, sounded through the bulkhead again.

'The message has been received and acknowledged. You may go ahead. I repeat, you may go ahead.'

'Good.' Tutschek spoke sharply. 'She has stopped.' After a moment's silence, Tutschek said, 'Switch on the lights. Start up.'

There was a thump from astern as the engines turned. They felt the boat's motion lessen as the propellers gripped the water and the M.F.V. swung into the waves.

On the faces of the men about him, Venner could read a variety of emotions: anxiety, speculation, even fear.

Lemon took a deep drag at his cigarette, threw it down, and screwed it out against the deck with his foot. Then he seemed to glance down at the leading seaman's badges he wore, his expression faintly puzzled. As he lifted his head, he saw Venner's eyes on him, and that wide, sly smile that had so worried Second Officer Margaret Pratt slid across his wide mouth.

'Well,' he said, his voice unsteady. ' 'Ere we go.'

192

Chapter Ten

At H.M.S. *Dolphin*, on the little tongue of land that stretched into the Solent from the western side of the entrance to Portsmouth harbour, a puzzled radio operator was staring at his log book, startled by what he'd written down. He turned and called to the chief petty officer working at the table behind him.

C. P. O. Rawbone lifted his head.

'What the hell do you make of this, Chief?'

Rawbone rose from his table and crossed the room to look at the signal. 'Keep listening,' he said.

Leading Telegraphist Clark copied the message on a signal pad as his other hand moved over the dials of his set. Rawbone took the message he'd scribbled and headed from the radio room. In the corridor he knocked on a door marked 'Lt. Phemister' and went in.

The Communications Officer looked up. 'What is it, Chief?'

'I dunno, sir,' Rawbone said. 'But it seems damn funny to me. Clark picked this up.'

Lieutenant Phemister looked at the flimsy. ' "Orders cancelled," ' he read aloud. ' "Change in destination..." ' What the hell is this?' He frowned. 'It originated at the Admiralty,' he said.

Rawbone shrugged. 'That's what Clark handed to me, sir.'

Phemister pushed back his chair. 'Let's go and see Clark,' he said.

The wave length was quiet when they arrived, but Clark was still moving the dials gently, trying to pick up the mysterious signaller again.

'What's this, Clark?'

The radio operator his ears tuned to his set, turned in his

seat. 'I picked it up, sir,' he said. 'That's just as I got it.'

'Where did it come from?'

'I dunno, sir. It was originated by C.-in-C., Fleet, and was marked "Most Urgent".'

'Did they acknowledge?'

'Yes, sir.' Clark pushed his log book forward to be examined. 'Straight away. It's all down, sir.'

Phemister read the book and frowned again. 'Think it could be some amateur arsing about, Chief?'

'If it is, sir, he's got the prefixes and procedure right.'

'We'd better have a fix on him and haul him in,' Phemister said. 'The bastard should be in jail. He's using naval prefixes he ought not to know. I'll see the Old Man.'

The Chief Communications Officer, Lieutenant-Commander Witty, was sipping a cup of coffee in his office, waiting for the evening's operation to be wrapped up so he could go home. He wasn't normally on duty late at night, not with a perfectly capable officer to deal with anything that came in, but, because of the importance of the occasion, the Admiralty had insisted on all senior officers being present. Even the Admiral was on tap. Witty was just beginning to eye his cap behind the door when the telephone rang. Moving slowly, because he was a big man and a little overweight, he picked it up. As he listened, Phemister appeared, apparently about to burst with excitement.

'Sir—!'

The voice in Witty's ear sounded angry and a little alarmed. He held up a hand to silence the eager Phemister. As he continued to listen, his placid expression changed and his broad features tightened. 'I'll look into it at once,' he said, and slammed the instrument down.

'Sir—!' Phemister started forward again immediately.

'Spit it out, Phemister,' Witty said. 'What's happened? I've just had the C.-in-C.'s office on the phone.'

Phemister thrust the signal at him. 'It's this, sir! We've just picked it up!'

Witty stared at the flimsy and began barking questions. Phemister had all the answers, because he'd just asked the same questions himself of Rawbone.

'The C.-in-C.'s office picked it up, too,' Witty said. 'They claim it didn't come from them. Did they acknowledge?'

'Yes, sir. No reason why not. It's all in order.'

'How about the operator? Not the sort to have a brain-storm and start hearing things, is he?'

'Not a chance sir. It's Clark – the best we have. You put him up for promotion yourself, and he was put on tonight specially.'

'Let's have a word with him.'

By the time they reached Clark's side, he and the Chief were both listening, their heads bent.

'What the hell's the bastard havering about?' Rawbone was saying. Then he saw Witty behind him and straightened up quickly. 'He's there again, sir,' he said. 'But he's sending pure gibberish now.'

'Have we got a fix on him?' Witty demanded.

'Doing it now, sir.'

'Hurry it up, and then tell him for Christ's sake to get off the air.'

Rawbone looked puzzled. 'How do we address him, sir?' he asked. 'He's using *our* call sign.'

Glaring, Witty said, 'Get off a signal, then, telling them that his message isn't to be obeyed.'

'Not that easy, sir! The bastard's hogging the wave band; we can't get in. He's got a powerful transmitter. He's just confusing our signals.'

'What the hell's he doing?' Witty demanded. 'Who's he talking to?'

'Nobody in particular, sir. There was just a whole array of call signs. Devonport. *Vernon. Daedalus. Centurion.* Lee-on-Solent. Whale Island. As though he was sending to everybody who came into his head. Even one or two Army call signs. Aldershot and Salisbury, for instance.'

'What's he sending?'

195

'God knows, sir. Just plain bloody rubbish. Almost as if he's trying to keep us from raising 'em again.'

A leading seaman appeared at Witty's side. 'Here's the fix, sir,' he said. 'It appears to come from Itchenor somewhere.'

'Itchenor, for God's sake!' Witty looked startled. 'There isn't a station anywhere near *there*!'

'It's been checked, sir.'

'Get a detector van down there!' Witty turned to Phemister. 'And inform the police. There's something bloody fishy going on.' He swung round to Rawbone. 'Raise 'em again as soon as this bastard stops sending. Tell 'em that message is not – repeat not – to be obeyed. Write it out in clear, and I'll authorise it. I'll get in touch with the Captain.'

By the time Rawbone pushed the new message at Clark, several more minutes had passed. 'Here,' he said. 'Give 'em that as soon as this bastard dries up. And make sure they acknowledge.'

Unfortunately, they were already too late. The mysterious signal had been too carefully timed. Even as it was being acknowledged, the big M.F.V. loomed up out of the darkness, almost on the spot where the submarine had shut down her engines.

'By God,' the submarine's captain said admiringly, 'somebody's efficient, for a change. Right on the button.'

As the submarine's searchlight snapped on, illuminating the water and lighting the tips of the waves, so that they shone green and transparent, a rubber dinghy powered by an outboard motor bumped softly against the saddle tanks. The four men in it all appeared to be carrying canvas bags. Whatever the orders were to be, they looked bulky. A bearded officer with gold leaves on his cap was clutching a brief case that looked big enough to carry the Encyclopaedia Britannica.

'No one else on the casing,' the Captain said, diving for the hatch, 'except for one seaman.'

The hatch in the fin was open now, and a seaman was already stepping into the glare of the light. As he followed

196

him, the Captain wondered at the elaborate artifice Their Lordships of the Admiralty were showing merely to hand him new orders. Knowing the nature of his cargo, he could only believe it was considered so important that these precautions had been carefully thought out and put into motion. After all, the officer in the dinghy, he could see now, was a full captain, no less.

The seaman on the casing grabbed the dinghy's painter, and the bearded captain scrambled aboard.

'We'd better go to your cabin,' he said, returning the submarine commander's salute.

The latter indicated the hatchway in the fin.

'Anybody in there?'

'Just one of the crew.'

'Send him below.'

The submariner decided that the Navy was going to extraordinary lengths for secrecy, but he complied.

'What about up there?' The bearded captain indicated the bridge ladder.

'First Lieutenant, sir, and one look-out.'

'No one else?'

'No, sir.'

'Right.' The newcomer gestured at the hatchway. 'We'll go into the fin, and I'll explain. There's been a big change of plan. The Prime Minister's had a hand in this.'

The submariner led the way into the fin.

'Change to motors,' the bearded captain said. 'Close the lower hatch. And be quick about it.'

The submarine's captain was growing more intrigued by the urgency and the continued secrecy, but he did as he was told. Stepping into the wind-tunnel draught of air roaring down from the bridge as it was sucked in by the pounding diesels, he gave the appropriate orders to the officer below. As the repeater telegraphs clanged, the electrician on duty in the motor room leapt to the main switches, while the mechanics in the engine room flung themselves at the engines. The rush of air down the shaft of the fin stopped, and the submariner

197

dropped the hatch. In the control room below, the sub-lieutenant looked up at it. 'Talk about cloak and dagger,' he said to the engineer officer who had appeared in the control room to find out what was happening.

As the submarine commander straightened up, above their heads, the bearded captain was behind him, and he didn't even see the silenced Luger that killed him. He slumped quietly across the lid of the hatch without a sound.

Tutschek dropped the bag he'd brought on board and, shoving the pistol out of sight, began to climb the ladder to the bridge. The First Lieutenant, huddled in his spray-wet bridge suit, was surprised to see the gold-braided cap appear through the upper hatch, but he concluded that his commanding officer was by the lower hatch studying his orders and that this captain was probably an old submariner come to have a look round. Because of the noise of the wind and the slap of the water, he had not heard the soft thump of the silenced gun by the lower hatch. Now, he saw no more than a gleam of metal before he, too, died. The look-out, who was studiously facing the other way so that he couldn't be accused of listening to the officers' conversation, didn't even have *that* pleasure.

Immediately, Tutschek leaned over the bridge coaming to shout to the men on the casing. With the smack of waves near his feet and the buffeting of the wind, the seaman by the dinghy painter had also failed to hear the soft thumps of the Luger and had failed to notice that he could no longer see the First Lieutenant on the bridge above him. He came to attention as a man from the dinghy in a commander's uniform approached. It was the last thing he did. As the officer turned and headed for the fin, one of the other men pushed the sea-man's body from the casing. It bumped heavily on the saddle tanks and rolled into the sea.

The helmsman of the M.F.V., who was watching the scene, saw the other men from the dinghy begin to scramble into the submarine's fin with their canvas bags. He turned to speak to the man alongside him.

'They're in control,' he said. 'Call the shore. Tell them they can stop sending. And then get the other lot across.'

No more than five minutes had elapsed since the rendezvous signal had been received aboard the submarine. When a second powered dinghy full of men left the M.F.V., the men from the first were already out of sight inside the fin. Below them, in the control room, the sub-lieutenant heard the hatch cover being lifted and felt the cold bite of night air again. Navy-clad legs descended the ladder, and, to his suprise, he saw they did not belong to his commanding officer, but to another man, in a captain's uniform and wearing a beard. He snapped to attention. The captain was followed by another officer, with the three rings of a commander, and two petty officers, all carrying canvas bags.

The whole operation had taken no more than seven minutes, and Leading Telegraphist White was again bent over the set. For several minutes he had been listening to what he had assumed was a Royal Navy signal station transmitting in-decipherable nonsense, almost blasting his eardrums and drowning all other signals, but now suddenly it had stopped, and he was picking up Nobby Clark in Portsmouth loud and clear once more. He stared at what he'd written for a second. Then he yanked off his headphones and put his head out of his office to call the officer of the watch.

The man in the commander's uniform, who was alongside the door, put a Luger against the back of White's neck.

'Sir—!' White had time to get out only that one word before the trigger was pulled and he fell from the office to the deck of the control room with a crash.

The young sub-lieutenant was shocked into immobility. The engineer officer, a man of greater experience and confidence, stepped forward, but one of the men in petty officer's uniform hit him behind the ear. He, too, slipped to the deck without a sound. The helmsman and the other men at the submarine's controls swung round in alarm and found themselves staring into the muzzles of machine pistols.

Seven miles away, Chief Petty Officer Rawbone stood

behind Leading Telegraphist Clark's chair, waiting, his eyes bewildered. Behind him, Phemister stood with the Chief Communications Officer.

'Anything, son?' Rawbone asked.

Clark shook his head. 'She acknowledged receipt,' he said. 'That's all. That was ten minutes ago.'

Rawbone looked down at the signal in front of Clark. IGNORE REPEAT IGNORE MY 2150 SIGNAL STOP NOT SENT FROM THIS STATION ACKNOWLEDGE IMMEDIATELY.

'They'll be coming up in a second,' Clark said.

Witty glanced at Phemister. 'What about that other damn station?'

'Disappeared,' Phemister said. 'Suddenly dried up. We haven't heard a cheep since.'

'What about the detector van?'

'It's on its way, sir. And the police have been informed. They'll have a job finding him, though, unless he starts sending again.'

Witty looked grim. In all his naval career he'd never before come across a case of an unknown shore station sending movement orders to naval ships with naval prefixes.

'Any minute now,' Clark said, licking his lips.

There was a long silence.

'You're sure they acknowledged receipt, lad?' Rawbone asked.

'Yes, Chief. It was them, all right. It was Chalky White, Chief. I know his fist. They're bound to come up again in a second.'

There was another long silence.

'Send again, Chief,' Witty said.

'Right, sir.' Rawbone leaned down to Clark. 'Send it again, Nobby.'

Clark nodded, and his hand began to flutter over the key. There was no response.

He tried again. Again there was no response.

'He's not coming up, Chief,' he said.

'Check everything, then give it him again, lad. Slower. Nice and deliberate, so he can't miss it. They're probably having trouble.'

They were indeed having trouble. The men in the control room had been joined by the men from the fore-ends, the cook, and the officers' steward. There weren't many of them because they were a reduced crew. Now they had been backed up against the bulkhead.

The intercom squawked. 'Bridge here,' the voice said. 'Our people are all aboard. Have you got your men posted?'

'All posted.'

'Send the crew up.'

Meyer, in the commander's uniform, turned and gestured with his pistol at the submariners. 'Up you go,' he said.

Unwillingly, the men began to pull themselves up the ladder. Though they were the crew of what was probably the deadliest of modern weapons, the individual men were unarmed, and they climbed reluctantly, bitter and angry. Just above them, by the lower hatch, another man was waiting with a machine pistol, and he directed them through the door to the casing.

Standing in a group on the wet deck, near where a couple of rubber dinghies bobbed, was another group of men, all dressed in naval working rig, jerseys, oilskins, and caps, and a naval captain, with a white-streaked beard, in full uniform. Thirty yards away in the darkness they could just make out a big M.F.V. wallowing in the sea.

'All right, get below,' Tutschek said to the newcomers, who began to push inside the fin.

The machine pistols jerked. 'Into the dinghy,' Tutschek said.

The original crew climbed into one of the dinghies. It was crowded and dangerously low in the water. Tutschek cast off the painter.

'All you have to do is stay afloat until morning,' he said. 'Someone will find you.'

As the dinghy drifted away from the side of the submarine, the men in it realised that the M.F.V. was swinging round and heading for the mouth of Chichester harbour. They were alone on the dark sea.

'It's no good, Chief,' Clark said at last. 'They're not acknowledging.'

Lieutenant-Commander Witty rubbed his nose, made a dive for the telephone, and pressed a button.

'Ops room!'

'Chief Communications Officer here. We seem to be having trouble. Have you still got Operation Peardrop on your screen.'

'Hang on, sir.'

After a short silence, the voice came back. 'Yes, sir, she's right there. Off the mouth of Chichester harbour. She's been stopped for some time. According to our instructions, she shouldn't be.'

'No, by God,' Witty said, 'she damn well shouldn't! There's been some damn funny radio traffic going on. She's been told to stop. But not by us.'

'C.-in-C., perhaps, sir?'

'Not on their radio.' Slamming down the telephone, Witty crossed to where Phemister and Rawbone waited by Clark.

'You sure, Clark?' Rawbone was asking.

'Not a whisper, Chief.'

The Chief turned to Phemister, who swung round to Witty. But Witty had heard.

'Never mind now,' he said. 'Get Captain Beaufort.'

'He was dining out, sir. He left a telephone number.'

'Then ring it, damn it! I've got to speak to him. Something's wrong. We appear to have lost *Achates*.'

Part III

Chapter One

Just as the telephone was ringing at the house where Captain Beaufort was dining, Mostyn's car was heading towards the docks. His visit to Daphne Eltney had not produced much.

'No,' she had insisted wearily, 'Jimmy Nanjizel never mentioned any ships' names. That other chap – Jimmy Venner – he kept coming and coming.' It was news to Mostyn, and he didn't fail to notice the first name. 'I kept on telling him the same thing. The only thing Jimmy Nanjizel ever mentioned was that old tub he was stripping down.'

Mostyn was silent as they drove into Portsmouth. Daisy sat alongside him, pawing through a *Hampshire Telegraph and Naval Chronicle* Mostyn had bought as they'd entered the outskirts of the city, in the hope that its column on ships' movements might indicate a lead.

'*Achates*,' she said. 'Isn't that the submarine Nanjizel was working on?'

'That's right,' Mostyn said. 'She's due for the breakers.'

'No.' Daisy shook her head. 'It's not that.' Her finger ran down the narrow column of naval appointments. 'It's got a new commanding officer – a Lieutenant-Commander H. St. J. Addams.'

'*Who*?' Mostyn's head jerked round.

'Addams. It's in the lieutenant-commanders' list – H. St. J. Addams.'

The car slowed noticeably. 'I know him,' Mostyn said sharply. 'Admiral Addams's son. Got the caste mark of high promotion on his forehead. The Appointments Board must be off its chump sending *him* to a clapped-out old ship going to the breakers' yard. A sub-lieutenant with a couple of good petty officers under him could have done the job as well.'

He was still puzzling over it when the car radio, which had been softly playing music, changed to the news. He had kept it on only in case of a flash message, because he was *expecting* a flash message, certain that the next forty-eight hours would produce something that would have them all on their toes. The first words brought him bolt upright in his seat, reaching for the volume control.

'The Prime Minister announced in the House tonight,' the voice said, 'that containers of the over-produced X gas from Ewerton had been placed aboard the old submarine *Achates* in Portsmouth, and that he had received confirmation that she had left the quayside for an unknown destination in the South Atlantic. The announcement stated that the news of the operation – known as Operation Peardrop – had been left until so late to prevent trouble from the organisations which had been staging noisy demonstrations at Ewerton for some months.'

Mostyn pulled the car over to the curb and turned the volume up again.

'This it?' Daisy whispered.

He didn't appear to hear her.

'The gas, the Prime Minister said, had been sealed into specially built pressure containers which had been transported secretly from Ewerton under heavy Army and police guard to the submarine base at Gosport. *Achates*, damaged last year by an explosion, had been due to go to the breakers' yard, and had been stripped of all her weapons systems. Since X gas has a life of only ten years, and submarines have been raised in good watertight condition twenty years after sinking, the Prime Minister said, it was considered that no more suitable container could have been found. The loss to the country's revenue of the scrap value of *Achates*, he went on, was nothing compared with the knowledge that the gas had been safely disposed of. The submarine will be escorted by a Royal Navy frigate to the position of sinking, which is to take place near one of the Atlantic deeps. The depot ship *Commando* will meet her there and take off the crew after the sea cocks have been opened. The Leader of the Opposition expressed his satisfaction at the secrecy of the operation.'

Mostyn was quiet as he turned down the volume and started the car again, moving in a deliberate fashion that told Daisy he was worried. Then he jammed his foot down on the accelerator, shot past a lorry heading into the city, swung violently round a sports car driven by a young man with long hair, who looked terrified as he hurtled past, and began to roar southwards again.

'Right!' Daisy screamed. 'Right!'

The car screeched round the corner and headed west towards the docks. Mostyn was scowling. The thing was obvious now, he thought. *Achates* was the answer to the whole thing! That was why Nanjizel had been approached, why he could think of nothing but 'the old tub' he was stripping. Someone had known all along that *Achates* was to be used for the gas. She was the perfect container, as the Prime Minister had said. That was what she was built for. They had been watching the wrong submarines all the time, keeping their eyes on the big nuclear vessels, when, all along, the target had been the oldest and most valueless submersible in the Navy.

This was why the mock-up of *Thunderer* had been so valuable. By all the normal standards, it was out of date, but for Latisse's use it was perfect – *Achates* was just an improvement on *Thunderer* – and was why someone as old as Galbraith, in Princetown, would have had his value. In addition to being a navigator, he could handle *Achates*'s power plant, even if he didn't know a damn thing about *Resolution* and *Jellicoe* and the new nuclear ships.

But how had Latisse discovered that *Achates* was to be used? Aubrey, of course! That whey-faced, limp-legged son of a bitch! He'd been feeding information on the gas to the Home Office all along. The whole thing suddenly began to fit together, as though the last missing piece in a jigsaw had dropped into place. It followed the pattern. What had a man to hide? Who could twist his arm? Where did he get his money? Aubrey belonged to an expensive intellectual club, though his income wasn't the sort that went with it, and he was clearly the link between Ewerton and Latisse, via Dorothea Holcombe and her brother, who was 'one of those'.

He'd been cleared for security, Mostyn knew, but it looked as though the security boys had boobed again. The spitefulness, the pale, fleshy face and the podgy white hands, and the secretive, almost old-maidenly jealousy he showed over the affairs of his department all seemed to fit.

The car screeched to a stop at the barrier of H.M.S. *Vernon*, which was the first naval establishment they came to. The naval sentry, smart in white cap, belt, and gaiters, stepped forward.

'Pass, sir,' he demanded.

'I must see Captain, Submarines,' Mostyn snapped.

'You need Fort Blockhouse, sir,' the sentry said. 'You go round by Gosport.'

Mostyn gestured irritably. 'That'll take hours. I've got to get a boat laid on.'

The sentry decided Mostyn was a nut case and kept the barrier firmly down. 'Sorry, sir,' he said. 'You can't come in here without a pass.'

Mostyn dragged out his pass. It was impressive by any standards, but it wasn't the one the sentry was expecting to see.

'Sorry, sir,' he said.

'Look, what I want to see him about is a matter of great moment to him.'

'Sorry, sir.' The sentry was young, pink-faced, and looked like a schoolboy, but he was heavy with strapped and gaitered authority and he wasn't budging an inch.

Mostyn sighed, trapped by the precautions he himself had insisted on. He climbed from the car. 'Perhaps I can use your telephone,' he said.

Looking round the stripped control room of *Achates*, Venner was wondering why it was the oldest submersible that they'd taken over, the least valuable, the least saleable. She didn't

208

seem a good prospect for a man like Latisse, because, even if he found a customer for her, it would cost a fortune to put back the weapons systems that would make her a threat. He decided they must be going to use her to run guns or heroin, then he remembered she wasn't cleared for diving and he was left as puzzled as when he'd started.

Battened down on the M.F.V., the new crew had not seen the murder of the men on the submarine, and they were standing about the control room at a loss what to do, their faces pale and strained, when Tutschek jerked a hand.

'McAvoy, Arteguy – engine room! The rest of you know where to go!'

Awkwardly, the men moved to their positions: Ekke to the helm, Bonser to the foreplanes, Luck to the afterplanes, Madura to the blowing panel, Venner to the chart table, where, incongruously, he found at his feet two white mice in a cage. What were they were doing, he wondered. It was sixty years since submariners had carried mice to warn them of escaping chlorine gas.

As Lemon settled himself in the W/T office, Tutschek took up a position by the periscope. 'So!' he said. 'Radio operator, first of all we will find out what the B.B.C. has to say. I think we will have it connected to the Tannoy. You can do that?'

Lemon nodded. 'Yes,' he said. 'I reckon so.'

As they waited, Tutschek signed to Meyer, who produced a roll of charts from one of the canvas bags and laid them before Venner.

'A course, Herr Venner,' Tutschek said. 'To Cap de la Hague. Then past the north side of the Channel Islands as close as it's safe, and by Roches Douvres, Sept Iles, and along the coast round by the Ile d'Ouessant, Pointe de St Mathieu, and Pointe du Raz.'

'Hugging the shore a bit, aren't you?' Venner said.

Tutschek smiled. 'That is exactly what I want to do,' he pointed out.

A breathless and angry Mostyn was ushered into Beaufort's office at last.

The Captain's normally cheerful disposition had been considerably tested by Liversedge's insistence on examining *Achates*'s orders, and he'd been thrown into an icy fury by what he'd heard from Lieutenant-Commander Witty.

'She's gone off the air,' he said in answer to Mostyn's questions. 'We can't raise her. We've been waiting ever since the signal was sent for that radio station to transmit again so we can take another fix on it and pin it down, and find out who the devil they are. There's nothing else we can do unless they do start, and it seems to me they won't. Their job seems to have been finished. They were there only to stop *Achates*. What happened after that we don't know. *Holdfast*'s moving in to investigate.'

Mostyn was guessing wildly, but he knew his guesses were good ones. 'I've got good reason to believe,' he said, 'that *Achates* has been taken over.'

Beaufort's jaw dropped. 'Taken over, for God's sake! People don't take over H.M. submarines!'

'People have taken over this one,' Mostyn insisted. 'Or can you offer any other explanation for the message and the silence since?'

Beaufort couldn't. But he was no fool, and was ready with ideas. 'If she *has* been taken over,' he said, 'they've picked the wrong place to do it. Radar shows she's still in the Solent. She isn't clear until she passes Selsey Bill.'

He turned to a chart of the area on the wall and indicated small red-capped pins stuck into it. His hand moved over the Isle of Wight to a point just off the entrance to Chichester harbour. That's where I place her,' he said.

Mostyn studied the chart. 'Can't we bottle her in?'

'By God we can! I've already contacted the C.-in-C. and sent off a signal to *Holdfast* and *Gladiator*. *Launceston* was actually due to escort her south. It was sheer bloody luck that *Holdfast* was there. I've suggested *Launceston* moves up towards *Holdfast* to narrow the gap between them.'

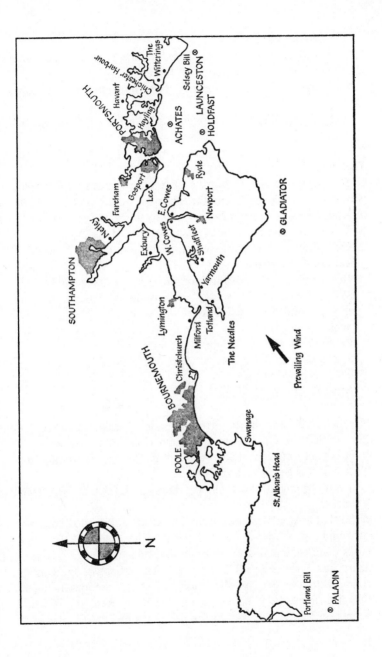

'What about the other end?'

'I've also sent a signal to *Paladin*. She's off Portland Bill about now, on passage to the West Indies.'

'Have *Holdfast* and *Launceston* been informed what to look for?'

'They have indeed. They ought to have her on their screens by now.'

They had.

'She's right there,' *Holdfast*'s Operations Room Officer said, pointing with his finger to the phosphorescent green blob on the radar screen. 'That's *Launceston* to the right.'

'What's all the fuss about?' his deputy asked.

'God knows. We were just told to watch her, and not – repeat not – to lose her.'

'But we're due to move in half an hour. Up to Iceland.'

'Well, if she moves south, we'll probably have to go the long way round. Via the South Pole.'

'What's going on?'

'God knows. But she's right there. Stopped.'

'She ought to have passed us a quarter of an hour ago. What's she stopped for?'

'Must be having trouble.'

She certainly was having trouble, but it wasn't the sort of trouble that the Ops Room Officer on *Holdfast* envisaged.

They had not yet had word from the engine room, and Tutschek was gesturing angrily.

'What's going on back there?' he said. 'Call them up, Herr Venner.'

'Sir!' The reaction was automatic and unintended, but the surroundings made it seem normal. The smell of fuel oil, grease, and damp was all too familiar, and had made Venner's heart jerk awkwardly. The cramped atmosphere of the control room, with the two polished tubes of the periscopes rising to the fin, filled him with nostalgia, which even the missing panels on the bulkheads and the hanging wires didn't change.

He picked up the telephone and called the engine room. There was a click.

'Engine room.'

'Control here. What's the delay?'

'A slight argument. All settled now. Our people are in control. They'll be coming out in a moment, but McAvoy's causing trouble.'

'How long?' Tutschek demanded.

'In a minute,' Venner said. 'McAvoy's unhappy with the engines. He says they're old.'

'So am I! Hurry! Hurry! We're taking too long!'

The Ops Room Officer on *Holdfast* had been joined now by the ship's captain. 'She's still stationary, sir,' he said.

As he spoke, a signal flimsy arrived. It was hard to read in the darkened operations room. The Captain moved to his chair and switched on a small shaded light.

'What do we do, sir,' the Ops Room Officer asked, 'if she begins to move off the screen.'

'We follow her.'

'South, sir?'

'Wherever she goes.'

The Captain had finished reading the message and he crossed back to the radar screen. 'There's something damn funny going on,' he said. 'We're not to allow her to pass now.'

'Not allow her to pass, sir?'

'Those are the orders. They're emphatic and quite distinct.'

'How do we stop her, sir?'

'I don't suppose it includes firing on her. They've gone to *Launceston*, too, though, and they've called *Paladin* back and put *her* in the chase.'

'They'll enjoy that,' the Ops Room Officer said.

On board *Paladin*, heading west through the darkness, everyone had been expecting a quiet night. To the north, land was just visible in the form of occasional lights and a dark loom against the sky. The wind brought flurries of drizzle on the

213

prevailing wind from the south-east, rattling against the bridge and sweeping on beyond the ship to wet the roofs in little Dorset towns like Abbotsbury and Lyme Regis.

The Officer of the Watch was thinking of his wife. He was only recently married, and the last time he'd been in the West Indies, as a free agent, there had been an American girl as eager as he had been, and for a horrible moment he found himself thinking, 'What have I done?'

The Communications Officer appeared alongside him. 'This'll shake you,' he said.

The Officer of the Watch stared at the signal that was thrust into his hand, and all at once he didn't know whether to be glad or disappointed.

'Captain's going to be pleased,' the Communications Officer said. 'He's sent his wife off to the South of France for two months to friends. When he gets home he's going to have to cook for himself.'

'Better dig him out,' the Officer of the Watch said.

Three minutes later, the able seaman on look-out on the port side was startled as the deck heeled abruptly. Then he became aware that the revolutions from the engines had increased. The bow of *Paladin* was lifting out of the water, the stern dragged deeper by her revolving propellers into a froth of racing foam. Instead of the flurries of drizzle hitting him on the left cheek, they were driving into his face as the ship swung southwards.

'Hello, hello, hello,' he said aloud.

But the turn didn't stop at southwards; the ship continued to swing, heeling at full speed until she was heading due east, and he was sheltered from the buffeting of the wind and the driving drizzle by the bridge structure. *Paladin* was bashing into the waves now with a violence that set things rattling, plunging downward into the troughs with the powerful drive of her propellers. A wall of water, grey in the blackness, flooded over her; she shuddered, then shot skywards once more, the sea cascading in arching bands of foam from the rising bows to be whipped away by the breeze.

Down below, in one of the mess decks, a cup had slid across a mess table and crashed to the floor, and, as a cupboard burst open, a shower of knives, forks, and spoons hit the deck.

'Now what, for Christ's sake?' someone said bitterly. 'Has war broken out or something?'

Chapter Two

Captain Beaufort looked at the signals flimsy in his hand and turned to Mostyn.

'*Launceston* and *Holdfast* are closing in,' he said. '*Paladin*'s turned back. She'll be stopping up the gap at the other end before long. *Gladiator*'s moving up.'

Mostyn drew a sigh of relief. 'Think we ought to have more on the job?' he asked.

'The signals have already gone off. There'll be more A.S. ships out soon. Their crews are ashore, but are being rounded up now. The Admiral will be here soon.' He seemed somewhat relieved that someone with superior authority was going to take over. What was happening seemed to call for it.

Mostyn glanced at Daisy, who was standing in the background, sipping a cup of coffee the Wren officer had produced. She smiled back at him uncertainly.

'I have a little job to do,' he said to Beaufort. 'I'll be back. Would there be a telephone when I arrive that I could use without interfering with your own lines?'

The Captain turned to the Wren officer, and she gestured to the door.

'You could use my office,' she said. 'I'll make arrangements.'

Mostyn nodded his thanks and turned to Daisy. 'I want Packer,' he said. 'Get him, will you? Try the man on the switchboard at the hotel. He'll know where to find him. Tell him I'm coming over.' He glanced at Beaufort. 'Has *Achates* moved yet?' he asked.

'Not yet.'

She was just about to, however.

216

When the armed men had burst into the engine room, shouting to the crew to stop what they were doing, there had been a moment of confusion because of the noise, and Chief Engine Room Artificer Riddings, a big man who'd boxed for the Navy, had floored one of the men with the machine pistols. He was now unconscious, with a split head, and locked in the crew's bathroom with the rest of the engine-room staff. The call had come through at last that the engine room was properly under control.

'So!' Tutschek spoke into the telephone. 'Send the rest of the crew up to the casing. One at a time.' He paused. 'All but the Chief Petty Officer and one other. We have old engines and a long way to go, and our own Herr McAvoy is not so good, I think. Perhaps we should keep them aboard in case we need assistance. A couple of hostages will do no harm.'

Shepherded by the machine pistols, the men from the engine room appeared in the control room in a gust of warm air and the smell of oil and sea water, and were sent up the ladder.

After a while the intercom crackled. 'Bridge. Last of the crew in the second dinghy.'

'Cast them adrift,' Tutschek ordered.

A moment later the intercom spoke again. 'Dinghy adrift.'

Tutschek grinned and seemed to stretch with relief. 'That is better,' he said. 'I feel safer now we have no enemies aboard.' He glanced round, and his eyes fell on the two white mice. 'A pretty touch,' he commented. 'And good for safety. They breathe more quickly than we do and will show sooner if we have chlorine or other dangerous gases aboard.' He smiled gaily at the control-room crew and picked up the intercom microphone. 'Now, gentlemen, don't let us forget our friends with the machine pistols. We will have no funny business.'

His eyes were on Venner as he went on. 'You once had a saying in your country, Herr Venner, from the days of Francis Drake and Walter Raleigh, when your gentlemen commanded the ships and your sailors only sailed them. You will remember

217

it: "The sailors were not gentlemen and the gentlemen were not sailors." ' His eyes danced merrily, and he indicated the men with the pistols. 'These gentlemen, who are under the orders of my good friend from the United States, Mr Meyer, are not sailors.' He gave a laugh. 'But unhappily they are not gentlemen either. There are six of them: Meyer, O'Hare, Blomberg, Sentini, Salis, and Noltenius. They are well armed and have been picked for one duty only: to make sure that everyone does as I say. They know their job.' He gestured at Blomberg, a small, tight-faced youngster with spectacles. 'Herr Blomberg is from East Germany and is also an expert on weapons, particularly *modern* weapons.'

Blomberg didn't look like an expert – he looked more like a scientist – but Tutschek seemed to enjoy his own jokes, and he now spoke into the microphone so that the men in the engine room could hear. 'There will be one of my friends with the pistols in the control room at all times,' he announced, 'and one in the engine room. There will be three off duty and one to prepare food. From now on, with the exception of Number Three, which is damaged, all bulkhead doors between compartments will be kept closed. Nobody will move from one compartment to the other without permission from me. There is only one watch, so you will get what sleep you can at your posts. Food will be brought to you. Unhappily, we shall have to live off sandwiches, soup, and coffee until we are finished, but it will only be for a day or two, and you are being well paid. That is all.'

He replaced the instrument. Venner saw Bonser glance at Luck. Madura gave him a deep, brooding, indignant stare.

Tutschek looked at Venner. 'Now that we have the submarine to ourselves,' he said, 'I think we can make a start. I will go to the bridge. It is quite like old times. What a pity we do not have torpedoes!'

He climbed stiffly up the iron ladder, and Venner watched his legs disappear, his mind racing, his eyes flickering about the control room. But Meyer was leaning in the doorway that led to the wardroom and the officers' tiny galley, with the

218

machine pistol cradled in his arms. Little could take place without his seeing it.

The intercom buzzed. 'Stop together. In both engine clutches. Slow ahead together. Course one three oh, Herr Venner.'

The telegraphs clanged, and a shudder ran through the submarine as the powerful diesels thrust her forward, dragging their monstrous gulps of air down the shaft of the fin. It was possible to hear the bang of the water outside and feel the vibration from the engine room. The motion of the vessel slowly changed from aimless rolling to a steadier lifting surge as she swung into the sea under power.

Nobody spoke. Ekke, on the wheel, was watching Venner.

'Course one three oh,' Venner said.

'Vun dree oh!' Ekke swung the wheel, watching the tape of the gyro compass repeater.

For a long time there was silence, except for the steady throb of the engines and the sound of the seas breaking against the hull. Then the loud-speaker clicked.

'Captain here. Herr Venner to the bridge.'

Venner glanced at Meyer, who gestured consent. He crossed to the ladder and began to climb. Inside the steel tower, his thoughts were racing as his legs drove him upwards. He was still trying to work out why anyone should go to so much trouble to steal an old submarine like *Achates*, and he was troubled now by the absence of the ship's captain. Whoever had been in command of *Achates* seemed to have disappeared. He had seen no commanding officer, no officers at all, in fact, beyond those he'd seen in the dinghy.

He thrust his head against the violent draught and the bitter cold dragged down by the pounding diesels. In the open air, he could see Tutschek's shape against the bridge, but the German didn't bother to turn his head. Noltenius was there, too, holding a gun.

Tutschek's head moved slightly as Venner appeared alongside him. He jerked a hand. 'What do you make of those lights ahead, Herr Venner?' he asked.

The night was dark, and little flurries of rain beat against

Venner's face. The bridge was illuminated only by the feeble phosphorescent glimmer from the compass. Behind them he could see the lights of Southampton and Portsmouth and the sodium street lamps on Portsdown Hill. On his right were the strings of coloured bulbs along the coast of the Isle of Wight, full of visitors for the holiday week-end. Tutschek pointed again, and ahead, fine on the starboard bow, Venner saw a red light moving across their course. Fine on the port bow he could see a green light, which appeared to be stationary.

Tutscheck handed over a pair of night glasses, and with their aid Venner was able to make out the shadows of the vessels behind the lights. For a long time neither of them spoke as the submarine headed slowly south-east for the open water, drawing nearer all the time to the two lights ahead.

'What do you make of them?' Tutschek demanded. 'My eyes aren't what they were.'

Venner lowered the glasses. 'I think they're closing the channel,' he said.

After a pause, Tutschek spoke briskly. 'We will bluff our way past.'

But as he spoke, a light started winking from one of the ships.

'Do you read Morse, Herr Venner?'

'Badly.' It was a lie, but Venner had no intention of offering anything in the way of help.

'Can you make out what they are saying?'

'No.'

'What are they?'

'A.S. frigates.'

'You're sure?'

'I recognise them. One of them's *Launceston* class. The other's a type-15. Last-war destroyer, but she still has a bite.'

Tutschek huddled deeper in his coat. 'We will chance it,' he said.

A searchlight came on, swept the sea for a second, and came to rest on the fin of the submarine. Immediately, a searchlight on the other ship came to life. *Achates* was caught in the converging beams.

'You'll not bluff your way past *those* two,' Venner said, with a faint trace of pride that the Navy wasn't such a set of fools as Tutschek had expected.

Tutschek frowned as he reached for the intercom. 'Stop together,' he said. He turned to Venner. 'Clear the bridge. We'll try the other channel.'

They clattered down the ladder to the control room, Tutschek closing the hatch behind him and pushing home the long-handled clips. He blinked in the glare of the control room.

'Check main vents and that we're opened up for diving, Herr Venner,' he said.

Venner's eyes flew to the older man's face. 'This vessel's not cleared for diving,' he said.

'So?' Tutschek seemed unperturbed.

'The bulkheads aren't all watertight. You know they're not.'

'She will still dive. Everything works, I think.'

Venner was conscious of startled glances from the men about him.

'The bloody thing'll come apart at the seams,' Ryan said abruptly.

Madura seemed about to join in, but apparently changed his mind. No one else spoke.

'Please carry on with the check, Herr Venner.' Tutschek smiled. 'I think you'll find we're opened up.'

'How do you know?'

Tutschek's smile widened. 'Because she did a trim dive in Stokes Bay before she left,' he said. 'She was watched.'

The control room was quiet as Venner finished the check. There were still a few alarmed glances, but nobody said anything. They were submariners and they knew why they were there. They had rehearsed together and they had all guessed there was a possibility of submerging, though none of them had expected to do the job with a condemned vessel that was unsafe for the operation.

221

Tutschek spoke again. 'Periscope depth, Herr Venner. She is quite sound. I have information that she is.'

Ryan tried one last protest. 'I don't give a monkey's if you have,' he growled. 'She's not cleared for diving! She can't be! Not with that damaged bulkhead.'

Tutschek remained quite unperturbed. 'Just a Royal Navy regulation, I think,' he said, and Ryan's eyes fell. 'The Royal Navy are always over-cautious about these things in peacetime, and this is an emergency. I think we will dive. Below, I think we shall not feel the motion so much.' He looked at Venner. 'I hope you are still skilled at keeping the trim, Herr Venner. We had better warn the engine room you may be a little rusty.'

Henry Latisse, born Franz Chudoba, in Brno, Czechoslovakia, was enjoying a drink at the bar in the Vernon's Head Hotel. He expected to drive the following morning to Heathrow for a flight to Paris. From there, he could be in India within a matter of hours. He felt secure and well content.

He finished his drink and moved to a telephone booth next to the men's room. Pushing coins into the box, he dialled a number.

'Latisse here,' he said.

'Everything going,' he was told. 'They're aboard and the M.F.V.'s back. We're clearing up and disappearing.'

Latisse quietly replaced the receiver. He felt he deserved another drink. When he opened the door, he was surprised to find two men waiting. Without a word, they took his arms and bundled him into the men's room. He was whipped round and placed against the wall while practised hands ran over his body.

'Nothing,' one of the men said.

As he turned, a third man, tall and languid, standing with his hands in his pockets, smiled and limped forward.

'Remember me, Latisse?'

As Latisse was being escorted quietly from the hotel by two plain-clothes policemen, Mostyn turned to Packer and

Haggard, who were by the door. Two more plain-clothes men and a woman detective were with them.

'Now for Dorothea,' he said.

Packer looked uneasy. 'I hope you know what you're doing,' he observed. 'She's got a lot of influence in her family, you know.'

Mostyn looked at him icily. 'I have a few big guns in mine, too,' he said.

Dorothea Holcombe had just stepped out of the bath when the manager of the hotel unlocked the bedroom door. He didn't enjoy doing it and was nervous.

The detectives with Mostyn pushed into the bedroom. Clothes were scattered across the bed, and water could be heard running in the bathroom. Mostyn stepped across to the door and opened it. Dorothea was standing by the mirror working on her hair. When she saw Mostyn's face in the mirror, she screamed and reached for a towel.

Mostyn tossed her a bathrobe. 'Hello, Dorothea,' he said. 'What a splendid figure you have!'

Forty minutes later he was back at H.M.S. *Dolphin*, speaking into the telephone in the office of Beaufort's Wren secretary.

'Pick him up,' he was saying. 'Yes, Charles Francis Aubrey. I don't think he'll give you any trouble. And search his office and his apartment. See if you can find a hint of where this bloody ship's going.'

Beaufort appeared from the outer office, looking bewildered. 'You were right,' he said. 'She *has* been taken over. *Launceston*'s picked up her crew. Fifteen of them from the control room and fore-ends. They were put in a dinghy when she was first boarded. There are no officers, so they must be still on board. They have no idea what happened to them.' He frowned but continued with the report, giving the facts concisely, with no waste of words. 'There's one known death. The leading telegraphist, who was shot through the head. His body was hoisted to the casing and hasn't been seen since. I expect they dumped him. The third hand is making a report.

223

It seems that the engineer officer was hit on the head with a pistol. That's all we know.'

Lieutenant-Commander Witty entered the office and handed over a signals flimsy.

Beaufort's eyes widened as he scanned it. 'She's submerged!' he said.

'I thought she couldn't submerge,' Mostyn snapped.

'She *did*, by God!' Beaufort sounded as though he didn't know whether to be shocked at the contravention of Queen's Regulations and Admiralty Instructions or proud that men trained at *Dolphin* could do what they had with the vessel at their disposal.

'I understood diving would be against regulations!'

'It is. But we're bending a lot of rules for this job. She's quite capable of diving. It's safety regulations that say she shouldn't. But she might have to when she's on position in the South Atlantic – in case something goes wrong – so Addams did a trim dive before he left. There was an M.F.V. and a lifting vessel standing by, mind you. It might be bloody different if she has to do it in an emergency.'

Mostyn absorbed this information thoughtfully. 'Where is she now?' he asked.

Beaufort glanced at the signal and crossed to the chart on the wall. He jabbed with a thick forefinger. 'There! They lost sight of her, but they have her on their screens because she's got her periscope and snort mast up. *Launceston* and *Holdfast* are following her, waiting orders. She's heading on a reciprocal course now and she's off the Langstone Bar Light again. It looks as though she's trying to get out at the other end.'

'Where's *Paladin*?'

'Off St Alban's Head now, but she can move a damn sight faster in open water than *Achates* can in the Solent. She'll be off the Needles before they can get clear. Especially with the machinery *Achates* has.'

Beaufort was right, McAvoy's responsibility seemed to be

224

bearing heavily on him. The noise coming from the engine room through the open bulkhead made him shout.

'We've got to surface,' he said.

'Why?' Tutschek's eyes were glittering and angry.

'Because the engines are bloody old, and the place's full of smoke.'

'What smoke?'

'Exhaust.' McAvoy's face looked blue from holding his breath. 'Something's wrong with it.'

'There cannot be anything wrong,' Tutschek said irritably. 'This ship was checked for her voyage.'

'Christ, she was only going to Devonport to have the engines out!'

Tutschek's look was cold. 'She was going further than that, I think.'

'Not that I heard,' McAvoy said. 'And anyway, she was never intended to submerge. Or she'd have been repaired and cleared for diving. She's perfectly all right up top. We've *got* to surface.'

'No!'

McAvoy had a nagged look. 'Why can't we go on main motors, then?' he demanded. 'The batteries have got a good charge on.'

Tutschek replied patiently, like a parent talking to a difficult small boy. 'We may need the batteries later.'

'Well, we'll have to get that exhaust right before you use the snort,' McAvoy persisted, 'or we'll suffocate in there. You want to come and see? It's enough to choke you. When I volunteered for this lark, I didn't think you were going to pick *this* old tub. I thought we were going for something that was serviceable.'

'Unfortunately,' Tutschek snapped, 'the serviceable submarines did not carry what we wanted.' He seemed to grow tired of the discussion. 'Very well,' he said. He turned to Venner. 'What's the depth of water?'

Venner told him. It seemed precious little, but Tutschek nodded. 'We'll lie on the bottom,' he said.

Ryan swung round from his position, eyebrows raised. 'Christ, man,' he said, 'there are bloody great tankers in and out of here all the time, and the *QE 2*'s due out. They draw a lot of water!'

'That's a chance we must take,' Tutschek said. 'We will stop together, Herr McAvoy, and wait.' He seemed infuriated by this minor miscalculation that was throwing his plans awry. 'We will wait until you have finished. So hurry. Be quick, be quick!'

McAvoy had looked exhausted when he vanished back to the engine room in a waft of hot diesel oil. As the door closed, the noise had dwindled, and the control room had become silent again. Venner glanced at the complex array of instruments. They were resting gently on the bottom now, and there was nothing else to do but look – and think. The two gleaming columns of the periscopes appeared to support the bulkhead. On the port bulkhead the dials of the depth gauges stared into the compartment like the eyes of a sea monster. The diving and blowing panel was a complex of levers and wheels. Close to the passageway was the helm, with its brass-spoked wheel and gyro compass repeater. Just forward of the engine room were the asdic and radar compartments.

The men at the controls were behaving instinctively, waiting quietly for orders. One or two of them looked nervous, as though aware of the monstrous thing they'd done. Leaning against the forward periscope, Tutschek watched them carefully.

Venner had felt strange when they pulled the hatch cover down over their heads. The thud of it slamming had seemed like the end of his previous life. It had seemed stranger still when Tutschek had barked his orders – 'Slow ahead together. Open main vents. Take her down' – like a faint memory coming to him from long ago and far away.

It had been hard getting the trim of the old boat. Despite the rehearsals, he was out of practice, and his reactions had been slow. It was a measure of Tutschek's confidence that he hadn't lost his temper, hadn't even grown impatient. Because Venner was a former officer, he'd treated him as though he were a being apart, his attitude different from the one he showed to Meyer – whom he clearly regarded only as a hired gunman. He allowed him to sort matters out without interference, even smiling and thanking him when he'd finished.

'Perhaps layers of fresh water from the River Hamble,' he had suggested calmly. 'Making the boat difficult to control.' He had seemed, in fact, almost *too* calm. Venner wondered again what he had up his sleeve.

In the silence, a high-pitched tapping sound was suddenly heard. It jerked heads up at once as it came like an electronic hammer bouncing off the old vessel's hull. Venner recognised it at once.

'What's that?' Meyer demanded, eyes wide.

'Asdic,' Tutschek said unemotionally.

'What's that?'

'An anti-submarine detection beam. They have found us.'

Meyer looked at the deck-head, where the tapping continued relentlessly, holding them firmly, persisting with all the nerve-wracking insistency of a finger scraped across a wet window pane.

'What'll they do?'

'Nothing,' Tutschek said. 'And keep your eyes down, Meyer. It's not your job to worry about that. It's mine.'

Meyer's eyes jerked down, sweeping the silent control room as the tapping persisted.

'Enough to give you the screamers, innit?' Ryan said with a nervous laugh. 'They'll hang us from *Victory*'s yard-arm for this if they catch us.'

'Be quiet, you fool!'

Tutschek's voice was sharp and commanding. In the silence, they heard a soft thud-thud in the water above them, a throbbing beat that increased and grew louder, like a train moving towards them through a tunnel.

Meyer's eyes jerked up again. He brought them down, but,

almost as though they resisted his will, they jerked up once more.

'What's *that*?' he said.

'Silence,' Tutschek snapped. 'I want silence.'

'*What is it?*' Meyer insisted. 'I've got a goddam right to know!'

Tutschek looked at him coldly. '*That* is a destroyer,' he said.

'After us?'

'What did you expect? We are not playing games. You are quite safe. They will not use depth charges.'

'How the hell do you know?'

'You will have to take my word,' Tutschek said. 'They will be armed, of course, I'm sure. Limbo, it is called, I think, is it not, Herr Venner? A three-barrelled omni-directional depth charge mortar now becoming obsolete, and used in conjunction with variable-depth sonar.'

Venner said nothing. The old bastard knew his facts. He obviously considered he was safe, and he probably was. With two of the engine-room crew still aboard, there would be no depth-charging – not yet, anyway. It would, to put it mildly, go against the grain for the Navy to have one of its submarines stolen – even an old one – but the hostages' lives would be considered of first importance. It was a hijacking, pure and simple, with the usual hostages to make sure they were allowed to go.

The tapping came again, probing along the hull like cold fingers. Venner felt his chest muscles tighten as the tension in the control room rose. It was almost possible to feel it, like a physical presence, even though, apart from Tutschek, none of the men was old enough to have experienced depth-charging or the relentless searching of surface forces. He saw heads turn nervously, and Ryan's eyes were wide, uncertain, and angry. He tried to relax and force himself to breathe more slowly, but the tiny clicking sound of the gyro repeater, loud in the silence, seemed to beat like a metronome in his brain. He was aware of them all seemingly holding their breath, as though they felt the ships above could hear their inhalations and exhalations. When Meyer spoke, it made him jump.

'There it is again,' he said.

Tutschek didn't even lift his eyes. The old rogue was completely in charge of himself, the only man in the control room who was, drawing his confidence from his vast fund of experience and his knowledge of undersea dangers.

Venner almost wanted to scream as the tapping continued. In that moment of claustrophobic nausea he realised he'd changed, that the torpedo that had injured him had done more than merely crush bones. He'd been away from submarines too long, had grown older and used to comfort and safety. Something had gone, some elasticity of spirit.

'What are you going to do about it?' Meyer demanded.

Tutschek shrugged. 'Nothing,' he said. 'It will do no harm. It is not explosive.'

'It gets on your tits.'

'It is sad we cannot have some music,' Tutschek said sarcastically. 'Music while you work. It would soothe a few tattered nerves.'

Meyer scowled. Hired killer that he was, he resented the taunt that he was edgy with fear. 'Nothing wrong with my nerves,' he growled.

Tutschek, leaning against the periscope, shoulders hunched, body inclined forward, forearm resting on the handles, ignored him. His battered wrinkled face made him look vaguely like a vulture. At least, Venner thought, the old rogue was a true submariner.

Meyer moved uncomfortably. 'What'll they do?' he asked again.

'What *can* they do?' Tutschek said. 'Nothing, my friend. They won't harm us. They daren't. They have to wait. We have them in a cleft stick.'

His continued untroubled confidence puzzled Venner, even though he was as certain as Tutschek that there would be no firing.

'Could we surface by accident?' Meyer asked.

'Of course not!'

There was silence for a while. Then, almost as though he were giving a lecture, his equanimity magnificent, Tutschek said, 'Submarines are easy these days. Surfacing in my day was a very tricky business. Especially in rough weather before we reached full buoyancy and the water had drained out of the bridge casing. The boat was extremely unstable then, and if you surfaced with your beam to the waves there was always a danger of being rolled over. We used to come up heading into the sea; and turn beam-on to dive, because the waves prevented us forcing our bows down.'

Nobody seemed interested. McAvoy came to report that the exhaust trouble had been cleared up. He looked even wearier and Venner guessed he was going to be one of their problems.

'Very good.' Tutschek accepted the report with the imperious indifference of a captain who *expected* troubles to be cleared up. 'Stand by, Herr Venner. Put a puff of air in Three Main Ballast to get her off the bottom.'

The pointer on the depth gauge crept slowly up. Tutschek seemed satisfied. 'Slow ahead both,' he ordered. 'Open Three Main vents. Periscope depth. Stand by to snort.'

As they got under way again, Venner looked at the clock. It was midnight now, and they were snorting slowly back up the Solent to the entrance to Southampton Water again. To port of them the lights of Cowes would be going out for the night, though the glow from Southampton, to the north, would be illuminating the sky still. Portsmouth Docks and Netley Hospital lay in that direction, with the sandy beaches of Hampshire and the New Forest country off the starboard bow. The green lawns of the Royal Yacht Squadron at West Cowes lay to port, with Cowes in front and Osborne Bay, with its low sea wall and encircling woodlands, and Ryde, with its long pier running out beyond the spit and the white-walled houses rising, tier on tier, up the hillside.

Tutschek crossed to the table where Venner stood over the charts.

'Where do you place us, Herr Venner?' he asked.

Venner placed his finger on the chart where the thin pencil line he'd drawn stabbed away to the north-west.

'We will have a new course past the Needles.'

Venner nodded and moved the parallel rule on the paper.

'But we will take it very slowly,' Tutschek said. 'In case our stupid Herr McAvoy panics once more.'

Chapter Three

Crawling during the hours of darkness through the Solent was an eerie sensation and Venner was beginning to feel tired. It was all so familiar, yet he was horrifyingly out of practice. In addition, many of the lights in the control room were missing, probably stolen by dockyard mateys, and the place had a dank obscure look that gave the operation an unreal, incomplete feeling.

Off West Cowes they had changed course for a south-westerly direction, towards the Needles, groping for an outlet to the sea. Several times they'd heard the steady beat of propellers, dangerously close, it seemed, in the shallow waters. Venner had guessed they were the ferry boats from Portsmouth and Lymington to the Isle of Wight. Every now and again, they'd picked up the faster beat of one of the two ships which were shadowing them as it drew nearer, propellers thudding over the relentless pinging of the asdic beam.

Remarkably little had been said since the argument with McAvoy, except for Tutschek's laconic orders and a few nervous questions from Meyer. Tutschek hadn't bothered to answer them, remaining terse and thoughtful and completely in control of his strangely assorted command.

'Periscope!'

Half a dozen pairs of eyes watched Tutschek reach for the handles as the periscope came hissing out of the well. He thrust his face against the contoured mask of the moulded rubber eyepiece and, with a jerk of his wrist, brought the lens into high power. The seat swung in an arc, carrying him round as he scanned the horizon.

'So!' he said, and Venner saw his teeth gleam in a grin.

232

'Daylight. A good English dawn. Full of rain.'

No one spoke. Made uneasy by the knowledge of what they were doing, and tired of the game of cat-and-mouse they'd been playing all night, they were all nursing private thoughts. None of them was at top pitch of skill, or even of bodily health; most of them had been away from the job too long. Venner could almost smell the anxiety.

Tutschek's voice brought him back to his duties. 'Watch her, Herr Venner. Hold her!'

Several pairs of eyes were on the bubble of the depth gauge, where Venner's gaze was glued.

'I have her,' he said.

Tutschek's chair was still turning. When it stopped, Venner saw him tense and his expression change. 'And there, Herr Venner, goes the *QE 2*. Heading west as if the hounds of hell were after her. I have no doubt that her owners felt they couldn't afford to risk the ire of her American passengers by missing the tide, and doubtless the Royal Navy made sure she was well out of our reach.' He grinned at Venner. 'I once saw *QE 1* – her mother, you might say – like that during the war. A mile nearer and I might have put a torpedo in her. Such a pity. She had about ten thousand Americans on board.'

He gave another little chuckle, but when he looked into the periscope again, Venner saw his brows come down.

'So! I thought it might happen! Especially with the delay caused by the stupid Herr McAvoy. They have stopped up this end, too.' He swung the chair, his eyes to the periscope. 'There is a frigate off the Needles,' he said. 'And I imagine there will shortly be another. I expect they have picked us up already on their radar. Yes, here she comes, busily flashing our escorts. Perhaps you'd care to see, Herr Venner.'

He leaned back in the chair so that Venner could look into the eyepiece. Through the pale blue-grey glass, Venner saw the sea the colour of lead and the frigate, with the white bone of foam in her teeth, and the winking signal light, with, just beyond her in the distance, the bulky shape of the liner.

'We will once more have a reciprocal course, Herr Venner,' Tutschek said.

'Reciprocal course,' Venner repeated. 'Helmsman, course please?'

'Course two five vun!' The crew continued behaving as though this were a real submarine, not a maverick.

'Make it oh seven one for the time being.'

Meyer moved forward, and Tutschek looked up.

'Stay where you are, Meyer,' he snapped over his shoulder. 'I am the captain of this ship. You are only a guard. Behave like one.'

'I want to know what the hell you're up to,' Meyer said. 'We should have been clear by this time – and we would have been if that goddam fool in the engine room knew his stuff.'

'Submariners are trained to deal with emergencies,' Tutschek said coldly. 'You are not a submariner. Leave it to me.'

'Why the hell are we going back in again then, when we're nearly out?'

'Because we cannot take chances. By this time they will have picked up the dinghies and will know we have two hostages on board.'

'For God's sake, they might depth-charge us!'

'I think not.'

They all turned their heads, watching, as Meyer's voice rose. 'They *might!*'

Tutschek smiled. 'I hope not. Not with Herr McAvoy to repair the damage.'

'Look—' Meyer's voice grated '—why go back? Why don't we chance it if they're not going to depth-charge?'

'Because they might try other things. Such as ramming.'

Meyer's jaw dropped. 'For God's sake – ramming?'

'Smashing the snort mast so that we have to surface. I do not want that.' Tutschek's eyes fell on the white mice by the chart table, and he grinned. 'And because we have something up our sleeve. Something they will not argue with when I remind them. Which way blows the wind, Herr Venner?'

'Round to south-west now. Force four.'

'Nice and steady. So! Herr Meyer, tell Blomberg to come here. Where is the radioman?'

Lemon appeared.

'We will raise the radio mast, Lemon,' Tutschek said, as polite as ever. 'Herr Venner, please make sure we remain at periscope depth.'

Though it was still barely light, it could be seen that the clouds that had brought the rain the night before had been torn to shreds by the veering wind. The only sounds that disturbed the early-morning quiet were the putt-putting of a motor somewhere about the base and the wild rising cry of the wakening gulls. Across the Solent a long swell, cold and grey and menacing, was rolling up from the south-west, lifting the bows of the vessels anchored off Spithead.

In Beaufort's office, a group of officers bent over the chart.

'*Paladin*'s picked her up off the Needles.' The Captain sounded relieved, as though he felt for the first time that they were bringing some control to the situation.

Mostyn lit a cigarette, saying nothing. They had been joined by Rear-Admiral Gillam-Smith, the Flag Officer, Submarines, and Admiral Haythornthwaite, the C.-in-C.

'That second dinghy,' Haythornthwaite said, 'did *they* see any sign of Addams or any of the other missing men?'

'No, sir. But they say they've got two of the engine-room staff on board. C. P. O. Riddings and Leading Seaman Crankshawe. They have no idea where the Captain or the rest of the crew are. Perhaps they're still on board with Riddings and Crankshawe. As hostages.'

Mostyn glanced at Haythornthwaite. The Admiral had picked up the threads of command as soon as he had arrived, but he seemed a little baffled, not only by the disappearance of a Royal Navy submarine, but also by the threat which it imposed on them.

'What happens now?' Mostyn asked.

235

Haythornthwaite frowned. 'I'm damned if I know,' he admitted. 'We can hardly depth-charge the bastards with what they've got on board.'

'Where are they?'

'Right here.' Beaufort placed his finger on the chart by the entrance to Southampton Water. 'Submerged,' he added. '*Launceston* and *Holdfast* can't use radar now, but they have her on asdic.'

A lieutenant appeared with the figures of a new plot on a sheet of paper. '*Holdfast* reports she's at periscope depth, sir,' he said. 'They have her on radar again.'

'The old bastard knows his stuff,' Beaufort said, unable to keep the admiration from his voice. 'It's a good job we've got them properly boxed in. *Holdfast*'s within five hundred yards of her now. All non-naval ships have been warned to keep clear.' He frowned. 'It's going to play hell with the traffic in the Solent. Now we've got *QE 2* away, we've stopped all sailings and all ferries to the island. There'll be a few angry voices raised tomorrow.' He looked towards Mostyn, who was standing at the window, staring out at the grey sky of a new day. 'Those people your men picked up, do *they* know where they're heading?'

'They're not talking,' Mostyn answered. 'Expect it'll come out in the wash before long, though. My chaps are working on 'em.'

Beaufort glanced uneasily at him. He wasn't sure what Mostyn meant by 'working on,' but he had his suspicions, and he couldn't find it in his heart to condemn it.

'Where were they supposed to dump this stuff?' Mostyn asked.

'A point west of the South-eastern Atlantic Basin.'

'Why there?'

'Correct depth. Too deep to raise but not too deep to damage her. If she were sunk in the deep itself, the hull would collapse like a crushed matchbox under the pressure, and that would defeat the whole object of the exercise.'

The room had filled up by this time. In addition to the

senior officers, there was an expert from Ewerton, who had been flown south during the night.

Admiral Gillam-Smith was looking vicious. 'That bloody man Aubrey,' he growled. 'I had him here in my office! During Navy Week. To arrange for some German ex-naval officers to go on board *Tiger*. Everything was in order. Clearance. Security. Everything.'

'I bet Aubrey fixed that,' Mostyn said.

'He got two of them on *Confounder*,' Gillam-Smith snorted. 'I bet this bastard running *Achates* was one of 'em.'

He saw Mostyn looking at him and seemed to feel it needed explanation. 'Policy,' he said. 'Good for the crews. Nothing to show why we shouldn't have had 'em. Friendly power now.'

'If one of 'em was Tutschek,' Mostyn said, 'he's distinctly unfriendly.'

'Communist?'

'No. Just as bent as a corkscrew.'

'I wish we'd known.'

'I wish *we'd* known,' Mostyn said with feeling.

The door opened, and Witty appeared. He looked as tired as the others. He spoke to Beaufort, who glanced at the chart on the table.

'Here,' he said, placing a finger opposite Gosport. 'She's stopped again. Wonder what the hell she's up to.'

Unable to bear the tension, Mostyn took a turn up and down the office. Daisy had disappeared; he guessed she was dozing in the Wren officer's room. The Wren officer was still on duty, still looking remarkably pretty. Her hair looked a little less tidy, and her white collar was crumpled, but she'd kept the coffee and sandwiches coming up at all the right times. There was a long silence as they stared through the rain beyond the window.

'Doesn't this chap Aubrey know where they're heading?' Beaufort asked.

'No,' Mostyn said. 'I expect he was just the paid hand.'

Beaufort was digesting this information when the door opened and Phemister appeared.

237

Beaufort read the signal he'd brought. 'They've found Addams,' he said, and everyone turned. Something in the way he said it sounded ominous.

'Dead?' Gillam-Smith asked.

Beaufort nodded. 'He's been fished out of the sea off the Nab. Tide must have carried him there. Shot through the back of the head. They've also found the first lieutenant and two of the crew. The look-out and the man who was on the casing. Also dead.' He stared at the flimsy in his hand. 'The bastards,' he said.

As they were talking the C.-in-C. walked in. He lit a cigarette and passed a signal to Mostyn.

CAPTAIN ACHATES TO C.-IN-C. SPITHEAD, Mostyn read. REQUEST FREE PASSAGE FROM SOLENT. ALL SHIPS TO BE WITHDRAWN. NO HOSTILE MOVEMENTS. REMIND YOU OF WHAT I HAVE ON BOARD. VERY EASY TO RELEASE BY EVACUATOR VALVE. HAVE EXPERT ON BOARD. ALSO HAVE MASKS. CHARTS SHOW US SURROUNDED BY BUILT-UP AREAS.

Mostyn passed it to Beaufort, who read it quickly. 'Good God!' he said. 'They'd never dare!'

'I think they might,' Mostyn said. 'They've already spent a small fortune on this operation, and they've nothing to lose. They've killed five men we know about. Six counting Nanjizel. Why shouldn't they be prepared to kill more? Wherever they're taking this damn stuff, they can reckon on getting a fortune for it.'

'Think we ought to get in touch with the civil authorities?' Gillam-Smith turned to the C.-in-C. 'Order an evacuation?'

Haythornthwaite shook his head. 'It mustn't come to that. There'd be a hell of a panic.'

'The man's right, though,' Beaufort said, staring at the chart. 'Whichever way the wind blows he's surrounded by people. The Solent's only seven miles wide at its widest.' He turned to the scientist from Ewerton. 'How far is this stuff effective?'

The expert looked uncomfortable. 'A hell of a way,' he said. 'It's filthy stuff. It's not one we invented.'

'What a miserable way to wage war,' Haythornthwaite growled.

'How's it delivered?' Mostyn asked.

'Chiefly by offshore submarines. It draws oxygen from the atmosphere and builds up in volume until it runs out. It rides on water, and it doesn't disperse. It's primarily for use from the sea.'

'It's delivered submerged,' Beaufort added. 'Submarines these days are exactly what the name suggests. Missiles can be released from underwater, and so can gas.' He ran his fingers through his hair. 'Good God, though,' he ended, 'I never thought we'd see it done!'

The man from Ewerton had a defensive look. 'We had to be ready,' he said. 'In case the other side used it. We had to produce a defence against it.'

'What is the defence?'

The expert looked uncomfortable. 'So far,' he said, 'the only one we've found is concentrated spraying, or just to issue everyone a gas mask. It sounds bloody awful, but it would have sounded a damn sight worse if everybody else had had it and we hadn't.'

Mostyn felt that events were pressing in on him. 'Surely to God they could have sealed the valve against something like this,' he said.

Beaufort looked at him pityingly; he felt that Mostyn had no conception of the thought that had gone into the operation. 'It *is* sealed,' he said. 'From the outside. Neither the government nor the Navy nor Ewerton expected that when *Achates* went down there'd be anyone *inside*.'

He turned away, his hands deep in his pockets, his thick shoulders slumped. As he did so, Haythornthwaite, who had been deep in conversation in a corner with Gillam-Smith, turned to the staff officer behind him.

'I'm not prepared to take any chances,' he said. 'Get me the Ministry of Defence.'

Chapter Four

Despite the early hour, the naval operations room at the Ministry of Defence was fully manned, and had been from the moment *Achates* had disappeared. It was not a room with any great tradition, because it was part of the new unified Services Ministry, and it remained largely anonymous, which, under the circumstances that now surrounded Operation Peardrop, was just as well.

Vice-Admiral Peverell, the Vice-Chief of Naval Staff, a short dark man with bright, black restless eyes, stood in front of a large chart of the North and South Atlantic. With him were the Assistant Chief of Naval Staff, Operations, Rear-Admiral Frayne; the Director of Naval Operations and Trade, Captain Hew; the Deputy Director, and the Duty Signals Officer. Though ratings came and went with signals, and Wrens moved about with messages, the room was quiet and they all looked tired.

Peverell stood with his hands in his jacket pockets, his feet apart, his heavy brows down, his whole attitude one of quivering concentration so that he looked a little like an angry terrier at a rathole. 'I can't see what he hopes to do,' he said. 'He can never get out, with both ends of the Solent sealed up. We can stop him any time we want. He'll have to surface eventually, and they've already brought everything they've got into the operation. The chief problem will be keeping it from the Press.'

'The nerve of the damned man,' Frayne said. 'Why the devil wasn't he stopped earlier?'

'The usual,' Peverell observed. 'The political boys being so secretive about the damned operation, we were having to spy on each other to find out anything.'

A red telephone on the desk rang. One of the Wrens answered it. She listened, then put the instrument down and turned to Peverell. 'Sir. On the scrambler. C.-in-C., Portsmouth, would like to speak to you.'

Peverell and Frayne looked at each other, immediately suspecting trouble. Peverell crossed to the telephone and picked it up. 'Yes,' he said. 'Yes. What? *What's that?*'

The heads of the other officers jerked round at his tone. Something was clearly in the wind.

'Good God!' Peverell said. 'When? Five minutes ago? How long does he give us? Yes, I've got that. Yes. Right. Stand by the telephone. I'll call you back as soon as possible.'

He replaced the instrument and turned to the other officers. 'Gentlemen, excuse me.' He tapped Frayne on the shoulder and inclined his head to indicate he should follow as he left the room for his own office. There, he closed the door carefully. Producing a chart of the Solent, he spread it on the desk and laid his finger on a spot roughly opposite Gosport.

'He's there, Richard,' he said. 'At periscope depth now and proceeding slowly back towards Portsmouth. He demands that we call off the hunt.'

'Call it off?' Frayne's eyebrows shot up.

'Yes.' Peverell's eyes glittered. 'And he says if we don't he'll release the bloody gas.'

'Good God!' Frayne's reaction was exactly the same as the Vice-Chief's had been. 'Who else knows about this?'

'No one here, thank God, except me – and now you. But if we don't get on with it, half Portsmouth will know before long. The message wasn't in code and could easily have been picked up by some enthusiastic ham.'

Frayne's face tautened. 'What's he up to?' he asked. 'Where's he taking it?'

'If he's taking it to Russia,' Peverell commented, 'he'll head into the South Atlantic.'

'China perhaps?' Frayne suggested.

'It's a possibility.' Peverell frowned. 'But, dammit, I don't see it. I just don't.'

'There are quite a few lesser powers en route who'd like what he's got on board,' Frayne pointed out. 'People less concerned with the international scene.'

This was something neither of them cared to think about, and Frayne waited for Peverell to make up his mind, aware that his heartbeat had quickened.

'I must speak to the First,' Peverell said. 'Personally. This'll be his pigeon. I'd be glad if you'd contact him yourself for me, Richard.'

'I'll try the Mall House flat. He'll be there, I expect. I should think he's still in bed at this time. Especially since he was at a dinner party with the Chief of Air Staff at Hyde Park Gate last night.'

'Get him out, Richard. You'd better use my office. The fewer people who know about this the better. Then you – you yourself, personally – call Portsmouth and put a security blanket over the whole thing. No one allowed out of camp. No one allowed in. Have no nonsense, Richard.'

'How about the Press? They're bound to find out.'

'We'll think about that one later. For the moment, nothing must leak out. Nothing. Arrange for everyone who knows what was in that message to remain on duty. They're to be isolated. They're not to be in contact with another soul. And think up something to explain it in case some damn fool wants to know why. Cholera scare. Anything. As soon as you've made contact with the First Sea Lord, let me know. I'll be in the operations room.'

The policeman outside Number Ten Downing Street, watching the early-morning traffic moving down Whitehall, jerked at his jacket and straightened his back as a big black car turned in from the direction of Westminster. It arrived in a tearing hurry, and he wondered what had happened. As it stopped, he saluted the tall figure, much taller than he was, which unfolded itself awkwardly and then straightened itself to a height that caused him to look up. The First Sea Lord, Admiral Sir Robert Forsyth, was looking sombre as he crossed the pavement and didn't even notice the salute.

The door of Number Ten opened before Forsyth reached it. A man in a blue Office of Works uniform stepped forward. 'Good morning, sir.'

Forsyth nodded, unspeaking. He wasn't in the habit of rudeness, but he had too much on his mind. The Royal Navy had had a bad time from politicians in recent years, and the chances were that it was going to grow worse. He crossed the entrance hall and took the long corridor leading to the Prime Minister's room, striding over the red carpet past the photographs of imperial conferences and the busts of Pitt, Melbourne, and Disraeli. As he reached the hallway at the end of the corridor, which served as an ante-room, the Principal Private Secretary came forward quickly. He looked grave.

'This way, Sir Robert,' he said. 'He's waiting.'

'Sorry to stir everyone up at this hour,' Forsyth said. 'But it can't wait. Does he know what it's all about?'

'Yes, Sir Robert. He knows what's happened. Have there been further developments?'

Forsyth's heavy brows came down. 'By God, there have,' he said.

The Principal Private Secretary disappeared. A few minutes later, a door opened and he popped through it like the demon in a pantomime. 'This way, Sir Robert.'

Forsyth followed him into the famous cabinet room. He had been there more than once, of course – the last time not more than three weeks before, when the decision to use *Achates* for the X gas had been made. Forsyth hadn't liked it. He hadn't liked *Achates* being sunk like a decrepit collier with a broken back to serve as the container for some filthy gas produced by a lot of half-crazy scientists just because some other power was producing it. It seemed a despicable way to conduct warfare. But then, perhaps it was no worse than any other. It didn't matter much to a dead man whether he was shot, blown up, burned alive, or had his limbs and nerves paralysed by

243

poison gas. War had moved past the state of having ethics.

The Prime Minister was sitting in his chair at the head of the table, with the panel of the internal telephones and the scrambler in front of him. Seated opposite were the Minister of Defence and the Secretary of State for Home Affairs. They both looked a little ruffled at the early hour.

'Admiral,' the Prime Minister said. 'Please sit down.'

'I'd rather stand, Prime Minister.' Forsyth's restless limbs wouldn't have fitted easily into a chair. The Prime Minister seemed remarkably calm, he thought. Damned calm. A damned sight calmer than he felt.

'You got my message?' he said.

The Prime Minister nodded, looking grave. 'This is a beastly business,' he said. 'You'd better tell me everything.'

Forsyth started at the beginning. 'The stuff was placed aboard,' he said. 'Everything went straightforwardly until she was stopped off Chichester harbour.'

'How?'

'Signal from a shore station. It sounded like a genuine one. It was heard at Fort Blockhouse, and the man on the set there confirms all this.'

The Prime Minister frowned. 'I can't imagine why Colonel Mostyn let the thing slip through his fingers. He knew what was happening.'

'No, Prime Minister. I can explain that. The top-secret file from you was marked to go to Mostyn, and his signature was on it. But it never went beyond Aubrey. Mostyn's signature was forged.'

The Prime Minister looked shaken. 'Where's Mostyn now?' he asked.

'Fort Blockhouse. But only because his suspicions had been aroused. Apart from myself, no one was allowed to know we were to use *Achates*. Mostyn learned what was happening only by working it out for himself. Neither of the telegraphists these people picked up had spotless records, and both would know procedure and call signs.' Forsyth coughed. 'Under the circumstances, Prime Minister – the secrecy that's attended this opera-

244

tion right from the beginning – Addams would have had good reason to suspect that plans *might* be changed and new orders despatched. The whole nature of the operation – your own speech – made it possible.'

'I'm afraid I have to admit that it is so,' the Prime Minister agreed. He managed a sad smile. 'I'm afraid we've all been very secretive. It seemed necessary. But, surely, with the submarine trapped in the Solent, did we need to fear?'

Forsyth looked irritated as he outlined the facts. 'Yes, Prime Minister, we did. She was trapped if we wished her to be. But, Prime Minister, if it had come to the final decision, would you have wanted us to sink her *there* – with what she's got on board? She was virtually surrounded by people. There are houses along every shore of the Solent. Bournemouth. Lymington. Southampton. Portsmouth. Havant. Chichester. The Witterings. To say nothing of all those holiday camps along the coast, which are all full at the moment owing to the bank holiday. On the other side are Yarmouth, Cowes, Ryde. None of them big, but all big enough to be a matter of concern.'

'Where is Addams in all this?' the Prime Minister asked. 'He was suggested for his skill and care.'

'Commander Addams is dead,' Forsyth said. 'Together with his first lieutenant and several other members of the crew. They've just been picked up. My duty was to stop the submarine, but, knowing what she contains and the government's concern with it, I had to make my decision and make it fast, and I have to have your approval. We couldn't take a chance on the gas being released.'

'What would have happened if the submarine had been destroyed where she was?'

Forsyth drew a deep breath. 'There was no knowing whether we wouldn't be releasing the gas. We couldn't guarantee what sort of damage depth charges or an A.S. torpedo would have done. There was no certainty that the gas wouldn't come to the surface and disperse towards the shore.' He paused to let the information sink in. 'This was a decision that in the final estimate was not mine to make, though I had to make it. It was yours, Prime Minister. I let her go because, as Colonel Mostyn and the C.-in-C., Spithead, agreed, I had no option. I let her go, but we'll be shadowing her wherever she goes. Now we must pick our spot and move in to destroy her.'

'And the men you have aboard her?'

'Them, too.'

The Prime Minister considered; then he nodded. 'We must keep this thing quiet,' he said. 'It would create a tremendous panic. Not only here, but abroad. Where do you feel *Achates* is likely to head?'

'We have no idea, Prime Minister. But it's my guess that wherever she goes, she'll hug the coast deliberately, knowing we won't dare damage her. If this stuff escaped and the wind were wrong, the loss of life would be immense.'

'Can we do what we have to do without any other government finding out?'

'We'll try as long as we can.'

'Everybody involved must be sworn to secrecy.'

'That precaution's already been taken, Prime Minister. I've no doubt there'll be some speculation, though.'

Forsyth's telephone call arrived in Portsmouth shortly afterwards. The C.-in-C. rang Gillam-Smith, who turned to the other officers, his face grave.

'It's been confirmed,' he said. 'They've rightly decided we couldn't take any chances. Arrange for us to be put aboard *Holdfast*.'

Beaufort reached for the telephone. 'I take it Colonel Mostyn will be with us, sir?'

'Since he knows more about the affair than anybody else, that would seem sense. Also the expert from Ewerton. We might need him. Treat it as extremely urgent, and warn all ships to have their best men on asdic and other apparatus. We'll be staying with *Achates* and we'll decide what to do when she's clear of land.'

It was Beaufort, his cheerful pugnacious face troubled, who informed Mostyn of the decision that had been taken. 'We're

246

being airlifted out to *Holdfast*,' he said. 'With the Admiral and the gas expert. We're going to shadow the bastards. I expect we'll drop a few cans on them when we've got them in the right spot.'

'If they ever reach the right spot,' Mostyn said. 'For all we know, they'll hug the coast all the way to Riga or Archangel. Or Shanghai. Or God knows where. You can't sink her in territorial waters, or even on the edge of them, in case she's damaged and the stuff leaks.' He managed a twisted smile. 'Besides,' he said. 'No depth charges. You've got two men on board and I've got one.'

Beaufort's face was gloomy. Even the way he held his thick-set figure seemed to indicate his unhappiness. 'It'll not be as straightforward as all that,' he said. 'We shall *have* to weigh what to do eventually. And if it's a case of them or the lives of thousands of other people and an international incident, you can bet we shan't be able to come down on the side of Venner.'

Chapter Five

Daisy watched the helicopters leave. Then she climbed into Mostyn's car and drove into Portsmouth.

She was dog-tired by this time and longing for a bath, but she had one last thing to do. Packer had called to say that Susie Gore had turned up at the Vernon's Head Hotel demanding to know what had happened to Venner. She had gone to the police to report him missing and had seen the tail-end of the Latisse-Holcombe arrest. She had put two and two together and Packer, tired of pushing her aside, had called for help.

The morning air was cool. Despite the early hour, the hotel's first guests were already downstairs sniffing for their breakfasts, fresh, clean, and well rested. They made Daisy feel even grimier and tireder.

'I'm looking for a Miss Gore,' she said.

The man behind the desk jerked his head towards the lounge, where Susie was curled up in a chair, her head among the cushions. She looked about sixteen.

'Has she been there all night?'

'I gather so, Madam. Said something about waiting for some news. Has there been a collision somewhere? We heard a rumour about some bodies.'

How the hell did it leak out, Daisy wondered, making a mental note to alert Beaufort's secretary about it.

She looked at Susie Gore again. 'Is it possible to get a drink?' she asked.

The clerk looked shocked. 'At this time of the morning?'

'Coffee, then?'

'I can arrange that!'

'How about a brandy?'

'The bar's closed, Madam.'

'This is an emergency, and she's going to need one. Me, too, come to that.'

Forcing her fatigue away, Daisy turned and crossed to Susie. When Daisy touched her, she woke, alert at once.

'Steady on,' Daisy said.

Susie blinked twice, then sat bolt upright, pushing her hair from her face.

'I know you,' she said clearly and steadily, in her high autocratic voice. 'You work for Mostyn.'

Daisy smiled. 'Doesn't make me an enemy,' she said. 'Just now I'm as tired as you are.' She paused. 'And just as anxious.'

'Where's James Venner?' Susie was not to be lulled by sweet talk.

'We don't know,' Daisy admitted. 'Except that he appears to be where he ought to be.'

'Where's that?'

Daisy drew a deep breath. There was no point in beating about the bush. 'On board *Achates* – and *Achates* has been stolen.'

Susie's eyes widened, and Daisy hurried on. 'That's for you,' she said firmly. 'Not the newspapers.'

'I'm not interested in the newspapers,' Susie said. 'Right now I'm interested only in James Venner.'

'You in love with him?' Daisy asked.

'Yes.'

'Will he marry you?'

'I think so. Now. Why are *you* here?'

'To stay with you, I suppose,' Daisy said. 'As a matter of fact Colonel Mostyn sent me.'

'I don't believe you.'

'He has hidden depths. Coffee's coming up, and, with a bit of luck, a spot of brandy. That might help. After that we might just as well sit back and hold hands. Figuratively, of course. It's going to be a long wait, and it's started to rain again.'

The rain had come down all morning in a shining curtain. By noon the ships were grey metallic shapes across the sea. But with the last of the daylight, the clouds parted, and the waning sun began to drink the moisture from the pools on the decks. The air was like the inside of a velvet bag, hot, stuffy, stifling, and there was the constant mutter of thunder over the horizon to the east. The sea seemed to heave like glue.

The operations room behind and below the bridge of *Holdfast* was silent, the radar scanners sending their sweeps revolving across the screens with a cold phosphorescent fire that lit the faces of the men in front of them. Next door was the communications centre, with its batteries of radio receivers and transmitters and its clicking teleprinters, where the radio operators bent over their sets, plucking information from the cacophony of Morse signals that beat at their ears. Feet occasionally scurried past like restless rats, but the humming of the turbines was only a muted throb.

Mostyn glanced at Gillam-Smith and Beaufort, who were conferring with the ship's captain. They were standing over a chart, their hands moving across the paper, trying to weigh the pros and cons, trying to measure one fateful decision against another. When the ship had left, the newspapers had been too busy arguing over the Prime Minister's announcement in the House two nights before to be much concerned with where *Achates* was and what she was doing. There had been comments from grave-mannered individuals on television at home and abroad on the ethics of the Prime Minister's decision to send the gas out of the country, and louder comments at Ewerton from less grave-mannered individuals who felt they'd been cheated of the chance of a good demonstration.

The secrecy attending the movement of the gas to Portsmouth had knocked the ground from under their feet. Though there was a little anxious concern expressed by civic leaders on the south coast and in towns bordering the Solent, the fact that the gas had been loaded and apparently sent off without mishap seemed to satisfy everyone. As far as was known, it was now on its way to the South-eastern Atlantic Basin.

The news of Aubrey's arrest had then knocked the whole Fleet Street schedule sideways, and men who had been sent hurrying towards Portsmouth for the follow-up on *Achates* were hurriedly called back to London to hold the death watch outside Aubrey's house. They had barely made themselves comfortable when their editors had been handed another story, this one about an unscheduled fleet exercise in the Atlantic, which the Admiralty had dreamed up to obscure the reason for the number of ships heading south. It had sent accredited naval correspondents indignantly to the telephone to demand why they hadn't been informed. But for once their editors weren't concerned with their cries of protest, because yet another story had come in, of bodies being picked out of the sea off the Nab, which had set the newspapermen chasing to the coast again.

The fishing crew who'd picked up Addams's body had spotted the gold rings on his sleeves at once and knew enough about not minding the Navy's business not to interfere. They had not gone through his pockets and had therefore not identified him when a naval tender from Portsmouth had relieved them of their blanketed bundles. But one of the crew knew a man on the local paper at Portsmouth, who had been dragged from his bed as soon as the fisherman had set foot ashore, and had been quick to telephone the story to the nationals in London that his paper represented.

Newspapermen were now thin on the ground in Fleet Street, while Portsmouth was filled with agency men. The Navy, however, had managed to move fast. The fishermen had been shooed away by a motor patrol boat which had been deflected from target-towing, and the rest of the bodies were picked up by naval vessels. The story put out was that the dead officer had been commander of a new midget submarine which was being tested. Addams's identity was hidden with the usual phrase, 'The names are not being released until next of kin are informed.' That there were other bodies had also been admitted. The correspondents were now jumping to the conclusion that the midget had been involved in the announced fleet exercise and were preparing ponderous dissertations on the uncertain values of undersized submersibles. They were only making guesses, however, because no one in Portsmouth was available to confirm them owing to a typhoid scare which seemed to have affected H.M.S. *Vernon* and H.M.S. *Dolphin*, its neighbour, just opposite.

Listening to the radio, Mostyn frowned at the deliberate confusion that was being set up. Then noticing that the group at the chart table were looking at him as though in invitation, he followed them from the cabin to the glass-enclosed bridge.

Up ahead, a Shackleton was circling over a dark shape on the lifting sea, and there was another plane just beyond. No chances were being taken. The dark shape was *Achates*, and on her port quarter was *Launceston*. To right and left of *Holdfast* was *Paladin* and *Gladiator*, with a radar vessel on each wing of the flotilla. Behind them were *Nightjar*, a buoy-laying vessel, *Armourer*, a lifting vessel, the submarine *Archer*, and the helicopter ship *Diomede*, her aircraft armed with homing torpedoes. They could almost be on a mission of war.

If nothing else, Mostyn thought cynically, it was good training for the asdic and radar operators.

Beaufort's voice broke into his musings. 'It's becoming pretty obvious,' he said, 'that she's *not* heading for the rendezvous with *Commando*, so we can rule that one out.'

They were moving slowly between Madeira and the bulge of Africa, with Morocco just to port. They had crossed the Bay of Biscay under lowering clouds, with constant showers of rain, all the ships aware that they were being watched by French, Spanish, and Portuguese radar scanners along the coast. Several aircraft had flown over from the east, shining polished darts hurtling past with a howl of jets to disappear beyond the horizon almost before they had been sighted. But the electronic gear on the ships was working at full pitch, and the radio wave bands were noisy with querulous pipings as urgent requests for orders were transmitted. In every look-out position on every one of the ships, men were stationed with binoculars watching *Achates*. It was all they *could* do, though Mostyn was growing uneasily aware that in the minds of the Navy men at the opposite end of the bridge firm decisions were beginning to take shape.

They had followed *Achates* past the westernmost tip of France near Brest to Cape Finisterre, Lisbon, and Cape Saint Vincent, with a westerly wind butting on their right cheeks. The submarine had hugged the coast all the way, and they hadn't dared chase her into the territorial waters they had skirted. Any attempt to close up would have brought a hurried dash for land; and any firing, a threat to release the gas. Radio messages had warned them of Tutschek's intentions, and, confident of his safety, he had been able to surface. 'The nerve of the bloody man!' Beaufort had exploded, but they all knew that any move they made could produce an international incident of appalling proportions. There was no alternative but to keep their distance.

From Saint Vincent, they had curved south-eastwards by Gibraltar to Tangier, turning south-westwards once more to pass Rabat and Casablanca. South of the Canaries, Mostyn had half expected some action. The Navy men were growing more worried and were rapidly hardening to the decision to move in for a kill. But he knew also that they were hoping *Achates* would move further away from the shore first, because the sinking of the ship on the edge of foreign waters, especially if it became known what she carried, would entail an enormous responsibility and tremendous political danger.

'If she remains inshore like this,' Gillam-Smith remarked, 'we shall need a coastline that's desert and largely unsettled.'

Beaufort tapped the chart. 'Port Etienne to Dakar,' he said. 'After that it's heavily populated all the way to South-West Africa.'

Gillam-Smith thrust his hands into his pockets, his brows

253

down. It was clear that the thought of what he had to do weighed on him.

'Is there no other way?' Mostyn asked.

'None I see,' Gillam-Smith admitted.

'There are eighteen men aboard.'

'I'm fully aware of that. As I am of Venner and two loyal sailors. *And* that we know nothing of the others, how much they're responsible, even how much they know.'

Beaufort looked up from his study of the charts. 'We shall come to a deep soon,' he said. 'The Gadoon West Africa Trench. Off the island of Bougouni.'

'What's the depth?' Gillam-Smith asked.

'According to the hydrographers, just what we want. If we could only budge him off course a bit, we could have him over nine hundred feet, which would be perfect. We could do the job just as effectively there as we could on the edge of the South-eastern Atlantic Basin. The depths are the same, give or take a few fathoms.' Beaufort looked up, his eyes hard. 'And nobody,' he said, 'would be any the wiser when it was over.'

Chapter Six

'They are still there,' Tutschek said as he clattered down the ladder through the hatch. 'You wish to go up and see, Herr Venner?'

'I'll take your word for it,' Venner said.

He reached out to answer the telephone. It was McAvoy, complaining that the starboard engine's piston rings were breaking up.

'We've got to stop that engine again,' McAvoy said.

When Venner reported it, Tutschek frowned. 'Very well,' he said. 'We will proceed on the other.' He turned to the charts. 'Why do they not do something?' he mused. 'Doesn't it strike you as strange, Herr Venner?'

Venner shrugged. Ever since he had learned in the Solent what *Achates* carried, his mind had been searching for a safe solution. He had wondered if he could set a course which would run them aground, and several times he had scanned the *West Africa Pilot,* looking for shoals or hidden rocks or even currents that could set them ashore. But Tutschek, an expert navigator himself, was constantly checking their position. Though his expertise might be rusty, it wasn't so rusty he could be fooled. Despite the lines of strain running down his cheeks, he remained remarkably alert.

They were all exhausted now, with unshaven faces, and Venner's back felt as though it had iron bands round it. Food they could eat at their posts had come in the form of vast sandwiches of corned beef, opened tins of sardines, and mugs of coffee which immediately absorbed the stale taste of diesel oil and damp and the stink of their own unwashed bodies. Sleep had been snatched where they were. Meyer's gunmen, the only ones allowed off duty, had disappeared in turn to the officers' wardroom to rest.

Venner glanced at the charts, reflecting on the irony that his wish to go back to sea had been fulfilled by a madman in an ancient submarine carrying a cargo of deadly gas.

His thoughts were interrupted by Tutschek. 'Why do they not attempt something?' he said again, as though even he were beginning to grow worried by the inactivity of the ships above. 'Why?'

'Perhaps they're afraid you haven't got a gas mask,' Venner growled.

Tutschek chuckled. 'But we have,' he said. 'In the officers' wardroom. When *Achates* was fitted out for this job, they made sure that everything was considered.' He indicated the cage by the navigation table. 'Even the mice. Every precaution was taken.'

'Except that some bastard like you would come along to ruin everything. What are you going to do with this cargo, anyway? I take it you're not going to dump it for them.'

'We have better things to do with it than that,' Tutschek said. 'In the right quarters it could be worth millions.'

'And where, for God's sake, are the right quarters?' Venner asked. 'Russia? China? We've got a hell of a long way to go before we get to either, and this old tub doesn't carry the fuel for Vladivostok or Shanghai.'

Tutschek laughed. 'So!' he agreed. '*If* we were going to Vladivostok or Shanghai. Which we are not.'

'Where, then?'

'You will see, Herr Venner. Presently. We are all prepared. Herr Blomberg is a biochemist and knows exactly what to do.'

Venner wondered if arrangements had been made to transfer the deadly cylinders to another vessel somewhere in the South Atlantic. But the following warships seemed to preclude that possibility, and Tutschek was still surprisingly confident.

Lemon, the telegraphist, switched on the B.B.C. again. He

256

had continually broadcast the news through the ship so they could hear all that was going on. It had seemed to amuse Tutschek to let them know how little response there had been in England to the theft. Once again, the reaction was the same – the B.B.C. was ignoring them. Venner guessed that nothing was being released. Though there was a brief reference to the fact that dragging operations were in hand in the Solent for the midget submarine in which a naval commander and four other men had died, nothing was said about *Achates*.

Tutschek listened with interest, a smile on his face. 'Your Admiralty is like Br'er Rabbit, Herr Venner,' he said. 'They are lying low and saying nothing.'

The news continued. '... Chief Olmuhi...' The calm tones of the B.B.C. man were strangely disturbing in the tense silence of the control room. '... Continuing threats have led African leaders to make a joint statement to the effect that they consider Chief Olmuhi a danger to peace, and a conference has been called at Freetown to devise a concerted plan of action. Chief Olmuhi's reaction remains that he has nothing to fear, even if the whole of Africa turns against him. African governments are inclined to discount his boasts, however, because they claim to know exactly what weapons he possesses and they know that even if a big airlift were to be mounted at once, he would require time for experts to train his men in the use of modern sophisticated weapons. ...'

Venner hardly heard the last of the news story. He whipped round and stared at the chart. Suddenly the whole thing was as clear as crystal. 'Presently,' Tutschek had said. Presently! No wonder! They were already circling the bulge of Africa. In Olmuhi they had a ready-made customer, panting to get his hands on their cargo. No wonder he had been shouting the odds for so long. All he'd been saying now made sense.

Venner saw that Tutschek was watching him with a smile. 'You have guessed, Herr Venner,' he said. 'I can tell by your face.'

'You bastards!' Venner breathed.

Tutschek was undisturbed. 'What better place to try it out,'

257

he said, 'than West Africa? It might stop a few of them from emigrating to Europe.'

Bonser, Luck, and Ryan were looking at Venner. The knowledge of what Tutschek was up to had come to them at the same time as to Venner, and they were all as well aware as he was now that Olmuhi could make them outcasts for the rest of their lives. Every civilised government in the world, black, white, yellow, and brown, would be seeking them. Since this thought didn't seem to trouble Tutschek, Venner guessed he had some hideaway planned in South America, the Far East, or the United States.

'A course, Herr Venner,' he said, as though nothing had happened. 'I want a landfall on the island of Bougouni. We shall go in one mile to the north. That will land us in Gadoon. Right on Chief Olmuhi's doorstep.'

'Olmuhi! By God, Olmuhi!' The B.B.C. news had had the same effect on Mostyn as it had had on Venner. 'He's the only man in the world who'd handle it.'

'The man's a lunatic,' Gillam-Smith growled.

'Of course he is. And that's why. Nobody else would touch a thing like this. But Olmuhi's the sort of madman who *would* have a go. He's got the right dreams, the right kind of egalomania, and the right kind of gold mines to pay for it.'

Gillam-Smith bit at his lip. 'I think we'd better make a signal,' he said, heading for the door. 'Downing Street will want to know the present course of *Achates*. I think they'll draw their own conclusions.'

It wasn't very difficult.

'In the hands of Chief Olmuhi,' Sir Robert Forsyth was saying, 'the stuff would be like a hydrogen bomb run amok.'

The Prime Minister stared at his hands, clasped on the desk before him. From across the table, the Foreign Secretary, the Minister of Defence, the Home Secretary, and the Leader of the Opposition watched anxiously. Then the Prime Minister seemed to shelve the problem; as though he wanted to know what positive things had been done, rather than study the things they could not do.

'Home Secretary,' he asked, 'you said this radio station that sent the message had been found?'

'Yes, Prime Minister. At Itchenor. In a house on the waterfront.' The Home Secretary sounded fussed and faintly irritated. 'We also found the M.F.V. that put these men aboard *Achates*. The man who sent the signal has been picked up, too, and we've found the place where they trained the crew.'

The Prime Minister seemed to force himself back to the negative aspects of the affair. 'This could set off a chain reaction in Africa against the Western powers,' he pointed out. 'It could set up a period of distrust that could go on for generations.' He stared at his fingers again, then lifted his head. 'I think it's only right we should warn the French, Spanish, and Portuguese navies. *Achates* is passing coastal strips administered – or formerly administered – by their governments.'

'And have them join the party?' Forsyth's eyebrows went down. 'No, Prime Minister. I doubt if that's a good idea.'

'Surely they could be of help?'

'They'd get in the way,' Forsyth said bluntly, 'and you'd have an international crisis on your hands at once. A real one.'

The Prime Minister looked worried. 'We *must* inform the French,' he said. '*Achates* is going to former French territory.'

The Leader of the Opposition spoke. 'I would go along with you on that, Prime Minister.'

Forsyth shook his head. 'No,' he said. 'Not yet. Not yet.'

The Prime Minister sighed. 'Do we know exactly where *Achates* is?' he asked.

'We do.' Forsyth looked at the signal in his hand and crossed to the map of Africa that had been erected on a stand. He jabbed with a long brown finger. 'Right there. She's still being shadowed. Even if she submerges, every asdic operator in the fleet will be watching her. Every helicopter's armed with torpedoes, and they can be vectored on to the target from Gillam-Smith's ops room in *Holdfast*. The submarine *Archer* and every A.S. ship there is armed, too, with either depth charges or homing torpedoes which are effective at several miles' range. In addition, we've now called up *Laceby*, which was moving northwards from Simonstown. She should join the fleet at any time now.' He paused. 'We're treating it as an emergency. It would take only a matter of moments and there would be no mistake.'

The Prime Minister looked relieved, and the Admiral continued. 'Of course, we can do nothing yet. Anything that's done must be done in the right depth of water. We have to find a place that's deep enough to be safe but not deep enough to crush her.' He paused. 'There is one other complication. A Russian ship's now shadowing the fleet. We're not sure what she is. She could be a whaler or a fishing vessel. But, judging by the amount of radar she carries, it isn't an accident that she's there.'

'What's being done about her?' the Foreign Secretary asked.

'We're trying to disregard her. But she'll be watching us as closely as we're watching her, and if we start an attack, she'll want to know why. She'll have guessed long since that it's a submarine we're shadowing.'

'Doubtless messages have already gone to Moscow?'

'They most certainly have,' Forsyth agreed. '*Holdfast* reports considerable radio activity.'

'What makes you think they haven't guessed also that it's *Achates* we're following?' the Leader of the Opposition asked. 'They must have been prepared to watch her sink with her cargo after the Prime Minister's announcement. When she doesn't turn up, they'll guess it's because she's here instead.'

'We shall have to risk that.' The Prime Minister's face was deeply troubled and he looked very tired, but he tried hard to keep the discussion to the essential points. 'I think we must disregard the Russians for the time being. They're minor irritants at a time like this. What we're dealing with is of more importance than mere international repercussions.'

Forsyth waited, and the Prime Minister finally made up his

mind. 'Under the circumstances,' he said, 'I see no alternative but to do our duty to the rest of the world. I'm sorry for the loyal men on board, but we have no choice in the matter at all, really. The individuals must be sacrificed for the sake of the whole.'

As Mostyn peered ahead over the bows of *Holdfast*, the sea seemed to heave like lead. The bright day, with flying fish skittering into sparkling waves, had given way to fog, which was thickening perceptibly all the time. The light already had the faded quality of worn canvas, and the atmosphere seemed desolate and evil.

Beaufort looked bitter. 'Fog,' he said. 'Fog! Now! The long-term averages for August for this area show seven days of fog per year. And *we* have to have one of them!'

Tutschek had been so confident that they would not dare touch him that he had remained on the surface throughout the whole voyage until the fog had come down, and only then had he submerged and tried to throw off his pursuers. He had changed course, doubled back on his tracks, and gone in for rapid changes of speed in the hope of throwing them off, but they had clung to him like hounds on the scent of a fox, following every move he made despite the fog.

It was barely possible to see *Launceston* now, or even the vessels to port, starboard, and astern, and despite all the electronic equipment available, the danger of collision in the event of sudden manoeuvring had increased enormously. Moreover while it was still possible to know exactly where *Achates* was, in the event of an emergency the urgent need to spot her at once if she surfaced could not longer be relied upon.

Beaufort crossed to the Officer of the Watch. He, too, seemed affected by the tension.

'What's the range?'

'As ordered, sir. One mile. Bearing green oh one oh.'

'Warn all look-outs once more. It's important we know immediately if she surfaces.' He glanced at the barometer, then peered outside. 'Seven days a year,' he said once more.

'Only seven out of three hundred and sixty-five, and we get one.'

Despite the fog, the asdic calls came steadily – 'Echo bearing green oh oh one, range one mile,' 'Echo bearing oh-oh nine, going away, range eighteen hundred' – and men were crouching like terriers by the radar screens, watching for the tiny green blip that would indicate *Achates* had her periscope up. The mood on the bridge seemed to have run through the whole ship. Despite the efforts to keep quiet what was happening, it was known in the mess decks now and there was little talk, no speculation, and no jokes. The whole ship seemed to have been wound up tight as a spring.

Wisps of sea smoke lifted off the undulating surface of the water, the low bank of fog lying like a translucent grey wall between sea and sky. Out of it Mostyn saw the shadow of a vessel's superstructure materialise like that of a ghost ship as *Paladin*, keeping station to starboard, briefly emerged. For an awesome minute she seemed to be floating on air, the hull emerging only slowly, the tall foremast, with its lacing of halyards and aerials, crisply etched above the fog, the rotating radar antenna curiously unreal as it revolved.

The atmosphere of anxiety had not decreased when Gillam-Smith appeared with London's reply to his signal.

'They've caught on,' he said. He looked towards Mostyn. 'This makes our problem a little easier to solve, Colonel. Even if no easier to face up to.'

'What do you mean?'

'We knew what the reply would be. I know what mine would have been.'

Mostyn didn't bother to ask him what it was. He had guessed.

'They make it very clear,' Gillam-Smith went on. 'They say *Achates*' cargo must never be delivered. They leave it to us to decide how to prevent it.'

'How do you propose to do it?'

Gillam-Smith glanced at the chart. His eyes were bright and his look eager. 'All that dodging he did was a mistake,' he said. 'It's brought him outside the Gadoon Trench. To get in now he's got to cross it, and if he tries it, he's right where we want him – over the correct depth of water.'

'Surely to God you're not going to blow him to bits,' the man from Ewerton said. 'The gas would reach the shore.'

Gillam-Smith frowned. 'No,' he said. 'But if we could put a few holes in *Achates* aft, the cylinders wouldn't be touched and she'd sink right where we want her.'

Mostyn and the man from Ewerton exchanged uneasy glances.

'Give it a little more time,' Mostyn begged.

'We haven't got time,' Gillam-Smith said. 'We're only one day's steaming from Gadoon now. Once we get inside Olmuhi's territorial waters it'll be too late.'

'We still have twenty-four hours. Venner's bound to make a move.'

'What can he do?' Gillam-Smith's voice sounded edgy with responsibility. 'We've worked out that there must be half a dozen men on board that submarine with automatic weapons of some sort. That's what the crew said when they were picked up.'

'Venner's no fool,' Mostyn insisted. 'And he still has two members of the original crew on board – spirited enough to put up a fight, too, it seems.'

Gillam-Smith shook his head. 'We can't take a chance.'

'We can for a little longer. If the cure won't take more than a few seconds, surely we can risk another few hours.'

Gillam-Smith frowned. 'I've no wish to destroy Venner,' he said. 'God knows, he deserves to be saved. Nor Riddings or Crankshawe or, for that matter, any of the other men either. They may be entirely innocent of what's being done. But we can't take risks.'

'Another few hours.'

'Very well.' Gillam-Smith nodded. 'But no more. They'll be inside Olmuhi's territorial waters by this time tomorrow, and we must give ourselves plenty of elbow room.'

'And then?'

Gillam-Smith's face was grim. 'I have instructions to use my own initiative,' he said. 'I suspect the politicians have run short of ideas and, as usual, want us to pick up the pieces. I'm going to do just that. For the moment I'm going to try to frighten him to the surface.'

Chapter Seven

As the crash of the depth charges shook *Achates*, she seemed to reel, and a pattering of moisture-absorbing cork came down from the deck-head.

Meyer's eyes flew upwards. 'I told you they'd depth charge us,' he said hoarsely.

The terrifying cracks of the explosions seemed to come from right under the stern, making the whole control room seem to leap. A light bulb popped. Venner saw instruments and gauges blur in his vision as the compartment vibrated.

'Watch the trim, Herr Venner!' Tutschek said quietly.

They all had their eyes on the depth gauges, as they flickered uncertainly.

'If anything happens,' Venner heard Ryan mutter. 'That bloody bulkhead's not watertight.'

Kkkkrrrummmp! Krummmp! Krrummmp!

The submarine shook again, quivering under the blows, and there was the sound of breaking glass somewhere. The gunmen off duty in the wardroom appeared, their faces scared. When the telephone squawked, Venner picked it up and heard O'Hare's voice, harsh and alarmed. 'What's happening?' he demanded.

Tutschek smiled. The old villain was suprisingly calm. The crashes were alarming to Venner, who had never been depth-charged before, but Tutschek and the old German on the helm seemed quite at ease.

'Tell him not to worry, Herr Venner,' Tutschek said. 'They are too far away to harm us.'

'Ve heff hed vorse than this, I think, Herr Kapitän,' Ekke said, grinning.

'I goddam doubt it,' Meyer said.

'They are just to scare us,' Tutschek said. 'They will not dare break anything. They were trying to frighten us to the surface.'

'That's all right,' Ryan exploded. 'But this bloody submarine's not shut off for depth-charging! She's not even cleared for diving!'

'Be quiet!' Tutschek snapped, suddenly losing his patience. 'All of you! When the lights go out and oil comes from the blowing panel and all the pipes hang from the bulkheads, *then* you need to worry. This is no more dangerous than a flurry of snow in summer, and we are still fast and manoeuvrable in spite of our approaching senility.'

'Can't we do something?' Meyer demanded.

Tutschek ignored him. 'What would *you* do, Herr Venner?'

'Surface,' Venner said bluntly.

Tutschek grinned. 'But *you* are not wholeheartedly with us, are you? So! We will continue as we are. They will do no more.'

He was right. After the second depth-charge attack there were no more sounds.

'Periscope depth, Herr Venner,' Tutschek said.

As the submarine lifted, the German nodded to Lemon to raise the radar mast. Because the set was old and tired and there was a lot of interference from the engines and the electrical gear, it was hard to read through the mush.

Tutschek stared at the confused blobs on the screen, frowning heavily. 'Ten of them,' he said. 'Four anti-submarine vessels and six others. I am very flattered. There are enough of them to swamp us.'

'But they won't,' Venner said. 'Because, unlike you bastards, they've got some sense of responsibility and they know damn well you'll run for the shore like a shot rabbit and threaten to let the gas go.'

The relentless ping-ping of the asdic probe started again. Tutschek's eyes rose, and Venner saw him frown. There were too many hounds following the scent. They were on all sides of them – too many, perhaps, even for an old hand like Tutschek. Despite his cunning, he was out of date, and the men on the surface would by now have had their orders for the kill. The only thing Tutschek was doing was delaying the final moment. But he was skilful still and still remarkably confident.

'Up periscope!'

Clapping his face to the eyepiece, Tutschek moved in a circle. 'They are still there,' he announced. 'Like a lot of dogs round a skunk. They would love to bite, I think, but they are afraid of the smell they would start up if they did.'

'You're dealing with an experienced campaigner,' Mostyn pointed out to Gillam-Smith. 'I've seen his record. I dare bet he's guessed exactly what you're trying to do.'

Gillam-Smith turned to the charts, then looked at Beaufort, who was standing at his elbow. 'Signal all ships to take up position again,' he said.

He traced a course across the chart, jabbing with his blunt finger. Beneath it lay the words 'Gadoon West Africa Trench.'

'How long do we have?' Mostyn asked.

'An hour or so.' Gillam-Smith looked at him. 'That's as long as I'll give your man. No more.'

The telephone sounded. Beaufort answered it.

'Radar reports *Achates*' periscope is up,' he said.

'Warn the look-outs,' Gillam-Smith rapped. 'We must see her if she surfaces.'

'Keep her at periscope depth, Herr Venner,' Tutschek warned. 'We must have no mistake. How is she handling?'

'We have her.'

Tutschek bent to the periscope. 'We have fog, Herr Venner. I think I shall be lucky.'

By God, he *was* lucky, Venner thought. The number of days when fog appeared off the West African coast was infinitesimally small, he knew, and they'd struck one of them. His lips tightened. Time was running short. From the charts, he knew

267

they would make their landfall in a matter of hours. An hour after that, they would be surfacing inside Olmuhi's territorial waters and then – if nothing had happened before – it would be too late.

He glanced at the pencil lines on the chart and turned the pages of the *West Africa Pilot*, hardly seeing the words that danced before his eyes. His mind had been pounding with too much thinking ever since Tutschek had let it be known just where they were heading and why. He knew the political dangers inherent in the delivery of their cargo and was as well aware of the shadowing ships as Tutschek was and could guess just what decisions were being taken aboard them.

With the fog, Tutschek was gambling on a race for the coast. But, despite his experience, he was still fighting his battle with his pursuers as he'd fought them in 1945, and anti-submarine vessels were armed nowadays with more than mere depth charges. Radio-controlled ordnance could be used at much greater distances. Venner had long since guessed that there was a submarine with the surface forces armed with homing torpedoes which could be launched at a word from the officer commanding the fleet.

The buzzer went, and he picked up the telephone. It was McAvoy, whose voice sounded edgy from strain, weariness, and nerves.

'Tell that bloody Hun them piston rings are breaking up,' he said. 'On both engines. And those bloody explosions have started a leak in the port propeller gland, and the pumps are dicey. We'll have to stop one of the engines again soon for repairs.'

'How long do you need?'

'Three, four hours with these piles of scrap-iron—'

McAvoy seemed set for a long moan, but Venner cut him short. 'I'll report it,' he said.

Tutschek looked up as he replaced the telephone. 'What is it?'

'McAvoy reports more trouble.'

'Again? What sort of trouble?'

'Piston rings. On both engines. And a leak in the port propeller gland. He says we'll have to stop to clear it up. He needs three or four hours.'

Tutschek scowled. 'Three hours! Four hours! *Gottverdamte!*'

'I think he's been at the drugs.' Venner spoke almost instinctively, aware somehow that he'd been presented with an opportunity to do something. He didn't know what or how he could use it, but McAvoy's message seemed to suggest an opening.

'Impossible!' Tutschek snapped the word. He looked at Meyer. 'Was he searched for drugs?'

Meyer nodded and Tutschek turned to Venner. 'Very well. Stop starboard. Half ahead port.' He paused, chewing at his lower lip. 'I have an idea, Herr Venner, that our friend McAvoy is not the man he was.'

Venner passed on the order, and as he replaced the telephone Tutschek was looking thoughtful.

'Let us have the two men from the seaman's bathrooms brought out,' he said to Meyer. 'They can help. They are experts. We must take no chance of both engines stopping. We will proceed on one for the time being.'

As Meyer spoke into the telephone, Noltenius appeared and moved into the engine room. A few minutes later he reported that Riddings and Crankshawe were there, too, both carefully watched.

Tutschek was clearly growing nervous as they approached their destination, and, as his anxiety communicated itself to the rest of the men in the control room, an uneasy silence hung over it. With no vessel to give them a tow, the whole operation would fall apart if McAvoy's clumsy hands could not keep at least one engine turning.

'Call the engine room,' Tutschek said. 'Tell them they must hurry. We must have nothing go wrong.'

Venner crossed to the telephone. O'Hare answered at once.

'I want to speak to McAvoy.'

As he waited for McAvoy, Venner's mind was racing. His

269

chance might not come again. With two of Meyer's 'gentlemen' off watch in the wardroom with Blomberg, the scientist, it was his only opportunity to act.

'Tutschek says you're to hurry,' he told McAvoy carefully.

'Sod him,' McAvoy said sharply. 'I'll do what I can. I can't do any more. Nobody could with these engines. They're clapped out.'

'Are you all right, McAvoy?' Venner spoke sharply, deliberately, his voice raised, and he saw Tutschek's head turn quickly from the periscope.

'Sure I'm all right,' McAvoy said.

'You sound strange.'

'What the hell are you talking about? I'm as okay as you are.'

Venner replaced the telephone. Tutschek was busy with the periscope again.

'That McAvoy is a fool,' he said.

'His speech sounded slurred,' Venner said. 'Do you want me to see what's happening?'

Tutschek was still busy with the periscope. 'You had better,' he said. 'Tell O'Hare there must be no delay.'

Venner turned away from the chart table, his heart thumping. There was trouble. It was the first lieutenant's duty to look into it, and Tutschek had responded automatically to his suggestion. It had been instinct on Venner's part as much as on Tutschek's, but he knew that he'd been given an opportunity to move away from Meyer's gun and he had to take advantage of it. Next time, Tutschek wouldn't be so busy with the periscope and would be a little more alert.

He stepped up to Meyer. 'You heard what the Captain said.'

Meyer nodded, keeping the muzzle of the gun at Venner's stomach as he reached behind him and unclipped the bulkhead door.

Venner stepped through and clipped the door behind him. The port diesel was thundering away in a pandemonium of noise in the confined space. The racket was terrific, and the

270

room seemed like a madhouse, stinking of oil, hot brass, and steel, and moving pieces of metal.

O'Hare looked at him, and Venner saw him exchange glances with Noltenius, who was standing just behind Riddings. The E.R.A. was bending over the silent starboard engine. He looked up, his eyes curious under the bloodstained bandage that had been tied round his forehead. Just behind him, the Frenchman, Arteguy, was occupied with Crankshawe. McAvoy was at the rear of the compartment, staring at a gauge. Beyond him, Venner could see the panels of switches, voltmeters, and ammeters in the motor room, and beyond that into the stokers' mess deck, a nightmare of discomfort surrounded by machinery. McAvoy looked up and saw Venner. He seemed tired but in control.

'Make it quick,' O'Hare said.

Venner nodded and stepped past him. The gun followed him all the way.

As he pushed down the narrow catwalk alongside the howling port engine, his nostrils full of the smell of oil and the hot metal from the exhaust, Venner's nerves recoiled from the din. Stepping over the toolboxes that stood in his way, he pushed past Noltenius and reached McAvoy. Even with only one engine going, the noise was enough to make their conversation inaudible to anyone but each other.

McAvoy looked angry. 'Get the hook off your arm, chum,' he said. 'There's no bloody panic.'

'There's more than you think,' Venner said. 'Do you know where we're going?'

McAvoy looked hard at him, then shook his head. Venner put his mouth close to his ear. 'Gadoon,' he shouted. 'What used to be French West Africa.'

McAvoy's head turned, and Venner put a hand on his arm.

'You know what we're carrying, too, don't you?' he said.

McAvoy's eyes flickered. 'What the hell are we taking it there for?'

'I'll give you three guesses. Are you prepared to be the cause of the deaths of thousands of people?'

271

McAvoy stared at him, and Venner could see that the news had startled him. He was a fool and a weak man, but the thought of being held guilty for the use of the gas had shaken him.

'What are you going to do?' he said.

'You'll see. Just sit tight and don't do anything until you're told to. Carry on with what you're doing.'

He slapped McAvoy on his shoulder, and moved towards Riddings. Noltenius was behind him as he stopped alongside the E.R.A.

'Listen carefully, Riddings,' he said. The noise from the engine was almost enough to drown what he was saying, and he cupped his hand to shout into the E.R.A.'s ear above the hammering diesel. 'I'm going to try something. Are you with me?'

Riddings glanced briefly at him. 'Who the hell are you?'

'Not one of this lot. Will you help?'

Riddings bent over the engine again, nodding silently.

'What about Crankshawe?'

'He'll be with you, whoever you are.'

'Right. I'll explain later. I want to borrow a wrench. A heavy one.'

Riddings swallowed, and Venner saw his Adam's apple jerk. Moving across Noltenius' line of vision he indicated the tools lying alongside him behind the engine, out of sight of O'Hare. Among them was a large wrench. With Noltenius' view masked, Venner put his hand on it, pushing the grip slowly up his sleeve, so that his fist contained the heavy claw head. As he turned away, he saw Riddings' hand also reach down to the tool bag.

Taking a handkerchief from his pocket with his left hand, Venner wiped his nose, changed it to his right hand to cover the head of the wrench, then stepped back as though his business with Riddings were done. 'Okay,' he said as loudly as he could, for Noltenius to hear. 'Three hours.'

He could see O'Hare watching him carefully from the door, the gun never leaving his torso. Riddings nodded again, his

272

eyes down on the silent engine. Venner turned and headed back towards the bulkhead door.

O'Hare watched him all the way, but as he reached behind him for the clips that held the door, his groping hand missed, and, as his eyes flickered away for a second, Venner lunged forward. The fist with the wrench in it caught the gunman at the side of the jaw. The jarr ran up Venner's arm, and he heard bone crack. As O'Hare staggered back, he let the wrench slip down into his hand and swung at him again with the heavy steel head.

The gunman gave only a faint cry as he dropped to the deck, but Venner took no chances. Expecting bullets from Noltenius' gun to crash into his spine at any moment, he swung the wrench again, once, twice, three times, until O'Hare lay in a huddled heap by the bulkhead door, blood running from his nose and ears. As he snatched up the machine pistol and turned, he saw that McAvoy had risen to his feet and that Arteguy and Crankshawe were staring over the port engine. There was no sign of Noltenius, but when he moved back on to the catwalk, he saw him lying at Riddings' feet.

'How did you do it?' he shouted above the din.

Riddings' face was grim. 'Shoved him against the port engine when he pushed past towards you,' he said. 'He put his hand on the exhaust. I hit him while he was still yelling.'

'Is he dead?'

'He won't move much. He's probably got a fractured skull.' Riddings held up a heavy wrench like the one Venner had used.

Venner stuffed O'Hare's pistol into his belt and picked up the one lying near Noltenius.

'Can you use one of these?' he asked.

Riddings nodded. Venner handed it to him without a word, and the big E.R.A. stuffed it inside his overalls. Crankshawe and Arteguy were still watching, Arteguy frowning heavily.

'What is all this?' he demanded.

'Do you know what we're carrying?' Venner asked.

'That bloody gas!' McAvoy spoke loudly, indignantly, as

273

though he had been in the secret all the time and had just been waiting his chance. 'You know what it is, don't you?'

Riddings was staring at Venner. 'Who the hell *are* you?' he asked.

'It would take too long to explain, but my name's Venner and I'm Navy and submarines and I don't belong to that bloody crew in the control room.'

Arteguy had moved from his position behind the starboard engine now. He tried to push past them towards the telephone.

'Leave that alone,' Venner said.

The Frenchman paused. 'I am not interest in heroism,' he said. 'I am interest only in cash.'

He tried again to push past, and Venner didn't argue. As the Frenchman reached for the telephone, he swung the wrench again, and Arteguy fell on top of O'Hare.

'You've killed him,' McAvoy said. He sounded shocked.

'Probably,' Venner agreed. 'If necessary, I'll kill you, too. If it's of any interest to you, this submarine's been shadowed by the Navy ever since it left England. Any moment now, they're going to start an A.S. torpedo after us. Either we hand over the gas to Olmuhi, and several thousand people die, or we go to the bottom with it. Which do you prefer? One of those, or taking her over.'

McAvoy gulped but said nothing. Riddings' eyes were bright under the bandage, and Venner saw Crankshawe's mouth lift in a quick excited grin of anticipation.

'I'm going back to the control room now,' he said. 'Stay here till you hear from me. I'm getting Meyer first. He's got the gun.'

They dragged the bodies out of sight, and Venner dropped the clips on the bulkhead door to swing it open. Meyer's face turned towards him as he stepped through. Tutschek was at the periscope again, his eyes glued to the glass, but he looked up just as Venner placed the machine pistol against Meyer's head and pulled the trigger.

The shot hurled the American against the bulkhead, and he spun round on limp legs, his gun dropping to the deck, his arms flung wide like a rag doll's. Then he slid down, his

274

fingers clawing at the smooth steel, until he was kneeling on the deck and sagging slowly over his own feet.

Tutschek's reaction was automatic. His eyes widened as Meyer fell. Then, even as the clatter of the shot was still filling the control room with its echoes, he swung away from the periscope, his hand reaching for the button of the alarm.

'Emergency!' he yelled. 'Flood Q! Three hundred feet! Fifteen degrees bow down!'

Chapter Eight

As the klaxon roared, the men in the control room – still half turned from their tasks at the sound of the shot to see what had happened – snatched their eyes back instinctively to the gauges and levels, and, responding automatically to the shout of emergency, threw their weight against levers and wheels.

Five tons of negative buoyancy from the quick-flooding Q tank dragged at *Achates,* and the fifteen degrees of plane tilted her bow steeply down. Venner felt the deck lurch, and there was a crash of something falling beyond the wardroom alleyway as he was sent staggering forward, his groping fingers reaching for a handhold.

'Belay that order!' he roared, grabbing for the chart table. 'Blow Q! Level her off at a hundred and fifty!'

He was aware of startled faces turned in his direction, craning round to discover whose orders to obey.

'Level her off!' he roared again, turning to bring up the pistol towards Tutschek. But while they were all concerned with the position of the submarine and confused by the differing orders, the German had snatched Bonser's small body from his seat at the foreplanes and now, with a muscle-cracking heave, he swung him at Venner just as Venner pulled the trigger. Bonser yelled and collapsed against him so that he staggered back and slipped to his knees under Bonser's weight. Lemon half fell out of the W/T office, alarmed by the shots, the headphones still round his neck. As they struggled, the call of the depth kept coming automatically from Luck, at the control panel. 'One seventy, sir! One eighty! Two hundred, sir!'

'Bring her up, for God's sake!' Venner roared, pushing the

276

moaning Bonser aside and struggling to his feet. His plan had gone wildly wrong. Tutschek had his gun out now, and only the increasing angle of the deck saved Venner because the German was having to hang on to the periscope to retain his balance. As he lifted the pistol, Madura, who had been silent and brooding throughout the whole trip, suddenly came to life and brought his huge fist down across Tutschek's hand. The shot splintered woodwork by the W/T office and Lemon yelled and dived for safety. Madura's hand came down again, and the pistol clattered to the deck. As the Dutchman kicked it away, Tutschek swung round, shouting for help, and plunged across the sloping deck for the wardroom alleyway.

Venner saw a hand snatch aside the heavy curtain at the entrance to the corridor. It was Blomberg. Fighting to keep his balance, Venner fired towards the flash of his spectacles. The figure vanished at once, but Tutschek, slithering on the wildly tilting deck, his feet slipping on the blood that was trickling from where Meyer lay, managed to reach safety. Venner fired again, and splinters sprang from the woodwork of the officers' galley where he'd disappeared.

Meyer's body was still sliding across the deck, but the tilt was lessening at last. The terror in the frantic voice calling the depth subsided.

'One hundred and thirty, sir. One hundred and twenty. She's steady!'

'Hold her! Madura, level her off and hold her there!'

The confusion and the tilt of the vessel had clearly thrown the gunmen in the wardroom as much off balance as it had the control room crew, but Venner knew he had little time left before they tried to regain command.

The control room looked like a battlefield. The men at the panels were beginning to lift their heads from where they had ducked out of the line of fire and Bonser was groaning on the deck in a pool of his own blood. Meyer was huddled by the chart table, but, without looking, Venner knew he was dead.

Drained of emotion, he drew a deep breath. More than anything else he wanted to sit down to recover his wits, to bring some sanity to the situation. It seemed an effort to move, however. Somehow he managed to stoop to pick up Meyer's pistol and toss it to Madura.

The demands on his muscles seemed to bring him to life, and his brain started to function again, to wrestle with the problems that had been forced on him. 'Watch that door, Madura,' he said. 'What's the depth, Luck?'

'One hundred and twenty.'

'Hold her there, Madura! Take over. Bring her to periscope depth.'

As the Dutchman moved back to the panel, Venner turned to the chart table, his eyes on the alleyway to the wardroom. 'Let me know when we're back at periscope depth,' he said. 'And for God's sake, be quick about it!'

'Ninety feet, sir! Eighty feet!'

'How's the trim?'

'She's level.'

'Keep her there.' Still watching the entrance to the wardroom alleyway, Venner reached for the telegraphs. They clanged to 'Stop,' and he lifted the telephone and called the engine room. Riddings answered at once.

'Venner here,' he said. 'We have control, but we've lost Tutschek and there are three others with him forrard. You're in charge there, Riddings, but stay where you are for the moment. I'm taking over command. We'll be surfacing.'

'Aye aye.' Riddings' voice came crisp and clear, steady with confidence, and it did Venner's heart good to hear it.

'What the bloody hell's going on?' Lemon asked.

'Never mind what's going on,' Venner said. 'Let go the indicator buoy, Ryan.'

Ryan's mouth was open. 'What the hell for?' he demanded. 'What's going on? Get us up!'

'Let go the indicator buoy!' Venner roared.

Ryan jumped to turn the wheel that allowed the buoy to leap to the surface from its housing in the casing.

'Indicator buoy released,' Ryan said.

Lemon was staring at the groaning Bonser. The old helmsman, Ekke, was bent over him with Luck.

'This wasn't part of the bleeding plan, I'll bet,' Lemon said.

'No, it wasn't,' Venner agreed. 'Nor was being blown to smithereens by an A.S. torpedo, which is what *will* happen before long. Get to your stations. Lemon, grab your pad and shove up the aerial. I want to send a signal. I'm going to surface as soon as I know they won't blow us out of the water.'

'We're on the edge of the Gadoon Trench now, sir,' Beaufort said. 'He'd go down here in nine hundred feet. Too deep to salvage, but not too deep to crush the pressure hull.'

The operations room was dark and occupied by a number of shadowy shapes in front of the pale-green glow of screens where the sweepers revolved with a cold phosphorescent fire. Behind them, green, amber, and red lights pinpricked a control panel.

'That's *Achates*, sir,' the Operations Room Officer said, indicating a small pinpoint of light just ahead of their position. 'We have only her periscope. The bigger blobs are *Launceston*, *Paladin*, and *Gladiator*.' His hand moved over the screen. 'The blob over to starboard is *Archer*, and the one to port's the Russian.'

Gillam-Smith glanced at the clock over the chart table. Turning to Mostyn, he said, 'I'm afraid we have to act, Colonel.'

Mostyn's mouth tightened.

'You can't have any longer,' Gillam-Smith said. 'I've waited as long as I dare. In another hour or two he'll be inside territorial waters.' To Beaufort, he said, 'Signal *Archer* to move up. She'll go in first. *Launceston* and *Paladin* will follow behind, in case anything goes wrong. Signal *Diomede*'s helicopters to stand by. We can't afford to make a mistake on this one.'

Mostyn felt the deck heave as the ship began to vibrate like an excited horse, the eager rumble from her engine rooms and blowers giving her a living animal sound. The bow wave rose, the stern sank, and a plume of white foam lifted fanlike

279

in her wake. As the vibration increased, Mostyn stared at the radar screen, his eyes narrow, his thoughts grim; he hardly heard the telephone.

The O.N.O. answered it. He turned quickly. 'They've stopped, sir,' he announced.

'For God's sake!' Gillam-Smith snapped an order. Mostyn heard the telegraphs clang. The vibrations stopped, and he felt the bow fall as the ship began to wallow in the swell.

'Warn all ships,' Gillam-Smith said, crossing to the chart. 'What are the bastards up to now?'

The telephone sounded again. Beaufort snatched at it.

'Indicator buoy, sir,' he said. 'Fine on the starboard bow.'

'Do we see it?'

'No, sir. *Launceston* reports it. It popped up alongside her.'

'Tell her to keep an eye on it.'

Beaufort had hardly replaced the instrument when it buzzed again. He picked at it once more.

'*Achates*' aerial believed to be raised, sir,' he said.

Gillam-Smith turned at once and headed through the red-lit corridor towards the bridge. The fog seemed thinner now, and, staring ahead over the bows, Mostyn was aware of a growing excitement, a sense of approaching climax. Almost immediately, the door opened, and the Communications Officer appeared. Beaufort was behind him.

'Sir!' The Communications Officer's salute was hasty and indifferent, but no one noticed. '*Achates* is calling us up.'

'What!'

'We've just picked this up, sir. It was in clear.'

Gillam-Smith held out his hand for the message. He turned to Mostyn as he read it.

'Good God,' he said. 'It's from your man, Venner! He claims to be in control. Requests we hold off. He intends to surface, but he doesn't want any accidents.'

Mostyn saw that Beaufort was smiling, for the first time since he'd met him.

'Thank God,' he said.

Mostyn took the message from the Admiral. There were no

frills to it, not even any prefixes. It was originated, he noticed at once, not from *Achates*, but from Venner, who was clearly thinking of the repercussions that might come later if the name were picked up by foreign ships. It stated exactly what Gillam-Smith had said.

'Call off *Archer* and the others!' The Admiral was already making his arrangements. 'Fix her position. Let's have no mistakes. Warn all ships she's about to surface, and make sure we get acknowledgements – especially from *Archer*.' He spoke quickly to Beaufort, then turned to the ship's captain. 'We'll stop engines, please, and stand by. And warn all lookouts to be on the alert. We want to see her immediately she surfaces.'

The Captain crossed to the Officer of the Watch. The telegraphs clanged. A moment later Mostyn heard the hum of turbines subside. Crossing to the porthole, he saw *Gladiator*, which had appeared through the mist on the port quarter and was just working up to a good speed, drop her nose as her speed was cut. The bow wave disappeared, and she wallowed heavily as her wake lifted the stern.

Gillam-Smith was talking to Beaufort, frowning heavily, his eyes glinting below the visor of his cap as he turned again to *Holdfast*'s captain.

'Have the guns' crews close up,' he said. 'And call the Gunnery Officer. Load with live ammunition.'

Mostyn turned quickly. 'What the devil are you intending to do?' he demanded.

Gillam-Smith faced him, his features taut. 'I intend to open fire.'

'Venner's bringing her up,' Mostyn said.

'Yes,' Gillam-Smith agreed. 'And I shall give him every opportunity. But it's a chance I can't afford to waste, because we don't know how much control he has over those bastards down there and whether he'll keep it.' He turned to the ship's captain. 'Aft,' he said. 'Tell the Gunnery Officer he's to aim as far aft as he can get. There must be no mistake. The fog's thinning, and we're close enough *not* to have any mistakes.

281

Make it clear exactly what I want. And there's to be no shooting until I give the word.'

He turned again to Mostyn to explain. 'Captain Beaufort tells me *Achates* is watertight aft of the control room,' he said. 'I can put a couple of shells in the stern. With the bulkhead doors closed, nothing that's in the fore-ends can get through and escape. Not even gas. But with her stern full of water, *Achates* will sink, and she'll never surface again. Never.'

A figure appeared alongside them. 'She's just ahead now, sir. Range five hundred yards.'

'Very well.' Gillam-Smith turned to the Communications Officer. 'Radio Venner. In clear. Omit *Achates*' name. Address it simply to Venner. We don't want our Russian friends in on this. Tell him we're standing by with all ships stopped. And tell him to close Number Four watertight door. Then warn all other ships' captains to be on the alert in case this is some kind of trick.'

Chapter Nine

Venner had heard Lemon's radio begin to cheep and knew that his message to the surface had been received. Although he had control of the submarine, he knew it was only a very fragile control. Though there were three machine pistols in the control room, beyond the curtain of the wardroom alley-way Tutschek had at least two, probably three, unharmed men, all with weapons. They dared not put their heads beyond the curtain, but, equally, Venner dared not go in or send anyone in to fetch them out. In the narrow confines of the submarine, any attempt either way would be suicidal. But for the fact that he had the ship's controls, it was a stalemate, and even that had been made possible only because so far the men with him had done as he had told them without question. They weren't good men, but they weren't prepared to condemn thousands of human beings to death for the sake of a megalo-maniac dictator and a few lunatic crooks.

Unexpectedly, as he waited, he found himself wondering what Susie Gore was doing. More than likely playing hell with someone on his behalf, he decided. She didn't know much about the Navy, but when she picked up the news, her suspicions would make her a formidable opponent, white with indignation.

'Come on, Lemon,' he breathed, beating his hand softly against the chart table. 'Look slippy!'

He could have brought the submarine to the surface at once, and chanced the reception they would get, but he suspected that with the emergency that existed there would be no mercy and no questions asked. This was the moment the hunting pack had been waiting for. Since they were within a few hundred yards of *Achates* now, the appearance of the submarine could well have brought a grim slicing bow tearing a hole in her aft.

He lifted his head to glance towards the W/T office. Madura, Meyer's pistol in his hand, was watching the wardroom alleyway with a grim and brooding intensity. Ekke was with Bonser, trying to make him comfortable. The bullet had entered his stomach, and he was in great pain.

'Morphine,' the German said. 'Ve must heff morphine.'

'There is none,' Venner said.

'Never mind the bloody morphine,' Ryan snarled. 'Get us to the surface!'

'Why, dear?' Luck turned and spoke in a high effeminate voice, the old sarcastic Jolly Jack Tar, contemptuous of fear. 'You feelin' faint?'

It was almost the first time he'd spoken since he'd come aboard, and it made the insult stronger. Ryan glared at him, and Madura's eyes flickered towards the W/T office as the bleeping of the set came with the nervous probing of the asdic. Then the bleeping stopped and Lemon put his head out.

'In clear,' he said. 'They've called everybody off! We're to close Number Four watertight door aft of the control room.'

The message puzzled Venner, but he had no time to think about it. 'Right.' He glanced about him. 'Stand by to surface.'

There was an immediate lightening of the mood in the control room. Though they had long since realised that the operation had failed, the thought of seeing the light of day again was reviving morale and driving away the low spirits caused by fear and the need for sleep.

'Come on,' Ryan urged, tense and nervous. 'Get on with it! Get us up!'

'Aw, for Christ's sake,' Lemon said. 'Take a reef in it, mate. You're worse than a Wren with a round up the breech! I'm sick of hearin' you bleat. No wonder the Queen's Navee slung you out.'

'They slung you out, too,' Ryan snarled.

'No, mate, they didn't.' There was a hint of unexpected pride

284

in Lemon's voice. '*I* walked out. With an honourable discharge, too. I was no angel, but I only got panned by the regulating branch and the Sin Bosun.'

'Shut up,' Venner snapped. 'Both of you!' He found he was trembling. To be trapped inside the cold oily steel box of a submarine's control room was an agonising thought, but they'd all been trained in what to do, and his plans were clear.

Even as he was about to give the command, however, the telephone sounded. Expecting it to be Riddings, he lifted it from the hook. It was Tutschek.

'Herr Venner,' he said, 'we are now in a most interesting situation, are we not?'

'What the hell do you mean?'

'You are out there, wondering how to save yourselves, and we are sitting in here in the fore-ends surrounded by gas. We have masks, of course, because we were careful to store them in the wardroom. Do *you* have masks?'

Venner's heart went cold. 'What the hell are you getting at?' he demanded. 'I'm taking this submarine up.'

'I wouldn't do that, Herr Venner.' Tutschek sounded remarkably confident. 'You will be aware that forward of the control room there are three watertight bulkheads, each with a door. There is one forward of where we are now, so that doesn't matter. Aft of us, between us and you, Herr Venner, there is a second door which we have wide open. Between the control room and the wardroom there is a third, and that, as you will remember, was so damaged in the explosion it is useless.'

Venner's heart was thumping. 'So?'

'There are also holes where pipes and wires have been removed.' Tutschek sounded almost cheerful. 'So! It will not be difficult to release the gas, and you have no protection against it. None at all. In case you don't know, when it comes into contact with the air it builds up pressure and, when it does, it increases quickly in volume for a time. There is only one way it can go, Herr Venner. *Your* way. To help it, we have laid the evacuator pipes along the alleyway towards you.

It should find its way through to your compartment within two or three minutes of being released.' The voice hardened. 'Herr Venner, I still intend to take this submarine to Gadoon.'

Venner's mind raced. 'There are half a dozen ships waiting on the surface to stop you,' he said.

He heard Tutschek laugh. 'They will find it very difficult. I can find my way into Gadoon blindfolded. This is a grave-yard of German submarines. There are three on the bottom here – all full of my old comrades. If you look at the chart, you will see I have marked them. I know this because I escaped from one of them, and the others were from my flotilla. Your countrymen were waiting for us in 1945. They ought to cause considerable confusion to electronic equipment, don't you think? And, Herr Venner, the moment I hear you start the engines or blow tanks to surface, I shall release the gas. Not all, of course. I want some for Olmuhi. You would have perhaps three minutes.'

Venner found swallowing difficult. 'What do you want?' he asked.

Tutschek chuckled. 'We are at periscope depth, Herr Venner,' he said. 'I know because we have a depth gauge here, too. I can tell at once if you try to surface; so there will be no tricks. From where we are, we control the third bulkhead door as much as you do. We are armed, too, and anyone attempting to close it will be shot down at once. I hope you see your position, Herr Venner.'

Venner's gaze roved over the faces of the men in the control room. Their eyes were all on him, tense and alert and scared. 'Look, Tutschek,' he said, playing for time, 'you've made your point. But I'm having difficulty here. Nobody wants to stay aboard. Not now.'

'They have no option,' Tutschek said. 'You have five minutes to make up your minds. No more.'

There was a click as he hung up. Venner stared round at the rest of the men in the control room.

'What does the bastard want?' Ryan asked. When Venner

286

explained, his narrow face twisted. 'Then for Christ's sake,' he said, 'let the bastards out!'

'No!' Madura jerked a hand. 'Yoost a minute!'

'I say let the bastards out!' Ryan stepped towards the telephone, and Venner was surprised to see Madura's hand lift quickly. Ryan dropped to the deck.

He squirmed to a sitting position, rubbing the back of his head. 'We haven't a chance, you great bloody fool!' he screeched, and Lemon gave a ragged grin.

'Shit or bust, I always say,' he observed. 'Let's have a go!'

'*Ja*,' Madura agreed. 'Ve vill vait. I am a peaceful man. I am not clever, or I would not be here. Is there nothing ve can do?'

'Lemon—' Venner turned to the radioman '—get a signal off. Tell them there's been an emergency. Tell them we'll close the watertight door, but to stand by. Tell them we still have control.'

'Aye aye, sir.' Lemon was responding like a responsible submariner, and it occurred to Venner that *he* was behaving like a responsible commander. It was ironic that it should be now, when there was nothing he could do but scuttle his ship. It was so ironic he felt like weeping.

The intercom buzzed. 'You have four minutes, Herr Venner,' Tutschek said. 'Then I release the gas. It will take only another minute or two to start seeping through. I have no wish for this, however. I want to use this submarine again. It has a value, and the gas has a habit of hanging around in corners. Moreover, unhappily there is no known antidote. The gas would put it out of action for too long, and I do not wish to stay in Gadoon.'

There was a pause then Tutschek's voice came again, with numbing persistence, against Venner's tired brain. 'You now have three and a half minutes, Herr Venner.'

Venner forced himself to remain calm. 'Engine room, Luck,' he said as the intercom clicked. 'Get everyone in here. Quickly.'

His eyes were on the second hand of the control-room clock, and it seemed to take an age before everyone was assembled. He explained the situation as quickly as he could. 'We have no gas masks,' he pointed out. 'But we do have the controls. I'm going to take her to the surface. And then I'm going to scuttle her. We're on the edge of the Gadoon Trench, which is as safe a place to ditch her as any.' He saw their eyes flicker. 'We shall have very little time to get up that ladder once we're surfaced, because as soon as we blow tanks, those bastards forward are going to release the gas. Understood?'

There were nods. 'How about escape equipment, sir?' Crankshawe asked.

'We'll do without, because we have to move fast. But there are ships above, and a calm sea. And they'll know we're on our way. How long will it take to bring her to the surface, Riddings?'

'She's old, sir,' Riddings answered briskly. 'All of two minutes, I reckon. She'll go up faster with the motors running, of course, and the planes to rise.'

'Right. And to scuttle her? Giving us time to evacuate?'

'Open the vents, sir.'

'Is there any way when she goes down that I can guarantee she doesn't come up again.'

'I can wreck the blowing panel, sir. A few good clouts with a hammer will do it.'

'Get one. Smash anything you think necessary. And close the after bulkhead while you're there. And be quick.'

As Riddings disappeared, Venner turned to the others. 'It'll be touch and go,' he said. 'We shall have to pray we reach the surface before the gas comes through.'

Ryan's jaw was hanging open. 'You're nuts!' he burst out. Madura gave him a quick shove. He staggered against Lemon, who shoved him back again. He stood in front of Madura once more, surly and unwilling but without much option in the matter.

Venner continued. 'After that, we shall have about thirty seconds to get up that ladder. Understood?'

'Aye aye, sir.'

'I shall put her to slow ahead and dive her. I hope to get up after you before it's too late.'

Lemon indicated Bonser. 'What about him?'

'I vill carry him,' Madura said.

Venner looked at the Dutchman's vast frame. 'Right,' he said. 'Are we ready?'

The intercom sounded again.

'You have two minutes, Herr Venner,' Tutschek said.

The intercom clicked.

Lemon and Ekke had lifted Bonser across Madura's back, and the Dutchman was holding the smaller man's slim wrists in one great fist. Bonser was groaning with pain and almost unconscious.

'Can you make it up the ladder?' Venner asked.

'There will be room for both of us,' the Dutchman said stolidly.

'What about him?' Lemon indicated Meyer.

'He won't worry,' Venner said. He turned to the E.R.A. as he scrambled back into the control room. 'Riddings, stand by the blowing panel. Crankshawe – engine room. When you get the order, put the motors slow ahead both, and come back here as fast as you can. Close the watertight door behind you as you come.'

Crankshawe vanished.

Madura, standing by the ladder with the groaning Bonser over his shoulder, was like a great ox, silent and motionless, but patient despite the skin-thin tension.

'You'll be following him, Ekke,' Venner said. 'You're a big chap, so shove as much as you can. Understand?'

'*Jawohl*. I understand.'

'No waiting. If Bonser gets a bruised skull, it can't be helped. It's got to be fast. Riddings.'

'Sir.' Riddings glanced round from where he had taken up his position at the blowing panel. 'You'll be last up, before me.'

'Aye aye, sir.'

'Right. Open the lower lid, Luck.'

As the lid was opened, a few drops of water that had drained down from the bridge splashed on them.

'Right,' Venner said. 'Up to the bridge hatch, Luck. And remember, it's up to you. I want you out as soon as we break surface.'

'Aye aye, sir.'

'You next, Madura. Can you hang on to the ladder?'

'*Ja.* I hang on.'

As Madura started to climb, Venner turned. 'Ekke. You next. Shove all you can.'

'*Jawohl.* I shove.'

'Now you, McAvoy, and you, Ryan—'

As Ryan vanished up the ladder, Venner swung round to Lemon. 'Right, Lemon,' he said. 'In your office! Send "SOS Subsmash!"'

Chapter Ten

Gillam-Smith was standing with Mostyn and Beaufort when Venner's signal arrived.

The Communications Officer had just brought him a decoded flimsy, which he'd handed to Beaufort, who'd passed it on to Mostyn.

It had come from the depot ship *Commando*, waiting near the South-eastern Alantic Deep. SUBMARINE ACHATES OVERDUE, it read. REQUEST INSTRUCTIONS.

'Do we reply sir?' the Communications Officer asked.

Gillam-Smith was calm and unhurried now that things were moving. 'Tell them the plans have been changed. And tell them to keep off the air.'

The Communications Officer had just disappeared to the communications room when he returned. He looked excited.

' "Subsmash," sir,' he said. '*Achates* has signalled "Subsmash".'

' "Subsmash," for God's sake!' Gillam-Smith glanced at Beaufort. 'Is he going to sink the damn thing?'

Beaufort turned, his face excited, 'Why not, sir?' he said. '*We* were going to.'

Gillam-Smith slapped the chart with the flat of his hand. 'Give him every assistance,' he ordered. 'Have *Nightjar* and *Armourer* move up. All ships stand by for emergency. Do we still have him pin-pointed?'

'We do, sir.'

'Send the helicopters up and have the boats lowered and ready for casting off. Alert extra look-outs.'

As Beaufort vanished, the Admiral turned to Mostyn. 'He might save us all a lot of trouble,' he said.

Lemon appeared, wrenching off his headphones. 'They acknowledged, sir,' he said excitedly. 'They acknowledged!'

'Right!' Venner glanced at his watch. There was barely a minute left. 'Off you go, Lemon!'

Lemon vanished up the ladder, and Venner reached for the telegraphs. As they clanged under his hand, he knew that Crankshawe was leaping to put the motors in gear.

'Stand by to surface,' he snapped. 'Shut main vents.'

Riddings slammed the long levers home, and Venner heard the muffled thuds as the vents closed to seal off the upper openings of the buoyancy tanks, so that the compressed air blowing in could force the water out through the open lower inlets. 'Blow all main ballast!'

As Riddings moved, they heard the roaring and hissing of compressed air expelling the water from the tanks, like a railway engine blowing off steam. The needle of the depth gauge rose quickly as Venner turned the planes to rise, and he felt the submarine move beneath his feet, beginning to lift like a cork. Almost at once, he heard the hum of the engines increase, then Crankshawe came tumbling back into the control room, heaving the heavy door to behind him and slamming the clips home with flying hands.

'Stand by with that hatch, Luck,' Venner shouted.

Gillam-Smith and Mostyn were staring over the bows at the grey lifting sea. Through the mist, they could see ships beginning to move forward, their boats manned and lowered almost to water level. There was the sound of hurried feet on deck as extra look-outs ran to take up position.

'Something should be happening in a minute or two,' Gillam-Smith said. He picked up the telephone and spoke to Beaufort, who had disappeared to the deck above. 'Anything in sight?' he asked.

'Nothing yet, sir. It's damn difficult out here to see anything.'

'There'll be a few questions asked over this lot,' Gillam-Smith said reflectively to Mostyn.

'Doubtless it'll be possible to have them answered satisfactorily,' Mostyn rejoined.

Gillam-Smith nodded, his face still thoughtful. Then the Tannoy crackled.

'Forebridge!'

The call came from the asdic cabinet. '*Achates* is moving, sir, and she's started to blow tanks!'

'Here she comes!' Gillam-Smith snatched at the telephone and spoke to Beaufort. 'Warn the look-outs! We mustn't miss her! And warn the Gunnery Officer she's coming. It might still be a trick.'

Over the intercom, Tutschek sounded as though he were choking with rage.

'You are blowing tanks, Venner!' he shouted.

'We're surfacing.'

'I'm coming out.'

'Put your nose round the corner and I'll blow your head off!'

'I am turning the gas on!'

Venner's eyes went immediately to the mice, seeing them as though he'd never looked at them before. One of them had a patch of brown on its back, and they seemed so clear in his vision he felt he could see every whisker and hair as they moved about the floor of their cage, their eyes glinting redly in the subdued lighting.

His heart thumping, he stood watching the bulkhead door. Handing Tutschek's pistol to Crankshawe, he glanced at the two engineers. 'It's up to us now,' he said. 'Call out the depths, Crankshawe!'

'Call out the depths. Aye aye, sir!'

The noise of the compressed air roaring into the tanks almost drowned the words. Venner turned to glance at the mice, and even as he took his eyes off the wardroom alleyway, he saw a shadow appear. He fired at once from his position by the control panel and the shadow vanished.

'I think you got the bastard, sir,' Riddings said.

293

Venner slid the cage of mice across the deck with his foot. 'Can you keep your eye on the mice, too, Riddings?'

'I reckon so, sir.'

'Let me know what they're doing. Okay or otherwise.'

'Aye aye, sir! Mice okay, sir!'

The air was still roaring noisily into the tanks. Like a steel coffin, the submarine rose from the sea.

'Forty feet,' Crankshawe called.

'Mice still okay,' Riddings echoed.

Venner glanced at the clock, one eye on the wardroom alleyway.

'Smell anything, Riddings?'

'No, sir. Does it have a smell?'

'God knows!'

'Mice are okay, sir, anyway.'

The intercom squawked again. 'Venner!' The snarling voice suddenly sounded faintly mad. 'I have released the gas! It is all about us. Any moment now it will be coming through to your compartment.'

Venner didn't bother to reply. 'Keep your eye on those mice, Riddings,' he said.

'Aye aye, sir,' Riddings replied calmly. 'Mice okay.'

'Twenty-five feet,' Crankshawe called. 'Fifteen feet!'

'Stand by.'

'We're up, sir!'

They had burst out into the light of day, hitting the surface in an explosion of flying spray, the water streaming off the ship's flanks in torrents as the bows leapt from the waves.

Luck unclipped the hatch and flung it open. A shower of water from the cockpit fell on them in an icy deluge, and Lemon's voice came down in a scream. 'Hatch open, sir!'

Madura was already half-way out with Bonser. Staring up, Venner saw his feet disappear.

'Planes to dive, Crankshawe,' he shouted. As the E.R.A. swung the wheel, he called again. 'That'll do,' he said. 'Off you go!'

As Crankshawe leapt for the ladder, Riddings spoke, his voice calm. 'The mice, sir! One of 'em's going!'

Venner turned. The mouse with the brown patch had fallen on its side, its small feet pawing slowly at the air. Venner's heart started to pound. Then he remembered that a mouse's breathing was quicker and shallower than a human being's, and that, although the gas multiplied, it remained heavier than air, and there was still a little while before it lifted to their noses and mouths.

'Other mouse's going, too, I think, sir!'

Glancing up the ladder, Venner saw above him in the tall shaft of the fin the round opening of the hatch and the sky above, and felt a desperate urge to race after Crankshawe. Automatically, he was sniffing, though he realised he ought to be holding his breath.

'Open the main vents, Riddings,' he shouted. 'I'll watch the alleyway.'

He heard the vents open and the sound of water thundering back into the ballast tanks. Above him, he knew, great gouts of water were shooting up as the vents slammed open, and the deck was probably already awash.

The intercom went, but he ignored it, and it continued to squawk alongside him. Then he saw a figure wearing a gas mask appear in the wardroom alleyway, looking like some martian. It was impossible to tell who it was, but he fired at it, and the figure fell backwards. He saw the depth-gauge needle dropping back and, almost without being aware of it, he heard Riddings swinging the hammer.

'Get going, Riddings!' he said.

Riddings leapt for the ladder.

Venner looked again at the gauges, determined there should be no mistake. Even without the gas, he had no more than ninety seconds of life left as the submarine settled. He heard the roar of water about him, and Riddings screaming down the hatchway.

'She's going, sir!' he yelled.

Venner still stayed where he was. He must make certain

295

there would be no rescue attempt. With his heart thumping in panic, he had no idea whether he was already breathing gas or not.

There was another shot from the alleyway, but whoever was holding the pistol was not taking any chances, and it was wild. Venner fired back automatically, his eyes returning quickly to the depth gauges.

Riddings shouted again. 'For God's sake, sir!'

Venner turned and fired a last shot into the alleyway to dissuade anyone who might be thinking of bursting out. The intercom was still squawking as he jumped for the ladder. In his haste, he missed his step and barked his shin, then he was clattering up the rungs as fast as he could go.

But the ladder was already tilting. With the planes at dive, and no one at the controls to balance her, the submarine was settling unevenly by the bow, so that he was having to drag himself up every inch of the way.

Faintly, above the roar of the water, he heard someone shout in the control room as he scrambled through the lower hatchway, and he braced himself for death. Something hit him in the leg with the force of a hammer blow and spun him round, but, recovering his balance, he reached for the hatch cover and saw it fall. Clutching the polished rungs of the upper ladder, he began to drag himself up. The tilt had grown steeper now and climbing was more difficult.

Riddings was on the upper lid, reaching down. 'Hurry, sir, for Christ's sake!' he was yelling.

'Take off, man!'

'Sir—!' Then Riddings was brushed aside, and he saw Madura in his place, and a great arm like an ox's leg reaching down to him.

The ladder seemed to be slipping away from him. He was growing dizzy, too, dragging himself up entirely by his arms, because his leg dangled below him uselessly.

Dimly, he was aware of the whangg-whanngg of guns firing and almost fell from the ladder as the submarine shuddered. Good God, he thought, they're trying to sink us! This was the

296

submariner's bad dream, the nightmare come true: trapped below with thousands of tons of water falling on top of him. His mind was numb with fear as he fought his way upwards. *This* was death, not the glory people read of in books, not the stuff Kipling wrote about. Not God's wisdom or the peace of Heaven. After this horror there would be nothing more, nothing at all. Not even space. Just darkness and a dim green choking silence below the sea.

Madura's voice came dimly through the clatter and hiss of water. 'Hurry, Mynheer, hurry!'

A heavy slosh of ice-green sea almost tore him from his hold. He seemed to be dragging himself up against tons of water towards the opening. At last Madura's thick fingers grabbed his wrist, and he felt himself lifted bodily upwards. Vaguely, he saw Riddings there, too, before he was dragged on to the bridge, cracking his head a stunning blow on the hatchway as he went through. There appeared to be water all round him, surging and roaring as it poured through the hatchway.

'The hatch, Riddings,' he screamed. 'Close it! Close it!' As the water swept him off the bridge into the sea, he saw Riddings slam the hatch down. With the pressure that existed on the edge of the Gadoon Trench, nothing in the world would ever lift it again.

Just before the water closed over him, he saw the stern of *Achates* reach upwards like a drowning hand. Then it began to slide away, turning over slowly, so that the keel showed.

Faintly shocked by the speed of the deliberate destruction, he found himself swimming with Riddings and Madura beside him. Dimly, almost unconsciously, he was aware of a gun firing and saw flashes on the stern of the submarine as it lifted, and a piece of metal flying through the air. He saw, too, the simple ingenuity behind the closing of the bulkhead door. *Achates* would never surface again now, whatever Tutschek's experience might suggest. The weight of water pouring into the after compartment would be proof against all his skill.

As he watched, *Achates* dropped away, twisting on the axis of her own length and standing on her nose as she went down.

297

In his mind's eye, he could see the depth-gauge needle gyrating madly as she vanished, could imagine the men inside her sliding forward to the bow, frantic fingers grabbing for overhead pipes and other handholds as she dropped to the bottom of the Atlantic; everything that was not fastened hurtling from one end to the other and the men rolling across the slimy decks knowing the meaning of the death they had been proposing to deal out to others, as they looked down the image of a stair-well in a twenty-story building, perhaps even with the mad irony of Lemon's radio still bleeping out some call sign.

A last gout of water shot into the air as the stern vanished, the propellers still slowly turning, then the excitement was over and the pain came. He realised he was being held up by Madura, and Riddings and Crankshawe were grinning at him. Bonser was supported by Lemon and Ryan. Luck, Ekke, and McAvoy were further away. He had got every living man of his crew away safely.

He saw shadowy shapes in the thinning mist, which he knew were ships – almost on top of them, it seemed – and could hear the clatter of a helicopter unseen up above somewhere. Then boats were heading towards them, lifting on the swell, and not far away Luck and Ekke were already being dragged aboard.

A wave hit him in the face, and he choked on the water. Shaking his head and coughing, he glanced about him. There was no sign of *Achates* now, and as the events of the last weeks closed in on him he realised he was exhausted by long days and lack of sleep, and the final emotional moments of the sinking. For just one wild quarter of an hour, he had commanded his own ship. Somehow, with the knowledge, an old unhappy weight lifted from his shoulders.

A boat coming alongside him slopped water in his face with its bow wave, and he saw Riddings disappear over the side. Hands grabbed at him and he followed, crying out as his injured leg was scraped across the gunwale. Then he was lying on the bottom boards, among the feet of the crew, panting, numb, and desperately wishing he could be sick.

As they dragged him to safety, in the asdic room of *Holdfast* the operator snatched off his earphones to avoid listening to the last convulsive agony of *Achates* hundreds of feet below. He looked startled and a little pale. 'That's it, sir,' he said to the officer alongside his chair. 'She's gone.'

In the Vernon's Head Hotel, Daisy lifted the telephone on the reception clerk's desk. It was the Wren officer from Fort Blockhouse.

She listened for a while. The voice at the other end sounded as calm as if its owner had just come on duty, instead of being alert for days.

As she put the telephone down, Daisy felt desperately weary. Leaving the desk, she crossed to where Susie was sitting, still in the same chair she'd been in all the time – since God knows when, Daisy thought – bolt upright, her face chalk-white, her eyes, underscored by shadow, staring from her strained face.

'It's okay,' Daisy said. 'It's all over and they're all safe.'

Susie didn't say anything, and Daisy was surprised to see that the little self-assured face was self-assured no longer. It had crumpled suddenly, and she was crying quietly, her body sagging.

The manager was waiting just behind them. 'I don't know what it is,' he said hesitantly. 'Is there anything I can do?'

'Just don't worry.' Daisy smiled. 'Just find her a bed. And then find one for me.'